GW00400910

FREAKSLAW

FREAKSLAW

Jane Flett

doubleday

TRANSWORLD PUBLISHERS
Penguin Random House, One Embassy Gardens,
8 Viaduct Gardens, London SW11 7BW
www.penguin.co.uk

Transworld is part of the Penguin Random House group of companies
whose addresses can be found at global.penguinrandomhouse.com

First published in Great Britain in 2024 by Doubleday
an imprint of Transworld Publishers

A CIP catalogue record for this book
is available from the British Library.

ISBN 9780857529541

Typeset in 11.5/15.75 pt by Adobe Garamond by Falcon Oast Graphic Art Ltd.
Printed and bound in Great Britain by Clays Ltd, Elcograf S.p.A.

The authorized representative in the EEA is Penguin Random House Ireland,
Morrison Chambers, 32 Nassau Street, Dublin D02 YH68.

Penguin Random House is committed to a sustainable
future for our business, our readers and our planet. This book is
made from Forest Stewardship Council® certified paper.

For Alex, co-conspirator in Adventureland.

For Alex, co-conspirator in all adventures.

A NOTE ON LANGUAGE
AND REPRESENTATION

I've chosen to write a book about 'freaks' – a group of people who've been cast out of conventional society for one reason or another, whether that's sexuality, gender, race, weight or disability. In doing so, I wanted to honour the ways in which our marginalities are so often a source of power, community and triumph, rather than something we succeed in spite of.

At the same time, these are not all identities I share, and I particularly considered whether or not I wanted to write about disability and how people have been ostracized because of it. In the end, I felt writing a book about a 'freak show' while excluding the physicality of that would mean erasing the ableist history of these performances in a way that was both dishonest and unhelpful.

I hope I've done justice to the whole, complex lives of the Freakslaw's inhabitants, and this book can serve as both a love letter to community and a reminder of how our struggle is connected. I'm especially grateful to the readers with lived experience who offered their feedback on these topics – their insight is so appreciated, and any remaining inaccuracies are mine to own.

CAST OF CHARACTERS

Funfair Folk

MR PARTLETT: Proprietor of the Freakslaw, silver-haired and silver-tongued. Nominally in charge; in practice, defers important decisions to the women around him.

GLORIA THE TELLER: Fortune teller, worm charmer, mother of Nancy. Sees altogether too much of both past and future. A most excellent storyteller.

NANCY: Human contortionist and teen witch. Scorpio (obviously). Enjoys casting hexes and manifesting all kinds of lovely trouble.

ZED: The waltzer boy. An irrepressible flirt, and entirely too easy to fall in love with. One of those rare humans who just really enjoy living. Also makes excellent coffee.

MISS MARIA: The Fat Lady. A rare beauty, with more pheromones than many would allow, and a fiercely loyal friend.

GRETCHEN ETCETERA: Sardonic drag performer and self-proclaimed 'gender pest'. Right about most things and invariably the last person still awake at the party.

CASS: Illusionist and conjoined twin of Henry. Girlish, charming, attention-seeking. Takes a great pleasure in irritating her brother.

HENRY: Illusionist and conjoined twin of Cass. Logical, pretentious, easily embarrassed. A remarkably ingenious thief.

THE PIN GAL: Human pincushion. Gleeful mischief maker and former theatre kid. Sports an impressive array of tattoos.

WEREWOLF LOUIE: Tightrope walker with hypertrichosis and a heart of gold. Extremely proud of his ginger locks.

STRONGMEN 1–7: Seven men, who are all strong. Otherwise generally lacking in discerning features.

Townsfolk

RUTH MACNAMARA: Horny overachiever and maths geek. Too clever for her own good. Encyclopaedic knowledge of early punk music. Intends to get out of Pitlaw by any means possible.

MRS MACNAMARA: Ruth's mum. Tea drinker who loves a good blether. Keeps a nice house.

MR MACNAMARA: Ruth's dad. Works at the factory and is seldom around. Enjoys a comfortable silence.

STEPHANIE MACNAMARA: Ruth's older sister. Former tough girl, now teen mother. Had, and still has, a reputation at Pitlaw Academy.

KAYLEIGH MACNAMARA: Stephanie's daughter. A baby; tends to cry a lot and occasionally blow spit bubbles.

DEREK GEDDES: Dishwasher at the Skene Dhu and incurable romantic. Writes a lot of songs he'll never show anyone. Sensitive stomach, even more sensitive heart.

JUNE GEDDES: Derek's mum. Prioritizes keeping the peace and prides herself on being able to stick out a bad situation. Secret weakness for sweet things.

BOYD GEDDES: Derek's dad. Believes himself a fundamentally logical man, though has a soft spot for the horses and beer. Lives in fear of his son turning out 'like that'.

SHONA PETERSON: Local hairdresser, proprietor of Curl Up and Dye. More imagination than the vast majority of Pitlaw, and generally disliked for it.

NORMA MURRAY: Head of the town council and general busybody. Fully invested in the redemptive power of rules and regulations.

DOREEN ABBOTT: Gossipy widow who lives alone with her black lab, Stitches. Easily flustered.

GREG HASKETT: Drinking buddy of Boyd. An unpleasant man who is inordinately sure about everything.

CALLUM MCALLISTER: Drinking buddy of Boyd. Distrusts foreigners and doctors in equal measure.

JIM BARRIE: Drinking buddy of Boyd. Terminally glum.

LEWIS DUGUID: Drinking buddy of Boyd. Deems his own sense of humour hilarious.

PHILLIP BURNSTONE: Righteous local. Watches a lot of Nazi documentaries.

ALICE WILSON: Waitress at the greasy spoon. Chronically nervous.

JACK HASKETT: Schoolmate of Derek and general arsehole. Truly gifted at picking fights.

STEVEN MCLEOD: Schoolmate of Derek. A self-satisfied prankster who finds fart jokes hysterical.

EUAN CRUIKSHANK: A boy in Stephanie's year. Known to be gay, bullied mercilessly at Pitlaw Academy.

BEV: Proprietor of the Skene Dhu.

CHEF: Chef at the Skene Dhu.

JOE: Waiter at the Skene Dhu.

MR SCOTT: History teacher at Pitlaw Academy.

MR DOROTHY: Has a dachshund, Dolly.

MOIRA MCGINTY, LESLEY MACDERMID, BARRY DONALDSON, SIOBHAN MAGUIRE AND HER FIANCÉ COLIN: Visitors to the Freakslaw.

'We are the weirdos, mister.'
THE CRAFT

WELCOME TO THE
FUNHOUSE

THE TRUCKS SHOW up one afternoon like a parade of chorus girls with dirty knickers. Prancing down Main Street, all cackles and engine revs, purple feathers fluttering from their rear-view mirrors. In the dreich afternoon drizzle, they're as garish as a cartoon. If you have small children (or wayward teenagers, for that matter) you might want to take this moment to stop up their ears with cotton wool and clutch their sticky brat hands tight. The trucks are oh-so bright and oh-so tempting, and it's bad luck to start any tale with screeched brakes and an ambulance siren.

Beneath the polished steel tracks of the roller coaster, Gloria the Teller sits high in her cab – webbed fingers splayed on the steering wheel, zebra-print tophat askew. Snuggled on top of a neon waltzer, the Twins hiss secrets and plot in each other's ears. On their lap, they clutch a metal cash box with six thousand stolen pounds inside. And in the Haunted House's truck of ghosts, the Pin Gal props her feet on the dashboard and plays the marimba on the piercings of her rib-cage. Her music is jerky and ancient, a wind-up magic-box song that means everything is about to begin.

When they reach the end of Main Street, the procession snakes around the back of Costcutters, past the bus stop – the place of fag butts, first kisses, and the one escape route out of this town. Miss Maria peers from her specially strengthened lavender caravan and wraps her feather boa tight as three kids scarf the dregs of a bottle of Glen's. Gobby with vodka, the shortest one raises his middle finger at the caravans and hocks up a swear . . . but then Gloria the Teller shoots him a wink and the kid freezes as if he's forgotten what he intended. He's left holding his finger in the air while the folk in the cabs screech and blow kisses and take the turn towards Jimmy's field.

The laughter carries them over potholes of broken roads, past the Ladbrokes and the Poundland and the boarded-up shopfronts. Miss Maria's seventeen chins ripple like belly-dancers clad in copper coins and sparkly intent. The trucks jiggle along.

And then there's Nancy – teen witch, trouble dowser and human contortionist – sitting in the back of Gloria's lorry, every surface piled high with mystic altars. As they hit the potholes, things fall: a High Priestess tarot card, a tangle of prayer beads, three baby teeth. Nancy ignores them, too busy leaning out the window, taking in the lie of the land. A green-brown sludge for miles and miles with just a small eruption of streets like a pustule the earth's barfed out.

But potential. She can sense that too, beneath it all.

As this day-glo horror creeps through Pitlaw, the curtains huff and rustle. These lorries, they're not your good honest *normal* lorries. Instead of cable ties or tinned fruit or manure, they're all filled up with 'entertainment' and God Knows What Else. Why, if those painted monstrosities on the side are anything to go by, they must be stuffed with dirty pictures and horror shows and worse! So the townspeople say, as the phones leap and clatter in their cradles. Word of the arrival spreads through the mycelium of the town – gossip erupts in damp-tissue sitting rooms, rumour spores catch the wind. *They're Catholic heathens from the south, so they are, intent on total depravity. No, worse: they're foreign. It's not right. Pitlaw may have had a snatch of bother of late, but that's nothing outsiders can solve. The crops will come back the way they always have. The land will provide. The factory's still going, isn't it?*

Well, that Jimmy was always a tight bastard, he'd hold a tenpence piece between his teeth to cure seasickness.

Says the tourism'll help us all, fat chance!

And speaking of fat, did you see—

Oh, disgusting it is.

A real shame.

Whatever are they thinking? Coming here, of all places?

The trucks reach Jimmy's field and circle like wagons, tyres gouging fresh brown tracks in the earth. Mr Partlett slams on his brakes. The procession comes to a screeching halt.

The inhabitants fling open their doors and step out into the wet. Engines hiss and tick. Werewolf Louie angles his face to the sky, hopping from foot to foot, letting rain run rivulets down his fur. Zed offers his arm to Gretchen Etcetera – the world's most spectacular drag performer – and holds her up, giggling, as her glittered red heels plunge into the soil. The circle gathers around Mr Partlett, a fat wooden stake in his hands. Everyone makes their faces as eager as puppies in the pound. *Pick me, pick me, pick me!* In the grey light, Mr Partlett's scars are silver and luminous, sardine skin packed in a can. He smiles (the scars twist and bubble), he turns slowly, then he stops and holds the stake out to the Twins.

Four long and greedy arms reach out and grab it. The crowd whoops and hollers. A single pair of legs dip a respectful curtsey. Two identical smiles crack open four identical lips. The Twins are beaming, beatific saints – chosen ones for this summer season.

Here is the spot where things will take root. Shiny metal struts will plunge into primeval dirt. Long-forgotten grudges will be fanned into flame. Chaos and mischief will leak into the waterways, unsuspecting mothers will brew a cup of tea and end up with a bubbling intention to stumble off the narrow. Why not? It's just *trouble* after all.

The Twins lift the stake high. Everyone watches, breath held, as it traces an arc. The tip is sharp. The wet wood casts a shadow across the sky. For a moment, everything is still. Even the birds close their beaks.

And then the Twins drive the stake into the earth. The ground splits open to receive it. Just like that, the rain stops. Droplets of water reconsider their life's true destiny and head back to the sky. Gathered grey clouds puff and disappear like smoke.

A sunbeam spills upon the earth and it is hot and it is holy. A good omen.

The Freakslaw applaud. They have arrived.

DIRT CHARMS

NANCY WAKES AT the crack of dawn. All those other fuckers are still asleep (things got a little skewed after the delirium of the stake, as things always do), but that's okay. It's best to be alone for what she has to do in the sickly morning light. She's all riled up with the electric magic of sixteen-year-old girls, enough energy between her thighs to light up the entire Manhattan grid.

She stumbles out of her crooked red caravan into the field in socks, all wrapped up in a pink Nepalese carpet embroidered with elephants. Gloria the Teller was sprawled on the sofa this morning, and the last thing Nancy wanted was to wake her up rummaging through drawers. So no clothes, save for knickers and knee-high socks that are already sodden with dew. She looks fantastic. Like a filthy witch and a mountain mystic. She ought to be carrying a bow and arrow. A crown made of owl bones and tinfoil and peonies. Something to inspire a little worship.

None of the attractions are set up yet, but the border markers are in place. It's the first thing Mr Partlett does: declare the boundaries, lay the land. You've got to separate the fair from the world before you invite the world inside.

The thing is, magic needs a base to cling to. Earth for its roots. It's all very well casting hexes at any opportunity, but a spell without a proper base is like a topsoil plant: nice and pretty, but one strong gust and it'll blow away. Nancy's learned this the hard way, and she's not making that mistake twice.

But that's the problem with the funfair. What kind of bedrock can you build when every year's a new destination? It's one thing to shove a stake in the ground, but sometimes Nancy gets a hankering for really taking hold of a place, wrapping her fingers around its neck.

If you've got a house, you can keep it safe by hiding an old shoe in your walls. You can ward off bad spirits by filling a witch bottle with piss and fingernail clippings and rosemary and hair and red wine and sand and rusty screws and feathers and shells and salt and coins and ashes, bury it under the fireplace and count to ten. But what if you've got no proper walls? No fireplace? What's the girl in the caravan to do?

Well. That's where Nancy's charms come in.

From her knapsack, she takes a jar of menstrual blood. Six months' worth, a whole dreary winter of shed innards, the reek of rank and rotted meat. Her blood's turned brown and there are small globs floating. Really good bits. Nancy paces the perimeter of the field, dribbling an unholy breadcrumb trail. It sinks into the soil, leaving clots like Rorschach ink. To help the grass grow. Attract the bears.

What Nancy really wants is for the land to know it's hers. Everyone knows the best way to make something yours is to mark it with your stink. And Nancy has the best stink. It's incredible. Like heavy cream. Animal fur. Bitumen. Roast meat. Sweet rotting tropical fruits. Solar flares. Some kind of industrial, chemical wonderland. A rough rub on sore skin. She smells like a lovely shove in the face.

Or so Zed tells her anyway. And whenever he does, she'll

straddle him and pin him to the ground. Dip two fingers inside herself and stick them under his nose, make him screech like a delinquent lunatic.

But not today. Today, Zed's asleep – probably thick in hallucinatory dreams after last night – and she's doing the charms. If nothing else, a stink can serve to distract the previous owners. Like a baby bird rejected the moment you place your hands on it, rubbing your scent over the land messes with the old ghosts. It tells any inhabitants there's a new bitch in town. And when those ancient voices try to make themselves heard, Nancy turns stubbornly away.

Once the perimeter's done, Nancy pads to the hollow where the Houses of Horror and Fun will end up. She kneels in the muck, hiking the carpet under her armpits, and starts to dig. Soil gacks her fingernails. Small rocks dunt her knuckles. But she keeps going. She wants to get deep enough for her magic to seep into the ley lines.

Into the hole, she presses a single baby tooth, white and shiny against the dirt. It looks like a toy, but teeth have got all kinds of power lurking in their enamel. Some witches think your tongue's magic because it's the only muscle that lives inside and outside the body at once. Well, what about a bone that's both in and out of your flesh? That's teeth for you – bits of skeleton you can trace a finger across. And they don't stop growing when you die, so she's heard. Teeth, when it comes down to it, are definitely on her side.

The last charm's a sweet one: hair. Nancy takes a pair of golden scissors and snips off a lock. Her bad dye job looks like red paint. The hair's cheap and brittle, but who gives a fuck? She knots four sections around four screws nicked from Zed's toolbox. These for the compass points. With the aid of a screwdriver and a welter of elbow grease, she secures them in the approximating trees. The screws hold tight. The hair gusts like window-box geraniums.

Done! Nancy dusts her hands on her butt. The charms pulse in place, sending winks to their fellow workers. Just a little apotropaic magic – although that's a misnomer. Witchery doesn't work by repelling evil, any more than bug spray works by grossing a mosquito out. All either of them do is mess with the sensors, so the little friend can't even tell you're there.

What Nancy has done is make the funfair quiet to bad intent. Not invisible – she's not as powerful as that – but quiet. And, at the same time, she's amped-up the invitation to anyone yearning to send their ordinary life off the rails. Such a thing is very simple if you know how. It's like turning up the saturation on a photograph: everything is suddenly very bright and very tempting.

Nancy sits in the grass with the carpet around her shoulders like a tent. She bends her knee and twists her foot against her cheek, grazing dead skin on her face. The dew soaks into her knickers. The wet crotch makes her think about fucking. For that's something else the charms will attract: men.

Nancy's cheeks are studded with the scars of picked spots and her lips are always painted a lickable red and whenever she's alone with men, she likes to fill them with lies. She tells them the accident gave her synaesthesia, and now twos and sevens are purple, and E-minor chords taste like jelly beans. She tells them one time Gloria read her cards and said she used to be an Egyptian queen, and you can still see the snakebite scar behind her left ear. She tells them the second foetus, when it came out, had the beginning of a third eye blinking from its chest – and, if she'd kept it, it would have been the biggest money-spinner the fair had ever seen.

Men stick around to listen because Nancy, on form, is captivating. Better than Mr Partlett – better even than Gloria. And eventually she fucks the men too because Nancy really, really likes nerve endings. She can never quite believe how good sex feels. No matter how utterly ordinary a man is, there's just something about taking off your clothes in front of a new human being. Every time, it feels like a baptism. The girls are fun too, soft skin and suggestibility.

Of course, afterwards you can make them do whatever you please.

Nancy drums her fingers on the earth: an old worm-charmer trick to make them think it's raining. As she gets to her feet, the ground starts to writhe with brown and purple bodies. She darts around them and heads to Zed's cabin, to pound on his door.

CABBAGE & DEATH

DEREK GEDDES IS keeping his head down. That's the only thing to do when your da gets in a mood like this, unless you're the kind of total numpty who likes sticking a hand in wasps' nests. Who actually enjoys the thrill of poking bears.

Well, Derek's only a wee bit of a numpty and he thinks wasps are the biggest dicks of all insects, bar none. If he saw a bear, he'd do the smart thing and play dead – unless of course it was the kind of bear you were supposed to run from, in which case he'd scarper. But his da would not be happy with him hightailing it out of the kitchen, so.

He's looking at his plate. You could spend a whole lifetime looking at a plate like this. He bets there are monks in Tibet who'd kill to gain the kind of perspective he's getting right now. Well . . . maybe not kill. The monks probably have to take a vow they won't kill. If they get attacked by wasps, they probably just have to sit there and take it.

'More potatoes, Derek?' His mum's already holding the bowl of mash in his direction, pink hands quivering. There's something pure ridiculous about tatties for breakfast – just that, mash – but he doesn't need a fight and he doesn't point this out.

'I'm alright, Ma.'

The house smells like boiled cabbage and death. His da huffs. There's a long and dangerous pause while his mum holds the mash aloft. She might keep it up there for ever. Maybe they'll all die and the mash will still be hovering, waiting.

Then – 'Give us that, June.' His dad takes the bowl and ladles a huge mound on to his plate. A ridiculous portion. Mice could build ski slopes from that pile. If a horse ate it, it'd be called gluttony. It's a portion the size of a man.

'Sort it out, son.' His da piles three ladles on to Derek's own plate. 'It's good stuff, June.'

A thin trickle of potato water seeps out and Derek's mum gives a sweet little smile as if this is the greatest compliment she's ever been paid. 'Oh, it's nothing much,' she says. 'It's just tatties.'

'It's good stuff,' he says again.

That silence settles back. It weighs a tonne. A big wet rug over the kitchen, and they've all got to pretend to be happy campers underneath. But it's not working. Derek can feel sparks of frustration coming off his da as he shovels food. He's moving back and forth like he's revving up to have a go at someone. Derek thinks of a bull dragging a hoof through sawdust. He thinks of the genny they use at work when Bev wants to run a kitchen outside, the way it shudders when you first pull the cord. Then his mum meets his eye and he snaps out of it. He puts a forkful of wet potato in his mouth and makes his face blank as it turns to mush. The pile is bigger every time he looks down. He wouldn't be surprised if it was growing, if he'll blink to see it slathering across the table like sci-fi-movie slime.

'Well, did you see those lorries yesterday?' she says at last, and Derek knows the silence is over.

His da's face gets bright and dark at once. It makes Derek

think of a summer storm, purple clouds and surprise shafts of sunlight. 'Oh I did,' he says. 'Couldn't exactly miss them, could you?'

Derek doesn't know why his mum does things like this. Surely, quiet is better.

'Folk like that –' his dad jabs a fork at the table, punctuating his words – 'don't know they're born. Showing up with their fancy rags and their radios, nothing better to do than get all painted up to sit in a field? Bloody ridiculous.'

Derek's mum clucks sympathetically. 'I don't know what they're after. You wouldn't have thought Pitlaw's the place for a thing like that.'

'Not a bit! Might go down in Aberdeen or Dundee, but here?' He's warming to it now. Spit and potato fleck the table. 'Waste of time and money. It's kids' games, so it is. Anyone with half a brain would know better! You won't see me throwing an afternoon away to that rubbish.'

'Lord, no.' His mum looks at his da with an expression he can't read. As his voice gets louder, she unravels just a tick.

Derek's not going to say a word, though he knows it's got fuck all to do with throwing money away. Pitlaw's got more bookies than pubs, and his da's no stranger to either. But the lorries are something, it's true. Something, for a town where the most excitement in months was last Saturday night, when all the council house wheelie bins were dragged to the skate park, corralled in a circle and set on fire.

'Some of us have jobs to do, eh? You don't see them putting in an honest day. Most they'll do is find the one who'll fall for that shite.'

'Aye, so.'

His mum meets his dad's eyes. She gives a wee smile of

shared conspiracy. And Derek thinks then, maybe she's not so daft. Maybe it's better to get on the same team against a common enemy than wait for his dad to kick off. Like how they set the gas from the mines on fire, because it's better to burn it off than wait for it to explode. But then again, he read about the hole in Turkmenistan where they tried that and it just kept on burning. The name of the article was 'The Gates of Hell'. The pit's been burning for twenty-six years.

'And what about you, son?' His da turns to him. 'You got a plan for the summer? I won't be seeing you dossing round here every afternoon, will I?'

Derek does have a plan. He's got plenty. He's going to become a truck driver and have a horn he can hit with the palm of his hand. He's going to learn CPR and become a doctor, a helicopter doctor like the ones on TV. *Not* a nurse. He's going to pass his driving test. He's going to wait until his birthday, then stand on a wide stretch of flat road and stick his thumb into the air and see what happens next.

He's going to be a drifter, or a cowboy in tight stonewashed jeans and a dented copper belt buckle. A sailor, perhaps, with a tattoo of an anchor on his arm. Grow into his skinny frame, tan his skin till you can't see the freckles any more, get a real man's hairdo and not this ginger embarrassment.

He's going to get out.

'I'm working, Da. Doing the double shift now school's out.' He takes another forkful and fills his mouth. It's rude to speak with your mouth full, he knows that much, so the mash is an insurance against more questions. It sticks in his gums like the cotton wad at the dentist, wet and dry at once.

'Bout time,' his dad says. 'When I was your age, I was already doing ten hours a day in the factory.'

Derek swallows. A clod of potato slides down his throat. 'But I am. I said I'm doing the double shift.'

'Don't you speak to me with your mouth full!' His da smacks a palm on the table. He's pissed off, of course he is. Derek doesn't know why he pressed that button, but just like any big red button with a sign saying DO NOT TOUCH, he never can help himself. He swallows again. He has visions of trying to open his mouth to argue and wallpaper paste gluing it shut.

'Well, I am sorry, June.' Derek's dad is all head shakes, like he just can't believe the situation they've found themselves in. 'Here you are getting up early, slaving over a hot stove, trying to make something nice, and where does it get you?'

'Oh,' says his mum. 'Oh, it's nothing. It's just tatties.'

'Derek,' says his dad.

'I'm sorry, Mum.' He is too. He's sorry they're stuck here. Sorry he doesn't have it in him to fight back, sorry this is the best it gets. Some nights, when things get particularly rough, he's sorry Pitlaw isn't on a fault line, that he'll never be lucky enough to see the earth split open and swallow them. It's not that he wants to die, not really, but if it has to happen, it wouldn't be the worst to do it in an apocalypse, all fire and lava and epic brimstone.

'I worry about you, son.' His da frowns, like what's keeping him up at night is concern for Derek's general wellbeing. 'You might want to think about toughening up a bit.'

Derek looks at his plate again, trying to be a monk. He sits there and takes it. He doesn't flinch for wasps. And all the while, a dozen big red buttons light up in his brain saying DON'T TOUCH! DON'T TOUCH! DON'T TOUCH!

Derek's fingers twitch under the table. The buttons are so bright, so tempting. Derek shifts in his seat and sits on his hands.

THE WALTZER BOY

BAM-BAM-BAM-BAM-BAM! SAYS ZED'S door, and he's awake already, okay? He wasn't even asleep. Zed's been up for hours, just thinking. Sometimes in an early-morning loam, he gets wondering about whether roots are as deep as trees are high, or whether they're more like the whole iceberg thing. Sometimes he can't get back to sleep until he's figured it out. Would you have to dig them up to tell, or could you somehow do it while they're still alive? And what about the physics of pyramids – can they *actually* sharpen razor blades? How does a metal detector even work for that matter? Could you make detectors for other stuff, perhaps, like wood?

Important things, for sure. Besides, there's something not right about this too-early sun. It can burn through a loopy night delirium in less than ten minutes, so he's heard. That's why Scandinavians are such a sensible people, why they're good at carpentry but not interpretative dance, why they'll never design a piece of furniture with floofy bits.

BAM-bam-BAM-bam-BAM!

Umf.

That door really doesn't want to quit.

Zed throws his legs out of bed, one after the other in a cartwheel, and leaps to his feet. His hair's sticking this way and that way, and he smushes it down while he flings open the hot-pink caravan door.

'Nancy!' It comes out in a yelp. It took him halfway to the door to realize he hadn't just been thinking of tree roots and pyramids. The hard-on – endless curse of teenage-boy dreams! – is prodding out the front of his jogging bottoms, as if it'd like nothing more than to fling things open itself and go rushing out into the day. He puts one hand in front, shaking away visions of Boris Karloff and dancing girls in satin shoes.

Nancy pushes past and throws herself on his bed. She flings one hand over her eyes like a depressed movie star from the 1940s. 'Darling. I've been terribly busy.' Then she sits up in a cross-legged position and grins her witchiest grin. 'It's a good spot, Zed.'

'Yeah?' Zed's feeling a little mushy. Things got messy last night, messy and delicious. He has a brief and hilarious memory of Gretchen Etcetera limbo-dancing under a wicker switch, while the Twins chanted Bulgarian curses and recited the alphabet backwards. 'Coffee,' he says. 'How about that?'

'Thought you'd never ask.'

Zed squeezes past the bed to his tiny kitchen area and starts his small morning rituals. He takes the silver coffee maker in his long fingers, unscrews and empties it – and then, a reverse magic trick, it's assembled again, full of water and ground coffee, brewing away on a blue flame. Zed turns back to Nancy. She's sat on the bed like a Persian cat, surrounded by pillows, looking very pleased with herself.

'I have a good feeling about this year.' Nancy rummages in his sheets and finds the dregs of a packet of pickled onion Monster Munch. She dips her fingers into the crumbs, licking the powder off one by one. 'This place is ripe. They've been waiting for ever for something like us.'

Zed doesn't ask how she got all that just from the dirt. He knows how. 'So what's the plan?' he says instead, but Nancy's already nuzzling down under his cover, her scabby knees poking out. She looks like a crumpled piece of paper. There are grubby footprints traipsing the short distance from his door to his bed, and Zed feels a sudden jolt of happiness. It looks warm in there. Toasty and snoozy and utterly delightful.

Nancy yawns theatrically and tugs the cover to her hot little mouth. '*I'm* going to nap. I told you, I've been very busy. But *you* ought to get up. It's nearly noon. You've got –' another wee yawn – 'rides to assemble.'

'Noon?!' There's that yelp again.

'Bring me coffee first.'

He pours a shot into a little clay cup and places it on the shelf by her head. But Nancy's already got her eyes closed, slipping into those snuffling sounds in the back of her throat that she swears she doesn't make but are so damn cute. *Snarr . . . snarr . . . snarr.* Whatever. It's there if she needs it. If she finds out her dreams are too slow and needs to crank them up a notch.

He puts his own coffee in a jam jar, tops it up with hot water, wraps a tea towel around it, and spills out on to Jimmy's field. He hushes the door shut as quietly as he can behind him – even though he's never met anyone who can sleep quite like Nancy. He's seen her sleep propped up against the central thrust of the waltzers, the cars screaming and spinning around her. Back when they had the Loopin' Louie, one time the carriage came to a screeching halt and there she was, head askew, a trickle of drool from her lips. For one brief and terrible moment, he'd thought she was dead – but no, just another nap. Shit you not.

Zed takes a big oily sip as all around him caravan doors creak open. Nancy was lying, of course. It looks like it's ten, ten thirty at a push. But now he's up and about, the desire to go back to sleep is burning off. There's a lot to be done. And he loves this bit: the metamorphosis of dull old field into sparkling city. It makes Zed feel like a kid. It's like sitting in Gretchen's caravan first thing, when she's straight out of the shower, transforming into Gretchen Etcetera: princess of the iced cake and gemstone of the magpie's knicker drawer. Except it's not just her. It's their whole world.

Zed grabs his toolbox and heads to the stake, where Werewolf Louie is already stacking metal crates with his little arms, hefting them up on each other with an acrobatic writhe. The Strongmen are flocking everywhere, muscly and glistening, working in unison twice as fast as anyone else: hammer and dig and screw and pound. They move like a silent film, twitchy and wound-up.

Everyone's helping, including the Twins, who've got a huge electrical cable tangled round their shoulders. It's balanced precariously, but the Twins move with innate grace, prancing the earth with ease, bringing the plug to Mr Partlett who'll plug it in the mains.

All day long, Zed works in the heat. He hefts the metal poles on to the rig, feeling like a Strongman in a Victorian swimsuit himself. He lashes neon lights to trees. These tubes, he's heard, are filled with the crushed gas of distant planets – the red one over there's straight from the spot of Jupiter, the white the snipped rings of Saturn. They're as bright and as tempting as ice lollies, dripping with condensation in the sun.

He builds the Haunted House of Horrors together with the Pin Gal, who likes to whistle Broadway tunes while she works. Before the Pin Gal joined the funfair, she was an usher at a local theatre, but that never came close to satisfying her desire for the transformative power of the stage. She left in the night with a suitcase full of screwdrivers stolen from the set department, and she's been with the funfair ever since.

At the top of the Haunted House, Zed and the Pin Gal lash the Mummy with cable ties and duct tape and a confidence bordering on lunacy. The Mummy looms over the funfair mid-creep, bandages dangling in the breeze. He's so charming, Zed can hardly stand it. Imagine! The terror of being pursued by something so slow and so goofy. Zed could press his palms to his cheeks and scream and pretend to fall over, and still he doesn't think the Mummy would ever catch him.

The whole day, Zed is powered by coffee and Broadway, until finally the horn goes off and everyone drops their tools, right where they're standing, and heads to the feast.

The attractions are still only partially constructed and the field has all the odd charm of a clown in a business suit. Metal scaffolding juts into the sky. Airbrushed superheroes lean against trees in the wayward manner of old drunks.

But by the caravans, the feast tent is rigged and the huge table is groaning and Zed is famished. He takes his place. As everyone grabs plates piled high with charred meat and salted potato skins and crispy onions, the chatter rises: how it will be this season and what this summer has to offer and bless this happy family and let us eat, eat, eat.

ESCAPE ROUTES

MEANWHILE, IN THE last grey house on Westburn Avenue, the screaming starts up again through the wall. Ruth MacNamara is trying to ignore it – trying to write the personal statement that will persuade the grant authorities just how exquisitely suited she is for further study – but the screaming's getting louder. It sounds like an exotic bird trying to call forth the apocalypse.

Ruth buries her face in her pillow. She presses her palms against her ears, then twists on to her back and sighs dramatically. Of course, there's no one to notice just how frustrating this is. Mum's burying herself in a pile of ironing and Dad's inspecting bits at the factory and Stephanie, well Stephanie should be through the wall telling baby Kayleigh everything in the world is going to be alright, but it doesn't sound like that's true.

She doesn't have time for this. There's a very precise list of things that need to happen if Ruth's going to get out of Pitlaw. She needs an acceptance from a top university. She needs a full grant to pay the bills. She's already filled out the application forms for accountancy and she knows, in her absolute bones, they ought to take her. It's just maths. But the grant's something else. They want to know about participation: all the javelin societies and debate clubs and extracurricular commitments Pitlaw's never had time for. The problem here isn't just a lack of money – it's the belief, baked into the soil, that anyone who wants more has already got ideas above their station, so best not give them the tools to climb. Keep everyone on the same level, a comfortable kind of egalitarianism. Which is all very well if you're sticking around here for ever, but it's clear the world out there has all kinds of rankings.

So she needs to persuade them she's enough. She has to get it right.

The screech changes pitch, getting inexplicably higher. It doesn't seem possible a human could make such a noise. Perhaps Kayleigh's been snatched in the night, replaced with fairy's spawn. Not that Ruth's hoping that will happen, really, but it's a possibility. It doesn't hurt anyone to believe in possibilities.

Like this one: she can tread the balance between the weirdo she really is and the overachiever she needs to be. She can go on pretending just long enough for the rest of her life to begin.

The essay isn't working, so she does the only thing that ever helps. Goes to the stereo and puts on a Velvet Underground CD, cranks it up loud enough that the sound of Kayleigh is smothered. She lies on her bed again, eyes closed and lets the thrum, thrum, thrum of Lou Reed's guitar soothe her. It sounds like chemicals and glitter and bite marks and sex. It sounds like the gutter. Ruth wants to crawl inside this album, have it pull her hair and buy her a drink and smack her in the face. She wants to let it rub all over her, so she's for ever beautifully defiled. When the music fills her ears, she's no longer the good girl – master of the quadratic equation, the one first called upon in maths. No gawky nerd with red cheeks and too-long legs, always tripping over her own feet. She's someone else who is secretly, inexplicably, cool.

Ruth gets up and turns it up a little louder then throws herself on the covers, presses her face into the pillow and her hand against her knickers, and lets the song crash over her in waves.

It's getting to the good bit, it's building and it's biting, it feels like there's an animal growing inside her, and then – the music stops.

'Ruth MacNamara! What in the hell do you think you're doing?'

She rolls over and cracks an eye open. Her mum's standing there, a big sheet bundled in her arms, one hand on the stereo.

And in the silence, the air-raid siren starts again.

'You've only gone and woken the baby up. Christ's sake, Ruth. Do you not think you could help out a bit instead of causing more work for us all?'

Ruth sits up and blushes. It's not really fair. Kayleigh started it, she wants to stay, but even she can tell that placing the blame on a one-year-old isn't a good look. Not to mention the moment when she thought her mum was asking something else, and that's a conversation she doesn't want to have: not now, not ever.

She digs her fingernails into her palms and lets the throb inside her subside. Her head is swimmy. There's a big gulf between Max's Kansas City and her Pitlaw bedroom, and switching from one to the other so fast has given her the bends. There ought to be some acclimatization. She ought to remember to lock her door.

'Sorry, Mum. I'll turn it off.' It's already off. But it sounds like the right thing to say.

'If you've nothing better to do, why don't you come and help me with this ironing?'

Ruth sighs. 'Fine.' Ironing always seems the most pointless task – a job you do just to prove you're working. Does anyone really need flat socks? But people in Pitlaw really love ironing. When God makes his big decision about who's going up and who's going down, everyone here's convinced that creaseless corners are going to comprise a huge part of his decision-making process.

'Or you can get the messages. We're out of milk, there's a list on the—'

'I'll get it,' Ruth says. She's already halfway down the stairs.

'Money's in the drawer.'

'On it!' She throws on her backpack and clatters out the door. Her bike's propped by the house: a boy's red mountain bike with a basket from an old freezer drawer. The brakes don't work so good and the chain's a little rusty, but when she gets going, the bike is horse's hooves and a pact with gravity. When she's in the saddle, Ruth feels she can fly.

The moment she steps outside, she feels lighter. That stale choke of indoors slackens and the light is pink and tropical. The sky is bigger than usual, stretching all the way from one horizon to the other. She's already running when she grabs the handlebars. A few strides, then one foot's on the pedal and her leg's swinging up over the crossbar. Her thighs are pumping. Ruth and the bike pelt down the hill, gathering speed, her hair whipping in the wind. No one could catch them now. As she takes the bend, they send up clouds of dust. Then it's the rise, the burn in her legs, that impossible heat. She leans forward and lets momentum carry her, and before she knows it she's rising up up up to the top.

And then she stops. Blood thrums furiously beneath her skin.

In the weird pink evening light, Jimmy's field – that dull brown square – has cranked into life. Fat smears of colour everywhere: buildings and billboards and the half-assembled skeletons of rides. Neon slashes in the trees. She can hear something too, over the pant of her breath. Distant music filling the valley, a creaky, jolting wind-up song.

Ruth shakes her head. There's something odd about it. It's the light, the saturation. So shiny-bright and tempting. The shock of seeing this in Pitlaw, of all places.

She opens and closes her hands on the brakes. The bike is almost neighing now. It can smell what's going on down there: gasoline and candied almonds and wet dreams and escape routes. She could show up and hold out one hand and they'd yank her into the cab of a truck. Head off blaring down the motorway, purple feathers flapping in the wind.

But she's being ridiculous. That's not part of the plan. And if she ever wants to get out of Pitlaw, she's got better things to do than mess around with kids' games.

Ruth takes one last look, then cycles off to get the milk before the shop closes.

IT'S NOT OVER UNTIL
THE FAT LADY EATS

AND SO THE fair begins to unfurl, taking up the land like slow waters rising. Five days swell into radiant sunlight then retract into darkness. Five moons traverse five night skies. Roller coaster tracks make a path to the next thing: schnack, schnack, schnack. Ghosts coalesce behind haunted doors. And the freaks unbutton their caravans and start oozing into this perfectly normal town.

They have work to do. Miss Maria does, especially. It's not easy to maintain a body like hers – a lush and decadent fruit, one that requires fertile soil and a strict nourishment regime. Why, just the stress and hubbub of the set-up and she's already lost four pounds! At this morning's weigh-in, Mr Partlett was quite displeased. When he scowled, all his scars leaped. If things carried on like this, who's to say where she'd end up? Just another ordinary woman, in another ordinary skin.

No, it would not do! She was to go into town immediately and Rectify the Situation.

'You go with her,' he tells Gretchen Etcetera. 'See what delights our new home has to offer.'

His incisors flash a flickering smile.

Miss Maria and Gretchen Etcetera trot arm in arm down Main Street, giggling like schoolgirls bunking off. What a treat! These hours their own to do whatever it takes, the afternoon stretching out long and lovely.

Gretchen is resplendent today in mahogany powder and contoured cheekbones, a heart-shaped beauty mark on her left cheek. She flutters her false eyelashes at all the houses, and all the curtains twitch back.

By her side, Miss Maria's skin is bare: her complexion is the softest thing imaginable. Making love to Miss Maria is like sinking into a huge bed piled high with throw pillows and silk sheets. Norms have flocked from all corners of the earth, paid any price, just to spend a single night lolling in the glory of her flesh.

Both wear the identical shade of cherry-red lipstick. Their mouths are huge and wet under the glistening sun.

'Miss Gretchen, are you hungry?' Miss Maria smiles coyly at her friend.

'Ravenous!'

The girls turn the corner and head to the one caff in town.

They take up a great many seats. The long window table, which is big enough for three generations of a family, a whole shift's workers from the plant, is now commandeered. They sit across from one another, holding fork and knife aloft, Miss Maria filling the window.

The caff's not busy. But the few other customers – in drab clothes and drabber faces, perched at the tables by the wall – huff and mutter. *Who do these people think they are, so fat, so garish, so repulsively in your face? And taking up that whole table, when there's just the two of them!*

Miss Maria drums her fists and laughs prettily. The cutlery leaps like a troupe of Russian dancers made to perform for dinner. Gretchen pours a puddle of sugar on to the formica tabletop and drags her glittery gold fingernails through. She draws a smiley face. She dusts that out and draws an angry face. She dusts the mouth out and draws the smile back but keeps the eyebrows so there's a candy-sweet madman gnashing at his lot in life.

From across the room, the waitress looks rather upset. For this, Miss Maria feels a tiny pang of guilt. Everyone knows that people who make service staff sad are the most dreadful of all humans. There's a true hell – one crafted of fire and brimstone and mouthfuls of phlegmy spit – precisely for their kind. The waitress looks like her day might just be ruined.

But at the same time, Miss Maria knows that ruin can be a precious gift. She can remember being a little girl, before she herself was ruined, when she still believed that if she did everything right, all the time, then one day she'd get what she'd earned. How many girls have been tricked into believing that fairy tale? How much better can life be, when you understand it's all a fib?

There's something utterly wonderful about ruin, because once you've fallen far enough, you stop trying to impress anyone. It's only then that life's true opportunities make themselves known.

'What can I get for you today?' asks Alice Wilson, peering down a small and unfortunate chin that looks for all the world as if her neck's trying to swallow it.

'I'm glad you asked, my dear,' replies Miss Maria.

'One of everything!' says Gretchen Etcetera.

'Don't be silly,' says Miss Maria. For a moment, Gretchen looks chastened. Miss Maria shoots the waitress a look of heartfelt apology, and Alice Wilson lets out the breath she's been holding. These people might be huge and hideous, they might be Not From Round Here, but they're just going to get some lunch. They're going to order the food and she's going to serve the food and sooner or later her shift will be over, she'll be back in her living room watching *Brookside*, eating a Tesco oven pizza with salami and mushrooms, drinking a treat can of Tennent's she put in the freezer for an extra ten minutes so it's super duper cold. Everything's ordinary and everything's fine.

Then Miss Maria starts reading items from the menu, her voice ringing like a big glorious church bell. 'THREE bigger breakfasts,' she says, 'SIX bacon rolls, FOUR square sausage rolls – one with an extra egg please, TATTIE SCONES! You best just make a whole pile of those, love, don't skimp on the ketchup—'

'A cheese and onion toastie,' says Gretchen.

'Three! And baked beans, we'll be wanting cheese on those too . . .'

'You might as well just put cheese on all of it,' offers Gretchen. 'Save yourself time.'

'Omelettes and chips! We'll have one mushroom and ham, one sausage and cheese, one . . . let me see . . .'

'You could put the breakfast in the omelette. I bet that would be good.'

'Oh,' says Alice Wilson, 'oh, I don't know about that.' But before she can protest any more Miss Maria dips her hand in her glorious spilling cleavage and pulls out an enormous wad of cash, a roll the size of a fist. She throws it on the tabletop and it unfurls like a flower.

'It's really no bother,' says Miss Maria, with her brilliant wet smile. 'No bother at all.'

Alice Wilson shifts from foot to foot, like she might wet herself. 'No bother?'

'None!' agrees Gretchen, who by now has a whole army of sticky sugar faces leering up.

All the argument slumps out of the waitress's shoulders as she scribbles the order. 'Some tea?'

'Pots of it!'

'Black coffee,' says Gretchen. 'As short and as strong as you can.'

Alice Wilson paces back to the kitchen, knuckles white around the pad. The other customers are shooting glances at Miss Maria and Gretchen. They're gossiping and ruffling behind their palms. Around the caff, there's a crackle of energy.

Miss Maria giggles. Her plump legs kick delightedly, as soft and squeezable as chocolate eclairs.

The window table was the right choice. Soon, it's groaning. Dishes cover every available surface – at some point, Alice Wilson gives up on finding new space and simply piles them on top. There's a mountain of breakfast rolls towering like a Cambodian temple. Omelettes flopped in layers like plump mattresses. So many chips.

Miss Maria is in heaven. The air's alive with hot grease and fatty meat, the vinegary tang of ketchup. Her teeth burst through a taut sausage skin and the flesh explodes in her mouth. She rolls balls of white bread into perfect squidges, placing each ceremoniously upon her tongue. And what about those onion rings! She bites through the batter, sucks out the slippery innards, feeling like Lady and the Tramp.

Miss Maria ladles salt on everything until it makes her

mouth pucker. She washes it down with sparkly Irn Bru, so sweet her teeth ache.

Gretchen Etcetera eats the inside of her toastie – stretching out the molten cheese like mermaid hair – but leaves the crusts. She breaks these into little pieces. Gives one of her sugar faces a bread cigar.

They lick their fingers. Their lipstick is still perfect. Their movements are heavy and carnal. They are more corporeal than anyone else. Three-dimensional, twice as real. Miss Maria's flesh ripples as she places her entire thumb in her mouth, running her tongue over ridges slick with brown sauce.

After they mop the last goop from their plates, they recline in their chairs, drum their fingers upon their stomachs, and sigh happily. A lovely peace descends. And then –

'Disgusting.' The voice comes from a table in the back, only a mutter, but it carries across the whole room. 'Just disgusting!'

Miss Maria and Gretchen turn slowly. They are sleepy and sated, absolutely belly-full. They move like cats in sunbeams, rolling over to warm a new patch of fur.

'Me?!' Miss Maria's mouth falls open in a perfect O. 'Us?' She sounds genuinely surprised.

Then she smiles, that huge red glistening smile.

Later, when Norma Murray is describing the day's events to her family, she'll find it difficult to express exactly what made her so angry. She'll tell the same story five times, six – enlisting the indignation of her husband to buoy up her own unshakeable sense of rightness. 'Would you credit that?' she'll say. Her sons will start to laugh at the bit with the slippery egg pile, but they'll soon catch the look on their mother's face and go quiet.

One thing her husband will notice (although he'll never point it out to her, no – he's not so daft as that) is the point at which Norma's voice breaks on each retelling, where it twists to something so high and hysterical he worries she might just start screaming and never stop.

It won't be on the description of the man in the dress (although she's disgusted enough at that, make no mistake) and it won't be the spilled sugar on the tabletop. It won't even be the list of everything that woman – that pig! – consumed.

It'll be the moment Norma finally had enough, when she simply had to say something (someone did), and what did that hideous woman do?

She smiled!

Back in the caff, the spell is broken. In the lull that follows Norma's comment, displeasure glints and fizzes. The tension thrums. And the drab-faced people open their mouths to make themselves heard, say the things they've been nourishing in their hearts. For Pitlaw has long had a simmering anger in its soil, one that takes so little to catch.

'Perverts!' hisses Doreen Abbott – who, as a girl, used to tap-dance and dream of crocodiles, who hasn't had an orgasm in over four decades. She looks around, shocked at the strength of her own voice, and goes back to nibbling her egg sandwich, a folded napkin to dab the mustard from her lips.

'What a pig, what an absolute pig!' pronounces Phillip Burnstone, who once had an imaginary frog friend called Frogbert, but now entertains himself with Nazi documentaries and microwavable lasagne at the weekends. If Miss Maria could see this past, she'd feel a pang of sorrow for Frogbert, who never had the send-off he deserved. She'd wish him a good reincarnation, a second go at life with a more loyal companion.

'Degenerates, so they are.'

'Freaks!'

Because it's one thing to be in possession of a body that draws stares, and quite another to flaunt it. Sure, there are those in Pitlaw who may have disabilities or disfigurements, but here they at least have the decency to cover them up – the good sense to know what folk would rather not have to look at. That's how it should be, after all.

All around Miss Maria and Gretchen, the voices rise up up up like the Ferris wheel cresting the trees. People shift in chairs and crane their necks. Miss Maria and Gretchen take a certain delight in this reminder of who they are. Outsiders. Freaks, you say?

They smack their lips and purr, relishing the hubbub, the warm fizz of validation, as the man in the corner gets to his feet. He clears his throat. The guttural thrum cracks something open in the atmosphere. Jim Barrie is holding a butter knife and it would be hilarious if not for the way the air changes. An electric shift, a feeling the caff could combust any second. Violence smouldering just below the crust.

'You're looking to start something,' he says. 'You've got a nerve.'

'Oh no,' says Miss Maria, although that's not completely true. It's the beginning of summer, a time when just about anything might happen. And they have more than their share of nerve.

Alice Wilson picks at her cuticle. She scratches her hair

with her pen, then starts doing the one thing she knows how: stacking plates. Alice Wilson is a very good waitress. The tower of plates reaches all the way to her eyebrow. Balanced on one wrist like a bear on top of a shiny round ball. 'Maybe you should go,' she says.

Miss Maria turns to Gretchen. 'You are *so* disgusting,' she whispers lovingly. Swallowing down the crackle of fear that caught for a moment there, the dark ember that threatens to take hold.

Gretchen removes a cigarette from a rhinestone-encrusted case, places it between her lips, sparks it into life. She takes a long drag and sends a series of smoke shapes: pirate ship, rhododendron, three hummingbirds blowing kisses. 'I love you too.'

'Shall we?' Miss Maria eases herself to her feet. Her luscious body crests and swells, moving like the glowing pink goo in a lava lamp. She's distantly aware of a woman clutching her little boy closer, as if Miss Maria's fatness might be contagious – a hunk of it might leap off and attach itself to him, if he happens to get too close. But mainly she's looking at her friend. Gretchen always makes her think of popping candy and jazz trumpets and the flower they call Bird of Paradise. She makes Miss Maria laugh harder than anyone, until they're both bent over and clutching their stomachs, weeping big round tears, saying stop-oh-please-no-more-stop! If anyone hurt Gretchen, she'd have to kill them. And where would that end up? Trouble, again.

'Come on, then,' says Gretchen with a grin. 'Let's get out before we degenerate any further.'

They leave arm in arm, not once glancing back to where the town's fury is already brewing.

NOT ONE TO JUDGE

THE NEXT DAY, Ruth sits on the living room sofa, knees to her chin, while the television blares. It's been a bad morning for news, as far as she can tell. It's been a bad week and a bad month and a bad year. There are hurricanes in places that never used to have hurricanes, and whole swathes of land keep falling into the sea. Babies go missing as easily as pocket change, anyone can be walking down the street, trip over their shoelaces and end up held hostage in a basement for seventeen years. No one ever thought to tell the news good things happen sometimes too, so the news spends its days replaying the worst nightmares greatest hits reel. Sometimes, Ruth worries she'll end up in the headlines one day. And then she remembers Pitlaw's not that kind of place, and somehow that makes everything worse.

At the other end of the sofa, Stephanie stands Kayleigh on her knee and bounces her. Kayleigh pooches her cheeks and giggles.

'Who's a daft wee cunt?' Stephanie says. 'Who's going to have to walk the plank?' Kayleigh burps and Stephanie steers her to the edge and Ruth tugs her hoodie over her ears, smothering the noise. She's trying to read Sartre's *Nausea*. By the time she starts uni, Ruth needs to have read all The Classics. She needs to know how to drink coffee and balance a spreadsheet and which order to use her forks. She's terrified she's already too late.

But *Nausea* is terrifically dull. Roquentin's always mooning around, getting ever so upset over an old stone, a soggy bit of paper on the street.

Her mum appears in the doorway, holding a tray of mugs and a teapot in a red knitted cosy. She places the tray on the coffee table and pulls up a chair, so they're all angled like a Greek chorus round the TV. It's switched to the weather. The smiling lady predicts another week of drizzle and gales, a cold front moving down over the mountains. Funny. Ruth looks at the road, where the tarmac is shimmery under a blazing sun.

'I've just got off the phone with Doreen.' Her mum pours three mugs of tea and places one in front of each of them. 'You'll never guess where she was yesterday.'

Ruth peers over her book. 'I don't drink tea any more, remember?'

'Oh suit yourself.' Her mum tops up her own and Stephanie's with big slugs of milk.

'Tell me.' Stephanie adjusts Kayleigh and settles into the sofa like a hen, wriggling her butt back and forth. Her mum leans forward conspiratorially and Ruth tries to shut her ears, to sink back into *Nausea*. Roquentin's wishing he'd never picked up that stone. His hands are feeling sick.

'Well, she was going to get an egg roll at the cafe – you know how she's been about bacon since she saw that pig documentary – and she's just sitting there, minding her own business, when who comes in but two of them freaks from the carnival.'

'No!'

'I kid you not.'

Ruth holds her book perfectly still and stares at the sentences. The words have become ants swarming the page. They traipse in formation, start to parade up her fingertips. Soon, they're all the way to her elbows.

'They've got a man in a dress,' her mum says.

'What, like a bearded lady?'

'No, I mean a man. In a dress. Big hands and feet and all.'

Her mum nods sagely and both of them are silent to let this revelation sink in. They take long slurps of tea. Kayleigh blows a spit bubble. Ruth's ears burn. She feels a strange shame unfurling, like some small, secret part of herself's been made public. The same as when she confessed to Lisa she'd had that funny dream about Mr Clement, flinging off his tie in graphic communication, and Lisa pissed herself laughing and Ruth couldn't bear it. Just the thought made her cringe. And whenever she masturbated thinking of him after that, there was always two things: the desire and the embarrassment, rubbing up against each other and making the other bigger.

'That's not the worst of it. The other one, the fat one, she must have ordered everything in the kitchen. Doreen says she had to have three chairs: one for each leg and one for the stomach.'

'She did not!' Stephanie bursts into laughter. Kayleigh, eyes wide, opens her mouth and laughs back.

'I mean, I'm not one to judge, you know that, but can you imagine? If I looked like that, I'd eat my dinner inside, thank you very much.'

'Inside? I hope you'd skip it.' Stephanie gives a bitchy smirk and for a minute, Ruth can see the person she was before Kayleigh came along. The tough girl with the sunbed tan and Kappa tracksuit bottoms hung low on her hips, always with two or three mates backing her up whenever she decided to deck someone. Full of contempt for the eejits who lived here, certain her own path would be different. Stephanie's nicer now than she was back then. Sometimes.

'No, no, you're right,' her mum says. 'I'm laughing, but it's not funny really. It's sad, is what it is.'

'It's so gross.'

And the two of them get to talking about the horror of it, a body like that, what kind of greed it would take! Do you think she just didn't notice? Or is it some kind of compulsion, she can't stop herself? What it must do to her heart. What it must do to those poor ligaments.

Ruth tunes their voices out. Stretches her legs off the sofa and pinches the skin by her knee. Her bones are so close to the surface. She's the kind of person who could stand sideways and go unnoticed. How would it feel, to take up that much space? To be so impossibly, indubitably *there*?

It'd be too much. It'd lead to all the wrong things, it'd send her spiralling off in directions you can't take back. Ruth let herself snap back once against the girls at school – just once, just because of the things they were saying about Stephanie being a dumb whore who deserved exactly what she'd got – and what scared her most wasn't the beating she got for it (though that was bad enough; boys may punch but girls will yank your hair out by the handful). It wasn't the rumours they started afterwards about Ruth being the exact same kind of whore, because really, who cares about a thing like that? No, what scared her was the raw anger that grew in her chest, feral and uncontainable. She felt like a tinderbox that would set the whole town on fire if she didn't hurry up and tamp herself down.

Besides, she just has to look at Kayleigh to see what happens when you let yourself follow an impulse to its foolish conclusion. And though she'd fight anyone who had something smart to say about her sister, the fact remains that Stephanie had a whole life planned out and look how that went up in smoke. Desire, fury – both are as dangerous as each other if you let them get out of hand, both are hungry, hungry emotions that'll swallow your heart whole. It starts with taking up space and it ends up right here, stuck in a trap of your own making.

Not an option. No way. Her tea sits on the table. A thin film over the top that makes her think of spiderwebs. She stares at it, then picks it up and downs it in one.

Stephanie and her mum stop talking. 'You drinking tea again, love? The milk's here, you only had to ask.' If she's trying to hide a smile, she's doing a bad job.

Ruth stares at them helplessly. Then she rams *Nausea* down the side of the sofa, grabs her bag and strides to the door. 'I'm going out.' She needs to get away, to run all this crackling energy out of her body.

'Be back at seven for dinner!'

The air outside is sticky and close. It's never like this in a Pitlaw summer. For a moment, she feels kind of dreamy – she has an image of a big hall with polished wooden boards, line after line of silk slippers, all kicking in unison. A place to dance, where the tight yoke of the town gives way to fluid movement, loose and lithe at last.

Then she shakes her head and fixes her lace, and she's gone.

RUFFLE OF FEATHERS

MEANWHILE, IN THE shadowy big top that comprises the Freakslaw's swollen heart, Gretchen Etcetera is drumming her manicure against a candied nut crate, a rat-tat-tat marching-band drill to punctuate her progress report.

'They're a bunch of judgey dickholes,' she says. 'Evil-eyeing the hell out of us, as if their own farts don't stink.'

Mr Partlett crooks an eyebrow, a smile plucking the corner of his lips. 'Well, that sounds promising.' It's with the ones who are quickest to judge that they've seen the most dramatic results in the past, after all. There was the whole business at the petrol station in Aberystwyth. Porth, of course, where the locals surely still talk of the Incident with the Balloons that got out of hand. And who could forget Shepton Mallet, that town square spattered with sweat and watermelon guts after the revelry was done?

A pulse of laughter escapes his lips. One thing he has learned from the passage of time is that age does nothing to mellow a man. In fact, as the years go by, he sees more and more beauty in the prospect of trouble's delectable attendance. A certain elegance in chaos, the subtle pleasure of lives gone awry.

Gretchen's drumroll quickens. 'It is. But be prepared for shit kicking off. These arseholes are scared. They've got this place stuck under their skin like a splinter, and they're afraid to prise it out.'

Miss Maria moves a protective hand over her friend's. When the world quickens to violence, Gretchen's always been a fast target. Singled out for the contents of her underwear and the colour of her skin. Yet she's always the first to fight against the choke of bigotry, and god, Miss Maria loves her for that. Gretchen takes not a single shit from anyone, not even Miss Maria herself, but beneath her blunt honesty is a fierce and radical care.

Mr Partlett nods. 'Duly noted.'

The Pin Gal is listening intently, one ear cocked while she threads knitting needles through the worn holes of her flesh. Silver flashes against Technicolor tattoos. At Mr Partlett's words, she lets the needles fall and saunters over. 'My turn?!' she says in her xylophone voice, every syllable ringing out. She stands behind Miss Maria, runs her fingers through Miss Maria's hair. 'Let me take a gander at what's out there.' There's an unusual pink high in her cheeks, an itching for a fight. The Pin Gal – who chose the scissoring metal of her own freakishness – still believes the world's an essentially benign place. She can fling herself against it full pelt and the worst that'll happen is she'll bounce.

And Miss Maria loves that too. Sometimes she feels such a gleeful love for her family – for the entire world! – that it physically hurts. A deep and pleasurable ache for how much there is of everything, just waiting to be experienced. So despite the twinge of anxiety, she thrills to see what will happen next. Every small-town arrival is the same: the freaks ruffle feathers, the norms huff and bother, and every time the Freak-slaw's magic eventually takes hold. No one can resist the allure of the left-hand path for long, not when it's right there, yellow cobblestones glinting!

They will take the whole summer, if they need to. Stick it out in this scourge of a town until they get everything they've come for. The pleasure of being dubbed troublemaker is just the beginning.

'And if they try to run us out of town?'

'Well, we make them pay!'

Their cackles drift up towards the billowing ceiling. A moth bats against the dangling lamp. They watch as it collides once, twice, three times, wings charring on hot glass. Yet it just can't help itself. As the laughter reaches the lamp, there's a flash and a spark.

Whump!

And the small, scorched corpse falls to the floor.

DEREK & THE PIN GAL

DEREK PULLS HIS hands from the dishwater. His fingers are looking a wee bit puckered. His palms are crimson, all the way to his wrists. Like he put on red mittens, and forgot to take them off.

Still, there's the goofy edge of a smile. Because work's not so bad, really. Sure, he's not so into how Chef yells at him to hurry the rack. And yeah, at first getting up at five was a right pain in the arse, but the dishes themselves? They're alright. When he's alone in the back and it's just him and the steam. When he plunges his hands into a sink so hot he can't tell if it's icy or boiling or full of electric currents, it feels almost good. Or just that: good.

Derek fires the hose over the plates. Lumps of beef fat and tartare sauce go skiting. They catch in the mesh and he plucks out the phlegmy handful of gunk, chucks it into the slops bucket. He slides the big rack into the machine, moving like a conveyor belt, and presses the glowing green button. The red one lights up, the dishwasher vibrates and hums, and he takes the next set into the water to start the whole process again.

If it could just stay like this for ever, Derek would be fine. He's worked at the Skene Dhu for two years, since he turned fifteen and graduated from his paper round, and dishwashing is way, *way* better. There's no dogs in the kitchen for a start, there's no bampot pissing himself laughing as some beast tries to get a lump of flesh out of Derek's arse. When he's here, he doesn't have to think about his dad or his life, all the ways things might be already screwed. The machine gives a thunk like a coin clattering into a locker, and the green light's on again. He opens the dishwasher and out billows the steam and there's Derek parading through it, a celebrity makeover on *Stars in Their Eyes*.

'More plates!' yells Chef from the kitchen, and he's on it, plucking the hot ones with a dishtowel wrapped around his crabby red hands, stacking them in a big pile, and running through.

The kitchen's something else. The overhead lights are twice as glarey and everyone's always running around like headless chickens, hot dishes and order tickets in their hands. Derek's stood in the midst, clutching his plates, trying to suck in his bum so that he takes up less room. He looks around frantically.

'On the counter, Derek,' yells Chef, so Derek turns to place them there, but just as he does Joe the waiter runs up behind him, shouting, 'NEW ORDER!' and pushes on past.

Derek takes a step back. His foot lands right in the grease spill by the deep-fat fryer. And he loses his balance all slap-stick. All of a sudden, he's that guy in the black and white movie with his funny little moustache askew, kicking and slipping, cartwheeling one arm while the other clutches the plates to his chest.

'Derek!' yells Chef.

But how can he . . . no! He does it! He manages to right himself – and then the tower of plates slips and slides to the ground in slow motion. They smash in the most dramatic fashion, like sheets of iceberg falling into the sea.

'Oh shit,' Derek says.

'Derek Geddes, you absolute gobshite!' yells Chef.

'I'm sorry!' Derek yelps, and he's already hands and knees on the floor. It's not all bad – it could have been worse. Just the ones on the top. These in the middle, they're okay. Derek pulls out the unbroken plates and piles them on the counter, starts gathering the big shards between his palms.

'Get a dustpan and brush, Derek.' The kitchen hasn't stopped moving. Chef's still running from point to point, conjuring up fish and chips and steak pie and chips and chicken curry for those feeling a wee bit fancy, a bit foreign for a change. Pitlaw might be small, but you'd never tell from Saturday lunch rush at the pub.

'I'm fine, it's fine.'

Maybe it's because his hands are still so hot and numb that he doesn't notice it right away. Then he feels a twinge and looks down and he's convinced he's going to vomit, right there and then. His head goes light. The two sides of skin peel back and blood bubbles up and out like water from a stuck drain.

'Get out of the way, Derek!'

'I think . . . I need . . .'

And that's the last thing before everything goes black.

Derek's sat outside, big white bandage on his hand, holding his arm above his head. He feels a right twat but Bev said it's supposed to slow the bleeding, and he knows better than to argue.

It turned out the cut wasn't so bad. Once Bev poured the

hydrogen peroxide into it – which fizzed and frothed and hurt like shit – the bleeding slowed. She taped on a thick cotton wad, wrapped him up like a baby and sent him on break early, while Joe grumbled and finished sweeping the broken plates.

So he's not at the hospital. He's outside the pub, in an unlikely patch of sunshine, waving like he's trying to hitch a ride out of this place.

Derek can feel eyes on him, and he doesn't like that. He's spent a load of time and energy training himself to merge into the background, and now here he is, big white hand in the air like a gype. He puts his head down.

But that's when she emerges out of the car park. And he can't help himself staring, because this person – this girl – is like nothing Derek Geddes has ever seen.

He's not the only one. All conversation in the beer garden grinds to a halt. The blokes place their pint glasses down and a funny thin silence catches. Derek's impressed. He's lived in Pitlaw all his life – grown up around these men, felt their scorn and worse. His da's not here today, thank god, but he recognizes his mates sat at a table. It takes a whole lot to shut them up.

The girl is covered in tattoos. Not just one or two, but the entirety of her skin lit up like butterfly wings: hot pink and turquoise and blood red. Mermaids wrestling with Betty Boop, anchors tangled round jungle flowers, a tiger bursting through a torn patch of skin. And so much metal! Every inch of her face is studded with golden piercings that catch the light. Delicate chains dangle, rubies wink in her eyebrows. She looks like a pirate's treasure chest propped open on a beach.

The only part not pierced is her lips – and they're painted a bright, glistening red. The men stare. They've been silent but it's wearing off; all the men are thinking exactly what needs said to this dumb bit of stuff. What it'll take for her to learn a lesson. Whether they need to say it with their mouths or with their fists.

And then the Pin Gal smiles and the silence is broken.

'What the fuck's all this then?' Derek recognizes that voice – that's Jack Haskett's dad. Stepping out the pub door, pint in hand, he looks like an angry bouncer: all shaved head and broken blood vessels across his nose. He runs the car repair. He's got a bull terrier whose favourite time of day is always the delivery of the *Daily Mail*.

The girl smiles even sweeter. She pulls a pocket watch on a long golden chain from inside her shirt and holds it to the light. 'Beer?'

The word rings out like a glockenspiel, and the other men look to Jack Haskett's dad to see how he's going to take this. Because it's not just the tattoos and the piercings and the goddamn attitude. It's also the fact that the pub is *their* place. Men's. In Pitlaw, there's plenty of places for womenfolk to gather for their chats. There's the shop and the hairdresser, there's the back garden over the fence, there's the kitchen with a pot of tea and the fancy cups, the ones with gold trim on the handles. There's church.

But the pub? Oh no. The pub is the last bulwark in a world women are taking over, the last place you can have a proper talk without getting all tangled up in lassies' shite.

And the Pin Gal is definitely a lassie. She may be funny looking, may be some kind of mutant, but that's definitely tits under there. No doubt about it.

Jack Haskett's dad considers, then leers right on back at her. Lips stretch taut over his teeth. 'You can fuck off to wherever you're goin, hen. Just not here, eh?'

The Pin Gal shrugs. She tugs down her shirt, just a smidge, and fingers a piercing beneath her collarbone, a brass bear head with an emerald in its teeth. Her fingers wrap around it and give one fluid tug, and the thinnest sword emerges, thinner than a knitting needle and twice as long. Just like that! She executes a two-step and thrusts it out like a fencer.

Derek's mouth is open. Did it come from *inside* her ribcage? No way! It's impossible. It's a magic trick. The girl looks like she's trying not to laugh. Jack Haskett's dad slams his pint down on a table shaped like a barrel, reaches out one meaty fist and grabs the blade.

It twangs ludicrously under his grip. He yanks it from her and throws it on the ground where it bounces back and forth like a demented jack-in-the-box. By now, the Pin Gal is giggling.

'You're havin' a laugh,' says Jack Haskett's dad. He says it with disgust, like there's nothing worse in the world. Like they should all be on the lookout for laughs all the time, and if they find any, they should stamp them out with steel-toecapped boots.

The girl tilts her head. Derek can't tell if she understands English, if the man's ranting is making any sense. He wants to reach out. Sweep her under his wing, protect her from Pitlaw's pointy edges. No matter what language she speaks, surely anyone can see Jack Haskett's dad is not, in fact, a welcoming force? His forehead is gouged with great angry creases. Whole slabs of muscle slide as he takes a step towards her, gives an almost apologetic shake of his head. He doesn't want to do this, you see. It's never been in his nature to enjoy hitting a woman. But if you don't administer a little correctional tap now and again, well, we all know how that ends up.

He clutches his hands at his chest, as if in prayer, then draws one back and smacks the Pin Gal in the face.

BAM.

Except he doesn't. He draws his hand back, yes, he swings – but as he does, the Pin Gal weaves like a snake in hot grass. One fluid movement, and she's gone. Jack Haskett's dad stumbles forward, carried by momentum, but he doesn't fall.

Behind him, the Pin Gal stands at the table, smiling the sparkliest smile. She picks up his beer, holds it to the sunlight, and starts to drink. By the time he has turned around, the pint is empty.

Derek cannot believe what's happening. He's terrified and he's thrilled and he might pee a bit. Too many feelings, all at once. His hands are in his lap now, his palm pulsing, but he pays it no mind.

Jack Haskett's dad's face has gone a funny shade of purple. His eyes have sunk deeper than any Derek's ever seen. They look like pebbles at the bottom of a lake. He steps towards the girl with hands out in front of him: a lumbering, creeping Mummy with strangling on his mind.

None of the other men are getting involved – this is his game, no doubt – but they gather in a broad semi-circle, ready to holler however it kicks off. The air is thick with testosterone and scampi fries. The girl opens her eyes very wide and Derek can't stand it, but he can't move.

The Pin Gal raises one hand to her lips – smothering a

burp or feigning surprise, he can't tell – then she opens her mouth and a gust of fire leaps out. The flames, fast and orange, fly right into Jack Haskett's dad's face. He shrieks. Starts flapping around. At the centre of his chest, where his heart is, his T-shirt dances and burns.

The Pin Gal catches Derek's eye and winks, flicking a match to the ground. He looks away as quick as he can, feeling hot and cold at once. Her attention is like a bright light shone upon him, the kind you could spend a whole life trying to avoid. But there's something nice about it too. The bulb is warm on his skin.

'Oh, I am sorry.' The Pin Gal's voice is shockingly proper. She sounds like she's from that antiques show on the telly. 'That wasn't very ladylike.'

Jack Haskett's dad is smacking the flames, pounding himself in the chest, sending little embers flying.

And the Pin Gal plucks her sword from the dirt and stomps off, towards the road, striding like the gunslinger at the end of a movie.

Derek feels his breath coming out all fast. Any minute now, Jack Haskett's dad will look around to check who's seen this shameful display of emasculation, who's looking for a beating – so Derek scampers to his feet, in through the staff door, to the corridor where Bev's stood by the rota, tapping a pen on her teeth.

'How's the hand?'

Derek flings his arm above his head again, caught out. 'It's fine. It's better. I'm sorry about the plates, I didn't—'

'You'll wear gloves over that,' Bev interrupts. 'It's not going to slow you down?'

Derek nods. He shakes his head. 'It's okay.'

'Come in a half-hour early tomorrow. I'm not paying you to sit in that car park.'

'Oh, I will. Thank you, Bev, I really appreciate it.' But she's already walking away.

A smile wrestles on to Derek's face. He tries to swallow it, in case Chef comes out or Bev comes back, but it keeps bobbing up. The feeling isn't a crush or anything like that. The girl's way beyond such things. But just her existence, her glittering reality in the grey of Pitlaw, makes Derek wonder what else could be possible. He forms gentle fists and moves foot to foot, imagining himself boxing like a ballerina. It's not like any strength he's ever known, but it feels like something. It feels magic.

WORD FROM THE WORMS

MAGIC. THAT'S WHAT'S happening in the grass, by the stake, in the Freakslaw's hot centre. At least, Nancy thinks, that's how her mother would describe it. For here's Gloria again, laid down in the dirt, a sheet pulled over her face like an autopsy patient. Ears pricked towards the ground, practising the meditation that puts her in the fugue state so she can pick up the mutterings from the soil.

Whenever she's tried this herself, Nancy's mastered the knack of getting the worms' attention. That's not so tough: simply a matter of tap-tap-tapping the dirt in just the right configuration, a Morse code message that says, *I'm here, I'm ready to talk.*

She peers out from behind a tent flap, watching Gloria's fingers make that same motion now. Knock knock knock! The sheet twitches. An invitation is sent into the ground. The worms pause in whatever boneless behaviour they're getting up to, in order to rise up and initiate the conversation.

In the late-afternoon sunshine, the smell of hawthorn hangs heavy in the air. In the distance Nancy can hear the bell toll of hammer against metal but where they are there's just the swaddled quiet of anticipation, punctuated by her mother's throat breathing: slowly in, slowly out. Making herself an aerial, her consciousness a single metal wire.

Gloria tends to come back from her little worm chats full

of righteous indignation. She claims the worms are messengers who bridge the gap between the ancient ancestors and the corporeal realm, but who knows if that's true. All Nancy's ever got for her attempts is a damp back and earth in her ears.

Gloria's body, beneath the starched white, is quivering. A halo of writhing bodies forms around her, a purple and pink corona that turns her mother a saint. From her thrash and jolt, it's clear the broadcast has begun. And Nancy considers scrambling over there, screaming in the worms' ears – 'What's up, bitches?!' – but she holds her fire.

A gasp from the sheet, loud and theatrical. Her mother's stiff silhouette prepares to burst into life as a Frankenstein's Monster, animated by the dirt's electric whispers.

She waits.

Right now, Gloria could be gleaning all the secrets of the underworld, while Nancy is stuck here in the silence. Or perhaps the worms are just whispering hearsay, like the invertebrate rumourmongers they are. Gossipy little terrors who like nothing more than seeding chaos among the surface dwellers! Who can tell?

Her mother tells her she won't hear from the ancestors until she learns to respect her elders, but she would say that, wouldn't she? Eat your greens and brush your teeth and be a good little witch or you'll never get your transdimensional resuscitation. In her most frustrated moments, Nancy's even considered the possibility that the worms are just worms with nothing to say. That the chaos comes from her mother, with all her own reasons to cast it. But that seems unlikely. If anything, Gloria's the one always telling Nancy to slow down, listen to the earth, hold her fire.

Well. Fire is the most magical of all the elements. Fire is

the one that destroys and transforms. Fire contains all the potential for rebirth and revolution in its irrepressible roar, so why hold it when you can spark it and set it on its way?

Nancy sees all the ways the world's got trapped in a noxious routine. And she doesn't need cartomancy like Gloria to tell where it's going. Left to its own devices, power will keep on consolidating in all its prevailing pockets. Shit that's been stuck for years will get even more entrenched. Decades from now, the good guys will all still be wailing about how they're yet to get their chance.

Fuck that.

Nancy wants nothing less than a fiendish metamorphosis of all the structures keeping the world in place. She has the magick to make it happen, if her mother would just lay off and let her.

She bares her teeth in the shadows. Nancy has so many plans for how she'd like this summer to play out. But still, she can't help the grin that breaks out as Gloria throws herself upright, rips the sheet from her face. Her mother's expression is feral. Hellfire in her eyes, dirt smeared across her cheeks.

And what about that delicious word she screeches into the sunlight, a word that licks and paws and throws open a dozen doors to the future?

'Revenge!'

A NEW DOOR
GOUGED OPEN

RUTH REACHES THE rise, her thighs thrumming, her head a little clearer. The run took her all the way down Main Street, round the back of the library, past the bus stop and the Skene Dhu, where the Freakslaw's first disruptions were beginning to play out. Normally, this is the point where she'd skite down the slope and cut across Jimmy's field, a shortcut that shaves a good fifteen minutes off the trip home. But today, she's not so sure.

Down there lies the funfair, glinting in the evening light. From this vantage point, she can see everything. It's made up of concentric circles like onion layers, dusty paths tracing between them. People scurry around, hard at work, threading fat cables under plastic ramps, cranking levers, securing fluorescent tubes to the trees. Round the outskirts, the steel slats of rides are taking shape, sharp and mechanical. Next are half-constructed houses: one cobwebbed and dishevelled, another slathered in painted mouths. And in the glowing centre, the big top itself, and a cluster of white tents and painted caravans, oddly old fashioned against the garish surrounds.

The thought of cutting through is impossibly bold. Better, surely, to take the long route. She can still make it home in time, if she gets a wriggle on. No harm done.

But she's being ridiculous. This is Scotland, it's the Right of

Way. As long as she closes any gates and picks up her rubbish, it's allowed. Nothing's changed. So Ruth makes her way down, pebbles scuffing her Converse, brown streaks on hot-pink canvas. She skips over rocks, like a goat. A brave goat.

As she stumbles down the hill, she's convinced the strangers keep looking up at her, watching her approach. It's too far to see for sure, but the feeling of attention is unmistakeable. You don't spend seventeen years in Pitlaw without learning when you're making a spectacle of yourself, when you'd be better off putting your head down and avoiding anyone's gaze.

Still, the only thing worse than walking down into that place now would be turning around and climbing back up the hill. For everyone to watch her scuttle away, tail between her legs. An over-reactor and a coward.

So she keeps going. Now she's thinking about being observed, she can't help walking like a person doing an impression of a walk. She forces her feet to go slower, her hips to loosen, but now she's a parody of a sexy lady. Or she's a robot, a fool.

At the bottom, she pauses. The buildings have their backs to her and Ruth considers sneaking between them, but she can still sense the strangers' eyes upon her – insistent and intrusive as a security pat-down – so she decides otherwise. She follows the path round instead, walking her normal human walk, until she reaches the entrance to the fair.

It's a mouth. That's the first thing she notices and all she can see: a huge, glistening mouth. Overhead, white wooden teeth dangle back and forth in the wind. The top lip is done in a glitter paint that catches the light. Sawdust spills on to the dirt, a furred and yellow tongue.

And over the mouth, a sign of screwed lightbulbs, although what it says is difficult to tell with them switched off. She squints, tilts her head – and like a Magic Eye image it suddenly comes into focus.

WELCOME TO THE FREAKSLAW
LOCK UP YOUR DAUGHTERS

Ruth takes a deep breath. Then she takes a step forward and lets herself be eaten.

She trots down the path, head down and hurrying. Everything's drenched in colour. Airbrushed faces, twice as large as life, grin down. There's Marilyn, throwing her head back, giggling with her knickers full of secrets. Elvis is slack-lipped and sneering, lips as fat as baseballs.

But where's everyone else? Okay, it's not open yet – but just a minute ago, there were definitely people. Now that she's through the gate, the funfair's a ghost town. There's a petrol smell that makes her think of 1950s drive-thru movies, all thrumming engine Cadillac possibilities. Beneath that, something tropical: a mix of rum and suntan lotion.

It feels like the moment before a surprise party, where everyone's hidden in cupboards, ready to spill out shrieking. Except instead of confetti, it's pepper spray – and the cake has a sharpened dagger hidden inside.

Hah! That's her paranoia talking. A ghost town is fine. Ruth doesn't need to run into anyone. She tramps past metal roller coaster tracks and a hot-dog stand with huge wooden wheels. She's almost at the Haunted House when, in the very corner of her eye, her gaze snags on a puff of sawdust. A streak of colour: the same sparkle-red as the gaping mouth of the gate. She spins around, but it's already gone. Footsteps echoing into the distance. The fat summer sun beating down.

Well. That's weird. But Ruth's fine, Ruth's never been intimidated by footsteps running in the opposite direction. She's going to take the path down to her left, which she's pretty sure will lead her out of the funfair, on to the road that winds towards home. She's going to ignore the beating pulse in her throat. She's seen enough.

Ruth pads down the path, her breath thick in the strange heat. Walks faster, as fast as makes sense without actually running. Without accidentally making a sound.

But really, where the fuck is everyone? And why, though she was certain this path aimed straight for the exit, does it feel like she's being led deeper and deeper into the heart of the funfair? There's something trippy about the route, about the shifty alleyways that draw her in like a spiderweb. With every step, she's convinced she can hear the echoing clang of a door swinging shut behind her.

And then she turns the corner, the path opens up, and he's there. An old man, staring right into her eyes. Splat bang in the middle of the clearing, leaning against a big wooden stake. As he moves, the scarred side of his face catches the light. It makes her think of oil spills, of those huge bubbles street performers make, all the colours when the sunlight hits them. He's wearing a dark red suit that barely covers his gangling limbs.

Once, when Ruth was little, she came down for a glass of water one night when her dad was watching telly, and he scooped her on to his lap. On the screen was a music video, a teacher gathering every last child and chucking them into the school, grinding the school's handle. The children came out as mince.

She'd seen that teacher in her nightmares for a week – her

mum had been furious – but when she heard the song years later, it lit her insides up. *No education, no thought control.* She recorded it off the radio, and even though she missed the first lines it didn't stop her listening to it a hundred times, a thousand, rewinding the tape again and again, until one weekend when her dad was sick in bed he'd come through after the tenth time, wrapped in a dressing gown, and asked her to just maybe, please love, listen to something else for a change?

She'd stopped listening to it at all after that.

Anyway, that big long puppet, all dangling fingers and knock knees: that's what the man in the funfair makes her think of. She stares at him. He grins back, a smile like he could unhinge his jaw and swallow her whole. A scream rises up in her but before it can erupt he lifts those long fingers to his head – as if he's touching the brim of a hat, though he's not wearing a hat – and turns to wander away.

Ruth stands alone, chest pounding. Nothing happened, nothing real, so why does she feel so uncanny? Her heart is beating with the old cowardly refrain – *turn back, turn back* – but it's got to be better to keep going. Sometimes the fastest way out is through.

She walks across the clearing, carefully now. Who knows what else is lurking in these alleyways, waiting for obstinate girls to cross their path? As she passes the stake, she looks down, and her stomach goes. Tiny holes have opened up in the sawdust, like bubbles in pancake batter. Scattered around them, lolling against the blare of yellow, are the swollen bodies of so many worms, gross and pink and squirmy.

Ruth's never been squeamish but she doesn't like it. It hasn't rained in days, so what are they doing there? She takes a wide berth, keeping her eyes on the worms – not like they're going to follow her, but still.

She takes the first path, striding determinedly. But that's when she hears it, and stops in her tracks. A deep, belly-shuddering bass. A high, jangling guitar. A voice like gravel and hickeys. It reverberates through her bones. That music, it's meant for her. That sound is the secret siren of teenage girls everywhere, the ones who press their thighs together and believe that punk will save their lives – who don't know why their lives need saving yet, but are certain that they do.

And okay, this place is messed up, okay, she ought to get out of here. But though Ruth knows all of this, punk music's the one thing she's never been able to resist. It's X-Ray Spex. And who in Pitlaw has ever heard of X-Ray Spex? Just her, and now whoever's over there, blaring it into this balmy eve.

The sound of it brings her back inside herself, the way only music can. It makes her brave. The chords are electrifying, little shocks to the system.

And despite everything, she can't stop herself from getting a little closer. What's the worst that could happen?

This is the mantra she repeats as she winds her way back through the funfair, away from home. What's the worst, as she follows the musical notes like birdseed down the path. What's the worst, as she creeps past higgledy tents with metal skeletons askew. What's the worst, as she takes the corner and sees him there: the boy. Leaning out the window of a hot-pink caravan, his hair stuck up in every direction like a finger in an electric socket. The boy is propped on his elbows, skinny fingers resting against his chin, the music behind him stupid-loud. Ruth stills her feet. He flashes a big dopey smile that reveals a broken front tooth. Her heart thrums and there's mascara smeared in his sockets. Then the boy flicks the music off and they're plunged into silence, except she can still feel it in every bone of her body, sending her skeleton unhinged.

She's okay. Of course she can remember how to breathe: she's a human, she's practically a breathing machine. Ridiculous urges flap through her body, the desire to grab his palms and lick them, to confess all her secrets. Instead, she just stands there. She smiles back.

Then the boy's eyes flick up and out of focus, so he's not meeting her gaze. His smile gets even broader. And Ruth hears – she never thought such a thing was possible, but there it is – the sound of someone blinking behind her.

'I was listening to that, you fuckwit.'

Ruth spins around. A girl in a sparkling red catsuit opens her eyes very wide. She gives Ruth a half-salute that makes her think of playground games and promises. 'Your knee's bleeding.'

Ruth starts. The girl's right, there's a scuff and a bubble she doesn't remember making. A thin pink trickle. 'Oh. It's nothing.' She dusts it off with her fingertips, smearing the blood around.

'Still, wipe it up before your mum sees.' When the girl grins, it's a lovely kick in the teeth. The sort of friendliness that'll leave you covered in bruises. She holds out a handkerchief, and Ruth takes it, rubs her leg.

'That's better.' The girl plucks the hankie back. 'She's got enough to worry about with—'

'Nancy!' the boy yelps, scrambling out of the caravan. He sticks one hand out, all long fingers and silver rings. 'Hi! Zed.'

Things are all off-kilter. Ruth's convinced the moment she

reaches out to take his hand, he'll snatch it away, or the rings will squirt water, or there'll be a buzzer snuck in his palm that feels like the electric fence, no wellies. But her hand moves to his, she can't help it. His palm is rough with tiny calluses just below the fingers. Chafed blisters from hard work. She's pretty sure if she pulled it to her mouth, it would taste of petrol.

Then she drops the hand, concentrates on sending all the blood back down, blood that's trying to creep up her neck and into her cheeks. 'Ruth.'

'We're not open yet,' the girl – Nancy – says.

'Sorry,' says Ruth. 'The gate was.'

'She didn't mean it like that.' Zed doesn't elaborate. Nancy's got a card in her hand, twirling it around her fingers like a flick knife from the movies. Zed's leaning loosely on one hip. Ruth looks from one to the other. There's something about them, sticky and magnetic. She can't tell if she wants to be them or kiss them or jump on them and fight them to the ground. Then Zed shoots her another smile and his dimples deepen, and she can.

'You should go,' says Nancy. 'It's past seven, you're already late.'

Zed's foot darts out and kicks her in the ankle.

'Ow!' She rubs it and pouts, bright red lips like a beauty queen. 'What? She *is*.'

'Right.' Ruth looks at her watch, unsettled. Somehow, half an hour has passed since she entered the funfair – time has squished and dilated, or been swallowed entirely.

'But come back,' Nancy says. 'On Monday. That's when things'll be going properly. Better than all this.' She waves a hand towards the boarded-up stalls, the funfair paused like a held breath. 'We'll see you then.' And she grabs Zed's hand, yanking him past the pink caravan, deeper into the cluster. 'Bye!'

Ruth turns on her heel. Her head is spinning. Her stomach is full of grasshoppers. Nothing happened, she tells herself, but it doesn't stop the feeling like a door has been gouged open inside her. A corridor leading to something new. People like her, people who'd understand the secret heartbeat she keeps locked in her chest. But she doesn't need a new door, that's the thing. Ruth's got it all planned out. Just a few more months, and then she's out of here – she's set. She doesn't need distractions and she doesn't need trouble.

But then there's his smile. So maybe she does. What's the worst that could happen?

She looks at her watch again. She's totally late. Ruth starts to run.

TROUBLE & DRIED SUMMER

ZED FOLLOWS NANCY to her dilapidated red caravan and they sit side by side on the steps, knees pulled to their chins. She's still giggling. 'You shouldn't have done that,' says Zed, and gives her a poke in the ribs.

'Done what?!'

Her innocent look is charming, he'll give her that, but he shoves her again anyway, enjoying the hot little feeling of her ribs. Then he puts on his Nancy voice, a voice like fireworks and Christmas paper wrapping. *She's got enough to worry about! It's past seven!'*

She opens her eyes wider. 'It *was* past seven.'

'Right! And what was happening at seven?'

Her shrug is like a panther's. She grins. 'All good girls have to go home for seven, don't you know?'

'Well.' Zed tries to look very serious. He loves Nancy, he does, but how come she's always got to go sneaking looks? 'You shouldn't. It's like – I don't know, like peering at someone naked when they don't know you're there.'

It's the wrong example, he knows as soon as he says it. Nancy's told him before about the Mirror People. For ages, she was convinced they were watching from inside every reflective surface. Sat around a long table, like a war room, tucked just behind the glass. At first she'd go to every kind of measure to prevent the Mirror People from seeing her changing – pulling up her knickers under her dress, scrunching a bra into a sleeve, performing tricks where all the plates and cutlery stay on the table, but – tah-dah! – a brand new skirt appears beneath. But that got boring, and after a while she'd let the dress slip (Oh whoops, I didn't see you there!). At some point, the performer in her won out and she got right into it.

She'd pick out her sluttiest too-small shirt and the skirt she grew out of three summers ago. She'd shut all the curtains so that the caravan was dim, and she'd get dressed in the corner, out of the mirror's line of sight, for suspense's sake. Then she'd walk out in front of the mirror and bite her lower lip and look as hurt as a cartoon baby deer.

Thinking of this now, Zed blushes. Nancy's eyes light up all sparkly.

'Sounds *terrible*.'

She'd flash a tit and she'd stick her hand into her underwear and then (since the Mirror People said she *really* had to), Nancy would jerk off, keeping eye contact with herself, until all the muscles in her legs went limp, and she'd fall, like a magical spring donkey toy when you press the button . . .

Zed closes his eyes and presses his thumbs in the sockets, so his vision lights up in orange splotches and this lovely filthy troublesome image disappears. 'Well maybe for *you*.' He swallows the smile. 'But some of us need our secrets. How am I supposed to be your friend with all my terribly important thoughts out in the open?'

'I told you,' she says. 'Not to you. Never you! You're special.' She rubs her head against his arm like a cat. He wraps it around her and they sit, snuggled together, looking out at the world.

'I'm only playing anyway,' says Nancy. 'I thought you liked it.'

'I do!' It's just the girl had that whole vulnerable thing going on, and god knows, Zed's got the softest soft spot for people who can't stop blushing at the world. There was also an urgency there, though, like she knew exactly what she had to do and didn't want to stray an inch. That's what Nancy's responding to, he can tell.

'It'd be fun to see what happens. A push, just a little one!'

'Hmnn,' says Zed. He's seen Nancy's little pushes.

'I'll stop if it gets too much, you know what I'm like.'

He does know. That's the point. And he's wondering if Ruth's got something to stop her once she gets going. Humans are supposed to be full of them: emergency offs that kick in when need be. He's heard your jaw's strong enough to shatter teeth if you bite down hard enough, but the signal in your brain tells it that's not such a good idea. So is Ruth the kind to have a safety switch, or will she just combust once her spark catches?

And for that matter, would he even want her to stop? Or would it be the most fun, to see her get carried away with the unfurling magic the fair has to offer? He looks at Nancy, his absolute favourite thing in the world, and he squeezes her tight.

'You know I'm right,' she says. Well, she probably is.

And then Gloria the Teller stumbles round the corner, one arm held out dramatically like old-school Hollywood, her zebra-print hat so skeewiff it's impossible it's still on her head.

'Darlings!' she says, as the hat flaps. She pulls a silk scarf from her sleeve and dabs at her lipstick, then crouches in a squat, hands on red velvet thighs. 'Which of you angels is going to make Gloria a little drinkie?'

Zed feels Nancy tense. He digs his fingers into the bones of her arm, sends a Morse code signal that everything's fine, and gets to his feet. It's past seven, after all, and Gloria the Teller's eyes aren't *so* glassy. But there's some look in them he doesn't like – a manic glitter. He scoots into the caravan and rummages behind the purple curtain, emerging with the fanciest of bottles. A fat splash of bourbon, some orange bitters, just enough cherry brandy for the twang. He swishes it around in a jam jar and drops three carnation petals on the top – because it's Saturday and because Gloria's fancy and because he can't be bothered washing a glass. Zed takes a sip. It tastes like smoke and shivers and cherry pie, all with a bit of dried summer on top. He takes another and thinks of seedy alleyways stuffed with red lights and baker's windows. Then he looks at the jar, the pathetic measure that's left, and oops – Zed's back behind the curtain, topping up this, topping up that. Perfect.

'Oh, you are a good boy,' says Gloria the Teller. He leans out the window and she plucks it from him with her webbed fingers, then he scuttles back to Nancy's side. Gloria closes her eyes as she drinks, neck moving like a swan. She downs it in one and lets out a moan like a wounded animal.

'Don't be gross.' Nancy picks a pebble from the ground and bounces it off Gloria's ankle boot.

'Don't talk to your mother like that,' says Gloria tartly. She arches an eyebrow at Zed, as if she can't believe what she has to put up with. He shrugs. His lips taste delicious. When

Gloria goes, he's going to make a fresh one for himself and one for Nancy, and then he's going to change the subject. He's going to tell her all the facts he's been reading recently: that monster and demonstrate are totally the same 'mons'; when it comes to helicopter and pterodactyl, 'pter' means spiral wings. Or whirly finger, or terrifying sky thing, or something? Whatever! That—

'Listen.' Gloria takes a deep breath and pulls herself together somewhat. 'Change of plans. It's opening night tomorrow. You got your glad rags together?'

'Urgh. Why do you *always* do this?' Nancy's mouth twitches with irritation but Gloria just gives her that laissez-faire toss of the head, the one that makes her hat dance.

'New information has come to light, my dear. It changes everything.' With this, she spins on her heel and totters off. Zed feels a finger of curiosity tugging at his guts. Something that changes everything! Well, if that isn't just his favourite kind of thing. He squeezes Nancy's knee, but she doesn't say a word.

'You okay?'

Nancy's sometimes quiet when Gloria the Teller gets like this. He never can tell with them. Some days he'll show up and they'll be laughing in bed together like a teen-movie slumber party montage, tarot cards scattered, the air cloudy with the smell of sweet resin. But on others, Nancy turns into this shut book and all he wants to do is prise open her mouth and crawl into her brain and flip things over until he finds what's bothering her, then chuck it out her ear.

'Nance?' he asks again.

Then Nancy laughs, her glorious hammer laugh, and from her sleeve she produces a tiny hand mirror, the frame all bejewelled with mother of pearl, the glass itself the funny grey of old cats and turned-out pockets.

'She's drunk. She'll never notice.' Nancy props the mirror on her knees and drums her fingertips on the frame. 'Besides, I have to get some scrying in now, before it's too late. Don't you know any day it's going to *be* the future? Then it'll be just like reading anything else.'

Zed grins. He pinches Nancy hard on the thigh, but she doesn't flinch. She just looks up with those too-big innocent eyes.

'Now which of us angels is going to make me a drink?'

IT'S NOT RIGHT
BUT IT'S HERE

GLORIA THE TELLER was not drunk. She was a little loose, perhaps, as one is wont to get of an evening. What she heard, laid there in the dirt, shook her to the core.

Now, Gloria's no stranger to chattering voices. She's lived a terrifically long time, pawed inside a great many minds, and sometimes things regurgitate inside her. Sometimes her whole skull is stuffed with other people's memories until she can barely hear herself. They whirl around her, demanding attention, looking for the resolutions she can never give: *Confess your undying love! Admit you stole the lavender suitcase! Apologize to Mother before she dies!* The long-dead have a habit of gossiping endlessly and psychic activity is like driving in a lorry cab at night with an out-of-control radio, flipping wildly between a dozen different channels.

But normally when she has a cocktail or two, everything becomes slight and festive. The memories still chatter in the background, but by then it's like snatches of old gramophone music. She dances to other people's lives and swoons around the funfair, full of twice as many emotions as ordinary folk. When she thinks about it, actors are probably in the same boat – which must be why they're also so glamorous, so overwrought, so utterly alive.

Gloria reclines on Mr Partlett's chaise longue, stretching a boot in the air like the mast of a ship. She kicks the other up to join it. Throws her head back, tosses another shot of gin into her mouth. The caravan is covered in red velvet and dancing shadows. The gin is like skittering over wet cobblestones in high heels. It makes her feel pretty and raucous, like a young woman again. She considers fainting into a set of arms, demanding a string of men set off a series of ever-larger fireworks to impress her.

And then the echoes of the voices puncture through this happy place. Christ, but they're loud! Yattering and howling, and not enough drinks in all the world to tamp them down. So she sits up. Makes herself businesslike. Smoothes her hair and balances her hat. 'You should have heard the ancestors,' she says at last. 'They were furious.'

Mr Partlett leans close. His elbows are propped on his knees, making his suit jacket ride up, showing off the bones of his wrists. It's not the first time Gloria's come to him with gossip from the underworld, but today she seems particularly manic. Eager to act. 'Tell me everything.'

Gloria presses her fingers against her eyes. Despite the gin, the images flash through her mind with harrowing clarity. Their foremothers, led down to the village square with ropes around their waists and arms bound down. Tied to the stake, ankles lashed so they couldn't kick and stamp. Sure, the lucky ones – those who got wet wood and the right breeze – suffocated on smoke before too long. Or death by shock, a quick and merciful unconsciousness.

But other visions are harder to shake.

The ones who bled to death, their inflamed capillaries leaking wildly in haemorrhaged confusion. Those who saw their internal organs decompose: a heart seeping, a kidney grilling. The woman who was strangled by her own skin, which shrunk like hot plastic around her neck until it cut off the airway. She burned on for six hours while fat leaked through her split-open dermis, feeding that hungry fire.

'They killed them here. Thirty-six poor souls, taken in the great panic of 1597. Right on this very spot.'

Mr Partlett lets out a hiss, a low whistle from between his teeth. Of course they did. It's a sharp pain to hear it, but then again, it's no surprise at all. 'The usual accusations?'

'Midwifery, gossip. A divination to see if a sick child would live.' She shrugs, and in that studied carelessness, he can see all the pain wracked upon her heart. 'But as their descendants, we have a chance to help them. Do what they no longer can.'

'And what might that be?'

Gloria's gold tooth sparkles in the candlelight. 'Oh, you know. Just your ordinary little revenge.'

Because that's the long and the short of it. You'd think the dead would be above such petty recriminations, but anyone who's ever spent time conversing with them knows better. No one can hold a grudge like a corpse. It's the long nights; they give altogether too much time to mull things over.

'Four hundred years they've been waiting, can you imagine? Stuck in the netherworld, tossing and turning, no way to go up or go down.'

Mr Partlett winces. A shard of anger appears in his eye. 'They're trapped there now?'

'Yes. But there's a chance to get them out.' Gloria smiles, delectable and horrid. 'You know how tangible the dead get on the turn of their century.' It's the point where they're almost human again, animated by ancient resentment and calendar fortune. 'The proper ceremonies this summer, and we can set them to rest at last.'

Mr Partlett presses his fingertips together. 'By ceremonies, you mean . . .?'

'Of course.' She means sacrifice, both dreadful and deserved. Just the thought of it brings a twinkle to her eye. 'I suggest we act on Lùnastal. It's cutting it a little close to the anniversary, but such an auspicious day for revenge.'

Because Lùnastal, 1 August, has always been a fine time to reap. It's the first of the three harvest festivals: the harvest of the grain. Followed by 21 September, the equinox, harvest of the fruit; then by 31 October, Samhain, harvest of the meat. All times of certain deaths, when the walls between worlds are thinner than usual. By equinox it will be too late: the dead will be swaddled back down in their purgatory. Solstice could work but that's too soon, not nearly enough time to plot. But the feast of Lùnastal – when the great golden sun god is cut down with sharpened scythes, when his seeds are snatched and thrown back to the earth – is just right.

'Isn't there a risk that we miss our chance, leaving it so late?'

'Perhaps. But if we do, no bother.' She chuckles, and it's pip-bitter in her mouth. 'We can just come back in a hundred years and try again.'

'That won't be necessary.' Mr Partlett runs his hand across the red velvet, dragging the pile backwards. 'We'll make them suffer, just like ours have. It'll be sad, really.'

Gloria and Mr Partlett share a look, a snatch of laughter. Oh, it *will* be sad. The Freakslaw will mourn their dead here, they will do the necessary ceremonies. Gather their family close. But ancient imbalances must eventually be redressed. It's not evil, you understand. It's not good either. The carnival charms are from a time before such Christian binaries: amoral, not immoral, if you will. And what it really is – what it shall be – is *fun*.

Plans made, a wet smile paws across Gloria the Teller's face. 'Is that everything?'

Mr Partlett smiles back. The scars twist and writhe. 'Is it?'

Gloria throws back her head and laughs. Then she reaches forward and unbuckles Mr Partlett's belt, her fused fingers surprisingly deft in their urgency. She flicks the belt and it slithers across the floor, nestling under a chair to watch. Mr Partlett's dick is already swollen in Gloria's grasp. She yanks it to herself like a handle, buries her face in the grey nestle of his pubic hair. He smells of firewood and old books and a sharp tang of urine. She flickers her tongue. They balance for a moment as Mr Partlett's veins jolt like live wires, as power seeps into Gloria, turning her electric. Then somehow her trousers are off and the tables twist. He digs his bony fingers up into her, crooked and beckoning, and it chafes – but then his fingers find the hot knot inside her and press it and Gloria is unravelling, wet and slippery and undone. She lies back and howls. Mr Partlett grabs her tongue between thumb and finger and holds it tight, and her mouth is open, helpless, and his fingers keep on grinding. She is full of comets and scraps of old magic. She's getting faster. And then, just for one second, all the voices shut up and she's alone in her head – just her, herself – and she screams.

After she comes, Mr Partlett tucks her on to the chaise longue. Gloria collapses on to a thousand cushions, waits for her breath to return to normal. When she smiles up at him, her tongue is too big for her mouth.

'That'th everything?' she says.

It is.

BAKED BEANS &
HOT GOSSIP

MEANWHILE, IN THE shop across town, June Geddes is looking at baked beans, wondering if there's a way to make them anything other than what they are. They've had a lot of beans these past weeks, it's true, but when beans are on special there's nothing that'll bulk a dish out like them. In a push, they're good for any meal – that's the thing. You can eat baked beans for breakfast and not feel like a fool.

June stands in the aisle, feeling her face go pink. Well, it might not have been much, but they didn't go hungry! Still, Lord knows she'd rather not give Boyd anything else to get wound up about. You never can tell what'll be the thing that tips him over. And there's no saying this week won't end up like last, with a shrug and wet beer breath, a half-empty enve-lope at the end.

She holds the tin and does the sums in her head. If she puts back the mushrooms, that's four tins right there. Or she could swap out the rice, Boyd doesn't wholly trust rice anyway – is never sure if it should fall into the category of food known as 'foreign muck'. On the one hand, they do eat a lot of it over there. But on the other, it's white, the same as all your normal, unpretentious foods: flour, tatties, salt, lard. So maybe she should—

'June Geddes, is that you hidin back there? Well did ye see what's happening down in the field?'

– and her train of thought is gone. June looks up and it's Shona Peterson standing in the aisle, carrying not a single item, but round-cheeked and ready to blether all the same.

'Oh, it's a right bunch of nutters,' Shona carries on, without even pausing for an answer, 'strange folk, not just ones who can do your tricks but *proper* strange, like – those wee people and some kind of selkie bairn and this one eejit with a hand coming out his arse.'

June giggles and it feels sweet in her mouth. 'Don't be daft.'

'I'm no! June, we have *got* to get down there and see for ourselves.' And she carries on, telling June about what Lindsey said, which she heard from Frank down the way, who'd been talking to Jimmy himself . . .

June takes a peek at her watch. She ought to be getting on, she really should decide about these beans – but this is Shona. There was a time, back when Boyd was still in his courting phase, bringing her carnations from the petrol station every second date, when her and Shona used to get together on the regular. There was even that one time when Shona persuaded her to get the bus into town, and if she hadn't put on her new skirt and gone! They'd drunk candy-sweet glasses of Baileys and ended up sticky and giggling, they even went to the pool hall and somehow Shona Peterson landed every last shot.

They don't see each other as often these days, but whenever Shona does show up, it feels for a moment like all the colours in Pitlaw get just a wee bit brighter.

'And did your lad nae tell you what happened at the Skene Dhu? That's Derek's place, isn't it?'

It is. But Derek never tells her anything these days, so she lets Shona explain. All the while, Norma Murray (whose basket, June notices, is piled with chicken breasts and low-fat cream and a sneaky bottle of Chardonnay) is edging closer, towards the baked beans special, although June can't see her sitting down to beans on toast or fantasy bean pasta or even a baked bean chilli. Norma keeps shooting them pointed glances then looking back at the shelves, like she can't decide if she wants to deign to make the first move. Someone as important as Norma Murray, head of the town council no less, surely they should be asking her to talk? But eventually a desire to gossip will always win out and—

'I was there!' she interrupts, pointing at her chest, and June and Shona stop talking.

'In the pub?'

'In the cafe.' Norma Murray swallows, nods, and finds a more ordinary tone. 'It was disgusting . . .' And now Norma's the one to talk, while June shapes her face into the proper glower of disapproval.

'. . . and she just started smirking, like she didn't have a moment of shame. Someone who'd smile at a thing like that!' Norma shakes her head. 'I just don't know.'

'Awfae,' says Shona, but June can see giggles threatening to bubble over. 'What a to-do!' That's something else about Shona Peterson. She's never had a lot of time for busybodies like Norma Murray. If anyone was to tell her where to stuff it, it'd be Shona.

'Well, someone ought to go down there and talk to them,' says Norma.

'They should?' June doesn't feel like she's been contributing a lot to this conversation. But what's she going to say? She tries to imagine herself just walking down to Jimmy's field and giving them a talking to – as if she, June Geddes, has any kind of standing for a thing like that!

Shona breaks into a huge smile, a gleeful one that reminds June of when Shona used to hide in the loos when the train conductor came, then emerge cackling when he'd passed their carriage by.

'Somebody should,' she says. She winks at June and for a moment all their teenage trouble is hung there in the air between them. 'Some cunt absolutely should.'

GHOST TRAINS &
GLAD RAGS

THE NEXT DAY, everything's all aflutter as the rides take form and the final spells are cast upon the land. Hammering dirt, calibrating mechanics, spirit levelling of every sort – why, if this joint's a millimetre out of whack, who's to say our most esteemed guests won't end up with grass in their teeth? Or catapulted into space, halfway to the moon.

Everyone's working in hysterical stereo, twice the speed as usual, but Gloria the Teller just shrugs as if the flurry's got nothing to do with her, she waves her hands and says 'retrograde' with the same stunning finality as immigration officers say 'denied'.

Still, rumour of the ancestors whips through the Freakslaw, catching at the speed of wildfire. Word is, Miss Gloria's had a message from the underworld! – so Werewolf Louie whispers to the Twins, the news slicking from Cass to Henry, a gossip from the guts. His information's good, top notch – why it came direct from Strongman No. 3 who overheard the Pin Gal's whispers after she'd wheedled it out of Mr Partlett himself. And if they've learned one thing from such messages in the past, well, they can expect twice as much chaos in store . . .

And though Miss Maria bitterly resents being told to hurry, though the Strongmen bitch and carp at their heightened workload, though Gretchen dosses off throughout it all, perched in her dressing room with a powder puff and a Brandy Alexander and a Marlboro Light in a long golden holder – all the same, by the time the sun's over the yardarm, the funfair is ready. A debutante slapped and sparkled and brought to her very first ball, she sits ripe with anticipation, waiting to dance.

Which is all very well, all most splendid indeed. 'But what about us?' cry the Twins – or Cass, at least, who prefers a few more hours to ensure their asymmetrical undercuts are as balanced as any joist. (Henry, meanwhile, can take or leave the mirror, has never quite accepted the fact he'll never see his reflection alone.)

'Get dressed, my dears.' Mr Partlett claps in the air, and everyone scurries. In the final hour before the funfair opens, a shroud of hairspray materializes over Jimmy's field, thick and potent as any storm. In Werewolf Louie's caravan, Zed massages moustache wax into Louie's hair, twirling the tips into points like a child's drawing of waves. Miss Maria anoints herself in sweet jasmine and cupcake frosting: beneath the swell of her neck, on the backs of her knees, a wee dab here by the fold of a thigh. The Strongmen wax each other's backs for the third time this week (as they rip off the wax, all the Strongmen say *grrrraaaarghhhhhh*).

And Nancy, oh Nancy. She just can't stop herself sneaking out for the most final touches: a screw loosened here, a pin unfastened there, a slick of grease on the bad bit of the track. There are monks who strew imperfections in every piece of pottery in order to get closer to God, and there are teenage girls who strew chaos in the world because sometimes that's what the world needs. This is the funfair, after all, and where's the fun without a lick of danger, without the skew and shriek on the final bend?

At the appointed hour, the funfair folk regroup, spattered with glitter and backcombed to the gods. Mr Partlett lifts one hand – a hand that smells of kerosene and a salty trace of Gloria. He wraps it around the lever and he pulls the lever down.

Electricity crackles. Sparks flit like fireflies in the night. And then, finally, the bulbs turn on. They light up one after the other like a domino rally – plink plink plink – and the light catches and spreads, a wildfire of neon. There goes the Wild Mouse and the Casino of Souls, there goes Gloria the Teller's tent, up up up go all the trees. Colours splash across watching faces: strobes of green and pink, a sudden bleach that turns them all to ghosts. 'Ahhhh,' say the Freak-slaw and it's a sigh of coming home at last.

And over the gate, the big wooden teeth creak in the breeze.

For the first ten minutes, nothing happens. The funfair energy is strong but there's another older magic at work too, the spell of tribes and traditions, keeping yourself to your people and never mind the rest. Nobody wants to be the first, that's the thing. To be the first is to align yourself with the freaks, to confess there's a thirst in your bones for a change. To admit you *want*. It's very dangerous to live in a small town and want. It's like building a garden of tiny flowers on a race-course. Stick a head too high and be tramped to dirt. Besides, to want is to offer yourself up for disappointment, because change doesn't stand a fucking chance. The folk of Pitlaw have said they'll steer clear of this place, so steer clear they will.

And yet, and yet. The funfair sits in Jimmy's field winking neon. The music creeps out into the foundations of the town. An old flute plays a familiar tune. Curiosity (that killer of cats and mistress of the undecided) gets to work, whispering: *The others said they won't go there. So how will they see you if you do?* Eventually – in fits and bursts, and then more, then all at once – the people arrive.

They wander down sawdust trails into a world as bright and hectic as the centre of a firework. *Roll up, roll up – come on over and shoot the stars, pick them right out of the heavens . . . Here, quick, take your seat – for magical marvels and human curiosities, freakery of the likes you've never seen . . . Are you brave enough? Time to go headoverheels, arseovertit, stomachto-theceiling on the wild and wonderful Kraken!*

Well, Barry Donaldson was just coming with his mates to see what shite they had really, but now they're here, they might as well put on those boxing gloves and see who's the biggest wuss. His fist connects with the rattling punchball, all the bells clang like church, and suddenly Barry knows he's Rocky, the underdog made good, and he stands, arms over his head in triumph, as the credit music kicks in.

And Moira McGinty and the girls, normally they've got sewing group on Sundays, but Lesley couldn't make it this week, and it's always at Lesley's on the first Sunday of the month, so . . . They might as well, eh? Just come and check out the show. Later, in bed that night, all Moira will be able to think about is the moment the shiniest of the Strongmen – whose every muscle was polished to high gleam like her walnut cabinet – came straight for her chair and hiked it up, above the motorbike and the fridge and the marble slab, so that Moira was perched there at the top of it all. Everyone was looking (and who knows *what* they could see from down there) but she felt special, chosen, and it was the best thing since she was picked to play Mary in the Sunday School play as a girl.

And what about wee Siobhan Maguire, clutched under the arm of her fiancé? She has Colin lead her into the Haunted House and every time a skeleton rattles or a key turns all by itself in a dusty door, she screams and shrieks and throws herself deeper into his arms, lets his comforting hand creep another half inch up her ribcage. When they emerge, Siobhan is bright pink and can't stop giggling, while Colin, Colin might just walk straight into an iron pole if she wasn't still wrapped around his waist to guide him.

Nancy watches from behind the candied nut stall. It's working. She can taste it, the sweet tang of sweat and vows that are dying to be broken. Inhibitions are already beginning to unravel, and it needn't take much: just a few well-placed nails to snag their threads.

And then – walking alone, hands deep in her hoodie – she sees the girl. Ruth. She's all buried in that big jumper, although the air tonight is balmy. Almost tropical.

Nancy takes a handful of candied dregs and tips them into her mouth. There's some shards of nut in there, but mostly it's just the ridiculously sweet sugarspun that sticks the bits together. She crunches down and electricity fires up the nerves of her teeth, right into her jaw. She grins and it crackles. Ruth glances her way but Nancy shakes her head imperceptibly and her gaze slides off. No. Not yet.

Although she wants to practise. To peel the girl. Dig her fingernails under those bones, prise her open and throw her innards on the ground, read the secrets in them like tea leaves.

Then decide a new destiny and stuff her with that instead. Sew her tight. A tricksy sort of taxidermy. Nancy thinks of the way the girl looked at Zed – the blush lighting up her cheeks, the words stumbling to fall out her mouth. For a moment she scowls – her Zed, indeed! – but then a Cheshire Cat smile blinks into life. Here's the chance for a different kind of charm, a new thing to plant in the dirt. The beginning of so much fun . . .

But for now, Nancy fades herself into the background – just another face in the crowd. She leaves the stall and follows as Ruth scans the Pinball Paradise and rejects it, considers the Hall of Mirrors but keeps on. She takes the twist towards the stake and the centre of the funfair, and suddenly Nancy knows exactly where the girl is going.

GLORIA THE TELLER, QUEEN OF KISMET.
FIND YOUR FORTUNE, DISCOVER THY DESTINY!

Nancy watches as Ruth draws back the curtain and steps inside.

FORTUNE FAVOURS

THE TENT IS dim after the funfair's Technicolor intensity and Ruth lets her eyes adjust. There are candles on every surface, malformed wax mountains that flare and hunch. But no one here. Perhaps she shouldn't have walked in – perhaps the tent was closed, and she didn't notice – but there's something nice in this analogue flicker after all those electric elbows. She traces her fingertips along the old cycle-crash scar on her bottom lip, a gesture that never fails to comfort her. The walls are close and covered in shards of mirror, framed photographs, beaded curtains. The cabinets stacked high with curiosities. Jar after jar, neatly labelled in embossed dymo letters – AYAHUASCA. AXOLOTL. ARNICA. AMNIOTIC FLUID. ABORTION. Dusty old books: *A Modest Enquiry Into the Nature of Witchcraft, Compendium Maleficarum, Daemonologie in Forme of a Dialogue.* Then on the cabinet, a taxidermied vole, moss lashed in the shape of a doll, a hand suspended in liquid – it's not clear whether it's a wax model or a real one. The nails, dug into the doughy flesh of the fingers, look plastic but the scar, that small, puckered cat scratch: surely it has to be real? Ruth takes a step closer. She crouches down and tilts the jar, trying to get the bottom to bob up to see the stump. That's where it'll be obvious. The hand gives a wee Queen's wave but doesn't rise.

'Hello, dear,' says a voice behind her, and Ruth leaps right out of her skin. To her credit, she gets the jar back without dropping it. She whirls to her feet, hands in the air to show she's not touching anything, and puts a smile on. Her best student smile, the one that's done all the homework and extra exercises.

'Sorry,' she says. 'Hi.' Her pulse crashes a drumroll in her ears.

'Take a seat, darling.' The woman swoops an arm lazily at one chair, sleeve billowing like a curtain drawing back, and slides into the other. She looks like no one Ruth's ever seen, in her zebra-print tophat and crushed-velvet suit. Her face is framed with hair red as paint, all save for a white skunk streak. For a moment, they just look at each other, then the woman grins dementedly and Ruth notices with a start that one of her teeth is gold. She's never seen anyone with a gold tooth in real life before, especially not a woman. Gold teeth are for pirates, or the bald jailer in a prison movie. She thinks of Zed, his broken tooth, and she starts to wonder what it is about this place anyway, if they're always breaking teeth off. If her own teeth are in danger just by sitting here.

No! She's being ridiculous. The woman winks, like she knows exactly what Ruth's thinking, then gestures at the chair once more. 'Sit.'

Ruth's thighs twitch, thinking better of it, but she obeys.

'So what are you here for, love?'

'Me?' Of course her. Who else? But Ruth hadn't walked in expecting questions. If anything, Ruth wanted to sit in front of someone who'd take one look and see just how special she really is. Who'd beckon her close and tell her she's not like other people. Things are going to be different for her.

'You want to see the future, that's what I'm here for! Gloria the Teller, Queen of Kismet.' The woman laughs and it's all off-kilter – the sound of a waltzer car whipping by, gravity akimbo. 'But how do you want to look, that's the question. We've got everything here, my love. Tarot reading, mirror scrying, rune magic, augury with birds . . .'

Ruth stares helplessly.

'Or you have a specific question? You want to know whether you'll make the trip, charm the swain –' at this, Ruth's brain conjures a brief and thrilling vision of Zed, grabbing her hand and yanking her close, clothes flying off like calendar pages in a movie montage – 'pass the test, get the job?'

She doesn't need a fortune teller to divine her future, that's the thing. She knows, has spent the past seventeen years preparing. She'll be getting out of Pitlaw. She's not going to be like everyone else who started out with grand plans but at some point got snared by the yoke of the town. There's a sticky kind of gravity in Pitlaw, one that kicks in for the unwary, but Ruth's not going to slip.

'Where I end up.' She finds her voice at last. 'Tell me where I'll be, years from now.' Because the close future is easy. By September, she'll be at the University of St Andrews, studying accounting, grant cheque in hand. She'll be doing what she's good at, which is numbers, all lined up in their little boxes, checked and balanced and adding up to escape. It might not set her heart on fire but it's a lifeboat to another place, and who needs a lifeboat that's on fire? Not her. But after that, who knows? There are a million possible destinies, a multitude of embarrassing desires she keeps close in her secret heart. She's imagined moving to Paris for a summer to subsist on red wine and gooey camembert and crusty baguettes, meeting a wild-eyed, charcoal-smudged artist who can speak to her in an accent and make her his muse. Ever since she saw that BBC documentary, she's entertained the prospect of volunteering at a bat sanctuary, just for a month or two, wrapping their tiny bodies in fleece blankets and arranging baby bottles in their weird little hands. Ruth has always wanted to take a scuba diving lesson because she thinks it's probably the closest she'll ever come to being able to fly.

And though she doesn't believe in psychics, not really, there is so much future out there waiting. It would be nice to catch a glimpse.

'Very well,' says Gloria the Teller. 'Your name?'

'Ruth.'

'Okay, Ruth. Let's see where you're going, where you'll belong.' She tugs her sleeves back and her hands emerge. Ruth gives a gasp that she immediately smothers. The woman's fingers are fused together, the skin solid flesh right the way to her bent top knuckles. She wears no rings – that would be impossible – but around her palm, above the joint of her thumb, is a bracelet, an intricate bronze band studded with amber. There are things suspended in that amber, insects. The effect is grotesque and magnetic. Ruth wants to throw herself at those hands. Ruth wants to run.

Gloria the Teller paws at her pockets. She tries two and comes out empty and a small flicker of confusion crosses her brow. Then she shrugs her devil-may-care shrug and smiles a brilliant, insouciant smile.

'Hands.' She waves her own and their shadows dance on the tent walls. 'You're interested in hands.'

Ruth can't tell if she's talking about her own disfigurement or the thing in the jar. 'Yes, hands,' she says, feeling as foolish as a whole sack of kittens who haven't worked out they're here to be drowned.

'Then give me those.' Gloria the Teller reaches across the table and takes Ruth's hands in hers. Gloria's skin is so soft. The metal is warm. There's a pulse that must be coming from Gloria, but it feels like the bronze is breathing.

Gloria the Teller opens Ruth's palms and spreads them to the sky in supplication. She traces her own thumbs across them. Together, they look down, where the secrets of her future are written in creases.

'Let's take a look.'

Ruth's never paid attention to her palms before. She thought she'd examined every inch of her body – the moles of her thighs and the goosebump skin round her nipples, the scar on her left knee, which looks like a wave cresting over bone. She's waged an eternity of wars against the redness of her cheeks: talcum powder and fancy foundation and a tube of green concealer, which the beauty assistant swore up and down wouldn't make her look like an alien.

But never her palms. And here they are. Seventeen years old and already covered in deep lines, and isn't it odd, really, when you think about it? Babies are born with these wrinkles; skin is always a bit too big for everyone and needs to be folded. And every time Ruth uses her hands, the creases get deeper and destiny becomes more entrenched and she'll end up exactly the thing that she is.

At the thought, a shiver goes through her. Once you go too far down that path, there's no turning back.

'Ah, now this –' Gloria traces a thumb along a crease – 'I see a big heart in you, girl. You're going to feel things, always. Twice as big as other people.'

Ruth blushes.

'And a drive, that too. This here's all your wanting, your ability to manifest the things you desire. See how deep that is? There's so much purpose in you. You're always in control, making sure you know where you're going.'

The words warm Ruth's guts. She does know. And when she gets there, she's going to be free.

Gloria the Teller pauses. She gives each hand a sharp tug and taps their sides, like she's on the pinball machine at the super bonus ball round, keeping everything in play. Then she drops them and looks at Ruth. Tilts her head, like she's trying to work out how to say it.

'You want to be careful with that, love,' Gloria says at last.

Ruth tightens in her seat. 'What do you mean?'

Gloria lifts her palm to the light. She draws her fingers along a line, her webbed skin brushing Ruth's palm. All of a sudden, it doesn't feel so magical. It makes Ruth think of tarantula hair, furred insects, dust on the wings of moths. Her stomach folds over itself.

'The future doesn't like it when you're too certain.'

'Don't be ridiculous,' says Ruth. That's not how it works, she knows. It's when you don't have a plan, that's when you end up trapped.

'And you're sure about that. But it's true.' Gloria's voice has become gentler now. It sounds like pity, like Ruth's a hysterical girl to be placated. 'Sometimes the future gets bored of people who clutch too hard to their destinies. Sometimes it tries to fuck with them.'

'That's not true,' Ruth says hotly. 'The future's not going to *fuck* with me.'

Gloria tips her head back and laughs, a belly laugh that

gets louder until the whole tent is sopping. She wipes her cheeks. Finally, she gets her breath. 'Okay. Let's pretend it's not. But a word of advice?' Gloria looks her dead in the eyes. 'Slacken your grip on the reins. Give up a bit. Do things without always knowing how they're going to turn out.'

'Or what? What if I don't?'

'It all comes back,' says Gloria, and a mineshaft plunges to Ruth's guts. 'You end up here, just where you began.'

'Here?' The tent walls are suddenly a little too close. The jars pulse like jellyfish. Outside, there are shrieks and hollers, someone is cackling and someone is screaming 'No, no, no!' and Ruth can't tell if it's one person or two people, if they're in ecstasy or agony, or both at the same time.

'Maybe this is your home, here in Pitlaw. Maybe this is where your future is waiting.'

Ruth shakes her head. 'You don't understand.'

'Perhaps not,' says Gloria.

Ruth snatches her hand back and leaps to her feet. The air is hot and close. She can taste metal and fingernails and burning rubber. She has to get out, has to be far away from this woman and her preposterous words. She needs fresh air and movement in her thighs.

'You didn't pay, dear!' says Gloria, but Ruth's outside, feet pounding in the sawdust. Ruth's already gone.

A TOE IN THE WATER

THE NIGHT SWOOPS and grinds and jolts towards moon-
fall. As the silhouettes of stars gouge holes in the sky, the
screams turn hysterical. In the Twins' tent, four arms yank
back a curtain flap, giggling, and release a dazed man – his
cuffs torn, his lips red and loose. He looks as if he's just been
slapped (he probably has). In the grass by his caravan, Werewolf Louie stretches his stomach muscles, which are tense and
cramped from keeping him balanced on the tightrope all
night long. And in hers, the Pin Gal removes a series of ruby-
studded daggers from folds of skin. Blood spills over the
tropical beachscape of her stomach tattoo, turning the sea a
peculiar shade of crimson. It will stop leaking by morning, in
time for the next show. She wipes the daggers clean, swallows
a handful of ibuprofen. The first days are always the worst.

The sawdust is littered with gnawed corn cobs, broken
bottles and sticky paper bags. By the Tilt-A-Whirl, a half-
decapitated polar bear slopes drunkenly, his innards tissuing
out like bath foam. The bear has been ravaged by desperate
hands. A crooked-stitch smile plays on his lips.

It turned out Pitlaw was hungry. There were all kinds of
desires that had waited so long to be satisfied: hearts rum-
bling in ribcages, fingers tensing into claws. A pulse had been
beating wildly below the surface, close enough you could
smell the blood through the skin.

Now, the town is tick-full. The townsfolk stumble home on bloated legs: blinking, trying to cast off what they've just seen. As they leave, the lights turn off: plink, plink, plink. All that's left are the painted bulbs in the main Freakslaw tent, casting a multicoloured glow over those who gather beneath.

'So,' says Mr Partlett. He's sitting on a bale of hay, a purple blown-glass shisha pipe in front of him. He takes a long drag and blows three question marks from the smoke. They hang in the air like inquisitive ghosts, then he shakes his head and they disappear.

Gloria's on Nancy's trapeze, her muscular thighs propelling her body, her many skirts billowing like flowers. She has an apple between her teeth which she spits into her hand; the punctures in its skin glow snow white. 'Not as adept at resisting temptation as they thought.' She laughs and catapults back into the air. 'No one ever is, in the end.'

In the corner, the Strongmen sit topless in a circle, massaging each other's stiff shoulders. Their muscles smell of grapefruit and castor oil, their fingers find and unravel the knots this evening has tied. Gloria sounds a sharp whistle between her teeth, and the Strongmen look up as one.

'A moment's privacy, my dears?' she says, and they tramp out in unison.

Gloria waits until the tent door hushes to speak again. 'It's a travesty, really. The way these people swan around as if they're clueless of their histories. Like they've no idea of the death that took place on this land, how many were killed in their name.'

'Maybe they don't,' offers Mr Partlett, and this brings a smile to Gloria's lips.

'Well, that'll change soon. But if we're going to punish them, we need to find their weak spot.' She tightens her hand around the apple, whose teeth marks are now browning. 'Find it, press a finger in, see what happens.' She pushes harder, holds her breath. In her fist, the apple explodes.

Mr Partlett smirks as wet hunks spatter the sawdust. 'So what now?'

And Nancy – who's snuck behind a hay bale in the shadows, folded upon herself out of sight – lets a wild grin burst open her face. Revenge and weak spots, power games and punishments. What fun! She angles her toe to her mouth and nibbles the black gunk from under the nail.

'Let's dip a gentle toe in the water,' says Gloria, 'and bring the first.'

A damp knock muffles against the tent fabric, and Mr Partlett arches an eyebrow. She nods: 'Come in!' and Werewolf Louie scurries inside, his blush barely visible beneath all that fur.

'You wanted to see me?'

Gloria grits her heels in sawdust. 'My sweet furred one,' she says. 'How would you feel about a very special task?'

'Him?' asks Mr Partlett.

Werewolf Louie looks from one to the other. His nostrils quiver, an ember glints in his eye. 'Me?'

Gloria cups a hand under Werewolf Louie's chin. A breeze tumbles through the tent, making the lightbulbs dance. Pink and green beams list crazily. 'Yes, you.'

Werewolf Louie nods, ecstatic, so Gloria explains, and behind her bale, Nancy rolls her eyes. A gentle dip, Gloria says – a toe in the water! When it's summer and it's so damn hot and the water is just begging for a swan dive. It's a good job Nancy's here, with her own magic to hurry things along. Her *scream-if-you-want-to-go-faster* magic, a two-handed push for the ones on the diving board who just can't get the grit to move.

'You ought to be careful,' Mr Partlett says. 'There's angry men here. Generations of them. They've their own type of dark magic.'

His eyes flicker and for a moment he is ancient and weary.

'Let them come willingly,' says Gloria, arching her toes. And her whole body casts up towards the Top.

THE FIRST

THE NEXT DAY, Monday morning up with the birds, the sun beats on Pitlaw for the ninth day in a row. In the terraces by Gaviston Avenue, Greg Haskett tosses in bed, clawing at the angry sunburn of his bald patch. It's already begun to peel, slivers of it like lemon flesh under his nails. Over by the shop, Mr Dorothy's dachshund, Dolly, lets out a whine, her ears twitching, her slack skin vibrating over the meat of her body. Dolly hasn't slept for eight nights, hasn't dreamed a single dream of rabbits. She pulls her leash taut, toenails clicking like a typist's manicure. Something is not right in the air. Wasps are gnawing at garden sheds, breaking shards of wood between their teeth. Moss is growing at twice the speed it ordinarily does (still, of course, infinitesimally slow). And all the while, Kayleigh MacNamara balls her hands into fists so small you could fit two in your mouth at once. She screams and she screams, and nothing Stephanie does can persuade her that the world is lovely, this day is lovely, the sun is shining and everything's going to be okay.

Funny that, what a wee bit of warmth can do to a bunch of folk who are always complaining about the weather. Funny how little it takes for reality to get an edge like a bunched carpet, a trip hazard you hadn't even noticed was there.

Back at the funfair, Werewolf Louie brushes his teeth carefully (his gums have a tendency to bleed) and grins foamily at the mirror. He's ready to do his bit – chomping at it, in fact. When he clambers off his upturned crate and heads out, it's at a scamper. If you shaved him to skin, you'd see deep grinning dimples.

Louie takes the back route and emerges on to Main Street. He offers Dolly a jaunty wave, sending her into a new frenzy of whines like an amp with nothing plugged in. 'Sorry!' he says. 'It's okay, it's okay!' Every gesture creates a new flurry of anxiety rippling through Dolly. 'It's okay!' but she doesn't believe a word, so he backs off, flinging apologies over his shoulder. Beneath the glowing ginger fur, Louie's cheeks are flaming. He trots as fast as his little legs will carry him without risk of overheating, and four doors down, he finds his destination.

Curl Up and Dye.

Werewolf Louie puts two hands on the glass to shelter the sun glare and peers through the window. Inside are swirly chairs and sinks deep enough to drown in. A line of gleaming turquoise hair dryers, the kind that look like they're from the future and the past at once. A space-age vision far more gleaming and ostentatious than the real future turned out to be.

A smile fills his whole face. There are many in Pitlaw who disapprove of calling a hairdresser Curl Up and Dye – who consider it essentially unserious, believe it's mocking them, specifically, in some hard to define way – but Werewolf Louie *loves* a pun. He also loves, in no particular order: citrus fruits, alpacas, stop-motion animation, being the passenger on a rowboat, and the feeling of strong fingers massaging shampoo into his scalp. Werewolf Louie doesn't like being shaved but he does feel that today, in Pitlaw, a bit of grooming could be just the ticket. It'd be nice to close his eyes and sink into the smell of ammonia. A comb around the chops, a soupçon of local gossip. A hairdresser is a great place to open your ears and listen.

Werewolf Louie pushes the door and steps inside. The bell rings out like a tiny church in a schoolteacher's hands. It's 9 a.m. on Monday and there's not a customer to be seen, but the tiled floor is dazzling and the air is already shiny-sharp. Werewolf Louie stands in the doorway, waiting, until a pair of high heels clack out. Scissor blades wink silver, twisting in the hairdresser's hand. She plants herself in front of him.

'Well look at you!' says Shona Peterson, and Werewolf Louie beams up at her with the most meek-sweet smile there's ever been. 'Look at you,' she says again, and she shakes her head.

Ever since it showed up, knicker stains on show, Shona Peterson's been thinking about the funfair. It's got embedded in her gums, stuck in a spot her tongue can't stop prodding. In fact, just this morning, as she was downing her second cup of builder's tea, Shona made a decision. She might've missed opening night but she doesn't need to miss a moment more. Tonight, she'll head down after work and see what's what. Never mind Norma Murray's pinched face like a cat's arse. Shona's always been a girl who picks at scabs and the thought of the funfair existing all the way over there, just waiting, is impossible. It's too much to resist.

But now this! A part of the funfair, broken off and delivered to her very door. Shona Peterson's never had a good reason to believe in fate or God or destinies in the bottom of teacups. She's always been open to the possibility, while also

97

considering the evidence against: the fact that somehow, she's still in Pitlaw. If there is someone pulling the strings, how come he's such a fucking arsehole? But say she *did* believe in fate or God or destinies at the bottom of teacups. Then, she might see this guy as a sign.

'What can I do you for, pal?'

Werewolf Louie raises his small, furred hands and gestures to his hair, his face, his body. 'A shampoo and set?'

Shona's never heard a voice like it. This wee guy – barely up to her shoulder, his entire body covered in thick orange fur like a young orangutan – has the sweetest, gentlest voice in the world. It sounds every bit as soft and furred as he is. She wants to pick up that voice and cradle it in her arms. She wants to tie pink ribbons to it, sit it on a plump satin cushion, protect that voice against anyone who would harm it. But though she thinks this, though the compulsion is very strong indeed, she moves on and gets down to business.

'Just a shampoo, eh? A bit of styling? You won't be wanting any off?'

'Oh no.' Werewolf Louie's eyes grow big as plums. He flicks his hands, as if bits of the very suggestion might have got on him.

'Aye, I suppose no.' Lord knows, it's probably better not to start. 'Get your arse over then.' Shona leads him to the sinks, flicks the radio on and lathers up her hands. In moments, the air is full of top-forty hits and soap lather.

Shona digs her fingers into his scalp and starts to chat. Werewolf Louie bats his lashes in the reflection. Their faces reflect in the mirrors in front and the mirrors behind. They bounce back and forth into infinity. And in this soft bubbled hush, a small magic begins. The oldest magic, from the time before tophats or even tablecloths. Nimble fingers unravel every knot. Shona tells that joke about the cheese and the small horse. Sodium lauryl sulfate breaks down two weeks of road grime. Tangled hair becomes sleek and smooth. Were-wolf Louie does an impression of an alpaca from the landed gentry, sending the pair of them into fits of giggles.

And Shona Peterson falls in love.

So Werewolf Louie dips a toe in Pitlaw's waters and comes out feeling fine. He has chosen well. This town may be small and fixed in its ways, but it's not immune to life's driving force – curiosity, that tricksy itch. The soil here is fertile. The people are ripe. As the afternoon segues into evening, Louie and Shona wander through the balmy air, where the pink trails of planes gouge the sky. Teasing one another with all the gleeful enthusiasm of a first crush, unearthing the splendid notions in common you can build a life upon. His small furred palm, her dry chapped fingers entwined.

By the time the week is over, Shona Peterson will be firmly entrenched in the world of the Freakslaw. The skills honed from years of running Curl Up and Dye will come in handy, sure, but she'll have not a single regret about leaving the shop behind. Shona will be among her people for the first time in her life, and if that's not a fucking fantastic feeling then she doesn't know what is.

But for now, she just lets Louie lead. She closes her eyes and feels the warmth on her cheeks. Possibility, cracking open like a dozen fat bulbs of tulips. Shona feels like the first spring shoot spearing through dirt. Like a glamorous wench paraded down the pirate ship plank. Like absolutely anything could happen, if only she decides to let it.

BEING & NOTHINGNESS

'SHIT!' RUTH SPREADS her palm on the desk, stabbing between her fingers with the compass needle. There are ants in her knickers. She feels like the surface of a frozen lake, like someone's just stepped on her, sending cracks in every direction. 'Shit, shit, shit.'

Ruth's spent the past five days bouncing from frustration to who cares and back. She's not the only one. The funfair's been working its way under all kinds of skin, gnawing at Pitlaw's subcutaneous layer with the insistence of a particularly focused parasite. In her ordered drawing room (*not* a living room), Norma Murray is making a bulleted list of evidence to submit to the town council. In the Ladbrokes on the corner, Boyd Geddes can barely tap into his usual hunches. Into the sunbaked pub table, Greg Haskett is carving a stick figure of a girl covered in pins, a silly little bitch he gives tits to and crosses for eyes and writes *SLAG* in block caps by her head, just for good measure.

And in Westburn Avenue, Ruth MacNamara is trying to read *Nausea* again. The words won't stick. She's too hot. She's itchy. She knows that fortune teller wasn't a scientist so really there's no reason to listen to her. Anyone can drape themselves in scarves and say *Oh ho ho here's your future*, and only an absolute tool would actually believe.

Stab stab stab. The surface of her desk smatters with tiny

holes. The problem isn't the fortune teller, it's this stupid book. She drops the compass, picks up *Nausea* again and forces her eyes to follow sentence after sentence, all the way to the end of the paragraph.

Never, until these last few days, had I understood the meaning of 'existence'. I was like the others, like the ones walking along the seashore, all dressed in their spring finery. I said, like them, 'The ocean is green; that white speck up there is a seagull,' but I didn't feel that it existed or that the seagull was an 'existing seagull'; usually existence hides itself. It is there, around us, in us, it is us, you can't say two words without mentioning it, but you can never touch it. When I believed I was thinking about it, I must believe that I was thinking nothing, my head was empty, or there was just one word in my head, the word 'to be'.

What's a girl supposed to do with a thing like that? Ruth flings it across the room and decides if she's ever in a smoky bar at one in the morning, listening to a flock of philosophers wax lyrical on the nature of being, she'll just nod sagely and say 'seagulls'. Besides, she's starving. No wonder her brain can't absorb existentialism. Sooner or later, she'll be nothingness herself.

Ruth thumps down the stairs and flings open the fridge. She peers under plates. Liberates a cherry tomato from a chunk of congealed macaroni, dips it in a tub of coleslaw and pops it in her mouth. At the back's a whole tray of cold lasagne. She cuts a slice. The pasta slithers from itself like a wet tongue.

'There some of that left for me?'

Dad's hovering behind her, folded newspaper clutched in

his hand. She didn't hear him come in. Lately, he's never around, and Mum and Stephanie don't seem to notice. The house has taken on a cantankerous womanly energy – all blood, gossip and problems – and she misses how it was before he started taking on those extra shifts at the factory. Driving out to Blockbuster Video on a Wednesday night, every third week her turn to pick the film. Holidays at the beach, standing atop a dune hollering while a gritty wind sanded their red cheeks raw.

'Sure there is.' Ruth cuts a second slice, grabs two forks and places them on the table. They sit opposite each other and eat in companionable silence. At some point, her dad gets the Heinz and they share a wee grin as they douse their plates in gory blobs.

'Gourmet,' says her dad.

'I think they call it fusion now.' She drags a finger through the ketchup and licks it off. 'Scottish–Italian fusion cuisine.'

'It's awful fancy. Chilled, too, for the man on the go. No burned tongues.'

She laughs. They finish their plates and Ruth takes them to the sink to rinse, prodding lumps of sauce down the plug-hole. The kitchen clock is unconscionably loud. It makes her think of a fascist army, marching in unison. Her dad spreads the newspaper on the table, sighs and leans back in his chair. He looks old. All her life he's looked exactly like a bear but in the past few months he's lost a lot of weight. A skinny bear just doesn't look right. The whole point in a bear is that it can wrap its whole body around you.

She doesn't know how to ask the questions in her mouth. She just wants someone to say it: Ruth, you've made all the right decisions. Ruth, things are going to be fine.

'Dad,' she says at last, slotting the plates into the rack, 'how can you make sure you get the life you're supposed to?'

He looks up at her and folds the paper in two. She waits for him to fold it again, and again, into an origami fortune teller. Flip it back and forth to find her destiny. Instead, he presses his thumbs against his eyes – sockets that seem to be getting deeper every day.

'Well, love, you can't. Not always.' His voice falters. 'You know how it is. Sometimes you just have to live it and hope that things work out.'

This is sublimely unhelpful. This is not what she was asking.

'Well, what if someone tells you it's not going to work? What then?' She grabs a cloth and starts wiping the counter-top. Cleaning feels like an act of spite.

'You prove them wrong.' Her dad's looking out the window. She follows his gaze. On the edge of the house is the wooden bird box they built when she was nine. For years, they'd had blue tits making a home inside every summer, popping in and out of the hole. Then one year something happened – after a noisy spring the box went quiet. They left it alone as long as they could, believing everything they'd been told about baby birds and a mother's rejection, until eventually her dad went up the ladder and took the box down. The skeletons were as fragile as moth's wings. When she petted one, it dissolved beneath her fingers. All that was left was the beak.

'As easy as that?'

'Easier.'

And although he'd hung the box back – after they buried the bodies in the garden, next to the remains of three hamsters and Florence the guinea pig – no blue tits ever nested there again. Every year they wait, but Ruth suspects the birds can smell what happened, deep in the grain of the wood. They know you can't build a home on all that death.

As a family, they don't talk about the dead birds. They don't talk about death at all, in fact. The months that her dad was sick four years ago were cloaked in euphemism and secrecy, and Ruth wasn't sure if no one knew what was going on or it was just her in the dark. There were appointments, and her mum sat up late at the kitchen table, new grey hairs sprouting from her temples, a tense crackling energy that felt like it could erupt into screaming at any moment. Then there were fewer appointments, and there were days when she'd come home from school to find her parents laughing. After a while it seemed the whole thing had just been a brief but unpleasant misunderstanding they could relegate to the past.

Ruth doesn't like to think about that time too closely. If she starts thinking about what it all might mean, then her carefully laid plans for the rest of her life start to look like such flimsy artifice. How can she run off to some big city and leave her family here if it turns out something's actually wrong?

And though there's a part of her that wants to grab her dad and shake him, get him to tell her everything, another treacherous part knows how easy it is to let all the dark, difficult things go unspoken. To believe his recent weight loss has nothing to do with anything but a few less fish suppers and a bit too much work. That life is long, as it turns out, and in all probability her dad will live for ever.

As long as the box is closed, the silence coming from the inside could mean anything.

Her dad lumbers over to her. He reaches up awkwardly and ruffles her hair, as if she's a puppy or a child.

'Dad!' she says. 'Gross.'

He doesn't take offence, just shrugs and goes to get his jacket from the hall cupboard. 'Don't be scared, love. Show the world what a MacNamara's made of, eh?'

This, she knows, is as close as she'll get to affirmation. The fork is in her hand, and she jabs her thigh through the denim. It doesn't hurt, not much. The prickling reminds her: she's still alive, she can run. She's going to get exactly where she needs to go.

BARBIE GIRL

THAT AFTERNOON, IN the depths of the Freakslaw, Nancy stands beneath an orange spotlight. The audience, who started out cynical and have spent the last twenty minutes watching feats of ever more grotesque contortions, lean forward. Nancy lifts one hand and holds finger to thumb in the OK symbol. She writhes her shoulders beneath the sticky light, dislocating bones, urging sinews into unlikely places. Then with a slick flourish, she points a single toe and steps through the O of her fingers. The audience scream, 'Ahh!'

It's impossible, of course. A trick of the light, a slip in the shade. In her beaded red catsuit, Nancy looks like a slash of blood. She carelessly lifts a foot to her mouth. What the audience see – hands over eyes, peering through fingers – is the lips spreading and the foot disappearing. The girl eats herself and emerges on the other side. She claps and the tent fills with sudden smoke, which gusts and blooms and becomes bats. As the crowd shrieks, women flinging their hands to their hair, Nancy bows. A cymbal crash, the bats are just smoke and shadows, of course, were they ever anything else? The music spirals louder and higher, and it must be the delirium of this hot tent, it must be a trick, because what seems to happen next is that she folds herself in half, in half again, again, again – her body becomes smaller until it's barely there, and then the last fold: poof!

Nancy is gone.

The tent erupts in terrified applause.

Back in her caravan, Nancy peels off her catsuit and flings it to the floor. It nestles among a dozen other silky swatches and when Gloria comes back, she's bound to get bitching. But that's not for, ooh, at least a couple of hours. Fortunes won't tell themselves, after all.

Nancy lights three fat red candles, fixes a jar of whisky, and sits on the bed in her knickers. Her joints are swollen – one elbow keeps pinging out of socket – but the Scotch takes the edge off. She yanks the drawer from under the bed and rummages for precious things. Objects of delicious power. Things that sparkle, that attract and repel.

Nancy grins. She's been thinking about this ever since she saw Ruth run from Gloria's tent, face red and fists balled. Whatever Gloria said, it clearly got under her skin. Which is nice. Under the skin's where all the soft and vulnerable bits are. Once someone's been got under the skin of, they're so much easier to play with.

And playing with girls is a game Nancy very much enjoys. What she wants is to plant another one of her charms – not in the dirt this time, but some place equally damp and susceptible. A gleeful little hook for her magic to hang upon. And isn't Ruth just the perfect soil: so good, so determined, so utterly set in her plans? The exact kind of girl who needs a helping hand to get where she ought to be going.

On the blanket, Nancy organizes the things. An old Barbie doll with a chewed foot. Three ribbons: one red, one yellow, one black. A blend of essential oils: frankincense, black pepper, vetiver, calamus, liquorice, bergamot and High John root. And, from her bag, that bloody handkerchief from Ruth's knee.

Nancy takes her golden scissors and snips a tiny square, buckled and brown. With a purple thread, she stitches it to Barbie's dress. Right where the heart would be, if the doll had a heart. She pokes it in the chest and kisses it on the nose.

She ties the three ribbons together and knots them nine times. With every knot, Nancy whispers her name: *Ruth, Ruth, Ruth* . . . Hilarity bubbles inside her. When she's done, she ties the knotted ribbon around Barbie's neck. The doll doesn't say a word, just looks at her with blank eyes.

To seal the deal, she grabs a fine black pen and writes across Barbie's plastic legs: nine times too, in tiny caps lock. *RUTH, RUTH, RUTH* . . .

She prises the wax seal from the glass bottle. The oil blend is spiced and musky and alive. Nancy lets a single drop fall on the doll's face, a drop on the heart, and one on the crotch. Is it enough? She thinks about ramming the whole thing in a mason jar and drowning it. But no. That'd be overkill. Instead, she dips her finger in her whisky and rubs it across Barbie's pink lipstick. She dips it again and sucks her finger. Delicious.

Then she rubs the Barbie across her chest and armpits, anointing it in naked sweat. After the spotlights, she's ripe. The plastic hair tickles. Nancy tugs her knickers aside and presses the doll's head into her crotch, grinding until the friction finds the spot. Closes one fist around her bedcover and rocks her body, mashing the doll against her cunt. Inside, she grows slick and feral. With every jerk of the doll, the power between her legs builds. A primordial magic, the original perpetual-motion machine. She feels herself thrum and the excitement makes her thrum harder. She leans into her own grossness, turning the air soupy. She moves the doll faster and a high mosquito whine starts up in her ears; and she moves the doll faster while the noise builds in amplifier feedback; and she moves the doll faster and right before the circuits trip, when the sound has reached a thrashing cacophony, the deep magic emerges, shuddering, sending her body into a holy spasm.

And she's done, she collapses against the cushions. Nancy sniffs the doll. It smells weird. Excellent. Now she's come, the energy is awake inside her. Full of snakes, she could do anything. It's too much to be trapped in the caravan. She has to leap out into the universe, smear herself over it as the day turns to night, lickety-split bright with the holler of the moon.

The world's out there, the glowy lights of the carnival rides. She's going to find Zed, that's what she's going to do, bite his most biteable cheek and drag him on the Orbiter until both of them have shaken something loose. They'll whip and whirl, turn their insides to blendered confusion, and then she'll drag him to the meat stall and get whoever's working to sneak them sausage and curly fries. Because she's hungry, now the work's done.

Nancy gets to her feet and flings some clothes on. She downs the last of the whisky and dabs the essential oil behind her ears along with the wet slick of her own fingers. She leaves everything on the floor, all over the place, so that when Gloria comes in for a break after a long afternoon rummaging around in other people's memories (that exhausting procession of loves lost and destinies wrought), she'll land one foot in a pile of silk scarves and skite on to her arse.

'Nancy!' she'll yell, but by this time Nancy will be already helter-skelter, hand in hand with Zed, upside down on the Orbiter. She won't be there to see Gloria get angrily to her feet, to help as she grabs handfuls of Nancy's dirty washing and flings them in the basket. Nancy will be terrifically busy screaming *faster faster faster* as Gloria notices what's on her bed, as she plucks her way across the room and picks up the doll. She won't see the frown that crosses Gloria's face as she takes in the thread and the tatter of blood, but even if she did, she wouldn't care.

Her mother has never appreciated Nancy's magic – loyal as she is to patience and books and all the tedious old ways. Gloria's got altogether too much fidelity to ancestral precedence, as if that's not just replicating the same old shit they're trying to subvert! She doesn't understand that tearing up the future sometimes requires a looser touch. A chaotic intuition. A whole new method of pressing your foot on the gas.

Nancy is feeling really good. As the axle whips around and all the air sucks out of her lungs, she's flying. She can do anything. She clutches tighter to Zed's hand and the power crackles in her fingers.

MEDITATION

'SHE'S A LITTLE shit sometimes.' Gloria rolls her shoulder and presses her head against the wooden beam, balanced in the centre of Mr Partlett's performance tent, which is quiet now in the hush between the shows. She's stiff, bound up with her wrists crossed above, her ankles tied, balance off-kilter. It's taking all her concentration to remain upright on tiptoes, adjusting and readjusting her weight.

Still, she can't deny it's relaxing. Her head's clearer than it's been all day.

'But no harm done?' Mr Partlett drifts the glowing ember of his cigarette towards her nipple, and Gloria's breath tightens. She watches in a kind of distant curiosity as the skin puckers into goosebumps. The tip edges closer with infinitesimal slowness and she feels it, hot as lava, hot as the centre of the earth, and then he moves his hand and there's nothing, not a mark.

Gloria sighs. 'Not yet.'

'Then to more important things.' His scars gleam. 'The revenge. How's it taking shape?'

'It's taking. The first has arrived.'

Mr Partlett grins. His belt slithers free and he wraps the buckle around his hand, letting the tongue hang loose. 'So what now?'

Gloria holds a breath, her mind emptying in this sublime

moment of anticipation. Here, in the pause before the pain, she can think clearly. Here is the one spot where the voices are quiet. 'We bring more!' she shrieks, as the first lash licks across her flesh.

'Just like that?'

'No.' For the plan requires a most delicate staging. Act too soon, and they'll reveal their hand, allow the town to gird itself for retaliation. This particular magic is best conducted as sleight of hand, an act in the night.

'So how?'

'Gently.'

Mr Partlett increases the speed of the belt. It snaps against Gloria's skin, turning her pale flesh mottled. Each crack is a firework exploding behind glass. She would like to throw open all her windows and angle her cheeks to the heavens. Tiny blood vessels bloom and explode, roman candles bloom and explode, the pressure builds.

'There's something bothering you,' Mr Partlett says. 'What is it?'

'Nancy!'

'What about her?'

Gloria takes a deep breath. The muscles in her calves are beginning to cramp. All the weight on her toes is sending pins and needles up her legs. 'She'll want trouble.'

'Yes.'

'Impossible,' she pants. 'To make that one. Slow down.'

'That's true.'

'A delicate. Balance. What if – what if it spills?'

Mr Partlett cracks the tip against her inner thigh and flickers a smile. 'Then we shall have to spill with it.'

A sharp exhale of laughter. 'True, that. But I'm afraid . . .'

'Afraid of what?' Mr Partlett catches the belt in one hand. He holds it high in the air and they both watch, wary, waiting for the leather to leap into life. Silence thick as sawdust. They can smell it, sweet and yellow, settling over everything. Gloria looks Mr Partlett in the eye –

And then three sharp knocks on the beam by the tent door, and the silence is broken.

Mr Partlett raises an eyebrow. She shrugs carelessly, as carelessly as one can when naked and bound to a single pole. 'Fine,' she says.

'Come in,' he says, wrapping the belt in his hands.

The flap swings open. Shona Peterson steps inside. Her cheeks are pink and a dazed, messy smile fills her mouth when she sees what's in front of her.

'Ach, I didnae mean to interrupt, I was just down in that Casino of Souls and we're lookin' for the big wrench, and that lad with the hair – Zed is it? – he said I'd best come up in here, so I—'

'No matter,' says Mr Partlett.

'Well, I wouldnae normally barge in. I ken how hard it must be getting a minute to yourselves in a place like this and—'

'We're almost done.' Gloria shifts her weight into one hip. Already, the sting of the belt is dissipating. Her skin is turning milky. The train of thought is gone. All that's left is a low thrumming fear, a twinge of danger on its way. Shona Peterson opens her mouth and then, catching the look in Gloria's eye, backs out, mouthing apologies. The tent flap hushes shut behind her.

'Afraid of what?' repeats Mr Partlett.

Gloria shakes her head. 'Let me down.'

Mr Partlett undoes her clasps obediently. He takes a hip flask and pours a shot into a burnished cup, while Gloria stamps her feet, digging her thumbs into her tingling calves. She throws it back in one. The liquor tastes like a campfire under an open sky bedazzled with stars.

Gloria walks over to a hay bale and collapses. From beneath, she plucks a thread of straw, glittering gold, and wraps it around one delicate wrist. Her fingers flex. It looks like it's worth a million dollars. But that's just the magic of the tent.

'Another?' says Mr Partlett, and Gloria lets him pour. The voices are so loud today. She can feel them in her bones, her liver. The pain somehow even worse than the last time. Her kidneys like old napkins, wrung between fists.

This time, the liquor tastes like a whole house fire. She knows exactly how this will go. The third drink will be gasoline on an empty school building. By the sixth, half of the Californian brush will be up in flames.

Gloria reclines, naked, letting the hay prickle her skin. She adjusts her tophat, channelling Marlene Dietrich, a leopard at her ankles. Tries to let go of this clawing fear for her family, a love so strong she sometimes worries it will devour her whole.

'You should have smelled it, though,' she says at last. 'That doll. The power in it.'

'She knows how to cast a spell, your girl. You should be proud.'

Gloria lets herself smile. She is. It could have all gone so differently. All pregnancy long, she was in a state of fret. Letting herself get knocked up by a norm, what had she been thinking? If she was going to do it, she could have at least kept the funfair in her bloodline! Three separate times, she'd stood before the mirror with a handful of peacock flowers. Ready to flush out the mistake before it overtook her entirely.

But something stilled her hand. She kept thinking, this is something I've never done before. And Gloria's always been so excited by that prospect. When you open yourself to things you've never done, the future licks its lips and lets itself multiply. It makes sense to excite the future. In a good mood, it'll lead you all kinds of interesting places.

So she let it happen. Her belly grew huge and grotesque, and her tattoos bulged and distended, and her feet expanded two whole sizes, and she ate raw steak and spearmint candy by the bucketful, and eventually a human oozed out. Nancy.

And it turned out all her fears were for nothing because right from the beginning, those huge green eyes were overflowing with trickery. If there's a glimmer of norm spunk in Nancy's making, Gloria hasn't seen it. So she is proud. But still, she keeps a small jar of peacock flowers on her shelf, because it's nice to have options. The future likes that too.

'I'm being foolish,' she says at last. 'Nancy is fine, the girl's fine. The first woman came easily.'

'So let's put things in motion for the rest.'

'Yes,' says Gloria, considering. 'We'll work with the year, with the moon.' At this, she throws her body back, kicks a leg in the air. Her embers are starting to fan. Her heart's becoming raucous again, the way it does every time. 'Solstice. Let's throw a great feast!'

'We'll come together,' says Mr Partlett. 'And then we'll break this place apart.'

'Of course.' She's sprawled and gleeful now, raising her cup to the rafters. A happiness floods her, dandelion-bright.

There's a season for everything – a time to plant, a time to reap. A time to spring into action, a time to hold fast. And after Solstice, when the sun begins its shrink, everything will speed up, the way it always does. Her plan will take delightful form. But until then, they will play, they will entertain, they will cast their spells.

'Let's enjoy this time,' she says. 'Let's not forget.'

'The revenge?'

'All of it.' Gloria's cheeks are pink. 'It's what we were brought here to do.'

THE SKY WILL WIN

THE WOODEN TEETH swing as another hot sun slopes from the sky. Ruth's sweating in jeans, her head hazy. It's hard to think straight when the air's like this. She supposes this is what the scientists were talking about, how we burned up the earth and will pay the price. Now it's happening, it doesn't feel real.

When she steps over the threshold, the good-girl part of herself hisses disapproval. It has a point. But that voice is drowned out by another, whispering about a shock of black hair and a broken tooth. The boy was cute, in a way no one in Pitlaw comes close to. The need to come back was a compulsion, an itch impossible not to scratch.

Ruth passes by the Haunted House of Horrors, the Mummy's bandages whipping in a makeshift breeze. An animatronic Frankenstein's Monster twists lazily and moans 'durrrrrr'. She kicks through grass, scattered with an endless confetti of tombola tickets. A group of kids from her year are shooting ceramic stars with a BB gun. When they aim it perfectly, the stars explode.

She follows the path, spiralling deeper like rings in a log, until she reaches the glowing centre. Here, Tiki torches are dug into the ground, each burning a different colour. Ruth recognizes the reactions from chemistry: the hot pink of lithium, cool lavender potassium, barium's emerald green. She notes Gloria's tent, its looping letters strung on carnival ribbons, and her spine tenses.

And then, her stomach performs an elaborate triple pike. A smile plucks at her lips. All of the sights suddenly line up perfectly. Zed.

In the distance, a star explodes.

Ruth cuts across the grass, so intent on her destination that she's halfway there before she notices he's not alone. By his side is the girl with the big mouth, the one who kept talking. She stops. They look up, Zed and the girl . . . Nancy, it was. Laughter breaks open their faces and Ruth considers running home again.

'Hi!' she says instead, and waves a big foolish hand in the air.

Zed and Nancy wave back. Their grins are shiny-sweet in the night. Ruth meets Nancy's gaze and something tugs at her. An odd twist. Ruth thinks about setting herself on fire. If she did, would Nancy leap on her, roll her around in the dirt to put out the flames? It'd be nice to be extinguished with flat-palmed slaps. The hands so loud and magical, she'd barely feel the burn.

Ruth shakes her head. The image is stupid, she has no idea where it came from.

'You came back.' Nancy flashes a shitkicker smirk, draws a hand through her traffic-light-red hair.

Ruth leans against an imaginary nothing and tries to look cool. 'Sure. What you up to?'

'All done for the night.'

'We are?' says Zed. 'You are. Some of us don't have such god-given talents. Some of us need to get back to the grift.'

He flexes an arm in his tight pink T-shirt. The muscle looks incredibly biteable. Ruth blinks and looks away.

'What a shame.' Nancy pulls out a silver thermos. 'I thought we could take some together. Get to know our new friend.'

Ruth doesn't say a word. Her head is reeling at the word *friend*. She doesn't have many of those right now. And the prospect of that changing, it's the same feeling as when she listens to punk at full volume, a loose thread in tarmac you can pull on, and the ground opens. Down there lurks a whole world you never knew existed, music and bruises and bars that stay open until dawn. She stands before them, arms too long for her body. With all the nonchalance she can muster, she folds one into the other.

'Give us a go.' Zed reaches for the thermos and Nancy snatches it back.

'Patience!' she huffs, and turns to Ruth. 'Do you like chai?'

'Sure.' The only tea Ruth's ever drunk is PG Tips, but she could be the kind of person who likes chai. Chai is probably like gin fizzes or Manhattans, something fabulous from a bygone age, the liking of which can almost be a character trait in itself.

'Ah, come on,' Zed says. 'I've got to get back, those waltzers won't spin themselves.'

'Okay, okay.' Nancy pours a cupful into the lid and hands it over. Zed swoops it into his mouth and swallows with a lovely shudder. He squeezes Nancy in a bear hug, kisses her cheek, and a spike of jealousy glides into Ruth's guts.

'Come see me later!' He's already striding off with great gangling legs. 'Nice to see ya again, Ruth.'

Oh. She wants to yell *wait*, wants to explain that he was the whole point in all of this, but she doesn't know how. Besides, Nancy's already poured another and is holding it out, dimples glinting. 'So how about it? Just a little dose, get the evening going.'

Ruth's stomach flops over itself again. 'A dose,' she says, understanding dawning.

'Half a dose,' Nancy amends. 'Enough to give the world a sparkle.'

'Ah,' says Ruth. She's never done drugs before. She's come close. She's listened to Jefferson Airplane while psychedelic rabbits rose up in her chest. She once took caffeine pills pretending they were speed, while Brian Molko gibbered about crawling skin and leather friends. And of course, she's heard everything Lou Reed has to growl about: uppers and downers and the terrifying candied seduction of smack. She's listened to that song a thousand times lying on her bed in Westburn Avenue, imagining sticky brown goo creeping through her veins, turning her liquid and apocalyptic. She's closed her eyes and she's swooned.

But this, perhaps, isn't the same as actually doing it. Not really. And now the opportunity's here, arms outstretched. Zed did it, just as if it was nothing. And Nancy's eyes are sparkling, and the thought of saying no is frankly impossible.

'Sure,' she says instead, as tough and certain as anybody. 'Give us one.'

Nancy passes her the cup.

The tea is golden. It smells of spice and honey, and something beneath that: a guttural earthy scent. Ruth downs it with the same tossed intensity she saw from Zed. It's tooth-achingly sweet. As she swallows, it turns dusty and ancient.

Like dirt. No, older than that. Dirt that's been left in an attic for a hundred years, while the dirt in the real world turns to soil to plants to soft summer rain. Another acquired taste, like coffee and olives. But she controls herself, she barely winces.

Nancy's grin is filthy. She drinks one herself, then pours a second. 'Another?'

'Thanks.' Why not? If she's going to try this, she might as well really commit. She can feel her whole body lighting up like a paper lantern, but the moment it hits her stomach, there's a wrench of regret. It's immediately too late to change her mind. Truth be told, it felt too late the moment Nancy offered. There's something about her that makes Ruth feel pliant, susceptible. There's something about giving over control that feels like relief. *If your new friend jumped off a cliff would you follow her?* Well no, of course she wouldn't. But maybe she'd stand on the edge, peer over, just to see how it felt. She refolds her arms in the opposite direction. 'What now?'

Nancy's hand darts out to grab hers, a hot little palm with nails bitten down to the quick. 'Come with me.' She yanks her arm, and Ruth follows, deeper and deeper into the Freakslaw.

Ruth sits quietly as the music builds. They're at the back of a tent, side by side on a bench, waiting for the show to begin. The song has a scuttering quality that makes her think of spiders, and she shivers. When they'd reached the ticket collector, a man with a strangely flat skull, Nancy had just waved her through. So now she's here. A part of the inside.

The spider-music rattles as three pink beams convene on the stage. In the dusky spotlight, there's nothing, and then – a cymbal kssh – the Pin Gal appears.

That's what the chalkboard outside pronounced her, what the ticket collector chanted: 'Pin-gal-pin-gal'. And as the show starts, Ruth understands. The Pin Gal opens her mouth wide and presses the tip of a fencing sword against the inside of her cheek. Her face bulges. The lights turn to polka dots. The tip of the sword punctures through. Flecks of blood scatter the sawdust: a jolt of silver, flashing metal. She holds the handle between her teeth and smiles awkwardly. Ruth feels a little sick.

Is it happening yet? Are they kicking in? Is she going to throw up?

No. Not yet. The Pin Gal tugs out her lower lip. Holding her skin taut in one hand, the other eases a second blade through it. The audience gasp and moan in unison. Her whole mouth splays open, a pink wound beset with gleaming knives. She reaches for a third.

Ruth holds her breath. She grabs her knees, making sure they stay in place.

Over the next half-hour, the Pin Gal's body becomes entirely punctured by metal. Just when you'd think there wasn't a single point left, she angles an arm behind her neck and discovers a whole new cushion. Spreads her toes wide and threads a needle between. She becomes a futuristic flower with knives for petals. The Pin Gal gets the audience involved, offering up her body as a palette to defile. The people cackle as their sharp objects slide through. Somehow, she won't stop beaming. Ruth looks at the Pin Gal's manic, metal mouth and then back at the men hollering to have a go on her, and something ratchets inside. Her stomach gurgles. She feels like someone's taken her in one hand and the world in the other, then made a half turn, so they no longer fit.

The two realities slip back into focus and the Pin Gal laughs like a bell. When she bows, the blades grind against each other like scissors. The fabric of Ruth's world warps once more.

'Nancy!' She reaches to tug on her new friend's sleeve. In horror, she watches her hand follow her hand follow her hand, a jittering series of selves, spread in a fan. When she lands on Nancy, they become one. 'I feel weird,' she hisses. She can still see where her hand dragged the air, disturbed like a dog's fur brushed in the wrong direction.

The Pin Gal starts whipping swords out of her body. She tosses them into a chest; they land swish swish swish. Ruth thinks of butterflies made of metal, moths made of metal, bat wings shearing through hair.

'*Really* weird.'

Nancy places a finger on Ruth's lips. 'Don't disturb her! This is very delicate work.' She grins witchily. The crowd hoots and hollers. Saliva creeps into Ruth's mouth. She doesn't normally have a weak stomach. But this is something else.

The Pin Gal reveals a tall glass of water from under a handkerchief. She tosses the fabric and it turns into a mushroom cloud, spreads, falls to the ground as atomic rain. The sawdust spends a nuclear winter trying to regenerate its crops while the Pin Gal raises the glass. She takes a long swallow, her pale throat bobbing up and down. For a minute, there's nothing.

And then the water pours.

From every puncture, a heady drizzle. Under the lights, the arcs are the same light yellow as piss. An image spasms into Ruth, the worst thing she ever saw, a clip of a man stood over a woman's face, urine spattering, and she can't remember if it's real or something she dredged from the filth of her imagination, but there it is, in three dimensions, there it is.

Ruth presses her fists against her eyes. When she opens them, the water is still drumming against dirt. 'Are you seeing this?'

Nancy's lashes open wide. She looks at Ruth like a whole field of poppies. 'Magnificent, no?'

There's something not right in Nancy's eyes. Her pupils are wide as fists. Her teeth all lined up like piano keys. Air tightens and solidifies in Ruth's throat.

She leaps to her feet as the crowd explodes in thunderous applause. She practically flips the bench. The walls are liquid and diaphanous, but Ruth parts them with a swimmer's crawl, slices through a clattering hellscape and the echo of Nancy calling, 'Hey, where you going? You need to see the end—'

And then she's outside in velvet darkness, pulse pounding. She presses one hand to her chest. If she pushed a little harder, she could reach right in and wrap her fingers around her rattling heart. In her fist, it would be soft and vulnerable as those baby birds. She'd wait and wait for it to spread its wings but it would never fly, its bones would already be broken. Her heart would turn to dust in her hand.

She looks up and there, above her, is endless ink.

'Gotcha.' A hot palm lands on her shoulder. Ruth doesn't know how long she's been here, eyeballing the sky. It's gone weird, that's the thing. There are far too many stars: the normal ones but then the extra ones behind, each a tiny door to an endless white corridor. When she concentrates, she can see all the way though.

'What's with the sky?'

'Relax.' Nancy clutches with her bony fingers. 'Why are you fighting it?'

Ruth doesn't know what she means. She's not trying to fight the sky. The sky would win, she knows that much. Just look at it. It goes on for ever. Ruth swallows and tastes it again, that old dirt, dusty soil in her teeth. She runs her tongue against her gums.

'Oh,' she says. 'Oh no.'

'What?' Nancy spreads her leather jacket on the dirt and pushes her down. 'You're with me, you're fine.'

How can she be fine? She's high, so very high. She never should have drunk that tea. A cartoon spatters into her brain: STRANGER DANGER! A leering man with eyes on springs, waving a bulging bag of sweets. The eyes bounce and boing. Beneath their feet, the ground is writhing. And what about everything that's going on above their heads?

'The sky would win.' Her words hang around them like wet washing and she hears it again, a damp echo. This guy. The sky.

'This guy would win.'

The giggles burst out of her before she can stop them. They launch to the surface as volcanic gas and her skin erupts. She looks at the craters in her arms, at the civilizations who have sacrificed virgins into these volcanos, at the rise and fall of empires between the moles.

'Nancy!' It's meant to sound like 'How could you?!' but it comes out as a shriek, a squeal, the delighted gasp of roller-coasters all the way down. Nancy's face is pure satisfaction. She looks like a little imp. An impette. The impette and the limpet, stuck together for ever. Ruth is wet flesh and a barnacle shell. Ruth didn't know that drugs made you so smart. All these associations flipping over like playing cards on a green baize table, and what even is baize anyway? It'd feel good to lie in now, whatever. She'd like to peel all her clothes off and rummage around in a big fuzzy astroturf.

'That looks comfortable,' says Nancy.

Ruth is somehow on her back. She's holding one foot in the air, her hand clasped around it like a baby's. 'Oh no,' she says.

Nancy starts to laugh. Ruth feels really good about making her laugh. Her heart expands until it takes up most of the room in her ribs. This is what she was always meant to do. The life she's been waiting for. The funfair is so weird. They're in a cocoon of neon. She tries to think back to what happened with the girl and the knives but it's already impossible. Ruth is all stretched out like an Irn Bru bar. Ruth is a lump of flesh without a past or a future. Limpet, she thinks, and laughs again.

'Let's go explore.' Nancy pulls herself to her feet as if she's made of ordinary girl bones. 'Come on.'

Are you sure? Ruth can't tell if she said that out loud. Going does not seem like a smart idea. Why would they want to go anywhere when they could lie liquid here with the ground? Nancy holds out a hand. Her eyes are so sparkly. She looks like she's pulled her pupils open and poured a handful of glitter inside. Ruth thinks about saying no. What About A Bad Trip? says her brain. Don't Have A Bad Trip. What if this magic spot is the home of all the feel-good feelings? She's reached a perfect equilibrium, it would be foolish to push it now. But Nancy's eyes are so sparkly. Ruth takes a deep breath. Puts her hand into Nancy's and lets the tug happen and she's standing.

Hand-in-hand with this strange, impossible creature who moves so fearlessly through the world.

'The things.' All their belongings, all over the earth. Impossible to organize. They might as well leave them here. But Nancy lets go of her and picks up the satchel, her leather jacket, magics them away. Ruth was wrong. Standing up feels terrific. Walking is even better. The balmy air licks at their faces and there's a glorious sheen over Nancy's cheeks. Ruth wants to bite them and see what's inside. A man staggers past clutching a huge stuffed panda. The panda's eyes are black holes studded with gleaming green buttons. Before the night is out, the bear will definitely have eaten him. Ruth nudges Nancy and points. Nancy cackles.

And Ruth realizes this is what she's been waiting for, this freedom to stop trying so hard and let the world swallow her whole.

THE WORLD
WHIPPING PAST

THE LIGHTS PLINK on from the centre of the waltzers, wap wap wap, a neon spiderweb bursting into being. Zed cranks the music. His head is full of vibrations and dancing animals. Everything's gooey in his legs. He assembles a broken-tooth smile and, with an effort that could be considered super-human, clatters over the spinning floor and closes his fists around the back of a car.

Three freckle-faced children look up at him, eyes wide. What doughy little puddings, slumped atop each other! Zed thinks about an advert for flour. A pudgy sack, a wooden spoon clasped in one hand.

'Doyouwannagofaster?!' His question's a shriek. An anthem. The dough boys squeal and wave their hands. Zed grins and grips the waltzer bar, then flings it away from him-self as hard as he can.

The car whips faster than a drag queen's wig. The boys become cows in the tornado, egg whites in the blender, paper boats in the drain. Their screams disperse somewhere around the ceiling, among the dry ice and the ghosts of all the other screams risen there before. He can see a thick layer hovering, an essence of terror and pure unfiltered delight.

Ooh la la! The cars today are electric
I WANNA SEE THE . . .

and he grabs the next and they dance. Zed and the waltzer, his dream date, one-step, two-step, hand-in-hand and then – seeyalater, forgetmenot! – he flings this one away too. It's not to be, my dear.

Zed leans into the music

. . . *BLUEBIRDS FLYING* . . .

and performs a new act of terror alchemy. The children scream uncontrollably, trying to grab a gasp of air, each breath whipped out and swallowed by the waltzers (Mine! mine! mine!). There's a car of grown men with frog faces, growing redder and redder, and is that sick rising up? Zed spins that car hardest of all. Oh dear, oh dear. Look at them tensing to hold on, as gravity slaps them back. They're resisting. Their rational minds know fine well that their innards are being crushed. Sooner or later, if they don't hold on to them, their brains will ooze out their ears. And then where will they be?!

The children let go of the bar. FASTER FASTER FASTER! Their bodies scramble. Someone's lungs turn inside out. A heart and a liver swap places, just to see how it feels. The song reaches the hundredth climax

. . . *OH WHERE IS THE SILVER LINING* . . .

and Zed gives them one last glorious shove, a holy tempest, and then stumbles back to the control desk. The dials and switches wink. This one, that one, off – and the ride wheezes to a close. The men stumble into the grass, weaving like broken boxers, clutching their stomachs. The kids lower their arms and sit tight in the cart. When he comes to help them out, they wriggle and squeal and refuse to pry their hands from the bar.

'AGAIN AGAIN AGAIN!'

Zed is delighted. His mouth's all sherbet fountains. 'Again?'

The children have the right idea. They know when to demand more and when to let go, when to have the world fling them and when to fight back.

'Let's go!' He clambers to the cabin and flicks every switch back on.

Time passes. The mushrooms give the world a delightful skee-wiff, mind rattling a million miles a minute. Every time Zed touches the cart – bzzzp! – an electric shock. His hair stands on end, his palms turn black, and here he is in the future. Here he is, bratty club-kid of New York in glittery cheekbones. Here he is, deep-sea diver, making faces at a Giant Pacific Octopus. Here he is, weather girl! Here, sixty years old and in charge of the Freakslaw. Him and Nancy, amateur sleuths in their secret detective agency. With that girl, Ruth, on stage with the world's fastest punk band. Here. Here. Here.

Do the people notice? Can they see this hyperactive goblin flickering in and out of reality, fizzing through timelines like a gurning zoetrope? Oh no. They're too busy trying to keep their guts in place, trying to stop the whole damn world from unravelling. Zed peers from his moving stage at the funfair stretching out. The streets are squish and sawdust. The rides are at high pelt, the air thick with endorphins and burned popcorn.

And in the tents, the others casting their own spells. The Twins will be neck-deep in trickery, sawing a victim in half, white rabbits leaping from their pockets. Gretchen will be astride some valley of filth: diamante knickers and a cabaret soundtrack, a headless chicken spurting blood. All the while, Miss Maria's tent will be hung heavy with musk and sugar. Those who wander in will sink all the way up to their necks.

Zed twirls deliciously. And that's when he sees them, weaving towards him. Nancy, stomping in her Docs, sending up puffs of dust. Ruth, walking as if the ground is swampland, alligators and islands. Nancy has one arm around Ruth, helping her or pushing her, and together they're heading straight for his side.

Oh no! he thinks – but the oh no is candy-sweet. Trouble! he thinks, and it's trouble like the Funhouse, like the tickle boat, like don't chase me! (please chase me), don't chase me! (catch me now). He's seen this happen before.

Left to her own devices, Nancy will make a girl unravel. She keeps pockets full of ruin, she barrels into every situation and flings things just to see what will happen. Nancy loves to tug a loose thread. She can't bear to see someone stood on the edge of a swimming pool without wanting to be the flat palms that shove them in.

It's all for good reason, of course. As Nancy tells him every time, teenage girls are a force for the future. And when the world's so hellbent on keeping them on the straight and narrow, it's only fair to balance that out with a little push for the other side. Why, without that, who knows what might happen? A future that the old men want, without a smidge of the sweet chaos that will save the world.

Zed doesn't like to get in her way – though he's curious as to how the drugs will affect her magic. Psychedelics have a tendency to turn everything very murky and very clear all at once. The dream soup goes strange. Will she still be able to fiddle with Ruth's future, the way she did with all the other girls? Bernice in the institution, skeleton visible through her skin, scribbling a million poems on the walls – the best she'd ever written. Or Dora in the police station, eyes glittering, char marks from the arson still black on her palms. Alive at last, but the policeman full of questions, the school up in flames. And Nancy stirring it all with her big stick. Finding those wide-eyed girls so full of potential, seeing how things may go if they skipped off the rails. Playing chicken on the tracks, and Nancy – her reflexes like a cat – playing the game too, but somehow always leaping at the last moment to safety while the others are hit with the whole force of the universe.

Was it wrong, how they ended up? Or was it just what happened?

Zed doesn't know. Zed couldn't be mad at Nancy even if it was. Look at her! She beams at him with her flashing eyes and clenched fists and black leather jacket slung over one arm. She makes him think of a perfectly wrapped birthday present with purple bows and razor edges, one that might contain your true heart's desire or a whole nest of angry wasps – and you know you're taking that risk, but still you want to rip off the paper because it looks so pretty and it could be the other, and you hold it to your ear and shake it, and that doesn't sound like buzzing. Does it? It's probably just your heart. It's probably just the excitement in your ears and –

Zed raises one hand in the air and waves it maniacally. 'Here!' as if they might not have noticed the waltzers scream-ing and sparking. The girls stop dead. Ruth blushes – he can see it from here, even over the strobing and the lasers and the dry ice. She stands wobbly on her too-long legs, a regular Bambi, and raises a hand to wave back. Nancy practically rolls her eyes. She clutches Ruth and stomps right up to the waltzer stairs. Zed brings the ride to a close. Time to take a little break. Poke a finger in the nest, see what's happening. Zed lollops to them, his grin stretched wide.

THE ACT OF A POOF

OVER THE WAY, without a single thought of arson and all the ways a life can skip out of orbit, Derek Geddes pads through the Freakslaw for the very first time. He does *not* want to be here. His dad's voice is hot in his ear, always. Derek can hear what a man would do and what a pure fucking embarrassment would do. The work of a bloke and the act of a poof.

But since that girl showed up at the pub, the funfair's all anyone's been talking about. Though the town had sworn they'd have nothing to do with it, apparently now it takes a real loser not to see for himself. That's what Joe said and even Chef stopped what he was doing – 'Aye, Derek, a UFO could land in the field and you'd still be awa in your heid.'

So here he is. The rides are sending him a-goggle. All that metal, just going for it, lit up like a space invader. At the sight, his stomach goes topsy-turvy and he has to concentrate on the ground for a sec. A place to make you puke, that's what it is.

When he first crept in, everything was day-glo bright and kid's play. The dodgems with their aerials spurting purple sparks on the ceiling. Huge airbrushed faces of clowns. Then, as he trod deeper, the rides got faster, darker. Men whipped upside down to certain death but laughing all the way through it. The Mummy leering, the demented cackle of asylum patients straining at the straitjackets.

And now he's reached the centre. Here, the light's different. Old fashioned and full of shadows. A winding path snakes between the tents, their flaps hanging open like mouths, ready to gobble you up.

That's where the Pin Gal is, no doubt. That's where they keep all the freaks. The ones who dance to a different song. (The poofs, the fucking fancy dancers.) Who've never played by the rules. (A shame to their folks, no less.)

He clenches his fists. He's not going to go there. Not today, not ever.

Derek wanders round the side of the tents and takes another fat path back to neon. His heart's rabbity in his chest, like it goes when he drinks too many Cokes on the night shift. Maybe he should get some chips, something to settle his stomach. But that's when he catches sight of her.

It's Ruth MacNamara, sat by the waltzers with a couple of kids he doesn't recognize. God, she's lovely. She's making her hand talk like a goose. The kids are laughing. The lights flash rainbows across her cheeks.

Daft notions flash through his head. Maybe he'll write a song about this tomorrow. When he's in the kitchen, suds to his elbows, writing songs is the best way to pass time. Fast, hard, loud songs, songs with baritone solos. He can't sing them aloud, because someone might hear, and he can't write them down (it's too wet for biros) so he writes them in his head.

Ruth reaches out her goose fingers and pecks at the girl, then covers her hand in giggles like she can't believe the audacity of that bird.

The song could be about tonight, how certain things fit in a certain world, how there's a universe of opportunity waiting to be grabbed if you can get up the guts.

And then he laughs – because he'd never do that, ha ha, wouldn't say a word, ha ha, definitely wouldn't sing her a song about herself because *that* would be the most awkward thing ever. Ha ha.

But if he did (just saying he did), she'd probably get it. Ruth's always going about with those big white headphones covered in stickers. Even if she didn't, Derek's pretty sure she wouldn't laugh at him or tell him to get back to sucking cock. Ruth's nice. He's never believed the rumours about her that started after her sister dropped out of school – in fact, it makes him blush to think about them. And even if they were true, he never understood why Ruth being the kind of girl who'd let a boy do whatever he wanted suddenly meant her whole crowd didn't like her any more. It's not like she'd be the only one in Pitlaw Academy. But girls are like that, he supposes, full of confusing logic when they get together as a group.

Anyway, the song – she'd probably just pretend not to get it, although she *would* get it (he's sure) because Ruth's well clever.

And she's got a blunt little fringe that looks like it's cut with kitchen scissors, and thighs that could kick seven shades of shit out of anyone who took the piss, and Derek Geddes has just a wee bit of a crush on her.

This is silly. He turns away, then takes a last longing glance over his shoulder. Watches as the boy dances into the waltzer booth, presses some buttons. Derek realizes with a shock: that's why he doesn't recognize them. They're not from Pitlaw. They *work* here.

An odd pride flickers in him. Odd because Ruth's not his, because he doesn't even like this place. Still, he thinks: *I knew it.*

Then –

'Hello!' yells Ruth and all the blood in Derek's body stops moving. 'Hellooo,' again, drawing out the O, sounding like a tape player whose batteries are running down.

She giggles. Hiccups, then swallows, looks over with huge Bambi eyes. 'It's Derek!' she says, and hearing his name in her mouth nearly makes his legs turn to spaghetti.

'Hi, Ruth.'

Ruth lights a cigarette, takes a drag. Her cheeks go very red and she coughs, 'Derek's from school.'

The others say nothing to this wisdom. The girl's sitting in the dirt by Ruth, picking at her grubby bare feet, looking like some kind of urchin. He looks over to the booth, where the boy twitches a hand through his shock of black hair, beaming a big broken-tooth smile that makes Derek think of the tenement buildings by the garage, their windows all smashed. Looking at it sends a strange, pleasant jolt to Derek's core. Makes his da's voice sound hotter in his ear.

The jolt feels dangerous, so he turns back to the girls. They seem to be moving in slow, underwater motion. The girl leans into Ruth and untangles the cigarette from her fingers, takes a long drag. She sends lazy rings into the air – bap-bap-bap-bap. The boy collapses in a swoon beside them. His limbs are altogether too long for his body. When he tilts his head back, Derek can't help staring at the vulnerable lump of his throat.

'You just going to stand there?' asks the girl. Derek shakes his head. He doesn't trust his mouth, so he kneels across from them and places his hands on his thighs. Maybe if he's very quiet and completely inconspicuous, he'll have a while before anyone thinks to ask him to leave.

Ruth and the girl are taking tiny sips from a bottle of supermarket own-brand whisky.

'Give us that.' The boy snatches it (earning an outraged shriek) and takes a swig, then hands it on to Derek.

'I'm Zed.' That smile again, Derek can almost hear bricks flying through glass. 'That's Nancy.'

He takes a sip. No one asks him what he thinks he's doing and that makes the burn just about tolerable as it creeps down his throat. He passes the bottle back to Zed and it makes its way around the circle again, and again. The others talk. Their chat is strange and disjointed, and Derek doesn't know how to make himself part of it. His foot falls asleep. He takes another drink, another. The lights of the fair get a little more glowy.

Nancy's holding forth on a million things and Ruth's sat beside her, in some kind of awe. He's never seen her like this, her personality drowned beneath someone else's, and he doesn't trust it. There's something about Nancy that makes his stomach twist. She seems like trouble, a black hole of it. Something you could trip into and you'd just keep on falling.

But then Ruth lets out her hammer of a laugh and Derek feels bad for being so petty. It's a good thing, surely. This promise that there's a whole fleet of people like him and Ruth who listen to punk and read books without indexes and wear clothes they make themselves in colours you can see in a brown field or a dark night.

People like Zed. Boys who somehow managed to move through the world soft but certain. Who do it looking like that. He focuses on Zed's soft interjections, and he feels himself nodding, and every so often a sharp animal bark escapes his lips. Hah!

Then Nancy stops her long reign of talking-talking-talking, and turns to Ruth. 'So what do you want to do?'

Just stay here, thinks Derek. Sit in this moment where things feel allowed.

But that's when Ruth decides they should have a go on the ride.

That's when she's looking so confident, Derek can hardly believe it. In a loose white vest with the edges of her black bra showing and bits of brown hair poking out under her arms. With her fringe sticking up and eyes forever darting, and he wants to – he does – say, 'I'm good, you guys go,' but then she takes his hand and says, 'Come on!' and her big stupid grin hits him, and her eyes light up like when you're driving down a country road at night and suddenly the head-lights catch a road sign and it's the whitest thing you've ever seen. He doesn't know if he wants to kiss her or to *be* her, if all this emotion ricocheting around his chest is for Ruth or for the night or for his entire life about to catch fire.

Okay.

And when it starts, when the metal bar comes down, feel-ing stupidly loose, for that moment, everything's perfect. The ride begins to twist, and she's pressed up against him. Her bony elbow digging his ribs. Her heat, her tensed legs. Zed clasps the side of the cart and shoots Derek a look that spins the world out of orbit, that says if he just stops worrying maybe anything (oh god), *anything* could happen.

Then, as gravity tosses them side to side, Ruth MacNa-mara grabs him by the arm and squeals in his ear. 'Eeeee!' she says, and, 'Shit! Jesus Christ!'

The lights are bright and hot and manic, and he lifts up the only arm that's holding on to reality, and he wraps it around her shoulders, and she rests her head against him.

Right here, right now: he could die.

*

And that could be the end of it, this could be the one perfect day in Derek Geddes's life.

But all of a sudden, his stomach wakes. His guts rise on their hooves and whinny. His muscles tense, he swallows, the music thrashes against their screams. And the lights start to blur and he has to gulp to keep what's in from coming out. Hold it together, Derek. Hold on until the fucking cart slows, and he flings the bar up and off him, before the ride's even over, he runs across the crests of the floor, feet echoing on metal. All the way down the stairs before everything catapults up and explodes, like a bucket of shit tipped out of an eighteenth-century Parisian tenement.

Derek stands over the grass, panting. Yes, he could die. He's going to die, sink into the ground, kick up a grave to be buried in. The second wave comes and he retches the last of the whisky on to the grass. The choke in his nose, that lumpy metallic stench.

'It's okay, Derek. Let it out.'

Zed's hand is rubbing his back. Zed's voice is hot in his ear, while the girls whoop and giggle. Derek sees everything in slow motion.

The smear on his cuff as he wipes his mouth. The hand on his shoulder. Zed's lizard smile when he turns around to face him. He can't let himself look at that smile or the ground will fall out from under him.

'You're good? It's okay. Don't worry about it.'

That slow, small kindness where his lips meet his teeth.

WHAT'S OWED

'SO, HOW YOU feeling about this place?' asks Gretchen Etcetera. The sun is casting its first beams across the sky, but she's sat with Miss Maria in the shadowy tent, chain-smoking pink cigarettes, turning the air a thick grey fog.

'There's potential,' says Miss Maria, nestled on a pile of plumped cushions. She has a platter of dusty doughnuts and is sampling them one by one, squeezing their plump centres, soothing herself with the spurt of jam. 'They came quick, didn't they?' Came the way they always do, and damned if Miss Maria's bed tent wasn't queued out: a revolving door of norms, young and old, keen to sample the whims of her flesh.

'I sense a *but*.' At the word, Gretchen slides a hand to her friend's vast buttock, pinching a sublime wedge of flesh between two fingers.

Miss Maria giggles and sighs at once, a sweetly conflicted sound. 'Potential for great things. And potential for terrible things, while we're at it.' Because she keeps coming back to that moment in the caff, how the locals snapped so quick to fury. As if they'd like nothing more than to crush them both. Yank their wild beating hearts from their chests, thrash the last gasp of love out of each of them.

'Oh, sure, ter-ri-ble things!' Gretchen flicks a finger to each syllable. Her diamante flashes like paparazzi. The way she says it sounds like beautiful ruction. 'Listen, I feel it. I *know* how brutal things could get. But what else are we going to do? Pack up and run?'

'Absolutely not.'

'Hell no,' Gretchen says. 'You know what happens when you choose that path.'

'You're right.' Miss Maria does know. She's seen it. What happens when you go through life only ever betting £2 on the favourite to win £2.10. If you never truly risk a thing, you'll never truly win either. And that's not the Freakslaw's way.

'I got you,' says Gretchen. 'We've got each other, all of us.' She plants a kiss on Miss Maria's cheek, and with it, a hot whisper against her ear: 'And we'll get *them*, too.'

Still, it's a thought Miss Maria comes back to all week. As each day ekes out longer than the last – the sun shining a garish June light over the fields and the hawthorn trees bursting into bloom – the niggling feeling remains. On Sunday, when Derek's blowing his hot hands and trampling down thoughts of a tricksy boy smile, Miss Maria will convince herself her worries were just loose gas. On Monday, when Greg Haskett is flinging a tennis ball across the garden, pissing himself laughing when the dog smashes against the broken fridge, she will pause rubbing shea butter into the folds of her belly, pinch a roll and ask, Maybe? – then discard the thought, continue with her slather. By Tuesday, as Norma Murray has the town council gathered to discuss the Problem of the Fun-fair (ten pages of neatly typed notes clutched to her grey cardigan, a battle plan in triplicate forms), Miss Maria will decide she must talk things over with Mr Partlett. A little chat, consideration for the gut that has never once steered her wrong. And she nearly does, she gets to his tent door but then the Twins run over – surprisingly quick for a body always tugging in two directions – and announce the feast for the weekend.

'Solstice,' chirrups Cass. 'We celebrate!'

Even Henry allows a twitched smirk to cross his lips. 'She has an announcement.' Miss Maria looks to Cass and he huffs. 'Gloria does. About the you-know-what.' This is punctuated with a self-important wink, a look of pure glee. It's the sight of them that seals it for her. Bad place or not, they need to stand their ground.

Midweek, the minister works a story into his sermon about the perils of Temptation and Sin. The folks go home brewing with preternatural resentment. Over pots of Tetley and rich tea biscuits, the waters of this discontent boil up the sides of the pan. Shona Peterson takes a last trip home to pack a suitcase of clean knickers and gleaming scissors, returning to the funfair to unpack them into Werewolf Louie's painted drawers. Ruth scoots over for another visit with wistful hopes of seeing a certain boy but runs into Nancy instead, never once thinking about fate or coincidence, the particular ways a particular body can be steered. Nancy issues her own invitation. Ruth stashes it deep in her satchel.

Thursday sees lines of opposition being drawn. Daughters storm out of kitchens yelling, 'You never listened to me, Mother!' Mothers lie awake to the ag-ag-ag of their husbands' snores, trying not to think of their own wild red teenage dreams. Husbands seethe at the sons who don't yet understand the importance of becoming a man.

And the ancient anger simmers.

And the ancestors holler and caw, sending fresh waves of agony rippling through Gloria's bones.

And the rumours, the anticipation, the gossip leaps . . .

And eventually it's Friday. The word now whispered from lips to lips – a word impossible to stop the spread of, even if one wanted to – is *revenge*. By the day before the feast, everyone in the Freakslaw has tried out the word once or twice. Miss Maria and Gretchen, plumped again on their stacked cushions, let its temptations hold them. They savour the texture in their mouths, faces slick and golden, teeth shiny-white.

'Revenge,' Gretchen whispers. She balls her beautiful hands into fists the size of feet and stomps them on her knees. 'Such a pretty little word.'

Miss Maria laughs. She can feel the hunger deep within herself, a place like a worn piece of fabric. A part of her that's been handled too often and is barely holding. She presses one hand to her stomachs and listens to them growl, scritching them like kittens. No, more than that: like big cats, the lions. 'Yes,' she says quietly. 'I want it.'

They all do. They want revenge, deserve revenge, have desires that need to be satisfied. They can feel the gap in their history. A holy lineage cut off at the roots, a generation of mentors slaughtered so they, the descendants, are left rummaging around the scraps. Trying to make something of them. Trying to get back to themselves.

The funfair folk know better than anyone how it is to be an outsider in a world that would prefer they didn't exist. Each and every one of them – those born freaks and those freakish by inclination, those with freakishness thrust upon them, those with it in the blood – understands the acrobatic feat of being oneself while surviving in the opposite ecosystem. It's a tricky balance, one that requires a great deal of concentration. Better freaks than them have perished under the weight.

The candles dance, blurry plumes turning the air shimmery and unfocused. They smell of burned matches, jasmine, and quiet anticipation. Gretchen's hand darts out and closes over Miss Maria's.

'Soon.' The word spills out of her red lips in a pale white light. It holds for a moment like smoke, then disperses.

Meanwhile, across the stake, the Strongmen are performing one-handed pushups in a perfect line. Their seven glistening bodies move like synchronized swimmers diving through sawdust. A hup and a one and a two; down they bob. Their back muscles crank and glide. All of the Strongmen swap arms at once. All are thinking of their own particular resentments – the times, before the Freakslaw, when their bodies were small and helpless, when they were kicked in the teeth, ran out of changing rooms, tripped in the mud.

In the silver caravan, the Pin Gal is polishing her jewellery, humming beneath her breath, wondering what ought to be the next tattoo she offers her skin. A rocket launcher, a Hawaiian skyscape, a lion wreathed in chrysanthemums? Personally, she doesn't like to think of the past, the things men took from her before she learned to make her body her own. But she hasn't forgotten it either: those hungry hands. When need be, she'll be the first to remember.

And then there's Gloria. Gloria has taken a handful of diet pills and the morning is stretching out, waiting for a Gloria to do what a Gloria needs doing. She jerks the tophat back. It dances, kicks and finds its balance. A little crooked, but then, aren't we all? She twists a toothpick with her tongue. The pick performs an elaborate backflip and lands between her teeth.

'My dears,' she says to the Twins, kicking back on to a bale of hay. 'You know what you have to do?'

The Twins nod.

'Well?'

'The feast!' They say it in unison. Tomorrow, they'll all gather beneath a swollen yellow light, flocking like daydrunk moths. The table stacked high with greasy platters and overflowing goblets of wine. Crisped potatoes and fluffy orange clouds of mashed carrot and a mayonnaise so thick and creamy it attains the exact texture of God.

'We're going to town,' says Cass. 'To get supplies for the feast. And we'll take whatever we want from the supermarket because we are owed.'

Cass licks her teeth at the word *owed*. A look passes between her and Henry that Gloria can't quite read. Sometimes it seems like the Twins tire of their proximity, carping and pinching each other, furious at their sibling for taking up too much of their body. Other times, they clutch each other close with protective adoration: Cass's right arm around Henry's shoulders, Henry's left arm around Cass's back, their stomachs pressed together, their hips as one.

Gloria loves the Twins fiercely. She would kill anyone who tried to hurt them.

'We *are* owed,' she says. 'We're owed so much.'

'We will not let the family down.' Henry talks briskly. Cass rolls her eyes. If he notices out the side of his gaze, he doesn't mention it. 'Everything we need, it shall be ours.'

Sometimes, Henry can be a little pretentious. This doesn't mean he isn't right. Sooner or later, things have a way of shifting. In the long run, gravity and cosmic justice tend to prevail. The universe, when viewed in the wide lens, would rather be sand. No matter the castles or the moats, the dunes or the valleys – eventually, the sea comes and finds the level setting.

'Go on then!' Gloria claps her hands. A cloud of chalk dust explodes like dry ice. Henry tightens the straps on his brown camping rucksack, practical pockets all in a row, while Cass's holographic pink gleams iridescent. She mimes a salute. Gloria waves and they head off through the morning light. The grass is wet with dew like spilled diamonds. The worms are cranky beneath the dirt, wondering how many more days they'll suffer without rain. By the time the Twins have completed their mission, the last of the moisture will have evaporated from the fields. It'll be balmy hot for the twenty-first day in a row, an entirely improbable number of days for this far north, for a stoic Scottish village more used to a thin grey soup of a sky. What a shame for those thirsty crops, gasping in the dry earth, withering on their vines. And how odd, that it would happen to be the same number of days as the tents have been erected, since the arrival of neon and delinquent flesh.

The weather isn't the first thing they'll complain about, not when there are so many others. But it'll come up sooner or later.

Eventually, everything always does.

AFTERSHOCKED

CASS AND HENRY step through the shop's automatic doors and are welcomed with a humble beep-boop. The door has no idea the people who just walked in are anything special. The door would give the same welcome to an axe murderer or the Queen. If a flock of ducklings gathered tight and tall enough to nod its sensor, the door would know just what to say.

'Beep-boop,' says the door.

'Thank you,' say Cass and Henry.

They step inside. The floor tiles are the brilliant white of fresh snow. The aisles stretch out in tundras, glittering under the Arctic glare of fluorescent tubes. Stacked high are boxes and jars and cans and baggies, all filled with every heart's desire.

The Twins steer the trolley with their inside arms, twisting their bodies away from one other and towards the shelves. Henry would like nothing more than to snatch what they need and leave, but he has a sinking feeling that such a wish is impossible. Already, Cass's eyes are gumball wide, her arms drifting like anemones.

To her left is a giant pyramid of baked beans, a big red sign screaming

BUY ONE GET ONE FREE!!!

Cass brings the trolley to a halt so quick they dunt their shin against it.

'Ow,' says Henry.

'Bog off!' Cass sighs happily. 'I love advertising.' Her voice is ripe with thrilled reverence, the same as she offers any shill who herds the hapless norms to their tent. Cass has always been far too impressed by a slick tongue.

'Leave it.' Henry tries to yank them onwards, but Cass holds still.

'It's so easy! You don't even need to decide what you want. You just let them tell you and there you go.'

'We're not here for beans,' he says, and Cass puts down the can. She pouts but of course Henry's right, there are more important things. She pinches him under the ribcage anyway (a piggy squeal and a twinge in both their sides) and they press further into the store.

As they walk, the other shoppers' conversation changes in pitch. Idle chat turns to silence turns to *oh my god, what do you think about that?* Cass lifts her chin. She beams. On days like this, Cass likes to think about statues of the Virgin Mary. Stone ones in small towns, who eventually tire of their silent stone lives and eke out a tear of blood. She can almost feel it trickling down her cheek. A crimson hoodoo that makes all the locals gasp.

Cass peers at the top shelf, showing off the long white column of her neck. Henry feels the blush rise in his own. His sister is a ham. A transparent, attention-seeking ham! Almost everyone in the Freakslaw is, to tell the truth – all of them take a pleasure in centre stage, watching the slack jaws of norms goggle. In the supermarket, the voices hiss louder.

'Did you ever see a thing like that?'

'Ah, it's a trick, bullshit so it is.'

'It is not! How do you do that as a trick? You go and show me how you could do that, come on. Right now.'

'Mummy, what are the—'

'Don't stare.'

'But how do they—'

'Shush!'

All said while staring. All said with their jaws to the floor.

This, to be fair, is part of the plan. Part of the Twins' beauty. One thing about being so perfectly malformed, so distracting, is the ability to distract even from yourselves. There's a form of old magic called hiding in plain sight. A sleight of hand that occurs when an audience can't wrench their eyes from the thing in front of them. The trick doesn't lie in the sly movement of hiding. It exists in the gleam of the other hand, a twist of light like the aurora borealis, a sight so mesmeric no one can rip their gaze away.

Cass lets go of the trolley and stretches her arms in a lovely yawn. The trolley glides forward like a ghost ship carrying its forgotten crew. Those in the shop are treated to a perfect view of the Twins' body. Their body roots through a willowy pair of legs (today, on Cass's insistence, clad in patent Mary Janes and purple tights and a pencil skirt that skims their knees), up through a shapely ass (one that attracts great attention and causes Henry endless torment) and then, somewhere around the waist (it's always hard to tell precisely where through their clothes) their bodies splay in two. And Cass knows exactly what all these nosy, leering, pretending-they're-more-interested-in-the-special-offer shoppers want to do: strip the Twins of their tailored outfit and peer close at that pivot. The precise point Cass becomes Henry, when one human becomes two.

Cass yawns her perfect yawn. She is impossible, but here she is. She smiles prettily, presses her fingertips to her lips. A society lady. A woman of most considered countenance.

A total ham! Henry refrains from rolling his eyes as he sneaks things into his rucksack and trench coat, precious delicacies for their perfect feast. Brown sauce and butter and billowy white sandwich bread. A bulb of garlic is easy to vanish up a sleeve – all that takes is one camp flick of the wrist. A bottle of Glenfiddich is harder, but not impossible. Henry waits until Cass starts whistling the riff from the *1812 Overture*, drumming her pink sherbet nails against a bottle of Aftershock in time, then uses the cannonball distraction to jostle it into Cass's backpack. Cass flings the Aftershock in the trolley, alongside two packs of birthday napkins and a jumbo box of bendy straws. The Aftershock is tacky and garish and looks like liquidized neon. It is exactly the right choice.

From across the aisle, June Geddes is trying not to look. She has shopping to do, so she does. It seems like every other day the cupboards have gone bare, shovelled into the mouths of her menfolk. June never comments on Derek and Boyd's ability to demolish in mere hours what seems like a week's worth of messages when it's stacked in plastic bags. She wonders about it though, and sometimes (in her darker moments) she thinks of locusts and biblical curses, exactly what she might have done to merit this punishment. God knows every hair on your head, so they say, and he's always watching. Here she is, staring at the baked beans again, and she'll be happier if she accepts her fate. But what about that rice?

Better to think about rice than the visit she had yesterday, anyway. The trouble that could cause if Boyd ever found out! Shona had come by in the afternoon, more bright-eyed than June had seen her for years. Only went and told June she'd cast her lot in with those folks from the funfair, and asked June to think about it too. Said she deserved better, as if June could just run away from all her responsibilities on a whim!

How to explain to Shona, who'd never gotten married, that having a husband sometimes meant putting your head down and persevering when things got tough? Yes, Boyd might not always make things easy. He's always had that temper on him. But June is a strong woman and if there's one thing she prides herself on, it's her ability to stick out a situation where anyone else might have given up.

Shona wouldn't understand. But gosh, she looked happy.

June sneaks a look at the Twins. Oh, but they are something! The girl reminds her of a young Doris Day – those shiny blonde locks and that golden smile. She makes June think of watching old Hollywood movies as a little girl, curled up in her aunt's living room by the tiny black and white box. And oh, if the girl can smile like that with the affliction she has, surely June ought to be able to. She tries it, crumpling in her cheeks, just to see if it makes her feel better. Does it work? The girl bobs her head as if she's listening to a secret radio. June can almost hear it, distant and jangling, increasing in speed. If she just focuses her ears . . .

Enough! No time for this foolishness, but plenty to be done. Somehow always twice as much to do as time there is to do it in. If she could just clone herself like that sheep from the news, maybe then she'd finally get on top. June wheels her trolley past the multipacks of Irn Bru and Coke, then places a two-litre bottle of own-brand cola inside. She doesn't even like the stuff, but being home alone of an afternoon, time stretching out, punctuated only by the washing and the drying and the ironing and the dusting, she finds herself drinking glass after glass. It clings to her teeth in gritty fur and bloats her stomach, and she convinces herself just one more will settle it. By the time the sun is low and the house is pristine, June can feel her whole body thrumming with that impotent sugar rush. Her heart has a caffeine jammer and she's too wrung out to do a single thing, but there's always more to be done, so she drinks one more glass. Just one.

When she looks up, the music has gone. The Twins have disappeared. All that's left is the crackled muffle of the tannoy. TWENTY PER CENT OFF PEDIGREE CHUM IN AISLE THREE! But there, on the tiles where the Twins were standing, June can see a set of footprints in silvery light snaking down the aisle. It makes her think of prints in sand, the point where the sea meets the shore. A trail leading off to . . .

June crushes her eyes shut and opens them again. There's nothing there, of course there's not. She looks in her trolley at the cola and another thought pops into her head, one so audacious and perfectly formed she blushes.

Fuck This, says the thought. A rush in her chest: she doesn't need the stuff, she doesn't even like it!

June reaches into her trolley and takes out the cola. Places it back on the shelf and swallows her smile.

Across the shop, Cass and Henry are stacking the few items they will pay for on the conveyor belt. Their long arms move like a factory machine. Cass's bag is heavy on her back. She always makes sure to carry the bulk of the weight (her spine is less curved than her brother's, the consequences lighter), but she'd never let on she was helping him. She'd never live it down.

The checkout boy concentrates on scanning. Trapped behind the till, he's acutely aware of the fact he has nowhere to go. All his confidence has leaked by the wayside. Up close, the Twins are something else entirely.

One hand closes around the bottle of Aftershock. He clears his throat. 'I'll need your ID for this, love.' Addressing only Cass, keeping his eyes firmly averted from the scowling boy by her side. From his angle, where only their torsos can be seen, he can almost convince himself they're just a pair of ordinary customers. The checkout boy doesn't want to get involved. The sooner he checks these final items off, the sooner he'll be done his shift and home to the telly.

'Eye dee?' Cass's voice is as bright as polished glass.

'Identification. You're over eighteen?'

Cass rolls her eyes. It's not the first time she's been infanti-lized by strangers, and it won't be the last.

'We are definitely totally grown-ups.' She picks up the bottle of Aftershock and starts shaking it. The checkout boy knows the bottle isn't fizzy, but part of him is convinced that any moment the cork will pop and he'll be sprayed with a fine red mist that turns his eyelashes to sticky cinnamon.

'Well, it's just, I'll need some proof.'

'No,' she says.

'Not a thing,' Henry adds.

'I can't sell you this.'

'Do we look like children?' she asks. Which isn't really fair. That sort of question demands the checkout boy look at her, at them, closely. He is suddenly terrifically interested in his own hands.

'The legislation . . .'

Cass slams the bottle down on the conveyor belt. Everyone waits for the delayed cracks to appear. For the bottle to shatter in triumphant fireworks, for everyone in the supermarket to say 'Woahhhhhh!'

Nothing happens.

'Oh, forget it. Come on, Henry.'

And she waltzes out the door with Henry alongside, their inner arms stretched out, hands held, fingers intertwined.

The checkout boy lets out a long breath. He picks up the Aftershock. There's a sound like Quality Street wrappers crumpled in a palm.

The bottle explodes.

It takes a while for the stammering checkout boy to clean up the sticky mess, but eventually June pays for her items, bags them up, and packs them neatly in her tartan wheelything. Waving off the checkout boy's apologies, which just make her feel flustered and the need to match them with her own, she scutters off.

June Geddes steps through the door ('beep-boop' says the door) and into the afternoon and a gasp escapes her. The Twins are stood in a patch of sticky sunlight, staring right at her. Their lips are very red. Their cheekbones catch the light. Something in the moment feels holy. June would never say this out loud, not in front of Boyd or Derek or even Shona, but for a second she's convinced the Twins are saints: beautiful, beleaguered saints, sent to bless those who truly believe.

The girl twists her head to the boy's ear. She whispers behind a cupped palm while the boy, eyes on June, flashes his teeth in a smile. He nods briskly, and then the Twins do something June can't fathom. The girl dips a curtsey and the boy performs a stiff bow. The movement together is crumpled and freakish, but not without a degree of respect.

The Twins walk straight for her. June finds herself frozen, legs of steel rods and rusted pins. It could be that she's made a terrible mistake. That they're not saints at all, they're exactly the devils they look like. June squeezes her hands into fists. She wants to say something, but what she has no idea. Four wide eyes are upon her and the sun rains down on those cheekbones and what's the difference, really, between something holy and something else? Lucifer was an angel too, that's what people always forget. Lucifer was an angel too.

June holds her breath. The Twins take one more step then, at the last possible moment, they loom left. Cass brushes June and she feels the girl's soft bare arm against her own. There's a thud as they scuff her tartan trolley but it doesn't fall. From behind her, she hears the Twins' footsteps, patent black shoes clacking away.

'Excuse me,' she says. 'Sorry.' Her heart is racing, the same breathless glory as when Boyd first kissed her in his Ford Sierra, his muscled arm reaching over the handbrake, her skirt hitched above her knees. A dizzying inevitability, a thing that's bound to happen, and all you have to do is nothing to stop it.

She stands until she remembers how to move her feet.

All walk home, her arms are heavy, the trolley dragging against the pavement, the sun high and hot. By the time she reaches Overview Terrace, all she wants is to collapse on to the sofa and raise her feet up high, until the fluid on her ankles drains.

But there's still the shopping to unpack. Always one more

thing, and plenty to be done. She opens the trolley and reaches a hand inside and for a moment, June wonders if she's lost her mind.

On the top of her trolley is a bottle of Baileys. A box of liqueur chocolates. Some bath salts, the fancy kind it looks like, bits of lavender and dried petals. What Boyd would describe as disgusting garden rubbish and a waste of money. She picks up the salts to take a sniff, and that's when she sees the invite.

A Special Feast at the Freakslaw,
and You Are Invited!
Saturday at High Moon.
Dress to Be Unforgotten.

June almost shrieks. She rips the paper in half, then half again, again, until it's an impossible confetti which she sprinkles in the bin. Her palms are sweating. She ties off the bin bag and takes it out to the garage and gets a fresh one, puts it in, and everything is normal.

Except there, still on the top of her trolley, perched on white bread and baked beans and rice: those fancy chocolates.

June doesn't make a decision, not as such, but her hand moves to open the box. She places a chocolate in her mouth. It melts under the heat of her tongue in a heady, boozy gush. She closes her eyes. She's not going to go, of course. She's going to hide this stuff. Brush her teeth, get rid of the smell.

But for now, for just one moment, she lets the chocolate melt, her body sinking into candied liqueur reverence.

CHEW IT WHOLE

IN THE ROOM upstairs, Derek doesn't hear his mother's soft animal moan as the chocolate melts. Derek's got other things on his mind. A mind that keeps skipping back like a stuck record, jagging again and again on that broken-toothed smile.

He doesn't need that. He sets it back to Ruth, a warm winking thought, one that is cute and normal and easy. But there goes his treacherous mind again: the fat bottom lip like a busted sofa. A bony thumb with a thick silver ring.

It's not an option. There's not a chance. But like all big red buttons you absolutely mustn't touch, Derek feels his hand creep towards it. He tries not to as the teeth get bigger and bigger, until they could bite out his heart and chew it whole.

Shit.

THE PIPER PLAYS
THE TUNE

AND SO THE great blue and green ball performs another somersault. Night looms large and passes, another day drenched in candyfloss skips by. The dirt sodden with roller-coaster screams, strangled yelps from the Haunted House, the stolen Freakslaw breath where the audience gasp in unison, *Ohhhh!* Finally, it's midnight. A bloat orange moon dunts the horizon and Mr Partlett closes the gate, sending the last giddy folk to stumble home, footless with adrenaline and hot hearts.

'Goodbye!' says Mr Partlett. 'Come again, my dears.' The women giggle and clutch at their handbags – having not been called dears in all too long, especially not by a long-fingered man with strange scars and a twinkle in his all-too-blue eyes. They hold each other's arms for the balance that has been leached by the shoogling Funhouse floor, and then they too are gone. A perfect hush falls.

Mr Partlett walks between rides, crunching through drinks cartons and discarded raffle tickets, napkins bright with mustard. They'll clean in the morning, no matter. In the dark, the machines are looming dinosaur skeletons, joints crooked and metal jaws askew. Among the usual smells, Mr Partlett catches a whiff of rosewater and strawberry jam and old book spines. He smiles at the guests who have left such traces, little stories of their little lives. It didn't take long for the town to give up its arrogance. It never does. Sooner rather than later, they all cede to the funfair's magic.

He turns the corner by the Funhouse, where the punch-bags bump happily like fat men's stomachs, ha ha ha. He strides beneath the trailing bandages of the Mummy, drifting like jellyfish tentacles. And down the hill to the heart of the Freakslaw, where the lights are toasty and the table is already unfurled on the grass outside. Where his family are waiting.

Tonight, they have outdone themselves. So Gloria thinks, as she lights candles with a silver Zippo, her face glowing over the wicks. The tables – three of them, stretched out in a long line – groan under the weight of food: sizzling platters of chicken wings and great hunks of parmesan and potatoes done every which way: roast and mashed and scalloped and fried. There's a dense cloud of glorious smells, so thick you could cut it with a knife. There are jugs of honeyed wine, their handles sticky, the Strongmen already laying in. They will eat well tonight. And when they do, they will be closer than ever before.

An irrepressible glee swells her cheeks. The benches fill as everyone leaves their work for the night to take part in something more important than entertaining norms. Family.

'What you looking so pleased about? You been off debating with Mr P?' Gretchen Etcetera's hand, heavy with silver rings, darts out to snatch the jam jar of liquor Gloria has laid on the table as she lights another candle. The flame whumps into life as Gretchen takes a huge gulp and her eyes grow wide and star-studded. 'What about some of these for the little people?' – gesturing to herself and Miss Maria, the whole width and breadth of them. Gloria laughs. She pulls a flask from the swirling pocket of her cloak and places it in front of them.

'Knock yourselves out, girls.' They do, pouring huge servings into their wine glasses and toasting, blowing kisses at Gloria's departing form. She winds down the table, finding another candle, leaning over Werewolf Louie. He's dressed in his smartest suit tonight, a red crushed-velvet number that looks gloriously textured against the curl of his fur.

'Gloria!' His voice is as sweet and bright as icing sugar. 'Gloria, this is our guest.'

'Aye, we met,' says Shona Peterson. She raises her glass. 'Shona.'

'I brought her, Gloria,' says Werewolf Louie, then claps a hand over his mouth.

'Welcome, my dear.' Gloria places a hand on Louie's arm, who is looking to Shona with hunger, needy and unashamed. By the time the jugs of honey wine are empty, Werewolf Louie will be sat on Shona's knee, her strong hairdresser's fingers running through his fur, the purr reverberating. While the first tendrils of dawn burrow into the sky, Shona Peterson will be hands and knees in the dirt, howling like an animal, as Werewolf Louie ruts her from behind. Mud will spatter her breasts and her palms will sink into soil and both will almost lose their minds, but Shona will leave a trail back to herself and, as the sun makes itself properly known, they will follow the scratches and return to their bodies, bruised and holy.

But for now, Gloria just smiles and welcomes the woman. The Freakslaw has magic yet to work. It will be interesting to see what Shona will become, what role she can play, but there'll be time later for that. She leaves them to their drinks and reaches the Twins, who drop what they're doing and turn to her.

'Did we do good?' Cass beams, dimples driving into her flesh, and Gloria wraps an arm around each of their shoulders.

'You did so good.'

Henry shrugs her off – 'It was nothing' – but Gloria notes the pink tips of his ears. She crouches behind the Twins and leans close, all hot breath and conspiracy. 'No one knows how to take like you do, my sweets. I'll bet it was masterful. My only regret is that I was not there to see.'

The Twins demur and giggle and Gloria hugs them close. She missed the supermarket, yes, but she's seen their work a hundred times: loaves-and-fishes tricks of criminal proportions. Train tickets multiplying impossibly before a goggling inspector; shopkeepers handing back change and payment both, hypnotized by Cass's prattling while Henry does the pocket work. The Twins do good grift and it's unnecessary, really: the funfair has no need of saving money. But they wouldn't be who they are if they didn't fuck with the system, and these small reparations taste so sweet.

Gloria plucks a chicken drumstick from the table and rips the skin with her teeth. It's black and sharp and gives way easily to the meat. She smiles at the Twins, her chin slick with grease, and carries on. A kiss and a compliment for everyone. One by one, the candles whump. A warm, tempting light, the kind to attract moths or gingerbread children. Eventually, everyone is bathed in this glow.

Gloria takes her place at the head of the table and grabs her glass. Mr Partlett squeezes her knee, his bony fingers sharp as twigs. This is home. This is family. The whole length of the table, voices rise in a festive flurry, battering against each other, shrieking and laughing and flinging declarations. She's one of them. She is here.

Gloria grabs her fork and drums it against the jug. The glass sings. A whole choir of dragonflies holler in unison: BIIING! and Mr Partlett lets go. The voices quiet. All faces turn her way. Gloria tosses her skunk hair, runs a tongue across her winking gold tooth.

'Welcome, my dears. Welcome to the feast.'

Everyone crows in return, clinks glasses, lets the loose promise of the word *feast* slide over them.

'We're gathered tonight, under the Midsummer sky, to drink and be merry –' at this, they all take a sip – 'to welcome new friends –' Werewolf Louie bats his eyelashes in Shona's direction – 'to celebrate family –' Cass pinches Henry – 'and to honour our histories.' This final declaration sends a flurry of delirium rippling up and down the table. The Strongmen lean in so their waxed moustaches sparkle in the candlelight. Miss Maria sets her chicken wing down, lets her glistening mouth fall open in an anticipatory *Oh*. Even Gretchen pauses, cigarette halfway to her perfect lips.

'Tell us, Gloria!'

Gloria clambers on to the table, kicking aside plates and gnawed bones with her black pirate boots. She lifts a goblet of mead high.

'A toast!' she says. 'And a story.'

'Story!' chant her family, looking up at her with smitten, hungry faces. They gather to listen, to be told. Voices lapping, chatters of excitement – then a great anticipatory hush, snagging the group and binding them close.

'Once upon a time,' Gloria says, 'there was a poor, sad town which was stricken by rats. These rats would gobble up the town's food and bite all the townspeople and spread the kind of disease that makes a dick turn black.' She takes a big drink and careens down the table, stottering between glasses. 'Terrible affair!' She finds her footing. 'But one day an outsider came to solve their problems. Sometimes it takes that, you see: sometimes the people of a place are the last to know what they need. He was a man, but no mind –' she smiles insouciantly at Mr Partlett, who raises his eyebrow back – 'and he made music. Because sometimes it takes an entertainer to do a politician's work.'

The table shrieks with delight.

'So our fine man makes a deal with the mayor: he'll rid the town of rats, for a price. A simple transaction, as money tends to be. Both would get what they needed, and that would be that. Our man played the rats right out of town with the song of his ancestors, a melody both ancient and blessed. The rats pricked their ears and thought, Why stay in this tedious suburb when out in the wide world there's magic and wild rivers?'

Around the table, there are mutters: why indeed? Gloria's a born storyteller, one who knows when to give, when to pause, when to hold it all back.

'Well, that mayor was very grateful the rats were gone, and they paid him handsomely, and that was that. The End!' Gloria performs a small bow, then stands and flicks the skunk strip from her eyes.

Her audience are furious. *'No!'* they yell, but it's a delighted fury, the howl of pantomimes, the big bad wolf behind you after all.

'Oh no,' Gloria says. 'No, you're right.' Her face darkens theatrically. She bends close. 'In fact, I think I remember . . . they didn't pay him at all. Said they didn't need to. Their problems were already over.'

'But they weren't over!' shrieks Cass, who is well familiar with this tale. She clutches a hand over her mouth as everyone's eyes flick her way.

'No. No, they were not. They were just beginning, if I remember rightly? But the town had the nerve to suggest that maybe he brought the rats himself! Maybe he was a trickster and a shyster, one who deserved nothing.'

A gasp circles the table at such insult. Imagine!

'Imagine, indeed! But worry not, my dear ones.' Gloria grins now: her filthy, devil-may-care grin, a grin that revs like a Cadillac about to drive off the highest cliff. 'This man wasn't one to roll over and accept such a grave injustice. If they would take from him, he would take something back . . . now what was it?' She presses a finger to her chin, looking dreamily to the sky as if the answer is floating, just out of reach.

This time, the voices crow together: *The children!*

'The children, of course!' She raises a finger. Those who catch the gesture at just the right angle see a lightbulb appear above her head, the moment all the roulette balls fall into holes.

Click!

'Our man comes back with his pipe and plays his song, the way us entertainers do. And they follow him, the children, because his song is so sweet. By the time the town realizes they should never have tried to trick a trickster –' she loves these words, practically licks her lips at them, so round and ripe – 'it's too late.'

The children are gone!

'The children are gone, indeed. To the trickster and the shyster! To the river! To the world of music and dance. So it was, and so it shall be!' Gloria beams now, her face beatific. 'That's all he took, all our kind ever take. What he was owed.'

An electric energy pinballs round the table. Implications reverberate in bells and multicoloured lights.

'And now? It is our turn. Because do you know what happened here, on this land we feast upon tonight?'

Her audience quiets in anticipation, ready to be told.

'Four centuries ago, in a community not so different to what we see here today, hostility broiled in Pitlaw. Season after season, the harvest failed. Crops rotted and died. Mass starvation trampled through the town and on its heels, like an animal that preys upon the weak: an early-summer plague.'

The freaks gasp and hiss, their own groaning bellies forgotten.

'The people sickened faster than they could be buried. Bodies turning black and swollen, bursting like overripe fruit. The stench hung so heady, every breath coated their insides with the sick-sweet mulch of death. Impossible that such a thing could happen, in this good honest Presbyterian town!'

They lean in close, enthralled.

'So who did they blame for this terrible forsaking? Why, the same they always blame: the ones God looks down upon. The quarrelsome women. Those with queer desires. The mentally ill and the physically disabled. Outsiders, foreigners, anyone who treads the left-hand path. And those, too, who dared impinge upon His power – midwives and herbalists, with their tricksy pocket sacks and terrible seeds. That is to say, the witches. Or, if you will, the freaks.'

The freaks!

'Us,' says Gloria, and the table hoots back in recognition: 'ONE OF US! ONE OF US!'

'Thirty-six poor souls, killed. Led to the village square, tied to the stake, to be licked up in flames before a hollering crowd. Watching gleeful as their skin seared and their blood vessels ruptured and their organs broiled. As these vibrant humans became nothing more than charred meat, the dripping fat from their split tissues only serving as further fuel for that hungry fire. A candle for each on the table tonight. Now those souls have called us back, to avenge them before the wheel of the year turns again. Before they're trapped for another century, wandering between worlds.'

A raucous delirium catches. It's not the first time they've heard such a story, not the first time Gloria has gathered them together to gripe about the treatment of their foremothers. But all stories contain magic, and the ones oft repeated cast the strongest spells.

'They took them from us. But now?' Gloria's teeth light up in the candlelight, she raises her voice to be heard above the drummed fists and stamped feet. 'We are taking from them in return!'

She lifts her glass. 'A toast. To what we are owed.' For oh, there are so many things! The ancestors may be Gloria's particular bugbear, but they all have their own reasons to seek revenge upon the world.

Miss Maria squeezes Gretchen's hand and remembers Christmas when she was fourteen years old. A dozen shimmering gifts piled high with her name, ripping each open to find a gown more beautiful than the one before, every last one three sizes too small. 'Something to aspire to,' her mother had said, and her father wouldn't look at her, and while her sisters played dress-up in their glory, she sat in jogging bottoms and wept.

Miss Maria raises her glass.

The Twins meet each other's eyes and allow themselves dimpled smiles. They remember drinking in the cobbled underbelly of a city, not long after their eighteenth birthday, followed into an alley by drunken men who cried out to know what lay beneath their diamante hotpants: whether they were one or the other or both. The men wouldn't stop with their grabbing hands until Cass brought a bottle down on one's head and they ran off in an explosion of green glass.

Cass and Henry raise theirs.

And Werewolf Louie remembers being cornered in the Asda car park by sniggering teenagers with a discount bag of Gillette razors. The hot slick of blood when the blade slipped, red mingling with red.

And Gretchen feels the twinge in her forearm that always aches when it rains, a bone so shattered in the beating it will never quite heal.

For the Pin Gal: one bad boss after another, history repeating itself like a magic trick. Another storeroom grope, another hand on her arse, just the ordinary indignity of a body the world believes it is owed.

And then there's Zed, left by a mother who walked away and never once looked back. Not even a phone call. Not a postcard in the decade or more that's passed since.

They all sit with their own moments – grave attacks and petty humiliations, oppressions and mockery and broken hearts.

They raise their glasses.

'To what we are owed!'

The table erupts into screams and applause. Gloria has to yell to be heard. 'Hold this story close in your hearts, and let us eat eat eat!'

They fall upon the food like ravenous animals. The feast has begun.

At the far end of the table, Nancy picks a bit of meat from her teeth with a shard of bone. She rolls her eyes. The prospect of revenge, it's delicious, but *this* is what they have to offer? A song and a dance, a future for a past, your average exchange. But not even a whisper of blood? Where's the fun in that?

No, Nancy's had enough of listening to the old guard – and that includes any long-dead ancestors who think this is the time to start rattling their gums. If you ask her, what's really called for is proper sacrifice. Slaughter. A red mist raining down like early-morning dew.

Nancy pictures a line of angry men with honed fists. She sees herself glint and wink, hears the high mosquito whine of a fast drill. In her mind, they come like a whole troupe of soldier ballerinas and when she presses the switch, truly, it is a holy thing.

Zed pokes her in the ribs. 'What are you smirking at?'

She turns to him and bats her lashes.

'I saw the future.' Her grin is every bit as beatific as Gloria's – the only difference is her teeth are sharper. 'And it was beautiful.'

ONE OF US

RUTH TIGHTENS THE black leather jacket around her shoulders and wheels her bike quietly out the front gate. She feels like a cat burglar. A fugitive and a debutante. Earlier in bed, waiting for the family to fall asleep, she'd listened to Lou Reed's *Transformer* three times in a row, her Walkman hot between her thighs. Now her heart's filled up with angry flowers. The music's given her extra layers of tough: a slick shellac like ten coats of mascara. Tonight, she's indestructible. She throws one leg over the bike and pushes off.

In the darkness, she can barely see the potholes, but it doesn't matter. Her feet pump the pedals. The wind gusts through her hair, blowing away any doubts she might have. No mistakes. She's going to seize the day, be the kind of girl who'll go out into the world and grab it by the neck.

She is.

Ruth doesn't know what's going to happen, but she has the feeling it's not going to be like any party she's been to. It's not going to be like the weekend farm affairs with boys from school, stunk witless with peach schnapps and Lynx body spray, drum of punch in the garden, slick of puke on the grass. It's not going to end with a glut of girls slumped on hay bales like disaster victims, petting the back of whoever failed to pull that evening. Cheeks mascara-blotched, breath a cloud of Red Bull and rejection.

Come back on Saturday, Nancy had said, *come at midnight –* and Ruth had opened her mouth to say she couldn't, but then she'd stopped. There was that door again, held open, a corridor down which absolutely anything could happen. *Okay,* she'd said. *I'll see you then.*

So here she is. The gate lights are already out. Ruth stashes her bike, grabs her satchel from the basket. The bottle in it dunts her leg like a dog reminding its owner it's dinner time. She unscrews the lid and takes a long drink. Practises not shuddering, alone in the dark. The vodka, pilfered from her parents' cabinet, is warm and wet and dead. It tastes like nothing, a hard nothing. A hole filled with grey metal. A filling in a tooth. It turns her insides invincible. Ruth bites her lip and a grin bursts out.

There, in the distant depths, lies the orange glow of the Freakslaw.

It doesn't take long to traverse the empty funfair, without garish distractions or pinballs to hoist her gaze. Something's growing inside Ruth as she creeps through the dark. Something's about to change.

As she weaves deeper, disembodied voices drift through the night. A feral chatter of happy discord. Until there, slap-bang in the middle of the noise, are the funfair people. Gathered around a long table, shrieking and laughing.

The invincibility that carried her this far begins to smatter, but Ruth pulls her jacket tight and wills it back. With every step, the table stretches away. The people multiply, but don't look up. It's worse than walking into lunch with a tray stacked high, searching for an empty seat. Except it's also better, because every seat in the lunch hall is a place she'd rather not be. But this? An entirely new arrangement. A track she hasn't yet played.

Right at the far end, beyond a line of muscle-vest men with skin so shiny it looks like plastic, sit Nancy and Zed. Zed is deep in elaborately gestured conversation with a woman so made-up she looks like a painting. The fat lady (Ruth remembers her mum's comments and can't keep from blushing) leans in and shakes a finger, and the flesh beneath her arm billows. Zed laughs. Ruth can't help noticing the way his eyes crease. She can't help noticing that Nancy isn't paying attention. She's playing with her plate: a bone between her fingers and a furrow in her brow.

None of them see the girl standing before them, the toughest girl, the girl who came over here alone in the dark to find her destiny. Ruth raises a hand.

'Hi,' she says quietly.

The conversation thrums. A cacophony of laughter, 'Take it off, take it all off!' Two siblings sit, half on each other's knees, eating a huge jar of cherries and spitting the stones against a candlestick. A tiny man with a furry face is licking a woman's ear, and when she turns her cheek – it can't be but it is – it's Shona! Shona from the hairdresser. Ruth gasps. A stone hits the flame and the candle snuffs out. Nancy's bone flicks like a pocket knife, and no one moves aside and makes a place for Ruth, no one offers her a drink. No one even turns her way.

She takes a deep breath, wondering how she's so invisible. Is this the way of black leather in a dark night? The chatter is all-encompassing. Two of the muscle men have started kissing and a girl with a face full of metal is inking a sailor ship on the back of a third and the fat lady has taken a wind-up T-Rex and set it loose and the big green dinosaur is tramping through the coleslaw and its tiny arms aren't long enough for hugging and no one is looking at Ruth, not after she came all this way, not after she snuck outside, and –

'HELLO!' she says again, and it comes out far too loud, and a hundred pairs of eyes turn to her.

The conversation stops dead.

Silence.

Ruth is suddenly falling. She's Wile E. Coyote, out over the cliff and no ground beneath. Everyone's looking now: the fat lady, the glamour woman, the man with fur for a face. Shona. Zed. Even a couple of other faces she recognizes from town. The quiet is so thick she can hardly breathe. She sees the fortune teller, draped over a man with a face full of scars. The woman looks at Ruth with an expression of curiosity. Any minute now, the ground's going to open up. Blood batters her cheeks, turning her futile and luminescent.

'I came to the party.' She gestures to herself.

And then Nancy looks up, at last. Her smile is a box of matches in a petrol station. It sparks and Ruth holds her breath and then Nancy's saying, 'Come on, then. Join us!' and the whole scene starts moving again. Like a wind-up machine, the chairs parting and someone slotting a new one next to Nancy, a plate materializing with slabs of meat and pickled vegetables, Zed's hand thrillingly on Ruth's arm, a glass pressed into her fingers, the surface cold and sticky, the smell saccharine. She takes a big drink, hoping for the sure tug of alcohol to stabilize her, but the sugar wallops her loopy.

'What took you so long?' Nancy says.

Ruth doesn't know. But she's here now, and she raises a glass.

And that is when the drinking truly begins.

After the fifth cup of sticky wine (or the sixth, the hundredth? the wine has seeped into itself and it's impossible to tell) things start to go a little peculiar. The time for feasting is over, and the music has begun: a spiky melody like static electricity in the fur of a cat. Ruth senses it crackling into her, turning her legs kicky and alive. For the past hour she's sat still, giving no one a reason to suggest she leave, but now she feels like dancing.

Some of the others are drifting to a nearby tent, where there's straw on the floor and red paper lanterns dangling. The moment they cross the threshold, they grab each other and cackle, flick their bodies madly as if trying to cast off bugs. The lanterns hew, casting dizzy red shadows, and in her ear Nancy says, 'You want to dance.'

It's not a question. Ruth turns, feeling her eyes open too wide for her face. Looks back at the tent, where someone's flipping their hair in a frantic whirlwind.

'Here.' Nancy opens her palm. Her hand is tiny, and in the centre lies an even tinier pink heart.

'What is it?'

'Candy.'

Ruth doesn't believe her. It's drugs, of course it's drugs. What a ridiculous question. But it's okay. She thinks about how the mushrooms opened her brain like a huge flower, all her worries peeling off like petals. How she could let herself become a different person, if she tried. The music tugs at her, impatient. The pill looks like it belongs to a doll. A small chemical magic, crafted in a tiny plastic kitchen. Her fingers twitch towards it. And then Nancy lifts her hand to her own mouth and places the heart inside.

'Oh,' says Ruth. There's a moment of terrible, giddy embarrassment with all her wanting on the outside, and then Nancy leans in. Her eyes glitter as she snakes her fingers into Ruth's hair. For a moment, Ruth thinks she's going to pull it, smack her in the face for being so presumptuous, then something shifts and she understands.

Nancy's lips are slick and soft. It's nothing like a boy face, that angled grind of stubble. This is fingers slipping into tiny satin gloves. It's placing your hand in a dark box and brushing against something living. Nancy's tongue is in her mouth and the first bitter rush of the pill dissolves between them. She closes her eyes. The kiss is a sherbet so strong it makes her teeth ache. Ruth doesn't care. She can't believe this is happening. Of all the things she expected, she'd never considered this. But it's so obvious now, the only possible outcome. It is *spectacular*. It hurts a bit and the hurt only makes Ruth want it more. She could be pinched all over. That hand in her hair. A kick in the shins and she'd know she was real.

'Eat it.' Nancy pulls away, wipes the back of her hand across her lips. The lipstick doesn't smear.

Ruth swallows. That's Nancy's saliva in her mouth, her spit and her tiny pink heart, which is already dissolving into her bloodstream, or perhaps that's just the kiss, and why did she wipe her mouth?

God, Ruth wants her attention. She'd almost forgotten how good it could feel to be under a girl's scrutiny. How girls will look at you and really see you, taking note of every little thing you try to keep hidden under your skin. It can be the worst thing in the world – when her schoolfriends stopped talking to her, Ruth swore she was done with girl friendship for ever – but at the same time, it can be the best. It can make you feel as if nothing else exists.

'Go dance if you're gonna.' There's a smirk playing on Nancy's face, a dimple of pure impishness. The music snaps into silver jacks. They roll on the floor, casting spiky shadows. Creep across straw and into Ruth's legs and remind her that was all she wanted. To move.

'But do you want to?' They could do that now. Run hand in hand to the tent and slam their bodies together. The inside of her mouth has gone all numb and plasticky. Every time she sniffs, a drip of metal trickles down her throat.

Nancy laughs. 'I'm busy,' she says, and gestures at the table: chewed bones and a cigarette impaled in mashed potatoes like a broken finger.

Ruth doesn't know what that means except no. 'Okay. I'm going to dance.'

'Yep.' Nancy turns away. A hot shame starts to rise in Ruth but she stands before it can get a hold. The movement is exhilarating. Her heart is higher in her chest than usual. It's beating very quickly and there's the chance that walking to the tent will kill her. *Thud-boom thud-boom.* Tiny hearts are multiplying in her veins. When she looks at her wrists, the blue lines are swollen ribbons. She watches, fascinated, as the veins pulse. Impossible it could have kicked in so quickly. Still, people have died of less stupid things. Her mum will be so disappointed if this is how it happens: on drugs, with these freaks, losing her hard-earned mind. But somehow none of that matters.

Ruth leaves Nancy, her small palms of treasures, leaves her to the bones. And then she's in the tent where the bass eats her whole. She flickers deliriously. This is the only important thing in the world: music. It's perfect, liquid, all-consuming. She's going to leap into it and find a boy with long fingers and a black shock of hair. Her insides wriggle. *Zed!* they shriek. She's going to find Zed, and he's going to kiss her, and all the lights will come on at once.

Through the smoke, she watches other bodies dance. The conjoined twins, the boy jerking around his robot arms and the girl exploding in giggles, their single pair of legs wide and sturdy on the ground. That glittering pierced lady, conducting an elaborate limbo manoeuvre beneath her own sword, snake-vine tattoos writhing with every shake. By the smoke machine, Shona Peterson is shimmying against that furred little man as if the world was about to end. Her eyes meet Ruth's for a second then both flick away, neither ready to acknowledge the other.

Why would they? To say something would mean letting the real world in, and Ruth couldn't bear that. Whatever else the fortune teller said, she was wrong about one thing. Ruth does not belong in Pitlaw. She's always known this, but now she knows something else: *this* is her place. Here, amid the weirdos and the magicians and the ones who got away.

She sneaks a look back at Nancy, sat alone at the table. A Barbie doll in her hands, stomping it through the detritus of dinner. She is so strange, thinks Ruth, and then there's a sharp tug in her insides and Nancy is forgotten. Her limbs need to move.

The music is getting louder. Ruth's body whirls. She's a dervish, a tornado. She's dancing her way into the secret true identity that's always been waiting. Her thighs chafe. Her heart opens, again and again, a rose blooming in time-lapse photography. These people, sweat-slick and beautiful. They're her people. All around, bodies crash into one another. Arms reach out. Ruth is so brutal with emotion she might explode. Her whole being is about to shatter into pieces that will fall on the crowd like confetti. The image is perfect. She wants to be spread.

And then she catches a glimpse: that shock of black hair above the thrash. The smile is upon her before she can swallow. *Hello you.* She parts the crowd like water, all her swimmer's muscles kicking in at once. This is easy. Everything she needs is already inside her, oiled and lubricated, ready for the reward. She's a manta ray. The world is yielding. She's moving through, she's in front of Zed, she's about to open her mouth and ask for what she wants . . .

But his back is to her. His attention is all turned towards the glamorous Black woman with the perfect make-up. They're dancing together, ignoring Ruth, as if they are of a kind and she is not, as if they can't see that she's part of this place now, she deserves to be here as much as anyone.

Ruth tries to shimmy into his line of vision. She waves her arms sexily, carelessly; she dances like the girl in the music video who has no idea the camera is panned to her. *See me, oh god, please see me.* She doesn't care, she's loose. At one with the music. *I'm here. I came.*

Finally Zed spins around and when their eyes catch, he grins. 'Hi!' A piano is dropped from a great height and explodes into never-to-be-repeated symphonies. Ruth swoons and Ruth says hi back but then Zed's turning around again, Zed's holding hands with that woman, Zed's laughing and being dragged out of the tent. He disappears in a cloud of dust. He doesn't say goodbye.

For a moment, she just stands in the midst of the thrumming people, alone. Her nerves are hiked up to maximum. A desperation she's never felt before claws at her joints. And so, when the man emerges from the smoke and holds out a hand, she lets him pull her close. She doesn't stop to question. His eyes are a polished blue and his muscles are hard and shiny and his tiny vest hangs off one shoulder, revealing a whole slab of meat.

Ruth is a hot throb of need, desire whiplashing inside her chest, as his hands close around her shoulders. She grasps out in the dark. The lips that meet hers are made of steel. A million tiny doors open in her chest.

This is a warm body in the darkness, and that is enough.

WHAT HAPPENS WHEN YOU STOP PAYING ATTENTION

A FAT ORANGE moon peers down from its low horizon. The moon nudges the evening star, as the Strongman slips a callused hand under the girl's shirt. Beneath the earth, the worms writhe. The girl falls into the dirt, racing against herself and her clothes, urging each to unbutton.

The vodka knew this was going to happen. The little witch is sat at the table, laughing.

Time plays catch-up while neon atoms bash each other in the tubes in the trees. The man spits into his hand. A pair of knickers is thrown into mud. Friction deigns to make an appearance, clad in silken party clothes.

Deep in the dirt, the ancestors cup their hands to their ears. The girl cries out. A hundred birds erupt in darkness. Sweat falls upon grass and fists close and that thumbprint bruise will still be there a week from now.

The moon creeps a little higher. The girl forgets her own name. Two bodies smash against each other while in the distance, a jerky wind-up box song is playing.

And the man lets go.

*

The girl doesn't know it yet, but this is a mistake for which she alone will pay. She swoons happily and leans her head against the man's chest.

The moon, who has seen the same thing happen a million times before, sighs.

Sleep comes onstage quickly and throws a cloak over our intrepid heroes. This night is the shortest, this act will be over soon.

GAPS IN THE CURTAINS

A THIN LICK of sunlight tongues over the horizon. The morning is hazy. Ruth is alone. She prises her eyes open, peels her face from the makeshift pillow. Her cheek is crosshatched from the straw. There are bits in her hair too, and when she reaches a hand to the throbbing melon of her skull, the back's a total rat nest.

Shit. Everything got squelchy and mixed up. Sometime in the night, she took her underwear off and put her jeans back on, and the denim crotch grates. Blearily, she takes in her surroundings: trampled straw, broken bottles, fairy lights still glowing Technicolor in the shaky dawn.

What happened?

The memory is quivering and vulnerable. She tries to approach it like a dog: hand outstretched, cooing. Bits remain cloaked in black curtains but others leap into day-glo focus.

Her leather jacket, tight around her shoulders (the vodka the vodka the vodka).

Flash!

A hundred eyes looking at her, but it's fine it's fine, she's made of steel.

Flash!

Nancy, her hot little mouth, that darting tongue.

Flash!

Sticky sweet wine.

Flash!

Dribbling laughter.

And then –

Dancing, all that music in her thighs. More kissing? A hard plastic chin, a whirl.

And then . . .?

The black curtains twitch and she catches a glimpse of something moving beyond. Ruth lifts a hand to her tit. Her heart beats erratically. She closes her eyes. She squeezes.

A jolt of pain goes through her, sweet and sharp.

And she remembers.

Ruth let that man take her. Right here in the dirt and the straw, where anyone could see. The thought is huge, terrifying, delicious. A snatch of lyrics repeats deliriously: *hunted like a crocodile, ravaged in the corn.* She imagines herself outside her body, looking down. The man is a dark shape on top of her: a crocodile, a monster, something ancient and outside of time. She's a slip of a thing. *Ravaged.* It doesn't seem possible, but it definitely happened. Her vagina is swollen. Her left nipple feels like it's been bitten. She can feel those hands, pressing into skin, claiming pieces. Now they'll never be hers again.

Ruth bites her lip to stop the smile breaking her mouth open. Not a good girl any more. A wild child, a creature of the night. Who knew? She did. She never admitted it, but she always knew. She leaps to her feet and her brain dunts against her skull and Ruth lets out a moan: 'Ohhh.'

She's going to be sick.

Ruth whirls around, clawing the hair from her mouth just in time. Her body wracks. A wet spatter covers the grass, hot and bitter, reeking of vodka. It comes out in a violent spray, desperate to get away from her as fast as possible.

When it's over, Ruth stares up at the sky. It's an astringent blue, toilet-cleaner bright. She feels purged. A spiritual baptism. Her insides emptied so she can start anew.

A dizzy smile plays on her as the funfair takes focus. Her surroundings are a garish mess. Broken wine glasses stamped into the earth. The fairy lights hang slackly from the trees, as if someone's yanked them in the night. Over in the tent (which she remembers as a feral writhe of possibility, all slick skin and glitter fuckery) the music has stopped. Two people are still dancing in slo-mo silence, heads on each other's shoulders, but their movements are hollow. By their side, there's a slack-eyed boy slumped on a hay bale, threading beads on to a blade of grass. The top half of his face is butterfly painted in iridescent pinks but the bottom's smeared off. His lips are red and fat as if they've been kissed (punched?) too many times. He gets six blue beads on, then the grass snaps and all the plastic scatters.

Something clicks. Ruth *knows* that boy. She didn't recognize him, what with the make-up, the last of the vodka oozing through her bones. But that's Euan Cruikshank. He used to be in Stephanie's class, he's the one that got the brunt of it at Pitlaw Academy last year. She remembers hearing about Euan showing up for drama class in a sequinned girl's blouse, how he'd memorized the whole of 'Memory' from *Cats*. How he'd sung in a quivering voice, how it was fucking hilarious. And for weeks after that, the canteen game: one point for ketchup on Euan's sleeve. Five for his T-shirt soaked in a full can of Coke. Ten whole points if you could sit him in a plate of gravy, so he'd spend the rest of the day with a jumper round his waist, hiding the brown sog on his arse.

Stephanie had told them about it over dinner, laughing through her fingers – she'd said Euan was a daft wee dickhole but it was a shame really, a total shame, and you could tell she didn't think it was a shame at all. Their mum had agreed but Ruth could see she was laughing too, or at least trying not to laugh, which is the same thing in your heart when it comes down to it.

Ruth shakes her hair violently. Stephanie. Mum! What's she doing dossing around here? She's got to get home before they wake, before they call her for breakfast and realize she's not there. That's when the questions will start, that's when they'll peel her open and see what she's been up to drawn in magic markers over her insides. All of a sudden, Ruth longs for a mirror. She wants to know, if you took one look at her face, whether you'd see that lovely ruin all over it. Is she old and full of knowing now?

Then Euan Cruikshank meets her gaze and smiles blearily and she thinks, No: that's what I look like. As if I've run into a brick wall. As if a flock of birds and stars are flying around my skull.

She takes one last look around the detritus, kicks at an empty bottle, and gives Euan a half-wave. Then Ruth turns and she runs.

SUNDAY MORNING
AND I'M FALLING

A FEW HOURS later, consciousness starts poking under Zed's ribs with an insistent finger. There's a pair of bony feet pressed against his stomach. An arm flung over his neck. Jabbed against his butt, something cold. He digs one hand under and pulls out a half-empty bottle of water.

There's a scurry in the covers, then Nancy's face surfaces, eyes flung open wide. 'That's mine.' How does she do this, go from dead sleep to bushy-tailed before he's even wiped the crust from his eyes? 'You can have a drink if you want.'

'Mmph,' says Zed. Water sounds good. There seem to be dead civilizations in his mouth. Desert animals crawling beneath rocks, the sun turning the world to grit and bleached bones. He takes a long, refreshing drink and . . .

'Fuck!' It's a punch in the throat. It's only by sheer force of will he doesn't spray it all over her, the bed, himself. The medicinal smell fills the caravan anyway. 'Vodka.'

'Breakfast vodka,' she amends. 'Have some but don't finish it. I need it.'

'I'm not going to finish it.' Oh my god, what's wrong with her? What kind of total pervert would finish the breakfast vodka? Not Zed, oh hell no. He's just going to swallow three times and all the bile will stay exactly where it's supposed to.

From the other end of the bed comes a deep groan, a

rumble like tectonic plates shifting. 'Breakfast vodka,' says a voice. Zed's stomach does a little high-ho silver lining and this is typical really. When the night gets squishy and impenetrable, when the party favours make an appearance, it's only a matter of time before he offers up his bed for the cuddle puddle. Zed is squashed against his friends and it's wonderful. He's battered and bilious and entirely in love. Of course the night itself is always brilliant, the party's wild, but is there anything more perfect than the morning after, wrung-out and draped over your fellow survivors of the small hours?

Another arm emerges and the hand clasps the air twice in lobster pincers. 'Breakfast vodka!'

Nancy grins. She plucks the bottle from Zed and passes it to Gretchen, whose head has also emerged now, filthy and radiant. Gretchen's fake lashes are stuck on her cheeks like furred caterpillars. Her red lips are a loose and lovely spill. Zed watches her take a generous sip, shudder once, then collapse back into the pillows – which, he notices, are all piled up on that end of the bed, Gretchen propped up on them, a precious invalid awaiting her visitors.

'This is really low-class service,' she says. 'I would have expected a Bloody Mary at least. So you know for next time.'

Nancy snatches the vodka and sticks it under the covers. 'Beggars,' she says. The tricksy grin flits back but she hides it quick, pulls an angelic face. Zed can practically see the halo glinting.

'Girl, what is that look?' Gretchen yanks the duvet, exposing Zed's chest, stripping Nancy. 'Tell me.'

Nancy flashes her smile of secrets. She's topless, of course, and she tucks her legs into a cross.

'Or don't.' Gretchen shrugs and turns to the bedside table,

her attention snatched by Zed's Casiotone keyboard and dinosaur stickers. 'Whatever you like.'

Nancy lets the moment drag out for a whole minute before she breaks it. 'Okay, fine! If you must know, it's voodoo.'

The word sloshes into Zed's brain, sweat-soaked and covered in swamp water. Nancy's never been one for subtle seductions. It's power or nothing, puppet strings all the way down. A glorious shiver runs through his spine, and he reminds himself to stay on her side, always and for ever. But of course he would, why wouldn't he? Nancy is the best.

'Someone in particular?' asks Gretchen.

'Of course.' Nancy runs the tip of her tongue over her teeth. 'That girl last night. Ruth.' She tilts the bottle at them. 'This is hers. Was.'

'So what? Down that and it makes her yours? That's a branch I never heard of. Hell, if I'd known, I'd have been nicking the ends of so many drinks . . .'

'No.' Nancy takes on a conspiratorial air. 'Maybe I drench the doll. Marinate it in this.'

'The doll?'

'Can't do voodoo without a doll.'

Gretchen rolls her eyes. 'Oh please. If you're going to be a thieving little witch, rummaging around in other people's magics, the least you can do is get them right.'

'Okay, fine.' Nancy sighs. 'I lie for effect, sue me. What do you want me to say? The doll's a cheap Hollywood obsession nicked from a whole religion because it looks good on camera?'

'Sounds about right.'

'It is. It's also *so* much fun.' She shakes the vodka. 'Anyway, this is just part voodoo. Part chaos magic. Part Nancy. The original mix.' Her mouth twists into a pout. 'You know I don't just *thieve* my magics. I do my best.'

She does too. Zed's seen it, a whole incomprehensible system of spell reparation, a practice that will see her locked away for days, focusing energies, sending magic back to the cultures she's borrowed from.

'Besides –' Nancy's dimples flash – 'the doll's a fine point of focus. It works fast. Doll magic gets right to those first emotions, all your childhood intuition. A love from the guts.'

At this, Gretchen relents. 'Maybe you're right there.'

'You're trouble.' Zed wraps his arms around her from behind. He thinks of Ruth last night, her dazed eyes, stumbling over herself to get what she wanted. What she thought she wanted. What Nancy wanted, anyway. His heart buckles a bit, but he knows better than to get involved.

'Well, what about you guys? Am I the only one doing any work around here?' Nancy wrinkles her nose at the word *work* and Gretchen laughs her glorious belly rumble.

'Ah yes. The revenge.'

The thought of those burned witches makes Zed's heart tweak. Tossing and turning in the halfway world, punished for being exactly the kind of person all of them are.

'Oh, I'll work it,' Gretchen says. 'But cut a gender pest some slack. They do like to keep their kids away from a gal like me.'

'True. But you?' Nancy squirms round in Zed's arms and starts pinching the skin beneath his hipbones. 'Typical dude. Dossing around while we get everything done.'

'I'm not!' Zed squeals. 'I'm on it.' Then he bites her bare shoulder until she shrieks for mercy. Rolls out of bed, flinging clothes on to his body, running a hand through his hair. This is good, actually. A purpose for the day. A lovely mission. Something warm and red and squidgy, a chance for rough palms and toffee apples. Perhaps a little bit of slippery zips. He closes his eyes and thinks about tidal currents, an eager riptide catching an ankle and running all the way back to sea. A force of nature, a thing out of control and –

'Where's our coffee?' says Nancy.

Zed blinks.

'Coffee? In bed? It's really the only way to start the day.' Her smile is so sweet. It's impossible a smile like that could come from such a monster.

'First things first,' Gretchen adds. 'If you ever want us out of here.'

'Of course. You're entirely right. Coffee must be served.' Zed's already at the stove, flicking it into life. 'And breakfast?'

'Naturally.'

And so they snuggle down as the hiss and spatter fills the caravan, the steam of coffee, the smell of hot toast. Butter. Molten cheese. Zed moves on autopilot, still thinking about the day ahead. He has a feeling finding his first mark will be simple. He already has an idea who it might be.

SAYING NO TO SAILORS

IT'S NOT STALKING if you're just going to check out the rides. It's research, in fact, cos Derek's going to write a song about the funfair and he can't quite remember if the waltzer shack's pink or purple. There's no point trawling the rhyming dictionary for things that end in –urple if he could've been coasting with –ink all along.

Ruth might even be there. He's heard she's been sneaking back, though folk have been saying all kinds of things about the funfair, and Derek's not so gullible he'd believe every one.

They've been saying that the neon's leaking into the water supply and if you drink too much it'll turn you doolally (like the man who runs the whole shebang, well have you seen those scars?).

They've been saying this time round, the fat lady doesn't even have the decency to blush.

They've been saying if we're not careful, ours'll end up like that. This funny business is contagious. So lock up your daughters. Tie a horse rope around your sons.

There's that, but there's also the way the Pin Gal shimmied from a punch that went nowhere. Her terrific confidence. An electric strength. Derek wants to feel like that too, even though he's scared. It makes him think of the small shocks that come from the tap by the dishwasher. They're not painful. In fact, they're kind of fuzzy. But there's always the fear they're attached to some big underground surge, and what's going to happen if you set that loose? Derek spends a lot of time with wet hands, and he worries.

It's fine. He'll go check the colours out, he'll keep his eyes peeled for Ruth. Maybe get some burned meat in a bap with red sauce, all charred and chewy. Maybe he'll find the girl with the magic metal and he'll bask in her shine. He's definitely going to avoid Nancy. And there's not a holy chance in hell he'll seek out Zed. No way. Derek remembers what happened at the waltzers last week, the hot gush and stinking embarrassment, and he has to press his hands to his cheeks to fan down the flames.

Not going to happen again! Derek chants greetings in his head to stop the shame spilling over: Hi! Hi! Hi!

And then – 'Hi,' says Zed, and Derek only goes and drops his bag. Fuck! His biros cartwheel like tiny apocalyptic logs, his papers catch the wind. Pogs scatter everywhere. Derek crouches to grab the stuff, but then Zed follows suit, and Derek stops.

Zed's staring up at him from a squat. Derek can see the line of thigh muscles in those tight mint jeans, which are ridiculous, but somehow Zed doesn't look ridiculous, even though there's no doubt in Derek's mind that he – Derek – would get decked if he ever showed up like that to school.

'Don't you want to pick them up?' says Zed.

Well what kind of question is that? Derek would. He totally would. Except he's watched movies before and he knows what happens when two people bend over to pick up a load of things from the ground. The first thing is that they'll bump heads, because they're not paying attention. Then, before you know it, one of them will stroke the other's cheek by way of apology. It doesn't matter what anyone's good intentions are: sooner or later, there'll be kissing.

Or they'll be reaching for the same thing when their hands will unexpectedly touch, and that static electricity will come parading up his fingers, and then somehow those fingers will be all wrapped up in each other's business. Intertwined.

Well, not this time. Derek's got this. He needs to scoop his stuff up quick. You don't just stumble into this kind of thing if you're paying attention. And once his stuff's back in his bag, there'll be no kissing and no entwine-y fingers and no rising chord sequences and—

Derek shakes his head, dislodging the things crowding his brain. Zed's still crouched, a wee grin twitching the corner of his mouth. *Is* it a grin? It could be a smirk – he could, just as easily, be laughing at Derek. And then he picks up a pen and hands it over and he's not.

'I'm sorry I threw up,' says Derek.

'It doesn't matter,' says Zed.

'Yeah, well.' Derek shrugs. 'I'm not like . . . I don't usually.'

'Okay.'

'I think it was the dinner. I mean, my mum did it too.'

'Okay.'

'She made the fish – you know what it's like with fish?'

'Sure.'

It's definitely a smirk now. There's a hook snagged in that fat lip, dragging it all the way up his cheek.

'So what about today?' asks Zed.

'What today?' Derek breaks his gaze and goes scrambling on the ground, sweeping everything into his bag, not worrying when the papers get scrunched, ignoring the gravel he'll be picking out for days.

'Are you still sick? Or did you come here to go on something? I can get the waltzers going if you like.' Zed's long, grasping fingers splay across a huge ring of keys hooked to his belt. 'I'm headed that way anyway, it's about time.'

No no no no no no no.

'Okay,' says Derek, and Zed's face breaks into an expression Derek can't read. He's laughing at him, or he's delighted, or he's both, or he's somewhere in between. Somewhere that hasn't worked out what Derek is yet, or somewhere that knows and likes it.

And so they wind through the concentric circles of the funfair, past the Casino of Souls and the Haunted House of Horrors and a dozen other things that don't spin one bit. The wibbly optical world of illusions – his guts could deal with that. But no. They're walking on. In fact, he's trotting, almost, a half step behind Zed, cos Zed's not only got the gangliest of legs but he also walks with mad purpose: stomp stomp stomp stomp.

They pass a row of food shacks, wooden fronts looming in a way that makes Derek think of dusty Westerns on afternoon TV. The way this road sags in the middle, you ought to clank down it with spurs. Except it's not as old fashioned as that: there are flickering neon bulbs, weirdly hollow under the sunlight. It doesn't smell old fashioned either. The air's stacked up with plastic: candyfloss and Slush Puppies and bubblegum. And underneath that, burned meat and engine grease, smells that make the muscles in Derek's stomach clench, just a wee bit, in ways he can't define.

And then – suddenly, impossibly – they're at the waltzers. Just looking at them is making Derek's belly want to give up the game.

Zed tosses his keychain, and the metal makes a clinky splish when the keys land in his palm.

Derek can already feel it crawling up his throat, even though the ride's dark and the cars are still. Is that the stain there, in the grass where he chucked up? It's paler, definitely, and – isn't that the smell? It's got to be. It can't be. It—

'Zed,' Derek says.

'Yup?'

'I don't . . . I don't think . . .'

'You don't?'

'I don't want to go on them again, actually, I think I'd rather, I, I want to, it'd be better if . . .'

The words all come out in one big long string, like those German compound words Mrs Mackie's always going on about, where you just keep adding things to make new things, except Derek's pretty sure whatever he made doesn't make a whole lot of sense.

Zed takes a step towards him. 'Come to my caravan instead?' He glances at his watch. 'It's bound to be free by now.'

'Free?'

'Vacant. Available. No troublemakers around.'

Well. Derek's spent his whole life avoiding this moment. A caravan's a wee place you live in, and places you live in have beds inside. That's a fact. Derek's mentally engineered a million methods never to be alone in a tight corner with a big bed and a cute boy, because he doesn't doubt that's where the ruckus starts. He's considered a thousand ways not to climb into the cab of the lorry with the burly stranger, the one with the tight gold rings around his knuckles. Just in case, Derek practises saying no to sailors, so when the sailors ask him aboard, he'll know exactly how to decline.

That's why he spends so much time imagining these things. No other reason at all. And Derek knows he's lucky, besides. The feeling he has when he looks at a girl is real too. It's real and it's normal. It's exactly what you're supposed to do. So who needs to have everything? Not him! Only an idiot would let a caravan complicate his life like that.

But on the other hand, there's a sudden feeling in his guts that everything he's built around himself is about to turn to dust. Or something slippier – oil, perhaps. He always believed that his preparations were amulets to ward off the world, but now they look more like shiny jewels designed to tempt magpies.

'I—'

'So, pray tell, what trouble are you sweethearts up to on this fine summer's day?'

The voice is all cut glass and polished metal. At the sound of it, the moment is broken. Derek whirls around and there's the Pin Gal, gleaming in the sun. Her smile is brilliant. The colours of her thrillingly vivid even against the funfair's backdrop.

And just like that, Derek isn't alone with Zed any more. Which is for the best, right? Never mind that Derek might never get an invitation like that again. He takes a shaky breath and attempts to steer his stomach back somewhere normal.

'Trying to tempt Derek here to sample some of our more delicious offerings. But he's a hard sell.'

The word *tempt* on Zed's lips. 'I'm not hard,' Derek insists, and it's only after the words fall out of his mouth that he hears what he's just said. The Pin Gal and Zed glance at each other, then back at him, delighted. 'I mean, I'm interested. In the funfair! The rides. Not the rides, the – the shows. What did you want to show me?' Dear god. Will he ever stop talking? The Pin Gal is smothering a giggle in one hand. Zed's looking at him now the way you might look at a baby goat, something cute and fragile and unsteady on its feet. That's not Derek. He needs to explain. Derek is tough and certain, or at least he can be, just give him a minute. If he's not quite a man's man, not yet, then at least he could be a boy's boy. But that doesn't sound right either. In fact, that sounds worse, it sounds like—

'I don't think this one is built for the centrifugal lifestyle, my dear.'

'Hmm, you might be right.'

'Of course I'm right.' The Pin Gal clacks her tongue. 'What he needs is a little more subtle than pure brute motion. Let him experience some of our joys of illusion and trickery. Let go of his anxieties about the ways things ought to be.'

Are they talking about him as if he's not even here? Well, truth be told, he doesn't mind that. Derek's often thought life would be sweeter if he didn't have to steer quite so much of it.

'A performance.' The Pin Gal drums one tiny silver sword against the metal of her collarbone. 'How about the Twins?'

'Potentially . . .'

'You want to bewitch your boy, that's the kind of magic that'll do it.'

His boy?

'Hush now!' Zed's yelp is firm but altogether gleeful. He grasps Derek's hands and squeezes them, bridging the gap between their not-touching and touching as if it was no bother at all. How does he do that? A big sappy grin that doesn't give a toss – as if all this is easy, as if they're just having fun.

'Eight p.m. tomorrow. You'll be my guest. Let me make up for ah . . . the trouble last time.'

The way he says it. It's a tease, but somehow Derek's not the butt of the joke. He says it like they're both in on it. And with a shock Derek realizes that maybe Zed's right. Maybe they are having fun, maybe this is easy.

'Okay.' Derek can barely believe the guts of himself. 'I'll be here.'

He will?

'I'll be waiting,' says Zed, and inside Derek a hundred doors blow open. The doors slam and smash, the wind howls. A delirious chill passes over his skin.

He will.

THOSE METAL JAWS

RUTH LIES IN bed, running her fingers over her shirt. There's her ribcage, the dents between her bones. She doesn't know how she got through breakfast, but she did. The worst part was inching open the garage door to stash her bike. That door always sounds like a whole orchestra, cymbals and steel drums.

But somehow – mercifully – no one appeared.

After that, it was just a matter of creeping upstairs, into the bathroom to rub the night off her face. The top layer came off easily with green soap, but she could still see a dozen other layers underneath. And when her mum and Stephanie sat across the breakfast table, gabbing about the calories in rosé versus red, she was certain they could see too.

Still, neither said a word. So maybe nothing's changed and she's just who she was before. Her hands move down to the bruise on her hip. She presses it, hard. Pain blooms deliciously. It feels like the only real thing about her. Her crotch tingles. In the distance, Kayleigh is crying. Further away than that, there's a man in a muscle vest going about his day. At some point he'll have to pee and when he pees he'll have to hold his dick and when he touches it, it'll be a dick that's been inside her, and maybe he'll think about that. How could he not?

I didn't even get his name, she thinks, and the thought is so huge and perfect she claps both hands over her mouth. For the rest of my life, it will be true: I was *deflowered* by a man and I don't even know his name!

Ruth giggles. There's a rap at the door. She tugs at her shirt, rearranging herself inside.

'What is it?'

The door swings open. Stephanie stands in the frame, Kayleigh on her hip. 'Post.' She chucks a big white envelope on the floor. Ruth doesn't move.

'Thanks,' she says.

Stephanie narrows her eyes. 'Why are you looking like that?'

'Like what? I'm not.'

Stephanie shoots her a glare. Kayleigh balls her tiny hands into fists, gathering a fresh scream from her throat. 'Gross, Ruth. Lock your door next time.'

'I wasn't doing anything!'

But the door is already slammed.

Ruth blushes. She prises herself from the bed and plucks the envelope from the floor. There's a jaunty little crest printed on the front and her heart skips out for a minute. University of St Andrews. Here it is. Her future, all sealed up with its decision, so why isn't she ripping the envelope open? Why isn't she already inside?

Saliva gathers in her throat. Ruth takes one fingernail and prises the glue. She peels the flap and just holds the envelope open like that, a numb clatter in her chest. Then she slides the page out and she reads:

We are pleased to inform you –

The words pulse. Everything she wanted. Unconditional Acceptance, Accountancy BSc (Hons). A ticket, a passport, the one-way train out of this place.

So why does it feel like a snare?

She stares at the letter. There's a glossy prospectus along with it, page after page of shiny white teeth – grinning at a microscope, at a stethoscope, at a man in glasses dissecting Kantian realities, so very certain in his certain knowledge.

Ruth flicks through with a growing sense of displacement. It suddenly seems very unlikely that this is the thing she's been waiting for. She tries to dredge up the fizzing excitement that usually lives in her belly. Closes her eyes and pastes on a smile, hoping her emotions will follow.

No.

Oh my god, thinks Ruth. I broke myself. She turns the pages faster. Here's a dorm room and here's a lecture theatre, a bunch of students in red cloaks, and who gives a toss? She does. Remember? She cares so much. So why is there this gaping cavern inside her, this desire to throw the whole thing in the kitchen bin?

Ruth grabs the form and takes it to her desk. She sits with a black pen and reads down the lines. They're really very simple. She knows all the answers already: her name, her address. A signature to confirm, *I do*. But she doesn't. Writing her name in that black box feels like putting her hand into the rusted metal jaws of a bear trap. Impossible.

Is this what sex does to you? It can't be. They would have told them in sex ed. They told them everything else: all the septic sores and screaming babies, the viruses that lurk in the bloodstream, death-warrant flowers in purple bruises. But now brushing up against *that* thought sends her heart into a skittering panic. She thinks of the Freakslaw instead. Then smashed windows, the terrific explosion of glass. The thoughts come out of nowhere, blinding-bright and alive. They crowd her brain and her heartbeat changes pitch – instead of the panicked thrum begins a manic syncopation of delight.

The form in her hand is shaking. She reaches to the bump in her jean pocket, the one which materialized last night in the midst of so many snuck cigarettes. When she strikes the lighter, the flame dances seductively. There's a breath where she sees what she's about to do and she can't quite believe it. What has twisted inside her, and how the fuck has it happened so quickly? She's been corrupted, broken; something sinister and uncanny has swept its way into her alongside the funfair trucks and bright lights. Some dark transformative magic.

But it only takes a moment for the page to catch. Ruth holds on to the form until the heat licks her fingertips, then drops it on the desk. For a second, she thinks it might set the room ablaze, but nothing happens. The ends curl up like autumn leaves. A smudge of grey ash, and the vice around her heart slackens.

And all the while, Nancy sits with Barbie, playing her childhood games. Nancy presses a pin into her unyielding plastic flesh. Nancy whispers *firebug* and *vandal* and *let's have some fun*.

Nancy laughs and laughs.

A HOT PINK GALAXY

THE NEXT DAY, it's five to eight and Zed's waiting by the big tent. He can't stop grinning. Of course, there's a chance Derek won't come. There's a chance all that nervousness and self-preservation will bubble over and put out his flames, that Derek will decide he's better off staying on the ordinary path, wayward opportunities ignored, unruly destinies shot down.

But will that happen? Zed doesn't think so. He saw the way Derek's cheeks turned pink when he crouched beside him, saw that eager little nod when he mentioned his caravan. When Derek agreed to come back, Zed thought Derek might slap both hands over his own mouth at the audacity of it all. And yet the moment the words were out, he looked absurdly pleased with himself, and holy heck that was adorable.

Zed wants to make him look that pleased again. He has a dozen different ideas how to do it, each more delectable than the last.

Three minutes to eight and Zed realizes he wants a gift for Derek's arrival. Of course he does! Giving boys presents is the best. There are few things in life as sweet as bestowing a shiny gift on a boy who's always been told that it's his job to be the initiator, not the spoiled, pretty thing. Derek is a pretty thing and making boys blush is a reason to get up in the morning and what better present for a sweetie than the sweetest thing of all?

Zed dashes over to the candyfloss maker and starts the whirl, pressing the big silver button that makes the sugar manifest. Is there anything so hypnotic as watching candyfloss coalesce around a stick? First there's nothing and then a hot pink galaxy conjures into being right before your eyes!

One minute to eight. Zed holds out the candyfloss like a huge bunch of flowers. He peers through the funfair, down the winding sawdust path, and holds his breath. Waiting, waiting. And then before him materializes a freckle-faced boy, picking his way down the path.

'Welcome!' Zed says, and presents his sugared bouquet. 'This is for you.'

Derek takes it from him, a little awestruck, peering at the pink cloud from every angle. 'Thank you.' Even the words seem to blush in the air. 'So, um, what are we going to do?' All nervous, like maybe this is a trick and Zed's going to strap him back in the waltzers and spin him round until he spews again. Which he never would. Never!

'Well, my dear,' (that hitch of breath at the word dear!), 'there's a little spectacle I hope will tickle your fancy.'

Zed went back and forth a bunch of times. The thing is, the Freakslaw has so many spells to cast, depending what mood you're in, what desires you care to evoke. The holy terror of Werewolf Louie's tightrope act might have Derek gasping and clutching at him, awareness of his own mortality swooshing in (we could all be about to plummet, so let's live first and kiss?!). Or Gretchen's drag show: a demonstration of gender euphoria and queerness so divine, it would surely push Derek out of the box of his own inhibitions. And there's not a human in the world who wouldn't leave Miss Maria's seductive burlesque all hot and bothered, swooning and sweaty, horny as hell.

But in the end he decided the Pin Gal was right. Magic is what's called for: spellwork and conjuring, gleeful illusions, an entire unbuttoning of the boundaries of reality.

'In here,' Zed says, and he ushers Derek into an already packed tent.

They sit in the darkness, perched on a wooden bench, close enough that Zed can feel Derek breathing beside him. That just gets Zed thinking about that air flowing in and out of Derek's body, swooshing through his lungs with impunity, and isn't that a thought to behold? Not for too long though, because everything is about to begin.

Roll up, roll up, roll up! And welcome to the mystical world of illusion . . .

As the Twins step out on to the sawdust stage, a murmur travels around the tent. *Ooooh,* like someone's dropped a tray in lunch, and Zed feels a twinge of love as Cass blows kisses to the audience and Henry shoots a brusque little finger-gun. Their body casts its own spells, sure, but the real magic comes after that: in the skills they've learned to hypnotize a crowd. The first flutters are your classic magic-show regalia – the dove exploding from the tophat, the playing card flying wildly round their faces, silk scarves flickering like snake tongues from a sleeve. Each trick hot on the foot of the last, a dizzying spectacle that leaves you no time to catch your breath.

Zed sneaks a look at Derek's face, and he is rapt, wide-eyed, besotted. Exactly how he ought to be!

Of all the acts the Freakslaw has to offer, it's the Twins' that Zed wishes he could emulate the most. He's always believed that magic tricks are the most honest form of deception. Sometimes he feels jealous his own contribution to the funfair is so pedestrian, but mainly he just likes to sneak in the back of the Twins' tent whenever possible and watch as they twist and tweak reality, see all the ways the world is possible to curve.

Cass flicks a cloak over their body and in an instant – a puff of smoke, small explosion of glitter! – their outfits have changed from black to diamante-encrusted white. The audience squeal appreciatively as Cass and Henry swivel before them, gemstones glinting in the light.

Zed remembers when the Twins first came to the Freakslaw. How they showed up in that small town in the West Country, eleven days in a row, watching every performance, until finally they'd gone to Mr Partlett's caravan directly and asked for a job. They'd had a strict demand along with their request: they were not there to be simply gawked at. Like every other act in the Freakslaw, they were there to perform, and if Mr Partlett had a problem with that, well, he could figure out where to shove it.

Of course, he had no problem at all.

The funfair is home for those who carve their own path. Like the others, both Cass and Henry have made a certain decision. If your very existence in the world is political, then you're already fucked before you try to behave by the world's rules. So why not live the exact life you've always desired?

Why not indeed? This is how it's been for all of them, for ever, all the way back to the ancestors. This is how they live.

A drumroll begins to echo around the tent and Zed feels Derek sit up a little straighter in his seat. The Twins are building up to the grand spectacle, the Big Trick: the one that really gets the audience going. It's all very well toying with small objects, but how about something larger? How about us in all our splendour, here and then not here, abracadabra, goodbye? To be honest, Zed always holds his breath a little at this point. He's seen it a hundred times, a thousand, and they always reappear again, and yet. There's a part of him that worries. A part that knows, bone-deep, that sometimes when people disappear, that's it. They're just . . . gone.

Take, for example, his mother. Zed doesn't know much about her, except that she was young when she had him, so young – probably the same age, in fact, as he is now. No age at all to be a mother, and still she lasted it out until he was five and a half. Zed thinks this was a good run, really. All things considered. He doesn't remember much of being a kid before that: a kitchen table with butter sandwiches, the red plastic bucket he was always filling with the prettiest of pebbles – oh he remembers pavement-chalk flowers covering the driveway, a blossoming hothouse, his mother kneeled beside him sketching great swooping vines. All suffused with a pink nostalgia the same exact colour as love.

What happened after is put together from stories he's gleaned from Gretchen or Miss Maria – stories he likes to tweak to be more romantic, invested as he is in his own lore. Did you know he was abandoned in a wicker basket like Moses, floated down the Atlantis Slider itself? Caught on a fishing rod by the Hook-A-Duck, plucked out of the water and presented to the Freakslaw, tah-dah!?

The truth, of course, is more mundane. A Tuesday afternoon, one July in Penzance. Gloria left one little bundle of trouble outside to play in the dirt, watched over by the worms, and came back to find two grubby monsters in its place.

Zed still has the note that was pinned to his shirt: *Forgive me. I love you. You deserve everything.* And if there's a hole in his life where biological family ought to be, Zed knows he's lucky. Jesus, is he lucky. Because there's another version of his story where he never found the Freakslaw. Never discovered how it felt to fit so perfectly in a place where you belong. A dodecahedron-shaped peg in a dodecahedron-shaped hole.

Maybe this is why he can't help himself, going about grabbing life with two hands. Or is it just because life is so very shiny, so very much fun for grabbing?

He turns to look at the boy sitting next to him and a delicious shudder crawls up his spine. Derek doesn't have a clue how cute he is, and that's the cutest thing of all. He's got those nervous hands that always seem to be about to knock things over. It's not a stutter as such, but the way he pauses in all the wrong places, the way he repeats himself when he's getting anxious? Adorable. The terrible part of Zed wants to leap over and perch upon his knee and give him a necklace of hickies, just to hear the ragged hitch in Derek's throat, just to mark him all over as one-of-us – the weirdos, the freaks – so he can never go back to his hidey-hole ever again.

On the stage, there's a huge explosion: kablam! A puff of smoke, the audience gasps.

And the good part of him knows he needs to take things slow. Let Derek come to him. This anticipation, it's so torturous and so sweet. How can something be so painful and yet utterly delicious? Well, it makes sense. The 'fer' in suffering has the same root as the 'phor' in euphoria, after all – torment has always been a part of pleasure, that's what makes it so fun.

'Derek,' Zed hisses, as the wonder circles the crowd, as the space where the Twins once stood now reveals nothing but a gaping hole.

'What?'

He knows Derek can't do it in the tent in front of all the people, not even in the darkness, not even with magic and possibility hung ripe in the air.

'You know how yesterday I invited you to my caravan?'

'Yes?'

'Were you going to come, if the Pin Gal hadn't shown up?'

Warm blush in the shadows. '. . . Yes.'

The music rises towards a crescendo, people peering and craning to find the Twins.

'Well, do you want to go now?'

And when Derek says yes a third time, he grabs his hand and pulls him outside.

Getting back to the caravan is like a magic trick in itself. One minute they're stumbling out of the dark tent, the next – suddenly, impossibly – here they are unlatching a door, clambering up a step, falling into a warm dark cavern.

Here they are on Zed's bed.

'Hi,' says Derek. He's turned the pinkest of pinks, and Zed's heart might just burst. They sit facing each other, legs touching, the spot of contact getting warmer all the time. If they wait too long, that spot will combust, so Zed takes one hand and places it on Derek's thigh.

'Oh,' Derek says.

'Did you like that?' Zed could be talking about the performance, but both of them know he's not. He's talking about that bold hand, a hand that is now pressing gently – not moving, not yet, but just giving the smallest, most-exploratory squeeze.

'I like it,' Derek squeaks.

The sound of that! A voice breaking against the shore of anticipation, that sees the hand and all it represents, the doors that hand could fling open.

'Do you want more?' Zed asks. Because there is so much more he wants to show Derek, to do to him (oh jesusfuck humans are lovely, aren't they? Covered in so much potential and skin!). There is so much delicious possibility, so many nerve endings, do you even know how deeply it's possible to feel? Zed just wants to hear that yes first, to confirm they're on the same page, suffering and euphoric, up for everything.

But in the end, Derek doesn't say yes. In fact, he doesn't say anything. In the end, he does the very last thing that Zed expected.

Derek leans in and kisses him first.

Closes his eyes and the distance between them, presses his soft fucking lips against Zed's, opens his mouth and there is a wet tongue, firm and certain, doing the one wild thing that tongue has ever done. Zed kisses him back. Their hands are all over each other, running up and down arms, trailing across thighs, reaching to unbutton, to peel, grasping to figure out how all these clothes can find their way to the floor.

And just for this moment, everything is perfect.

There is no thought of darkness, of revenge, of howling ancestors trapped between realms. No thought of fathers or consequences, no fists, no rules for how a boy ought to behave. There is just this: two creatures in a caravan where time has stopped, where one is crossing a threshold he's waited his entire life to cross and the other is yanking him gleefully over to the other side.

The kiss feels so fucking good. Let them have this. One last moment before everything changes. A soft, living moment, like a heartbeat quivering in the palm of a hand.

THE MYCELIUM CREEPS

AND SO THE summer twists and turns, sliding against itself like shoulder muscles. After the hump of solstice, the days get shorter, and faster with it. The last scraps of June evaporate in the baking sun and July gallops into its place.

Fuelled by the prospect of revenge, the sticky intention of the Freakslaw spreads. While the waltzers whoop and whirl – sweating light, cracking teeth – the mycelium creeps. All over Pitlaw, into tight stagnant living rooms, turning the air ripe. It gives off a warm, moist energy: the energy of souls and snuffed candles. Every night, it seeps into dreams. When the teenagers wake, they hear doll music through double glazing. Every day, they return to the world of electricity and carnival charms. And as the weeks go by, wayward minds begin to wonder: is this what they've been waiting for their entire lives?

In a black and white tent on a balmy evening, the Twins cast tricks in smoke and mirrors, while sixteen mischievous schoolchildren gasp in unison and lean close. One volatile Thursday – the kind of day where every moment of skin against skin is high friction, when just the sight of a flower blooming is inexplicably lewd – Miss Maria works long into the night and sets a new record of flesh. The Pin Gal swallows swords and spits out lassos. Gretchen dances the seven-veiled dance.

And the Freakslaw casts its spells, and Pitlaw drinks of this sweet strangeness with a high thirst. But not everyone is slaked. Gloria was right – there is another magic at work here. Generations of angry men, that pulsing Calvinist heart. One that's not so simple to smother.

Over mince and tatties, parents lecture about the foolishness of wasting time and money on childish games. Pocket money is docked. Curfews clack into place. But something's shifting. The message isn't sinking in. Teenagers find pinball funds in unmanned purses and gas-money drawers. A locked front door is no match for a window propped open to the balmy night.

And, worse. A division brews between parents themselves. Those loyal wives – oh, how they ought to back up their husbands! – find themselves contemplating the quaint allure of roast nuts. The sweet shriek of haunted houses. Most tamp this down but there are the few who let it stick. Those delinquent harpies forgo cooking the evening meal, sneak out along with their sons to be found white-knuckled on the crest of the roller coaster, screaming and laughing and clenching their thighs! The beleaguered husbands come home to an empty table. Some don't even get a note.

So is it any wonder, as the weeks go by, that frustration turns to violence?

The crack of a belt behind closed doors won't be discussed in the morning. A bruised collarbone can be brushed off as a slip on the stairs. The funfair folk will sense this shift but they'll be too busy with their own tasks to give it the attention it deserves. The smallest of mistakes but for want of a nail, the kingdom was lost. And later, when this violence is turned upon themselves, the Freakslaw will regret this moment with heavy hearts. In hindsight, every earlier moment is the right moment to act.

Because it doesn't stop there. As Lùnastal creeps closer, as the funfair accelerates its campaign of candied seduction, it bubbles over. One mid-July night, in the wee hours, some drunk takes out a string of coloured lightbulbs with a fistful of well-aimed rocks from the quarry. The explosions summon Gretchen (who rarely sleeps, truth be told) but by the time she arrives, it's all shards of glass and footprints in the dirt. A week later (again, under the cover of darkness, those cowards!) the popcorn cart is smashed. The dubious smell of piss among the husks in the grass.

Still, the Freakslaw could overlook such things if they stopped there. Who among us has never succumbed to the allure of destruction? We all clutch the spirit of Dionysus close.

But the attack is something else.

It happens on the cusp of Main Street and Haverston Avenue, on an evening so hot it's impossible to tell the difference between boiled water and blood. In the beer garden, just down the road, Greg Haskett, Boyd Geddes and Callum McAllister are sinking pints with the cross-eyed determination of monks. None would do anything as fucking pansied as apply suntan lotion, and this summer's inexplicable weather has blessed each with expanses of blistered red skin: the shoulder, the chest, the thinned patch of the scalp. Perhaps it's this endless chafe that puts them in the mood they're in. The sweat on their balls, the hot denim rash of their thighs. Perhaps it's the simmering fester that's been brewing all summer, getting under everyone's skin.

But they'd say it was none of that. It was the scream. What kind of a man wouldn't respond to that poor woman's scream?

That poor woman, Doreen Abbott, was just walking her dog – Stitches, the black lab – and never meant to cause a fuss. She was doing her daily brisk, you see. Her mind was on last night's *Taggart* when that . . . that wild man came running! Gave her the fright of her life, so he did. Clutching that fabric between his hairy little hands, about to leap up and strangle her. Terrifying, it was. And yes, she realized after a minute that it was her scarf, which must have fallen to the pavement. But by that time she was already screaming and it was difficult to stop. Her heart rat-tat-tatting in her chest and Stitches whining at a pitch that would shatter glass and there, hopping from foot to foot was that *beast* of a man . . .

'Help!' screams Doreen. 'Oh stop it, get off! Go away!'

Werewolf Louie stops, confused. He holds out the scarf as an explanation. Get off what? He's not on anything. Louie's fur twitches into a soft smile. Round the corner, in the beer garden, Greg Haskett slams his pint down so hard the glass cracks. 'The fuck?' and the three men are on their feet. When they turn on to Main Street, this is what they see: one of those freaks, a monster, terrorizing poor Doreen from down the way. Right here in broad daylight! Claws out, ready to attack.

'You get away from her,' shouts Callum McAllister, all fired up.

Doreen's breath is coming in shallow pants. It all happened so fast. That's her good silk scarf, the one Rory bought her before he died, and oh she'd never have forgiven herself if she'd lost it getting her exercise in!

'It's okay,' says Werewolf Louie in his wee high voice, 'she dropped her scarf, I just—'

Callum looks down and sees the pint glass in his hand. In a fluid motion of total bravery, he flings it at the wee bawbag.

'Owww,' howls Louie, as the glass scuffs his brow. He raises his hands to his forehead and they come away crimson. At the sight of these bloody palms, Greg Haskett loses his shit. There's a broken brolly in the gutter, dusty and useless under these new sun-soaked skies, and he grabs it, starts lashing Louie's back. The prongs bend under the force of each thrash.

'Get back,' instructs Boyd Geddes, and Doreen Abbott shuffles away from the fracas.

'Oh goodness,' she says. 'Oh I didn't mean . . .'

But it's much too late for what she didn't mean, so she just stands and watches as the blows rain down. He shouldn't have run at her like that! Not looking the way he does. He ought to be more careful.

After, Werewolf Louie scampers home to the Freakslaw: bruised, battered and terrified to his bones. Doreen plucks her discarded scarf from the pavement and winds it around her neck. Stitches sniffs the gutter, picking up a familiar old smell, bloody and elemental.

And the men congratulate themselves, a job well done. They might as well go back to the pub, drink another pint, put the world to rights. If not them, then who?

It's 23 July. Cancer ticks into Leo. Peaches, figs and cabbages ripen into fruit. Tomorrow will be three minutes and forty-three seconds shorter than today. Lùnastal is just around the corner, August waiting behind the curtain to make her most dramatic appearance yet. The ancestors are closer to the surface with each passing night, thrashing and half alive. Running memories of what was done to them through their fingers like rosary beads: this split flesh, this charred throat, this false accusation. Muttering *You KNOW what you DID and you KNOW what is COMING.* On a balmy evening, the sky shimmers with stars.

Derek Geddes lies in bed, one hand clasped around his cock. He's thinking about a pink caravan and a hot velvet clutch. A perfect thing. A sordid secret.

Across town, Ruth MacNamara can't keep a thought in her head. She's turned seven pages, traced her eyes over every word, but couldn't recite one for the life of her. She slides the book under her pillow, trying to ignore the panicked clatter of her heart.

In her caravan, Nancy is sat cross-legged, drawing tarot cards. She gets the good ones: the Tower crashing down, Death tramping the barren land with her skulls and her sickle. Her fury's stoked to a roaring flame. They tried a gentle revenge, a revenge without blood, and what happened? Blood, all the same! Their own, yet again. Well, things are about to change. She'll see to it.

And Zed is nursing Louie's cuts with hydrogen peroxide and Shona Peterson is soaping the blood from his hair and Gloria the Teller is three sheets to the wind, plotting what needs to be done. The funfair folk will review their spells. Consider how best to counterattack. But carefully. The town is a frightened animal and it has teeth.

And the mycelium creeps on – getting hotter, gathering energy, beneath all that hard, packed summer dirt.

BETTER THAN A HOLE
IN THE HEAD

FOR THREE DAYS, Nancy fumes. Sure, Werewolf Louie's already making jokes by the morning, but she can hear the twitch of fear, see him wince as he buttons the mirrored waistcoat to his chin. The other freaks are in full solicitous mode: Miss Maria sharing her rare lavender macarons, the Pin Gal stitching Louie a sling that looks like a sailboat. But Nancy's not the only one who's furious. On the second night, she sits with Gretchen until the wee hours, setting Gideon bibles on fire and stoking each other to a toasty frenzy. Who did those fucks think they were? And how did they think they'd get away with it?

It's all Nancy can think about. The doll is child's play now, discarded beneath a mound of dirty knickers. That's in motion anyway. There's bigger fish to fry. She expects her new plan to require some kind of plotted precision, so when the man shows up at the tent, it feels like fate.

It's ten minutes before her performance and she's pacing the sawdust, a hotbed of wired energy waiting to be earthed. She sneaks a look through the flap at the gathering queue, and a smile plays on her lips. Nancy's popular today. She blows a kiss to Louie – who's working the crowd, taking on the role of shill until his arm heals and he's back to the tightrope.

He catches the kiss in a furred fist, beaming. Lifts the megaphone and starts up again – *Roll up, Roll up, the Greatest*

Show on Earth! – his wee voice high and happy. Then the words catch in his mouth. Nancy sees his face turn pale beneath that glowing ginger mane. Louie's staring at a man who is smirking right back. His neck red, eyes small and piggy. The tips of his hair bleached yellow and so coated in gel you could snap them in two.

Louie holds out the megaphone like a shield and starts shuffling backwards. He's still talking, *Roll up! Roll up!*, but there's a crack on the high notes.

The man looks like he might piss himself laughing. And Nancy watches and thinks, Really? You'd show up here? This is the guy, it has to be. Delivered to her door for what needs to happen. A terrible smile plucks across her face. Oh, you shouldn't have, she thinks. And Oh, oh, this is going to be fun.

In the centre of the ring, Nancy flicks one ankle behind her ear, careless as brushing off a mosquito. She folds her body, feeling the crunch of organs as her waist contracts until she can fit through a hoop the circumference of a jam jar. She turns and twists ever-smaller – vase, milk bottle, pinky finger – contracting then expanding like a flasher flinging his coat. The kids in the front shirk back, clutching their hands as if she might bite their fingers off, but they can't stop staring. It's not them Nancy's interested in, though. She's aiming her gymnastics at the man in the third row, who has no idea what to make of the bird in the bright red catsuit.

The trumpet rises in pitch: an oompahpah and a wallop. A scuffed moon rises on a wire, cratered and captivating. A single beam of light falls to the sawdust. In the darkness, there's a rustle as a hundred moths shake the dust from their wings.

Nancy parades across the floor like a crab, limbs all back to front: grotesque and fucking beautiful. The beat of the wings gets louder. When she reaches the circle of orange light, she stands on one leg, holds her foot to her ear as if answering a telephone.

The trumpets are in carnage now. Three children have started to cry.

Nancy whispers into her foot. 'Come on, darlings. Come to me.'

And there's a great furred beating and the moths are upon her, covering her entirely as she twists on a single toe. They make a writhing, shivering cocoon. Just when you thought the trumpets couldn't get any more triumphant, they burst into a series of Catherine wheels. A beat, the moths pause their wings, and then scatter back to the rafters.

The audience blink, rub their eyes, and look again.

Nancy is gone.

Afterwards, the crowd snakes outside, not quite sure what that was. 'Trapdoor,' mutters someone dismissively, but it's not just the disappearance. The real question: how do you train an army of moths to do a thing like that? And, more importantly, why would you? Those leaving keep feeling that hideous flutter of wings. The otherworldly vibration of dust. Buh! When they get home, they'll shower before bed, do their best to scrub the feeling off, but bits of the moths will stay on their skin and dreams for a time to come.

The line curves away from the buttery yellow of the tent and towards the bright summer afternoon.

'Psst!' says Nancy.

Callum McAllister, who's been thinking hard about salt

and vinegar crisps, nearly jumps out of his skin. He corrects himself immediately. Turns around in a manly fashion, arms folded on his chest.

'Psst,' she says again. 'Come with me.'

It's the girl, the contortionist, all five foot nothing of her. She's leaning nonchalant, chewing gum with the laziest, devil-may-care attitude. It makes Callum think of those made-for-TV movies he'd watch as a kid, the bandits who'd waltz in to kick up trouble in some sleepy Western town. He always wanted to be the cowboy who showed the outsider a thing or two about . . . a thing or two.

Looking at this girl now, this bolshy wee bint, he thinks it might feel nice to rustle up a lesson.

'Alright hen?' he says.

Nancy stretches the pink gum out on a finger, then wraps it around, and around, beckoning. Callum shrugs a why-not and steps out of the departing line. He follows her across the parched grass, past the Whack-A-Mole and Pinball Wizard, past Miss Maria's tent lit up like a Hawaiian summertime. All the way to the dilapidated red caravan, where Nancy flings open the door.

'Get in,' she says.

Well, Callum's not about to take orders, not fucking likely, but then Nancy's past him and on the bed, her catsuit peeling off like a red gash, a Glasgow smile. It falls to the floor. She lies in front of him, a hot little streak of nakedness, and he steps inside.

Nancy is feeling terrific. Post-performance, she has the whole energy of the funfair inside her: firing around, lighting up scorecards. Her body is ringing and snapping back into place, the punchball and the fist at once. The adrenaline's almost enough to blast through the pain of her dislocated bones. She moves to him, feline and feral. Then the man is on the bed and she's astride his lap.

Nancy closes her eyes. The man's tongue is hot wax. His palms are sandpaper.

The taste he leaves in her mouth is burned underbrush left fifteen months to rot.

When they kiss, it's like she's dipped her clit in battery acid. The burning spreads up her guts and crawls out of her throat. When she probes his mouth with her tongue, sparks explode against the metal fillings of his molars.

She can't stop wriggling. She can't wait for him to get it up inside her. Fast and hot and violent, but a pretty kind of violence, a nuclear bomb in a field of jasmine, so all the petals leap up and ignite in the air, the reek of perfume and gunpowder. Nancy grabs his shoulders and slams herself against him. The man shudders like Frankenstein's Monster, the moment where lightning strikes and life ignites. Her hand is already on one butt cheek. Her hand is spreading them and working a slick finger inside. The man keens and thrashes and Nancy meets every movement, their bodies snapping together like clapperboards sounding ACTION, ACTION, START THE REEL.

When she comes, butterflies explode out her ass.

Afterwards, they slump under a cloud of post-coital haze, butterflies clattering against the lightbulb.

'That was . . .' says Callum McAllister, then he puts both palms on his face. The insects shrivel and wither and fall to the ground.

Nancy snaps her knickers on, runs a hand through her hair so it sticks up in a mullet. She's electric. When she feels like this, Nancy could vault the Empire State or strangle a panther. It's incredible. But the feeling never lasts, and so it's terrifically important to do what needs to be done while her adrenaline is spiked. She drops to all fours and crawls to him like a cat. She tilts her head. 'Do you want to feel like this all the time?' she whispers in his ear.

Callum twitches and considers. Like this. Like the man, the fucking man, like a thousand hands clapped on shoulders, a chant rising to climax, the ball in the top corner of the net. A flat palm on a mouthy bird, a bomb dropped on some foreign cunts, a hiss in the ear saying *That's* what *you* get, that's what you get, that's what you *get.*

'Yeah,' he says, his eyes closed, head loose and dreamy against the pillow. 'Yeah, doll, that sounds capital.'

'If you insist.' Nancy pulls out the drawer under her bed. She paws through a stack of dirty Victorian postcards, jars filled with armpit hair, a pair of pinking shears. The bottom of the drawer is dusty with used staples and rolling tobacco. Dirt sticks to the patches of spit and spunk on her palms. She reaches right in to the back and grasps what she's looking for.

The man in the bed isn't paying attention. He's drifting in and out of a nap. His dick, curled against the snarled hair on his stomach, looks like a moth's cocoon.

Nancy finds the extension cable and inserts the plug.

'It's scientific, really.' Her voice is soft, almost curious. She might as well be talking to herself. 'When you were a kid, you know none of your skull bones were fused together? Back when your brain had space to breathe.'

Callum snorts and burrows back into his dream.

'They found the same thing happening all over the world. Different societies, way far apart. Which makes you think, there must be something in it.' Nancy allows herself a Cheshire Cat kind of grin. If you turned out all the lights, her teeth would be floating above the bed. 'Enlightenment, they say. Visions, understanding, all that jazz.'

She straddles him. It's tricky to get her balance, with the weight of the drill in her hand, but she squeezes her thighs tight. Callum's hands drift on to her legs.

'Ah, sweetheart, give an old man a chance to reload before we go again, eh?'

She looks down at his ridiculous body, sprawled and stinking up the sheets, and shudders. 'Don't be *disgusting*.' She loves screwing, of course she does. But in the time after, the thought of touching them is repulsive. The magical temptation of grossness is long gone. 'Now hold still.'

Callum opens his eyes at the same moment the drill rattles into life. 'What the fuck?!' He starts to thrash but Nancy's thighs grip tighter.

'Jesus, I said, hold still! Do you want this going all the way through to the meat?'

Something in the word *meat* makes him freeze. He presses his head back into the pillow and watches with huge cross-eyes as the drill bit finds the spot on his forehead. The noise is incredible: a roar like a tsunami. Flecks of blood and skin spatter Nancy's arms. A thousand synapses fire and misfire: *run, fight, ball, attack, run.* His limbs weigh as much as mountains. And he watches, helpless, as this little bitch drives the drill into his head.

Then comes her favourite moment, that soft little *thock* as the skull gives way. A circle of bone the size of a ten pence piece plops out. His brain stops fighting, lets out a sigh it didn't know it had been holding. And the colours come –

pink, turquoise and a sweet, swirling lilac. Callum closes his eyes.

Nancy sews up the hole with neat little stitches. She's humming under her breath, an old song about snitches and what do they get? The bandage she wraps around Callum's skull immediately blooms with a fat red rose. She isn't worried. That's what scalp wounds do – all that blood flow to the brain – but her surgical technique is impeccable. It'll stop soon, it just needs to coagulate.

He's already coming round when the door flings open and Gloria the Teller waltzes in. She takes one look at the drill and the bandages, at the man trying to sit up.

'Nancy!' she says. 'What on earth is going on?'

Callum looks from one to the other, a dumbstruck smile lolling across his lips.

Nancy rolls her eyes. 'It's fine, Gloria. Really. Look how much nicer he is.'

'It's not fine!' Gloria presses her fingers to her temples for a moment. Her face contorts. Then she grabs the clothes from the floor and flings them at him. 'Here. Get dressed.'

He holds his shirt up like it's the Turin Shroud. 'Thank you,' he says. 'No, really – *thank* you.'

'You're welcome,' says Nancy.

Callum looks at the light falling through the caravan window. There are motes of dust suspended in a sunbeam and he's seen this before, seen it in a movie. These floating bits of dirt mean that everything is really beautiful. He tilts his head and the blood somersaults and he beams. 'Have you ever thought about the world?' he says. 'I mean, really? You know, it's bloody brilliant.'

'For fuck's sake,' says Gloria.

Nancy can't hide her snort of laughter. But Gloria's not smiling. Her hands have tightened into fists.

'Come on, go.'

Callum wanders out the door. He's thinking how it might feel to lie on the mount, watching the clouds pass by, naming his favourite ones after dinosaurs. When the wind changes and his plesiosaurus turns to meaningless fluff, there'll be a loss, but he'll soon get over it. There are so many other miracles. Magnets, for instance. Seeds, or bumblebees.

But Nancy, ah Nancy. She yanks out the plug and shoves the drill back in the drawer. Takes the sheet from the bed and togas it around herself, and shoots Gloria a look. 'A bit of privacy?'

The look her mother shoots her suggests Gloria is not to be fucked with. 'Clothes on. Now.'

Nancy changes gleefully. She looks out the window, where the sun is still high and hot. Not even twilight yet, and look at everything she's achieved for the day! Finally, things are moving in the right direction.

'Goddammit!' says Gloria. She slams a hand on Nancy's altar. Tiny jars and dog teeth leap into the air and fall back down. The Tower floats lazily to the floor: a card of lightning bolts and cascades, all the plans and the people falling. 'Can't you see?'

Nancy turns to her, eyes wide, the last of her sex magick still thrumming. She can, of course. She can see everything.

A BAD RECEPTION

'COME WITH ME!' Gloria yanks Nancy out. She thunders towards Mr Partlett's performance tent, hand clamped tight around her daughter's wrist, hair billowing in a great flame. She can feel it in her insides, a compass being yanked off course. Organs full of the ancestors screaming. Nancy lets herself be pulled. She doesn't say a word. When Gloria turns to her, she just lifts her hand and sniffs, a small, mocking smile playing across her lips.

'Get in there.' Gloria throws the tent flap open and pushes Nancy through. The girl saunters inside.

Gloria's hands are hot. The skin might start to blister. She wants to get Nancy away from herself, get her somewhere public, before the furies really take hold. Gloria doesn't want to do anything she'll regret. The voices are loud as fire.

Give me a moment, she thinks. Just a moment, just to shut them up.

She closes her eyes and counts to three. Thinks of the belt, the ropes, the glowing ember of the cigarette. Gloria holds one hand to her throat and tightens it, just a smidge, until it hurts to swallow. The voices don't stop, but they quieten. She squeezes harder and a choke blooms. The voices are further now – it's like listening through glass. Or a crackling phone line, a surprisingly bad reception from visiting area to prison room. She holds for one more moment then lets go, takes a deep, rattling breath.

All Gloria knows is that this little game of Nancy's wasn't the best idea. Everything had been rushing forward, plans streaming, intentions angled towards a single purpose. Preparations for the following week when they'd leave in the night like a magic trick, and the town would wake to find the children gone. It was working, seductions taking hold. But now it's all slipped off course. They need to sort it out. Get everything back on track before it's too late.

But her daughter has never cared about any of Gloria's carefully laid plans. All her life, Nancy's seen a track as a challenge, a line to push things off. And if it wasn't for that unfortunate bedrock of fierce motherly love she's never been able to shake, Gloria would be first in line to wring her daughter's troublesome little neck.

Then she steps into the tent and all the words fall out of her head.

'Hello darling,' says Gretchen Etcetera. She's in a latex nurse uniform, hypodermic needle in hand. Shona Peterson's sat in a medical chair, feet in stirrups. A batty grin on her face. Various implements litter the table: a screwdriver, pliers, a scalpel blade. Glue.

'We're just preparing for the surgery.' Gretchen gestures dramatically at her patient. 'Madame here's requested we find her inner freak.'

Nancy folds her arms and presses her tongue into her cheek. She looks at Gloria pointedly.

'Aye,' Shona says. 'I've always thought an upgrade would be pure brilliant.'

Gretchen rummages through the implements, picking

and discarding things with a flick of her hand. 'But what's it to be? Scarification? Subdermal implants? Tongue bifurcation, give you the snaky mouth of your dreams?'

Shona pouts. 'Can you no go bigger? A bonus limb, special delivery? Or a tail, Pritt-sticked direct on my arse there . . .'

Gloria doesn't have time for this now, when the future's hurtling towards them. Time is so short. July is running out like the last grains of sand, August will be here any moment. And there's a roughly bandaged man stumbling back to a fragile town, a smile plastered across his face. A most dangerous kind of happiness.

'Girls!' she shouts.

They stop and turn to her.

'Mr Partlett. Where is he?'

Gretchen opens her palms. Shona peers to the rafters, as if he might be lurking there. Nancy just examines her fingernails lazily, not one single care in the world. And all the while, the future gets closer. Then the tent hushes open again, and Mr Partlett steps inside.

'Gloria.' His voice is grave, understanding, but not without a twitch of humour. He moves carefully and with two steps he is beside her, placing a hand over hers. 'What happened?'

In the comfort of his papery touch, Gloria exhales. She turns to Nancy, still slumped on one hip, looking for all the world like the teenager that she is. And then the voices shriek back into her skull. *FUCKED IT UP! FUCKED IT UP!* Like the worst howl of hangover anxiety, like all the mornings after. The voices refuse to specify exactly how it's wrong, which only makes it worse. It could be anything and everything at once.

'Gloria!' says Mr Partlett, more sharply this time. The sound sends the recriminations rattling around her brain. They shatter into tiny pieces and fall to the earth. She takes a breath in the quiet. Sighs.

'This one –' she tilts her head at Nancy – 'thought it would be a nice idea to drill a hole in a man's skull.'

Gretchen snorts. Shona's eyes grow wide.

'It *was* a good idea,' Nancy says.

Mr Partlett tents his fingers together. 'Oh dear. And he's dead?' There's no tone of regret, just a tinge of curiosity.

'No! He's fine.' Nancy steps forward, taking centre stage. 'It was one of them who did Louie in. So I drilled him. Gave his brain room to breathe. He'll be nicer now. You *know* that.'

Gloria nods reluctantly. She's read the literature, knows what good a trepanning can do. Has considered it herself, once or twice.

'So what's the problem?' Mr Partlett asks. 'There *is* a problem, isn't there?'

Gloria nods again. It's hard to trust her voice. Open her lips and all those other voices are bound to come rushing over. And this new pain in her chest, spearing through. 'The plan was set,' she says. 'Everything was working out. We're supposed to be luring them in, not giving them ammunition to drive us away!'

'And we still will,' Nancy says. 'Whatever.'

But Gloria shakes her head. 'I don't know,' she says at last.

Mr Partlett tilts his head. 'What's wrong?'

She closes her eyes and presses her hands on her ears. It does nothing. The voices rise and overlap, thrashing upon each other like hectic shoals of fish. Their wet bodies glisten and thud against the deck of the boat. They pound so hard the wooden beams will break. No matter how she concentrates, things refuse to take shape. All she can feel is the energy, thick and black and gagging her lungs. The voices don't sound like they're about to be set free.

'There's an anger,' she says. 'A fury. An eye for an eye and a tooth for a tooth. Things are out of balance, things are coming back.'

On the last word, her voice cracks and she erupts into a fit of coughing. There's something caught in her throat, or deeper: a scream in her lungs. Every word from the ancestors is a difficult birth. A lump comes up. She spits into her silk handkerchief and it comes away crimson.

Gloria can feel it coming, fat and bright as a harvest moon. She can't stop it. It might be the end. The ancestors are enraged. And what's worse – she can't tell where the anger is pointed. Whether it's at the town, for the history, everything that's been done. Or whether it's at the Freakslaw, for getting their hopes up and failing. Gloria crumples the handkerchief into a ball before the others can see.

'Trouble,' she says.

All the while, inside her, the ancestors scream.

OFF THE BUS

CALLUM MCALLISTER WALKS down Main Street, whis-tling. It's a tune from when he was wee, when his ma took him to the theatre see the Singing Kettle (who came com-plete, no joke, with spout, handle *and* lid of metal). What a show! That kettle had some weird songs, though. One about a ghost fae Dundee who skelped a polisman on the chin. Another where naebody could believe John went to bed at night without pyjamas on. And the song that's stuck in his head now, about who in your family it's legit okay to chuck off a moving bus. Not your ma's ma, apparently (her being your ma's ma and important and all), but everyone else? Fair game. Even your da's ma. He disnae quite get it, but the world's full of things like that.

Callum's not thought of that kettle for fucking ages. But ever since he had blinding sex with the crazy bint, since she took the drill to him, he's been feeling like a kid. It's weird. But it's also a relief. He didnae ken how much effort it was to lug about all that fury until it was gone. Now, his feet could dance. All together now: *Oh you cannae push your granny* . . .

Callum stumbles a clumsy two-step. He touches his fore-head, where the bandage is still tied. She did a neat job too, he'll give her that. He was so pissed off with the drill at first and now all of it seems a wee bit unnecessary. The feeling's far away. It's a beautiful Sunday – the sun looking pure fucking brilliant in the sky – and Callum McAllister's off to the pub.

Fantastic.

When he reaches the Skene Dhu, Callum feels a funny twinge in his guts. Like a reminder: Callum, you left the gas on. Callum, you big gype, you forgot to lock the front door. But it's not those things, he knows it's not. It's probably nothing. He waits to see if the feeling will get any thicker but then it disappears. The song is back, his heart is light! He pushes open the pub door and steps inside.

'What the fuck happened to you, mate?' says Greg Haskett. He's stood at the bar with the lads: Boyd and Jim and Lewis. They burst into matching laughter.

'You get in a barney with your bird?'

'Aye, come on, like Callum's got a bird! It'll be his own right palm that took a disliking to him.'

'That or the toilet bowl.'

'I'll bet he was pure bleezin.'

'Alright, alright,' says Callum. He's smiling, a glut of love welling up inside. Not that he'd say that – he's not gonna sound like a total poof – but it's there. 'Who wants a pint?'

'Thought you'd never ask.'

He squeezes through, raises a hand to Bev. 'Five pints of the seventy.'

'Make mine a lager,' says Lewis. 'That seventy tastes like warm pish.'

'You'd know? You been drinking warm piss again?'

'Aye, shut your face.'

Callum feels a sappy elation cross his face. He takes a sip and he knows that Lewis is a total eejit, and it doesn't matter.

It tastes incredible, like off-the-hook good. He takes a second sip, a third. This is the drink of the gods, Ambrosia, Devon, whatever they called that custard. His Adam's apple bobs, delighted.

'You thirsty?' says Greg.

Callum looks down at his glass, which is somehow empty. 'I guess I am,' he says. 'Another?'

That's how it starts. And the way it goes on is how it always goes on: one pint becomes two pints becomes three, five, nine. Who can tell? Not Callum. Callum knows a few things at this point and all of them for sure. This beer is delicious. This pub is the best. His friends are good lads. That bird did him a favour. He's got better at noticing since yesterday, way better, and he sees this all at once. He's lucky, like. If only everyone could be as lucky as him.

Callum swallows another pint of the world's most perfect beer and gazes at Jim Barrie, who's sunk in a mournful slump over a packet of scampi fries. Poor Jim, thinks Callum. He's always been a quiet one, that long Eeyore face, convinced the world's out to get him.

Then Jim looks up and meets Callum's eyes. 'What's the grin aboot, McAllister?'

'Ah, nothing.' Callum smiles even wider and spreads his hands. 'It's all good.'

Jim snorts. 'Like fuck.'

Lewis leans over, sloshing beer, his own grin wet and loose. 'He's got a secret under there! You ever see him like this?'

'Aye? That it, Callum?'

Callum shakes his head. He's not going to say a thing. There's a tiny, smart part of him – deep down, smothered beneath the beer and the banter – that knows to explain would be a bad idea. He saw what happened with Doreen and the scarf, how quick a temper can get out of hand. Heck, he's seen it in Pitlaw for ever. Folk here kick off at the slightest. Still, the knowledge is bright inside him. It's like having a crush, all you want to do is say her name, squeeze it into the conversation. Callum giggles.

'See what I'm saying?' Lewis reaches to Callum's bandage, makes like he's going to whip it right off.

'Leave off!' He bats him away. But this just encourages Lewis, who's dumped his pint and is coming with both grabby, tickle-monster hands. Callum slaps at him helplessly. He can feel the blood in his skull, thudding against the bone. Any minute now, it's gonna spurt.

'Under there! Under there!'

'Alright!' he says at last. 'If I tell you, will you shut up?'

Lewis drops his hands and smirks. 'Aye. No need to make a big deal of it.'

So he tells the story. Which is a good story, it is. He gets so into it he barely looks up. He's spreading his palms, gesticulating to explain. When he gets to the bit about the anger, welling up inside him, he chuckles. Like can you believe it? It's pure shite.

'And then she only went and did it. Put the bit against my forehead and drilled.'

There's a moment of stunned silence where the magnitude of what's he's said sinks in, and then –

'She did WHAT?'

Jim's voice is a roar. A silence falls over the pub. Greg stops dead on his way from the bog, fingers jimmying at his fly. Boyd pauses, pint halfway to his mouth, and Lewis's cheeks pouch like he's about to do a comic spit take.

Callum shuts up. There's a part of him racing ahead, still convinced this story was an okay idea. Lewis will piss himself laughing, even Jim'll smile. But then, with the words out and un-take-back-able, that confidence seems fucking nuts.

'She DRILLED a HOLE in yer SKULL?'

'What's that?' Greg stalks over, plants himself in front of them. Callum can see the red blotches creeping up his neck, the way they do when he's angry or drunk, which end up the same thing often enough.

'Some wee bint at the funfair.' Jim's voice is the size of an artic lorry, pelting down the motorway. 'Callum's getting his end away and what does she do? Takes a power tool to him! He's lucky he's got any brains left.'

'It wasnae—'

'Oh, the funfair?' That's Boyd started now. 'I told you cunts about that . . . funfair.' He slams his pint down on the bar. It slops over the edge, but he pays it no mind. 'That place is a fucking monstrosity.'

'A drill? In your heid? Jesus Christ, Callum!' Lewis looks impressed as he slaps Callum on the back. 'And you're down here getting a round in rather than fannying off to the hospital? That's no bad, that is.' The smack is heavy with respect. It's the mark of every Scottish bloke who'd rather die than do anything as wet as see a doctor. It's taking an anvil to the head and shrugging it off with an ibuprofen. It's pissing blood and flushing twice to hide the evidence. Lewis pounds his back and Callum takes it, he says, 'Aye, it's fine, I'm alright' – and maybe the moment will pass like this. Because it *is* fine. He's better than alright, he's doing great. He beams at Lewis and Lewis nods back.

'Another round?' says Callum.

And then Boyd slams his fist down and all the glasses leap and shimmy. In the beer puddles, a rippling ring like that bit in *Jurassic Park*. Callum looks with horror. The big dinosaur is coming. It's heard them.

'It's not ALRIGHT,' Boyd says. 'You think that's alright? It's all hunky fucking dory?' His face scrunches into a ball. 'Some of us have kids, you know. My Derek's been down there. You happy to think of that kind of shite going on? Attacking Callum like that, what's next like?'

Greg's face darkens. 'They're asking for something, eh? Those cunts.'

The others – who don't have kids and don't care what shite happens down there – shrug uselessly. Callum holds his breath. Jim twirls his empty glass.

'What about that pint then?' he says.

'Aye,' says Callum desperately. 'Another round, mate.' And the drinks come back and the moment passes, although Boyd's still scowling and Greg's oddly quiet, he can almost hear the tick tick tick in his furrowed brow.

'So,' Lewis's hand comes crashing down on Callum's back, 'was she worth it? A good bit of stuff?'

'Oh aye,' says Callum. 'Pure magic.'

He sips his drink, and fuck if it doesn't taste good.

TIGHTENED LIKE A TRAP

WHILE THE MEN are in the pub, Derek's out in the sunshine on the dirt road down by the factory. He's got his head down, staring at rocks, but his thoughts are warm and squidgy. He's replaying a day that's never far from his mind.

The hitch in his throat as Zed's hand wrapped around it. The smell of their sweat, spiced and salty, a tang of burned onions. The softness of *that* skin, the softest thing he'd ever drawn a thumb across, but hard too, and hot, and *alive*.

A month since it happened and Derek thought time was supposed to make memories fade, so how come this one's only got more vibrant? How come whenever he gets Zed on his mind it's so real Derek can practically taste him? It doesn't make sense. Derek's starting to think the only way he'll shake it is if he goes back and sees him again, never mind that it's a terrible idea, never mind that it'll only fling open a whole load of doors that are best kept closed.

It's cos he's got his head down that he doesn't notice them. Jack Haskett and Steven McLeod, and the other boys who are always turning the Bunsen burners on in chemistry, who've got a black eye in their pocket for anyone who'd grass them up.

'Oi. What you looking at there, Geddes?'

The voice breaks through a perfect daydream where Zed's

hand is drifting up Derek's thigh, coming to rest somewhere around his—

'I *said*, what you looking at? You looking at me, are ye?'

Derek's heard this question before, once or twice, but he hasn't worked out the magic reply. The get-out-of-jail-free answer.

As for the question: the logic is perfect, infallible, Catch-22. It's the smartest thing he's ever heard from the mouth of Jack Haskett. There's no wiggle room. Either the answer's 'nothing' – in which case the response comes quicker than vomit, 'So you're calling me a liar then?' – or the answer's 'you' – in which case the response is going to be something along the lines of 'You fucking poof' or maybe, 'You trying to start something, like?', or perhaps just a slow incredulous smile across the face of Jack Haskett, a Rottweiler promised the gift of paperboys to fling bloodily across the lawn, again and again and again. So Derek says the only true answer he can think of: 'I don't know.'

'You don't know?' The boys look at each other with delight. 'He doesn't know!'

'You thinking about something nice, Derek?' That's Steven McLeod, who's always making fart noises in music class, who once waited until Mr Wright snuck to his office for a coffee halfway through German, then soaked six tampons in cherryade and left them floating in sad puddles all over his desk.

Mr Wright hadn't punished anyone, didn't even attempt to find out who it was. That was the worst thing. He'd just looked at the desk and sighed, then swept everything into a plastic bag. Asked them to do page seventeen of the exercises while he got a cloth. It would have been better if he'd yelled.

But that sigh said *This is your problem, not mine* and the infinite weariness behind it tightened like a trap round Derek's neck. A trap for boys who never got out – he could hear, in that sigh, that Mr Wright had already given up on them all. It wasn't worth yelling. It was already, for each and every one of them, too late.

'I'm . . .' Derek says. 'I don't.'

They can think he's stupid. That's not so bad – someone too stupid to be worth bothering.

'Where you headed, Derek?' Steven falls into step, like they're about to start a cèilidh. His arm claps on Derek's shoulder and he can see, from the corner of his eye, the gouge in the back of Steven's hand. They all have them from playing 99ers, a simple game, just drag the metal compass back and forth across your skin. If you can last ninety-nine times, you're a real tough guy. You're in the club and septic-sored. Derek's own hands are soft, the backs are smooth.

'I . . .' he says.

'Ye dinnae ken?'

'Ah,' he says.

Derek's mind is flailing wildly with half-truths and hopes. There's nowhere good to lead this group, not into a quiet dark place, not to his house, not to the shop where the world could watch him getting it: what he deserves.

But it's as if there's something in him that delights in picking the worst of all options. It can smell disaster and, for once, wants to be the small-town queer in the high-class boots, prancing wildly with smeared eyelids, yelling, 'Come on then, darling!' while a cigarette droops from his lips. The one who ends up bleeding out, who's lit a spotlight on his secret self for bad news to gather round.

'I'm going to the funfair.' The words hang in the air like a bad fart. But surely the funfair's just a steaming great pile of shite? Kid's play. Loserville. He wills them to laugh; he'd take any smack in the face over what he realizes is about to happen.

'You going to take us with you, then.' It's phrased like it could be a question, but Derek knows it isn't, not even a little bit. Shit.

And so he leads them to the place of all those red-velvet dreams. It's just as he remembers, a wild Technicolor tumble that makes him giddy. As they walk through the midst of everything, Derek tries to understand how this happened. Maybe it's just worth taking the piss out of. Maybe he is. Or maybe the funfair's got its fingernails under the town's skin, and even the ones who don't care about anything can't help but get a little snagged.

Because fuck, is he snagged. Fuck, he came back and now he's not sure he remembers how to leave.

'Over there,' says Jack, pushing Derek a half-step ahead. 'Let's get to that, eh?'

Of course they'd pick that one. The Tilt-A-Whirl. The big one, the one that whirls your universe round the centrifugal, the one where he's got no chance of keeping his lunch down. The one he can see, even from all the way over here, is manned by a boy with sticky-up hair and sticky-out lips, and the longest fingers he's ever held.

Of course it's Zed. And just the sight of him makes Derek's stomach turn over itself, stupid little butterflies flap flap flapping their wings. He wants to do something unthinkable to that mouth, but he can't, of course – not in front of these boys, and not away from them either, not again (or can he? He can't. Can he?).

As they walk closer, Derek's practising ways to make his face say: I didn't mean it, it wasn't me, don't open the door to them. If you get the chance? Run run run.

It's a lot of different emotions in a single grimace, and it's not worth shit because the moment Zed looks up, Derek's smile spreads over him, erupting like a big stupid sore.

'Derek!' says Zed. And Derek can't really regret anything, because for one lovely moment, Zed's face is as warm and open as a box of party tricks. 'You came back.'

Derek loses his breath. Zed can tell what's happening here, right? He's been up and down the country plenty. He surely knows the difference between boys that want to explore the secret magic of soft skin, and boys that want to smash your face in for thinking about it. It's not so subtle. These are the ones that don't like limp-wrist types (although limp wrist has got to be the worst kind of misnomer – nothing that happened in that hot-pink caravan was limp, was it?).

'A'right?' It's Jack who hisses that – Jack, whose eyes are a little too close together, in a way that only happens to boys who are a certain kind of cruel. As if always looking pure raging will eventually cause the cartilage to break down, make your eyes creep closer and closer until you end up as some kind of Cyclops. It's a known fact you never see a nice boy with eyes like that.

'We're here for a go on the Tilt-A-Whirl. Ain't that right?'

'Absolutely,' says Zed, and though he's talking to the boys he keeps beaming over at Derek, like he just can't believe they're both really here. 'You got your tokens?'

'No.'

Zed doesn't react. Derek would flinch, start grappling for answers and excuses, but Zed just smiles that slow lizard grin again, the one that isn't committed to anything.

'Go get them then. Your carriage will await!' He waves a hand towards the booth. None of them moves a muscle.

'Nah.'

They're quiet. The quiet is a thing that moves between the boys, not sticking to anyone, resting in the gaps. It's more threatening, somehow, than yelling or fists. Derek can hear it getting bigger, like they learned in geography, the beach before the tsunami, when the sea dredges back and every-thing's exposed.

And then Jack Haskett nudges Derek under the ribs. His elbow's a sharp stick with bad promise, and Derek doesn't like it, not one bit.

'You going to let him speak to us like that, Derek?'

(Like what like what like what?)

'You going to let him tell us what to do?'

'Hey,' says Derek. He can't raise his gaze right now, can't possibly look Zed in the eye. 'Come on. This is stupid anyway. Why don't we go . . . get a drink?' He can hear the begging dripping over everything, leaving it wet and weak, ready to dissolve.

'Oh yeah, he'd like that, wouldn't you?' Jack's pointing at Zed now, pointing with that sharp mean finger. 'We're not good enough to have a go on your fancy ride, is that it?'

Zed doesn't laugh out loud, which is something. But it's there, he can't help letting it flicker – Zed's clearly got the kind of face that spells out every cute crush and swallowed snigger, the kind you could read fortunes in, the kind that's never *ever* been able to keep a grin behind its gums.

'Ah, it's funny that, is it?'

'It *is* fancy!' says Zed. 'Been with us since the very beginning. That's real wrought iron, you know. Genuine!' Then, as
the lads refuse to entertain as much as a smile, he changes
tack. 'Hey, come on, we're cool. Okay?'

He doesn't get it. Derek can hear that; Zed might think he
knows what he's doing but he doesn't know Jack Haskett. The
Jack Hasketts of this world are never cool, and there's nothing
to be gained from telling them anything. Derek has learned,
from long and bitter experience, that it's best to avoid them
entirely, and he'd tell Zed this except Zed would have been
avoiding Jack, would have been fine, had Derek not led the
wolf right to his door.

'Don't tell me what we are.' Jack's voice has changed. It's
thicker, there's something pushing it forward with gleeful
palms, and Derek can hear the chain clink as the Rottweiler
strains. Derek knows – just *knows* – that Jack Haskett wants
to let that dog out. He won't bat an eyelid when it runs ram-
page, leaving everything shredded and bloodstained in its
wake.

The boys are around Zed now, stepping closer, and there's
a frantic slapping in Derek's chest. It's the feeling he gets in
football crowds, the smell of testosterone and angry muscle,
full up to here with no-fucking-place-to-go and cashless-on-
Fridays, needing to take it out on something, and Derek just
knows that he himself is that something, the rabbit to sink
their teeth into.

'Aye, this guy thinks he's the fuckin' boss of what's what.
You like that, Derek? You and your mate getting together and
seeing what's cool?'

The way he says it. The word 'mate' like what animals do,

like Steven can see right through Derek and everything he let happen. The disgust dripping off it. But Derek's not going to react. He's not like his da. He doesn't get angry, and if a feeling does come that's bigger than he can handle, Derek just closes his eyes and waits for it to go away. So that's what he does, he breathes, and—

'Aw, look at that, is our wee lad about to start bawling?'

(It's not tears. It's something worse, something darker, gathering like storm clouds in his guts.)

'He's no! Oh my god, you absolute homo.'

(Shut up shut up shut up.)

'That why you wanted to bring us here? You some kind of poof trying to get us alone?'

'Urgh gross!'

It's his dad's voice he hears in that moment. The one that says if anyone saw who he really was, they'd be horrified. He's a fucking embarrassment – and worse, a fucking queer.

That's when he does it. He feels his fist tighten while the voices get louder and he can't even tell what they're saying any more. He draws his arm back, or maybe it draws itself back – he's not sure what's his intent and what's the will of something else.

The ancestors writhe. Dark forces rise up from the soil, sucking him down, snaring him to repeat the same furies as have always been part of this place.

Derek looks up at Jack with his fist high in the air and Jack stares back, dead in the eye, because Jack's not scared, course not, he's got no reason to be. Maybe that's what makes the next thing happen. The thought of being not scared, just for a moment, and how that might taste.

His eyes flick to Zed. This boy – this careless, beautiful

boy – who'd have Derek believe that you can just go around following *impulses* all the time, that there's no retribution for listening to your heart. As if it could ever be that easy! He has no idea, no *fucking* idea what it actually means to be Derek, the impossibilities of his world. Up to your neck in shit and forever sinking deeper.

He doesn't realize he's doing it. It's not a conscious decision. But something deep in Derek's bones whirls his fist around, even as he's thinking he wants to stop, to leave, to be anywhere but here.

And when it makes contact with Zed's cheekbone, something in Derek's heart cracks a little bit.

He feels the punch travelling all the way up his arm, tingling pins and needles, like he's been lying on it funny and all the blood's just rushing back inside.

'Fuck!' Zed reels around, clutching his face, his lovely, long-fingered hand covering it, so Derek can't see if he's bleeding or not – not that either would be good, but he didn't mean it, he didn't! He can't believe he just did that. These feelings, they're welling up all over the place, and he didn't mean it, he really, really didn't –

'Hey – shit, Zed! Are you okay? Zed, I'm sorry. I didn't—'

Zed looks up, eyes wide, a spurt of blood dribbling out his nose.

'A'right, Derek!' That's when Jack's hand claps against his back and he feels it through his shirt, all that meanness seeping on through to his skin. 'Nice work.'

Nice work. That's what he's done. A job on Zed, a nice job, worked him over because Derek's a twat and a coward who couldn't tell the Jack Hasketts of the world to shove it. And now he's feeling what you get when you align yourself with these people, a hollow sickness, these fucking pins and needles running up and down his arm.

Derek stares at the ground, watching small rocks blur and congeal. He can't look Zed in the eye. He's scared if he does, he'll see something that makes him snap. The same look, maybe, that was in Mr Wright's eyes: the look that says you're not worth disappointment, I'm not even going to give you that.

And so he watches, watches as his feet move, his ankle twisting around, his foot scuffing the earth. He feels Jack's hand leave his back – or maybe it's his back leaving Jack's hand – and suddenly he's running.

Everything swells in his head. He thrashes his hands, trying to disperse the noises, but they stretch him out tight as a balloon. The laughter from behind him, and his own voice, a high-pitched keen, running the same phrase over and over, trying to force it out of his lips but getting stuck between his teeth: *I'm sorry, I'm sorry, I'm sorry.*

Stomp stomp stomp.

I'm sorry, Zed. I really, really am.

BAD GIRL

MEANWHILE, AS THE twilight fingers tug the sky, Ruth's got ants in her knickers and bees in her bonnet. She's been having weird dreams all week, scenarios that get wilder and more defined each night. In the dreams, things keep detonating like a Hollywood blockbuster movie. She wakes wanting nothing more than to throw a match over her shoulder, never looking back as the whole world explodes. No consequences, no pillar of salt.

In the month since she burned her university letter, Ruth's been waiting for regret to catch up with her. Every time she checks, it turns out she still doesn't give a fuck. Here she is, careening through life without the fixed path that's guided her every action until now. Here she is, racketing off the rails.

If she thinks about it too much, she can feel the beating of black bat wings of panic. The question in her mouth: what the fuck happened to her? How did she get like this, how did things change so fast? But the thought of caring about the things she used to is impossible. All there is to reckon with is the delirious presence of the right now.

Ruth keeps seeing herself in credit-sequence slo-mo. She sits on the bed and drags her fingernails up and down her calves. What would feel really good? Like, what would feel totally the best?

What she wants to do is check into a hotel and take a

room on the thirteenth floor and unplug the television and pitch it out the window and hold her breath all the way down until the thing explodes.

BOOM!

The shatter of glass, the detonation of the inner tube, scraps of wire flying through the sky.

Thinking about how terrific it would feel, her cunt twitches. *Bad girl*, she whispers, and the promise is delicious. There's only one problem: there are no multi-storey hotels in Pitlaw, no skyscrapers, no windows from which to pitch. In the other room, the TV is blaring *Gladiators* and Stephanie would definitely notice if Ruth tried to unplug it and run away.

So *think*. There must be something else. Ruth chews her lip. Sees herself running down Main Street, baseball bat clutched tight, smashing the windows one by one: CRASH. BANG. WALLOP.

But this, too, is a lie. She's not American, for Christ's sake. She doesn't own a baseball bat. She doesn't own bats of any sort, except for those ping pong bats in the garage, and she can't see herself putting those through a plate of glass.

It's impossible. The impulses are so strange. A hungry alien compulsion rampaging through her veins. If she looks at them too closely, they're terrifying, so she closes her eyes and lets them wash over. One hand drifting towards her underwear, thinking of that night. The bruise on her hipbone should have healed ages ago but she's kept it ripe by digging a thumb in every night. Here's the blue-eyed man in the muscle vest again, as she moves her hand in herself. If she'd ever known his face, it's long gone: what's left is the memory of the memory of the memory. That, and the clatter in her jaw as he threw her against the ground.

She clatters her own jaw again and it's exciting but also the worst. It's not enough. Lying here and wanking, staying stuck, never once throwing a TV out a window and fuck that, really? Fuck it.

Ruth lifts her fingers away. She pulls down her shirt. Without thinking about where she's going or what she's planning, she latches her jeans and slips her black leather jacket over her shoulders. Tugs her Converse on and she's already outside. She doesn't even take her bike, just starts running. The slap against the pavement is good. A reverberation up her legs. Past the poplar trees, past the supermarket, past Mr Dorothy walking his dazed little dog.

And then she reaches Main Street where all the windows wink and flutter in the dying light. She doesn't have a baseball bat and she doesn't need one. Of course not. She's her own weapon. Her body is an axe.

In the back of her throat, a scream surfaces – rising up too fast, she knows, you can't come up that fast, it's going to give her the bends. But the scream whoops out of her and into the night. She waits for someone to scream back, to stop her, but there's no one. The street is dead. The main street of town, nine thirty on a Sunday night with not a soul to speak of. Of course, this whole town is dead. Stuck in amber, trapped in resin. Here from today until the day they die. Is it any wonder a girl can't stand it?

Ruth thinks all of this, all at once, as she sprints, her Converse slap slap slapping on the tarmac. Shopfronts flip past like playing cards – Ladbrokes, Poundland, Sue Ryder, where the only goods are old things from dead people or cheap things that will die themselves any day. Her decision comes quick: not that one, not that one, not that one. *This.*

Ruth bends her head and goes shoulder-first into the front of Curl Up and Dye.

The window explodes. Glass flies in every direction. She twists, rolling into a ball as she does, while all around the shards fall like rain. She hits the ground and lies, curled in leather, as they spatter the pavement. It sounds like a ring pull on a shaken can of Coke. They keep falling for an epically long time.

Time stops in the glittering monsoon. Her heart keeps going. The spot where her shoulder hit the window is aflame, swarms of wasps buzzing in her ears. Her body, beneath the broken glass, already burns.

Ruth lies under the deluge and grins. It was everything she hoped for. Exactly what she needed. She waits for the sound of the burglar alarm, but there's nothing. Just dust settling to the metronome of her heart.

Eventually, she peels open her eyes. It's beautiful. The broken glass is fresh snow. She spreads her arms and grinds them back and forth, making a perfect angel.

Then she creaks gingerly to her feet, brushes the shards off, and examines her body. Through her jeans, her knee is bleeding again. She presses a finger to her cheek, and it comes away red. She's leaking, but not too much. Just enough to prove she's alive.

This is what bodies do, isn't it? They live and they leak, a reminder: I'm still here, I belong to you.

The thought makes her smile. All of a sudden, her life feels hard-earned and worthy. She stands up in the detritus, daring the world to notice her. But no one does. She's alone. Alone and alive.

Ruth brings the blood to her lips and tastes herself. Copper pennies, a metallic twinge. An adult taste, as acquired as coffee or olives. A woman who bleeds.

And she's about to start for home when another thought darts, minnow-quick, in her guts. Ruth stops. She grasps for it and it squirms out of reach, but something stays: a low, hollow terror. An unfamiliar dread.

Then, all in a rush, the thought is back: the thought of leaks, of blood, of how long has it been, how long? A sudden, unholy wonder if this is what led her here in the first place. Her subconscious screaming out for blood – because there should have been blood by now.

Ruth shakes her head. It's impossible. It can't be.

But of course it can.

She can't be.

But she is.

IF YOU FALL IN YOU'LL
MAKE IT BIGGER

DEREK PLACES A hand on the front door, wondering how he could have been such a shithead. So mean. So utterly typical. He closes his fist around the handle and a jolt of pain skitters to his elbow. The punch is still in his bones. Well, good. He deserves it.

This is why he can't have nice things – because when it comes down to it, he's no different from anyone else round here, no different from his father either. He thought he was, but he's not, and isn't that a thing to discover?

Derek thumps inside, keeping his head down. If he can just get upstairs, get to bed. It's only half nine, sure, but he's ready to put the day behind him. He's spent hours walking in circles, putting off the moment of getting home in the hope that everyone would have already got to bed. He wants to brush his teeth. Get out the taste of himself, furred disappointment, enough to turn his stomach.

He creeps through the hall to the stairs when –

'Derek, is that you?' shouts his ma. 'There's soup in the pot, come join.' Derek peers into the kitchen. She looks up from the stove, her face pink and sweated. And Derek loves her, he does, but what's she doing making soup at this time? Could they not, just once, eat like normal human beings? A meal now should be ice cream, or toast. Or chips. He could go some chips right now, that would be one thing.

'I ate already,' he says, shifting from one foot to the other.

'Aye?' says his da. 'Well, is it going to kill you to eat again with your folks?'

Not this. Not now. Derek can hear it in that voice: his da itching for a fight, itching to take his own day out on whoever has the sweet misfortune to bump into him after eight pints and whatever shite's rubbed him the wrong way.

'No,' he says.

'No what?'

'It's not. I mean, I'd love some.'

He grabs a spoon and takes a seat next to his dad. His mum wordlessly slops the broth in front of him. Pours him a lurid yellow glass of Sunny Delight. The carrots are disintegrating, the barley coated in a weird jelly substance. From the bowl, great billows of steam rise up, turning his cheeks damp and salty.

He blows on the surface. His dad starts again, about Callum, Greg, the pub, and Derek blows harder. Still, the first sip scalds his tongue. He gulps his yelp down and his dad doesn't pause. Derek swallows another spoonful. He can't taste a thing. His mouth is loud metal. By the morning, it'll be covered in tiny blisters.

Serves him right.

In his head, the same sentence keeps repeating in a grotesque sing-song: *You punched him in the face! You punched him in the face!* Chanted by a row of tiny toy soldiers. On the word *face* the army doubles in size, quadruples, sixteen times. He's so consumed with the crap of it all, he doesn't notice a word his dad's saying until he looks up and both of them are staring at him for a response.

'Well?' says his da.

Well. *A well's a well, a river's a river, if you fa in you'll mak it bigger.* That's what his dad says, and fucked if he knows what it means.

'You're right.' He rubs his palms to his eyes.

'I am that. That place is no good, you hear? Bunch of degenerates. Dangerous now to boot. Did I not say that when they first showed up?'

His mum places a limp hand on his arm. 'You did, Boyd.'

Derek pauses in his soup shovelling, ears prickling. Of course that's what's got his da all riled up. What else would it be?

'You haven't been gallivanting around there, have you, son?'

'The funfair?'

'No, Tescos. Of course, the bloody funfair.'

'I haven't,' Derek says, tightening his hand on his spoon. The twinge feels as close to absolution as he can muster. He never paid much attention in Sunday School, but the one thing he remembers is that God's a sucker for self-flagellation. If the Big Man can't be the one to stick the knife in, second best's that you do it to yourself.

'You'd better not. Because you know I hear things? And if you start chucking my hard-earned cash away down there, I'll be the first to find out.'

'I know.' It's impressive, really, this disconnect between confidence and reality. Derek wonders how it must feel: to be so certain of yourself, always convinced you're absolutely right. He doesn't want to grow up to be anything like his da – and he's determined he won't, despite what happened this afternoon. It was a mistake, that's all. It doesn't mean the anger lives inside him too. Does it?

'Aye. A bunch of filthy vagrants and perverts to boot. Coming round here and—'

'They're not perverts!' The words are out of his mouth before he can stop them. His ma's eyes grow saucer-wide. She reaches across the table, as if she can pluck the words from the air before his da hears them. Chuck them in the soup perhaps. Under the tablecloth. But her hands come away empty. Derek's throat is thick. 'They're alright, is all I'm saying.'

There's a silence, as the three of them digest this statement.

'They're alright?' his da says at last. And then again, louder: 'They're ALRIGHT?'

'Maybe,' says Derek.

'You haven't been down there, wouldn't know a thing, but they're alright?'

Derek winces. All of a sudden, he's sick of it all. Sick of placating his da, sick of pretending, sick of being a man when a man's such a rotten thing to be.

'Maybe they are. Maybe they're better than us, and that's what the trouble is.'

'Derek!' his mum gasps.

'Maybe we're lucky to have them. Maybe it's us who's no good, maybe it's Pitlaw, maybe the—'

And that's when his ear explodes. Someone hits a gong right beside his head and oh how it goes off: BONGGGGG! He's never heard anything so loud. His ear's suddenly hot and he's yanked off his seat, dragged across the floor. The fists come fast to his stomach, his ribs. The pain is crystal clear; he can see all the way through. For the first time in hours, Derek's not thinking of Zed, or of his own terrible self. He's just an object. Just another thing on the floor.

'Take that back.' Spit flecks across his cheeks, that sour oniony exhale. A weight comes down on his leg and his knee erupts into blackness. 'Learn a bit of respect, why don't you?' Another punch, and his cheekbone hollers.

'Oh Boyd. Okay. It's okay.' His mum's voice is gentle, so gentle. But surely any moment now it's gonna snap. 'It's okay,' she says again, and Derek almost laughs, because it's not, is it? It's so far from okay.

Then all at once, it stops.

Derek lies on the sticky linoleum. On the stove, the glop-glop-glop of the soup. His da's breath, coming in ragged tatters. A dark twinge beneath his ribs. Toast crumbs under the cabinets. Derek takes in everything: this happy family, this fucking nightmare.

'Alright,' says his da. The chair creaks as he yanks it out and sits back down at the table.

Derek closes his throbbing eye and listens to the clank of the spoon. The slurp of the soup. It's all so normal, so what's he doing lying here on the kitchen floor? He'll get up in a second. He'll sit back down at the table, and everything will be okay.

QUICKSAND

RUTH'S IN THE toilet, clutching her satchel to her chest, waiting for her hands to stop shaking. It's a precaution, that's all. A quick check to put her pulse at ease. It can't be anything else, because she had a plan and this was certainly not part of it.

Through the wall, Kayleigh is screaming again. The noise is like biting on metal and that's a good thing, surely, because if she was pregnant then she'd hear that scream and want to comfort the baby, and she definitely doesn't. If anyone needs comfort right now, it's her. Kayleigh can go bust a lung.

Ruth lets the bag slide to the floor. Getting the test was a nightmare – which is also a good thing, surely, because that means she's had her bad luck for the day. She'd walked into Boots first thing to see Mrs Mitchell and Ms Valentine from school, standing between the Slimfast and the bowel supplements, yattering about the ladies' jazz choir. Impossible to shop in front of them, she'd spent ten minutes at the Revlon shelf rubbing too-dark shades of foundation on the back of her hand until it was stained a paint-sample accordion. By then, the teachers had moved on to neutering Ms Valentine's tabby. Ruth started on the lipsticks. It was possible that they'd stand here talking for ever. There were so many subjects to exhaust.

That was when she'd heard a familiar burst of laughter

from the tills. Of course she had. Of course there were no secret pregnancy test purchases in Pitlaw. Everywhere you go there's someone who already knows your business or someone who wants to. Merrily scanning Pampers and a multipack of salt and vinegar Discos was Stephanie's friend Laura – and maybe she was able to keep a secret, but Ruth wasn't about to find out.

So where did that leave her? Only one option. And Ruth could barely believe how little time it had taken her to fall: once, a good girl; now, a thief. Heart ratcheting in her chest, she'd stomped over to where the tests were stacked, just next to the condoms in a mocking fuck-you. 'Hi dear,' Ms Valentine had cooed over the aisle and Ruth had grimaced some awkward smirk, the best she could muster. 'Nice weather,' she'd said, as her hands unzipped her satchel and rammed the box inside, and this inanity had sparked a whole new conversation about when the last time they'd had this many sunny days in a row might have been.

Under the cover of chatter, Ruth backed off, down the aisle to the exit, where she strode out of the shop trying to look more confident than she felt. This was the moment where a heavy hand would clamp down on her shoulder. She'd be pulled before the jury, made to confess. Stern-faced officials would shake her bag upside down, and the testing kit would come raining out amid grubby two pence coins and bag lint and broken biros. Hello hello, what's all this?

But nothing happened. She'd walked all the way to the end of the road, then home, and no one stopped her, no one said they were going to take it from here. Which was worse, somehow. She didn't know she was waiting to be caught until she got away.

Now, she's alone in the bathroom. The box is white and medical. The stick looks like a fat blue marker pen. Ruth has deja vu, a strange certainty she's done this before. She's seen it happen in a million movies, read this scene in too many books. This is the moment where the second line appears, and the stupid girl finds out exactly how little it takes to ruin a life.

Ruth pulls her knickers down and sits on the toilet, thighs sticky against the plastic. She angles the test between her legs and waits. Thinks of waterfalls, white-water rapids, thinks of dancing naked in a tropical monsoon. Her bladder clenches; it's holding its breath too. She stares at the ceiling. There's a crack in the plaster inching across. By the time she finally manages to piss, it'll have made it to the door. The roof will collapse. She'll drown in a flurry of white dust and the test will be knocked from her hand by wayward bricks and she'll never have to know what it says. Perhaps one will get her brain too. That would make for a simple ending.

The first drops begin to fall. A tiny spurt and then, as if it had been waiting for permission, her bladder opens and she pees all over her hand. Her piss is hot and smells like fear. Frantically, she waves the test under the gush, trying to make sure the tip gets wet. She should have done this in a jar. Is she getting it? She's getting it. She's got it.

A last spurt, and she's done.

Ruth manoeuvres the test from between her legs and holds it out with her soaked hand, waiting for the change. She wants to wash herself but she's terrified. What if she accidentally washes her pee off the stick and it says she's not pregnant and that's a lie? And she does nothing and the thing inside her grows until it's a real live human, what's she going to do then?

What's she going to do now, for that matter? It's impossible that she could be so foolish. Her, of all people. She saw what happened to Stephanie. She knows exactly how close you can get and still be sucked back down. That was the whole point of the plan. She should have known this would happen, how did she not know? They say Pitlaw girls are super fertile, it's something in the water, but she knows the truth. The town is a quicksand: the more you struggle, the faster it swallows you. Try too fast to howk a leg out and the earth will crush your limbs.

And so Ruth watches with a sick horror as the test changes. It's a mirage. She blinks.

The second line waves up at her. Hello, Ruth. Something squirms in her guts. She wants to scream, hang up the phone, stop this revelation. But she can't. The call is coming from inside the house.

She is so incredibly screwed.

WHAT'S FAIR

BY THE FUNFAIR gate, June Geddes stands beneath a row of creaking wooden teeth, her heart looping frantically. The moon is fat and yellow, leering down, and if Boyd wakes to find her gone, there'll be hell to pay.

He's not going to wake though, not likely, after the drinks he downed. It's been the same for days. The whole house frozen in glass: Derek creeping around avoiding Boyd, Boyd pacing determinedly towards drunkenness. Those crumpled cans, lined up on the kitchen table, and June not saying a word. Not about that, not about anything else.

She can't take the silence any more. Something has to shatter. Things were fine before the funfair came to town – they weren't perfect by any means, gosh no, but they got by. And when the fair leaves they'll get by once more, her son will be safe. She hears Norma Murray's voice in her ear again, *Well, someone ought to go down there and talk to them.* So, here she is. She's going to. She absolutely is.

June gathers all her confidence into the clearing of her throat. She raises a hand like she's going to knock one-two on the arch, but it freezes in mid-air. A figure takes shape in the darkness. It's late and the funfair is doused in black, but there's a man, a long-legged man in a fitted suit. Coming for her, cane outstretched.

'Hello?' she says.

The man steps out of the shadows and into the light. Her gaze moves over the side of his face – skin blistered and flaking like paint on a window frame by the sea – and lands on his eyes, without wavering. Much. She may have flickered momentarily, but June Geddes is a woman who was brought up right, and no matter the strangeness, the fear uncoiling in her stomach, she's not going to recoil.

Although it's strange alright. It's not just dead skin. In fact, it seems to be alive. Like there – that big pustule, right on the cheek – isn't there something moving inside it, wet and lapping? The kind of thing that, if you were to poke a hole in it, would start gushing and never stop? June doesn't intend to poke it, mind, but her hand twitches and rises even as she isn't quite thinking and—

'Mrs Geddes,' says the man from the funfair, and he smiles. 'I was wondering when you'd drop by.'

It just doesn't make sense, June explains stutteringly over coffee and cake, sat tight in the flickering candlelight of the man's caravan, perched on the edge of some fancy velvet sofa. He'd insisted they come here – wouldn't hear a word of June's resistance – so here they are. Talking things through. June's hands quiver and she tightens them around the hot cup, blows on its slick oily surface.

God knows, she'll never sleep tonight. As if she would have anyway. She hasn't slept all week.

'So, you'll be going soon?' She can hear her voice pitching higher, forces herself to take a breath. She's here to appeal to logic – June has talked to men before, knows just how to make them feel like the big fella with the good idea. 'You can see we're just a wee town, why, surely there's not the customers left here to be worth your while? Better you head on to Banchory, or Turriff, or or . . .'

At this, the man from the funfair lets out a soft laugh. Amusement sparkles across his face. And with it, realization, so crisp and sudden she cannot believe it's taken until now to arrive. Whatever they're here for, it has nothing to do with eking out a profit from the people who cross their gate. It's something darker.

So June takes a different tack. She tells the man that the town found its equilibrium before they came along. Things were what they were. And the funfair might be a bright salve for other places, but Pitlaw's different. He couldn't possibly understand, what with being an outsider and all, but there's anger burbling in these waterways. A fat stack of dynamite with a sputtering fuse. Things are about to kick off. It's best for everyone that the funfair should leave, before it causes any more bother. Best for the town, and the funfair, both.

'Absolutely.' The man's voice is as bright and proud as the wedge of Battenberg cake sat before them. All yellow vowels and pink consonants. Fat and honest and good.

Absolutely. Yes. Though June didn't expect him to agree so quickly. Truth be told, this sudden acquiescing throws her: she'd been hurling herself into a certain tug-o-war, and now the other team's dropped their side of the rope, sending her sprawling on to her behind.

'Yes,' says the man from the funfair. 'But if we're going to make a decision like that, we ought to make a deal.' He reaches across the table and places his big hand on hers. June (to her credit) barely flinches, although she can't help noticing the man's hand is very hot. Beneath it, her own feels like a trapped animal, sweating in a cage under the sun. 'Let's work out an agreement.'

'What do you want?' she asks, making her voice firm and real.

'What's fair,' says he.

The man has three suggestions for June. She can pick what she thinks best, and the man from the funfair – the folk from the funfair, all of them – will stick to it without a whimper of complaint.

June's breath tightens. She was carried here tonight on the back of her fear, after lying awake for days, counting her options. But now she's here, alone with this man, all her certainty has vanished. Now he's spelling out *options*. Telling June she's got to choose!

It's too fast, too ridiculous. She's no authority for such a thing. No one would listen to her. Still, the man talks on.

The first option: they leave Pitlaw now. Tonight. No questions asked, no liberties taken. By the time the sun sneaks over the horizon, every last light and bauble will be packed away, the lorries on the road south. But (of course, there's a but) the fair will come back next year, and the year after that, and every year for seven years.

In a year's time, June's own son will be grown, gone, out of harm's way. You see? And it'll be so nice for the people from the funfair to have seven years to make a home, put down roots; this soil a veritable feast. Don't you think?

June doesn't want to ask what the man means by *feast*. The warm thought instead is of Derek protected. Her son, her flesh and blood. The apple and the orchard of her eye. But he's not the only one, surely, who's been taken in by those sluttish neon lights. And seven years! How can she commit Pitlaw to such a thing? Potassium and water, so they are. It's the one thing she remembers from chemistry lessons, and that sputtering purple flame is all she can think of now. The reaction is starting. Best keep these things apart, for ever and on.

So, the second option: they leave the town now. Tonight. No questions asked, no liberties taken. By the time the sun sneaks over the horizon, every last light and bauble will be packed away, the lorries on the road north. But they won't leave alone: June will go with them. Her, and every other friend who's already learned to love the fair. At the word *friend*, the man from the funfair's eyebrows twitch, and June swallows her gasp. This is what she was worried about! This! A place of temptation, a creature that eats its young.

And even if it weren't so ridiculous – utterly, completely! – she couldn't leave Derek at home with Boyd. No. Better they stay the summer, and she keeps Derek inside. She'll ask him to keep his head down, maybe even apologize. It's not his fault, she knows it's not. But it could be easier. Even if her heart breaks at the thought.

Still, there's a third choice, the man explains. She might like this one. Perhaps? For the third and final option: the funfair stays tonight. And he has one chance to show June its magic. One night. All he asks is that she go into it with an open mind, no prejudices, and take a peek. And if, after that, when the sun sneaks over the horizon she still thinks they should leave? Done. They'll go, no questions asked. Pack their bags, be gone.

Does that sound reasonable?

'One night?' says June. 'And what, I have to prove that you're—'

No, no, nothing like that. Just take a look. Just see if you like it. And once you've done that: you decide.

Well, it sounds reasonable. Certainly the best of the three. And though, if asked, June would say she'd rather they just left, the truth is she's not set against taking a wee peek. There's something about the way the fairground glows in the darkness, lights bulging in the night like the many chins of a toad: *ribbet, ribbet, ribbet*. About those Twins outside the supermarket, bathed in the sun like saints. About the man. She doesn't like him, not exactly, but she can't help feeling a swell of respect. The sudden strange presence of these folks in Pitlaw has unlocked something within her, a door she thought was long closed. Through that door is a time before Boyd and his temper leached the colour from her life. It makes her mind skip traitorously to the day her first boyfriend screeched into her driveway on his Harley Davidson, all gleaming metal promise and shuddering escape. Her own mother furious, yelling at her to get back inside before the neighbours saw, but June was girl then and not yet woman, and still knew how to chase her own want rather than push it aside to keep the world happy. The judder of the engine between her thighs had been terrible-sweet. The heat coming off it had left her giddy. The funfair is something like that: a dangerous invitation that could lead just about anywhere if you let it.

The man holds out his hand, leads June out of the caravan, back into the world of the funfair. Past other glowing trailers – a huge purple one that smells of freshly baked scones, a dishevelled red one strobing into the dark. They walk by the Haunted House of Horrors and the Casino of Souls and the whirly cars – gosh, but June'd be sick just looking at them! A teenage boy saunters out from behind the ticket booth, raises a hand at them both – and she notices, with horror, the purple bruise swelling his eye shut. Such a dangerous place! So no, she won't weaken. There's nothing here that could make her change her mind. Bright and shiny, yes. But that's not endorsement. That's not nearly enough. And if she gets to pick (why her?), she picks an end to all of this. For their world to go back to how it was.

And then they stop walking, all of a sudden, so June nearly bumps right into his back. 'I think you'll like this,' says the man. He leads June through another archway, dangling with razor spikes. June shivers, but it's good clean fun, that's all, just a laugh. She steps forward: through the maw, behind a twitching curtain, down a very long, very straight corridor she's convinced is shrinking with every step. The man nudges June towards the door at the end and says, 'Go on,' so she reaches out a hand and pushes and the next thing she knows they're capsizing into another room, all glowing with fluorescent lights and . . .

'Mirrors!' cries June. And so it is. Mirrors on every surface, reflecting every angle of their bodies. A fat mirror where her stomach bulges, pregnant again, glowing. A tall mirror where her neck lunges like a diplodocus, head hanging loose and useless, a sunflower too big for its stalk. Mirrors where her hands turn to paddles, her fingers to wet columns of drool, her eyes to endless windsocks in the breeze. June looks from one to another, allowing herself a small private smile, which immediately leaps and multiplies, a Colosseum of teeth.

'It's nice, Mister . . .' she starts, her voice small. 'It's funny. It's all very nice and old fashioned and, well, sweet – but it's not enough to change my mind. No.' At this, her voice begins to rise. 'Are we nearly done yet? It's getting late, my husband, oh—'

Done, done, done. They are almost done, we are almost done, June. Nearly there.

The man from the funfair takes June's hand and says, 'Just one more thing. Just a little closer.' And he walks her into the centre where one mirror stands apart, its frame gold and ornate, twisted with vines and fruit and buds and barbs. He stands June in front of it and bids her look at herself, and so she does.

'What do you see?'

For a moment, June closes her eyes. She takes a breath. Then she looks. She meets her own eyes. There. Her face. Her big round what-have-we-here face, her face that looks, always, just a wee bit shocked when she catches it unawares. Like this here world is not to be trusted. A face that's never gazed in the mirror and beamed at what looks back. But not a monstrous face. Not grotesque. Just her, as much as she's always been.

The man from the funfair steps up, and she moves her gaze to his reflection. His eyes flicker, his lips twitch, the skin on his cheek glows like infected meat. She waits for the funhouse magic to start, for their images to be transformed. The man's scars to smooth away like a sudden quiet spilling over the surface of a lake. Nothing happens. They stare at the reflection: two old bodies, scarred, bulging, pocked and oozing, hunched and haggard, just that, the things that they are.

'What is it?' says June, her voice sudden, high and frightened. 'What are we looking at?'

'It's us,' says the man. His laugh is as rich and deep as freshly ploughed soil. 'What else were you looking for?'

'Well,' says June, and she puts her hands on her hips. This is a fine thing, a ridiculous thing, but that's all it is, and it's time for her to go.

There is something though. Something about their bodies next to each other that looks – well, she can't deny it – it looks almost right. June stands a little straighter, just to see how it will feel, and there's the breath of the man on the nape of her neck. The breath is warm. She feels it turn to condensation on her skin. She doesn't move. She can't. She is staring, very intently, at the skin on the man's face, thinking yes, some might say it's horrible, but there's something about it that's almost beautiful too. Like skate tracks on a frozen pond, or dew on a spiderweb, or . . .

The man from the funfair leans down, breath getting hotter, and brushes his lips against the spot just above her collar.

'Oh!' shrieks June.

He moves his small sharp teeth, and bites down, ever so gently, on her shoulder. The brush of dead ridges of skin.

'Ohh,' says June, feeling something loud and hot unspool inside of her. She turns to face the man. 'What is it? What do you want?' She's trying to sound angry, but something bright keeps bursting behind her words, like a spark plug, like two wires meeting.

'You'll join,' he says.

June snorts.

'You'll bring him too.'

'Who?' June asks, but her question is hollow.

'It's not us,' says the man from the funfair. 'We're not the issue here. You see?'

June closes her eyes. She can hear Boyd's voice, cracking in anger. Derek's frustrations all over the kitchen floor. Flat palms drowned out by the radio. And her back, her back bent over the hob, turned away from it all.

'I didn't ask for this, you know.'

The man from the funfair smiles his cat-paw smile. 'Of course.'

'It just ended up this way.'

'Yes.'

'Is that all?'

'No,' says the man from the funfair, and on every surface, a hundred gnarled hands close around her own.

A FUCKING CAR ALARM

THE NEXT MORNING, the noise goes off like a fucking car alarm, knocking a hole through a deep and dreamless sleep. Wrenched from that soft grey burrow, Boyd Geddes yanks the covers over his ear. June'll switch it off any second, if she knows what's good for her. He crushes his eyes tighter, tries to trick himself back to unconsciousness.

BEEP BEEP BEEP BEEP

Balls crash about his skull in every direction. The alarm's still going, how the fuck's it still going? As the last sleep scurries from him, Boyd rolls on to her side of the bed and smashes a fist down.

The alarm stops, never to be heard again.

'June!' he roars. His voice echoes inside his head: hot, sore and swollen. His mouth's a dead animal. There's something not right here. But what?

Boyd sits up in the tangled sheets, clawing a hand against his temple, trying to undo the knots in his brain. She's probably on the pisser, and she hates being shouted at when she's on the pisser. Too bad. Boyd hates being woken by that fucking alarm clock. Is it too much for a man to ask for – a man who works this hard to hold his family together – to start the day with a nice cup of tea instead of an empty bed and electronic caterwauling?

'June!' This time, he lets all his anger into it. And still, there's no answer. He yanks the covers off, scowls at her side as if by doing so he can make his wife materialize. The spot is empty. The sheets are bare. He presses a hand against them. Cold. She didn't just get up. She's not on the pisser. No, there's been no one on that side for quite the while.

Ding ding ding! Ten points to the man in the bed! But if she's not just got up, where the fuck is she? It's not time to panic yet, oh no, but Boyd's not happy. A few years back she'd started to get those sweats – the spells, she'd called them – and would leave him alone in bed to go stand in the cold shower. Boyd thought he made it clear back then. If she wants to fanny around in the morning, she better turn the alarm off. And when it comes to getting him up, a cup of tea and toast will do alright.

Now here we are. She's forgotten that lesson, and here's his skull caving in, and all the morning to deal with. Boyd throws his feet out of bed. Dresses quickly, steps into the corridor. At Derek's door, he wonders about getting him up to explain for his ma, then thinks better of it. The boy's been in a sulk ever since the other night. Things might have got a wee bit heated, but what did he expect? If the boy wasn't so soft, he wouldn't have to help him out. Boyd flexes his hand. The stiffness is gone, no real damage. When Derek's older, he'll get it. He'll come thank his old man, get down on his knees when he works out what he could have been, if not for the necessary corrections. The boy will understand in time. He did it out of *love*.

Boyd thunders down the stairs. There's still a part of him convinced that June'll be sat at the kitchen table, cutting coupons out of the newspaper or boiling old socks. She'll look up at him with that glaikit expression of hers and they'll have a few words and everything will go back to normal. A blip, but nothing that can't be quick forgotten.

But when he gets to the bottom, sees the empty table – that's when the real twist in his guts arrives. A cold steel finger that chills his intestines. It's empty. It's fucking empty. For a second, all the ground slips out beneath him, and Boyd Geddes begins to fall.

Five minutes later – just enough time for his heart to right itself – Boyd takes his chair. Phone in one hand, a big mug of steaming tea in the other, he hammers in the number. Takes a massive slurp. Four sugars will take the edge off a morning, and today he needs all the blunt he can get.

A tinny ring starts up on the other side.

June doesn't have many friends, that's the thing, but she's always had a soft spot for that dyke at the hairdresser. He takes another swig. Another ring. That lazy cow must not be up yet, though it's past ten. He grits his teeth. Boyd Geddes isn't here in a flap because his wife's ran out on him, oh no. He's not as fucked as all that. He knows what he's going to say, so why doesn't she hurry up and answer so they can get back to the script?

The phone just keeps ringing. He hasn't worked out what the next plan is yet. Cut a man some slack. He's about to slam the receiver down when – finally, about fucking time! – he gets through.

The muscles in his back relax. He makes his voice all casual like – 'Aye, Shona? June said she's going round your way today but the daft cow's only gone and left her purse here. Be a doll and put her on, would you?'

Shona won't like him calling her a doll. Or June a daft

272

cow, for that matter. She's just the kind to take offence, the sort who gets all fired up about Women's Lib, who has all sorts of theories about fish and about bicycles.

Shona doesn't say anything. Boyd can just see her fuming at the other end and a smile crosses his lips for the first time today. And then the person speaks and for the second time today, the third, his guts wrench.

'Is that you, Boyd?' says the voice, and it's a man's voice, it's not Shona at all. 'June's not here,' it says. 'Shona's not either, mate. Someone had a go at her window the other day, though. Glass all over the shop!'

'The window?'

'Aye, but she was gone before that.' The voice lowers: confidential and gossipy. Boyd can't place it and doesn't want to ask: the voice knows who *he* is, that's the thing. 'You know she's been gadding about the funfair, Shona has?' The voice laughs. 'Maybe your June's down there as well.'

Of course, that fucking place. Boyd's hand tightens on the receiver. 'Oh, I doubt that.' His own voice is creeping higher. He takes a superhuman effort and clears it, settles back into himself. 'She wouldn't dare.'

No response. In the silence, Boyd fills in a hundred ends to a thousand sentences. He's not going to explain himself – that's what the voice wants! Next thing, it'll be telling him he did the wrong thing with Derek. That the boy's just a wean, what's the harm? Why, he'd have gone off the rails himself had his own da not had the good sense to teach him about consequences. A soft touch isn't love. It's just being too feart to do the right thing.

He slams the phone down. His blood is pumping in his veins now, having a good go at it. Here we go, here we fucking go. The receiver stares up at him like a total dick and he lifts it up and slams it down again.

It doesn't make him feel any better. Funny that.

So what to do? Boyd closes his eyes. In the darkness, grotesque charades leap into being. A world of pervy thighs spread open. A curtain covered in round holes, yellow marigolds sewn into them, all those hands grabbing. He sees June – how she looked when they first met, kiss-me curls quick around her face. In the darkness, June presses a finger to her lips and giggles. All the marigolds paw at her, hungry for flesh. They grasp chunks, and she's happy to be torn apart. She's actually laughing!

He picks up the phone again. Someone has to pay for this, that's the thing. He has to take action. The thought he could be wrong never crosses his mind. He sees it all. Carnival skin. Long pinchy fingers. Wet mouths with missing teeth and whistling trouble. He dials the number.

'Hello?' says Greg Haskett, who's been waiting his entire life for a call like this.

'You've got to help me, mate. It's June.'

He can hear Greg smiling through the phone.

And so Boyd explains the situation. As he talks, the frantic fog in his skull starts to disperse. The window was smashed. Shona wasn't there. And June, she's got to be at the funfair. Got to be! These things, they're tied together in perfect logic, he's sure of it. Isn't he?

If it sounds ridiculous, Greg doesn't let on. He's all for this story, he's riling Boyd up to let it all out. 'Go on,' says Greg. He listens all the way to the end and his only interruption is to say, 'aye', 'go on' and 'tell me'. It's encouragement, it's no interruption at all.

'And with what happened to Callum,' says Boyd. 'A fucking hole in his fucking skull! They're lunatics over there, so they are.'

'You're right.' Greg's voice is sure as bricks, and Boyd lets himself loosen. This is why he called Greg. When you're flailing and fucked, when you cannae make head nor tail of it, Greg'll get in there with his bricks and show you how. 'Only one thing for it.'

'Tell me,' says Boyd.

'Burn the fuckers down.'

There's silence. Boyd waits for him to elaborate, but that's it.

'Burn them?'

'Aye.'

'The lot of them?'

'The whole fucking fair!'

'Right,' says Boyd. He's not sure how it follows. How fire will get June back. He doesn't want to hurt her – does he? No. He definitely doesn't. But then there's that fog again, the haze of anger suffocating his skull. He's got to do something. And he can't scream and he can't cry. And what was she thinking, really, wandering off and leaving him? How could she? Boyd passes the receiver from one hand to the other. 'We'll put the scare up them.'

'And the rest.' Greg laughs like a sack of broken bottles. Boyd matches it with his own. This'll be a laugh, a riot, just like old times. Setting the world to rights. But Greg keeps laughing and Boyd can't quite get there – there's other things in that laugh. There's the summer when they were just daft lads, bored out of their skulls with Pitlaw, yet another year drifting by with all the life squeezed out of their bodies. The summer of the dead cats. That was when Greg had discovered the magic of playing God, sardine cans in an emptied rubbish bin, so the strays would get tempted inside and he could slam a lid on top. Boyd would have to hold that lid down while Greg got the bricks, feeling the vibrations as the cat thrashed against the metal. They'd leave them round the back of the tenements, ignoring the yowls. They'd walk away as if they owned the world, as if life and death was theirs to proclaim.

Greg loved that game. It made Boyd want to boak, when they'd open the bin and there was the cat with its paws clawed down to blood, green spittle matting its fur. Thirteen years old and Boyd believed in vampires, and he didn't like to think how long the cat had been howling and ravaging, alive and not quite alive at the same time. Greg called the cats 'soft kids', a name Boyd never understood and didn't want to get close to. There was laughter like this then.

'The rest,' says Boyd.

'Oh yes,' says Greg.

Well, what else are they going to do? What would a man do, if a man found himself in this situation? That's the thing. A man would protect his own. His town, his wife, his soft sack of a son.

'Let's call the lads in,' says Greg. 'Get this job on the road.'

So Boyd says yes. Boyd hangs up the phone.

STRINGS OF
LIGHTBULBS EXPLODING

MEANWHILE, IN THE red caravan with the dirty underwear scattering the floor, Gloria the Teller flings open her eyes. She slept late today, and her mid-morning doze carved out a conduit to the future. Anyone can do this trick, if they practise. Squirrel out the hypnosis lurking in the moments of semi-consciousness when all the doors are flung open. Strip off their clothes and dip in the dream soup. Part the waters, slip between worlds.

But today, Gloria was dragged under by a ferocious riptide. Not a minute to catch her breath before the ragged bottom of the ocean. The visions down there! A stench of gasoline, the soft whump of a thing catching. She could hear her ancestors screaming, charred skin tightening across flesh. Oh, how those witches burned. Skin blackening, peeling back, the wet sizzle of bursting blood from beneath. The bitter reek of hair on fire.

But then, in the depths of the dream soup, something changed. The current shifted and it wasn't just the ancestors any more. It was her family. It was now. The *splish splish splish* of a string of lightbulbs exploding, eyes streaming in black smoke. The tattered end of the Mummy's bandage sending a scatter of orange stars across the sky. The screams of the Freakslaw, so agonized and loud.

Fire, fire, everywhere. Mad yellow and ravenous. And on its way.

Gloria sits up straight in bed, clawing at her eyelids. Another fit of coughing wracks her, blood spatters in the tissue. Across the caravan, Nancy is still sleeping – one thumb between her lips. She pumps her legs under the covers, a dog dreaming of running. Gloria's heart jack-knifes. This can't be right. Tonight's the night to enact their final temptations. A sweet flute melody, the kind any wayward child might get hooked upon. A time to play, a time to reap, a time for bare feet padding across the grass, mouths open singing *Yes, take me, yes.*

There's no time for this carnage! For torture or flames! Here they are, the future rushing to meet them. The past in the benches, hollering instructions. This pain in her chest, sharper with each breath. And time ticking madly, all out of plans, furious at the approaching finish line.

Oh, Nancy. What have you wrought? Gloria clenches her fists in the bedsheets. There's only one thing for it. A closer look.

She must go desperate to the dark place.

In the tent, Mr Partlett brings out the necessary items: the sack, the spade. A snatch of silk to keep the soil from her lips.

He cups a gnarled hand against Gloria's cheek and she pushes against it like a cat. 'You're certain?' There's ancient regret in his voice – the more things change, the more they stay the same, it seems.

'Not certain at all,' Gloria replies. 'But I will be.'

He lights a gas camping stove and places a tin pan upon it. Fills it with water, shakes in the herbs. They clump on the surface, but as it heats, they'll disperse. Turn the brew bitter and charmed.

'You have the rest?'

'Of course.'

From the very bottom of the sack, Mr Partlett removes a tiny vial. They don't carry a lot of this in from year to year. It's not easy to source and besides, Gloria doesn't quite trust it. The venom, extracted from the liver of the puffer fish, will make a heart slow to the frequency of postcards. If Nancy decided she wanted a go, Gloria doesn't like to think what might happen. Though her daughter's wild impetuousness will no doubt change the world, it also leaves her so very vulnerable to the crueller whims of fate. If anything hurt her, it would be more than Gloria could bear.

Dosing is a delicate balance. A Goldilocks kind of procedure. She plucks it from him and uncorks the vial. Holds it above the pan, now leaping at an angry boil, and lets a single drop fall. Is it enough? Gloria closes her eyes and thinks of yellow madness, how a flame will gallop. She drops another.

As the mixture roils, Mr Partlett spades the sawdust from a person-sized rectangle of ground. He tightens his grip on the handle and begins to dig.

Gloria tries to steady her breath. She's done this before. Not often, but enough. It's a simple act, so long as the mixture is the right balance. Just enough to slow her breath, her pulse, so when the soil falls on her, she doesn't suffocate.

Then it's just a matter of lying there and listening. For the ancestors in the dirt, for the worms. She'll stay until she knows what to do and then, when the venom wears off, she'll emerge. Fat with knowledge. Prepared.

The grave Mr Partlett is digging looks soft and warm in

the darkness of the tent. Gloria is ready. She drags a hand through the white skunk of her hair. Flicks off the gas so the mixture has the chance to cool before she drinks it.

She doesn't want to burn her mouth, after all. She doesn't want to be uncomfortable, not when she's being buried alive.

CLOSER TO A HUMAN

'LUNCH'S READY!' HER mum's voice hollers up and Ruth takes a last look in the mirror, sucking her stomach in. She presses her fingertips against her skin. It doesn't feel different. It doesn't feel like there's a creature inside, lashed to her innards by a bloody flesh tube. If you looked, you wouldn't be able to tell there's a leech siphoning the nutrients from every meal, feeding and growing and becoming closer to a human with each passing day.

This week has been hell. She feels like something suspended in liquid. She has no idea how to act. All she can think is: How could this have happened? But she knows, of course she does. Any idiot would, and that's what makes it worse.

She thuds down to the kitchen, where everyone's sat round the table for once. There's a huge colander of steaming spaghetti, curled against itself like cat tails. Her mum ladles a slithering mass into each bowl. The air is hot and damp and smells of garlic.

'Not so much for me.' Her dad holds up his hand. His portion is barely a kitten's worth. Her mum frowns but doesn't say anything. For a moment, Ruth is furious, but the anger passes as fast as it came. This is how it is, how it's always been. Every difficult conversation, kept under a blanket, dark and warm. Sometimes one of them will stick a hand under, grasp around, but never at the same time.

'Gobshite gobshite, princess gobshite!' sings Stephanie as she bounces Kayleigh on her knee. 'Who's the queen of all the gobshites?' Kayleigh looks around for a second, dinner-plate eyes filled with horror, and bursts into a fresh bout of screaming.

'Oh great,' says Ruth. The shriek hits deep in her belly. She jabs her fork into spaghetti and starts twisting. 'I thought she was the princess, anyway? She can't be the queen and the princess.'

'Of course she fucking can,' says Stephanie. 'How do you think royalty works?'

'Girls,' warns her mum.

Ruth rolls her eyes. Stephanie sticks her tongue into her cheek, twitches a fist in the international sign for blow job. Kayleigh stops crying and looks from one to the other. Giggles. Lifts her own chubby fist up and mimics. Stephanie pisses herself laughing.

'Oh no,' she says. 'You don't do that. Not yet.'

Ruth watches as her sister yanks Kayleigh closer and holds her tiny hands between her fingers. She's smiling, but Ruth wants to grab her and ask: Don't you hate this? Stephanie had plans, plans to get a degree in beauty therapy and take a salon apprenticeship in Dundee. She was going to work hard in the week and drink Archers and lemonade on a Friday night. Take holidays in Gran Canaria. It's not what Ruth would have chosen but Stephanie wanted it. Now she's still here, she doesn't go on holidays, her nails are bare. There's sick on her shirt. She's exchanging blow job faces with a child.

'Are you going to eat that or just stare at it all night?'

Ruth looks at her mum. Nods. Takes a mouthful and tries to swallow but the spaghetti dangles at her throat. It feels like fingers and that's when the bile leaps up, the sick's already in her mouth. She barely makes it to the toilet. But she does, on to her knees, vomiting great dangling threads of pasta. The way it feels slithering out is so repulsive it starts a fresh batch of retching, thinner and greener, frothing in the toilet water.

'Ruth!' her mum shouts. 'Are you okay?' Sweat leaps on to Ruth's brow. She grits her teeth and clutches the toilet rim.

When she turns her head, her parents are both there, crowded in the corridor, matching expressions of shocked concern.

'I'm fine,' she says. The smell of bile wafts up and it takes a superhuman effort not to start again.

'What happened?' says her mum.

Sick floats in the toilet. The question doesn't seem to require an answer.

'Was it something you ate?'

Ruth manages a wan smile. 'Or a bug. Your cooking's not that bad.' The joke takes a similar effort, but it's worth it for the relief that slackens both their faces.

'Go have a lie down,' her mum says. 'I'll bring some peppermint tea.'

Ruth eases to her knees. Her hands are shaking, but she clenches them and flushes the toilet. Strands of frothy pasta disappear. It's miraculous, how simple it is. A single flush, and everything is clear.

'Don't worry about the tea,' she says. 'I'm going to have a nap.'

Her dad pats her on the back. Ruth lets him, then creeps upstairs and lies on her bed. The ceiling whirls. Her skin is studded with goose pimples. She lays a hand on her stomach. Is it her imagination, or is something still roiling inside? Not her imagination. The thing is multiplying. Cells dividing. And who knows what kind of strange creature it's turning into, given its origins. Every second, it gets twice as big, twice the problem. Twice as close to the destruction of her future.

A single flush, and everything is clear. Could she do that? No. Not here. Not in Pitlaw, where there's one doctor in town and it's old Dr Wilby who has a cross hung up in his waiting room, who actually recommends praying sometimes like it's a fucking prescription. Even if he could actually help, there's no way she could open her thighs and let him poke his old man fingers inside. She was examined by him once, after she ran into a tree stump in some daft game and ended up pissing blood. Turned out she was fine but the horror of undressing, letting Dr Wilby peer over his spectacles into her vagina, has never left her. So it's not an option. But what else is?

There are other places. Cities where things like this must happen every day. But how would she even go about that? Take a train to Aberdeen and show up at the A & E and just start screaming? She doesn't think they'd consider it an emergency. They'd be wrong, but that's not the point.

Which leaves her parents. But she saw how Mum reacted to Stephanie – she had a whole speech and everything. She was keeping it. They would raise it, if it came to that, but she was keeping it. 'You're going to do good by this wean, Stephanie Anne MacNamara.' Using her full name so you know she really meant it. 'You've made this life, and that's that, you're going to see it through.'

Ruth doesn't even know what Stephanie wanted. It didn't matter; it was a done deal. It's stupid. They don't even go to church. But the one time it mattered, her mum was suddenly, stubbornly religious. God doesn't give a toss about shellfish and mixed fibres any more, but he's terrifically strict about the destinies of teenage girls.

Ruth balls her hands into fists and presses them against her eyes. She's exhausted. She has to do this on her own, and it's impossible. It is so unfair. She's just a kid, really, a kid herself. The thing inside her absolutely cannot be happening. Why her? Why is she the one that has to deal?

That's when the anger hits her: fast and loud, thrumming like a bass line. Fuck this, Ruth thinks, fuck this very much. What about the man? The fucking man, where is he? Why doesn't he do something to sort it out?

You don't even know his name, comes the judging voice from deep inside.

And it's true. She doesn't. But she knows where he is.

SHIT AND LUMPS

DEREK STANDS BEHIND the door, listening for footsteps. If he can get through one more day without talking to his da, that'll be something. If he can get through the rest of his life. His ribs are still a little tender. His eye's blue and swollen, but it's not so bad. What's worse is the memory of black toast crumbs, the kitchen linoleum. The embarrassment. How did things get to this?

The corridor is silent. Derek creeps down the stairs, soft steps on threadbare carpet. When he gets to the bottom, he hears his da's voice, and how did he miss it before? There it is: big, loud and fucking furious. Derek had been clutching a wee hope that the other night let some of his pressure out. For the past few days, things have been quiet – though tense as anything, the kind of tension that would smash if you dropped it.

But now here he is, all riled up. Maybe it's the football. He sounds like he gets then – as if all the players need is a toxic pep talk screamed through the telly, as if they'd never even thought of kicking the ball into the net.

Derek waits in the hallway, hand tight on the bannister.

'They've taken her, Callum,' his dad says. 'June and god knows who else. Believe you me, what happened with your heid was just the start.'

His mum? Who has *taken* her? Panic flutters in Derek's throat, an image of her bound and gagged and hoisted off by kidnappers.

'Time we took matters into our own hands, like. Me and Greg and the lads, we're heading down tonight.' A pause, and in the silence Derek dies seventeen times and is born again. 'Nah, it'll be no bother. They're no hard men. They're just freaks.'

Freaks! All of sudden, the pieces fall into place. It's the funfair again, of course it is. Another excuse to get riled up against them. In all likelihood, no one's taken his mum anywhere (they wouldn't, right? She'll be off at the shops or, or . . . somewhere). It's just his da has a bee in his bonnet, and when Boyd takes against something, he doesn't stop until he's satisfied that thing is back where it belongs.

Derek listens with growing horror. The plan is full of mob mentality and burning sticks. It sounds fucking medieval. They're going to torch the place? To save the town, the families, the good honest working folk? Derek doesn't understand, can't follow the logic. His da's gone and lost the plot. Someone could get hurt. Someone could die! Not just anyone. Zed . . . Derek did the worst thing in the world and punched the best boy in the face. And now his da's going to set them on fire!

Oh my god, oh my god. It's this town, it's his family. There's something deeply wrong, something in the waterways and the bloodline. A plague that takes a simple nice thing and turns it to shit. A fucked-up chemistry. Put a good thing in Pitlaw, just for once, and it curdles. Turns to shit and lumps. That's all they're good for.

But it's not too late. Derek can still make it right. Forewarned is forearmed, that's what they say, isn't it? This is better than an apology. This is being the hero, being the one who *acts* for once in his entire fucking life.

He'll get there first. He'll find Zed. And they'll make a plan together.

THE STICKY SURFACE
OF LOLLIPOPS

ZED'S IN HIS caravan, pouting in the mirror, admiring the gravitas and glamour of his black eye again. It looks terrific. He's always wanted one. Always! Ever since Patti Smith talking about Anouk Aimée in *La Dolce Vita*, longing for a guy to knock her around, dark glasses and a black dress. Ever since every Bette Davis movie.

And it's just so hard to give one to yourself. That smear of purple-blue across the cheekbone, the swelling around the lid. Smudge in the socket. The face of cute cowboys and prison bait, those who've been deliberately hanging round the wrong dark alleyways. Tempting danger because danger's just too much fun, the sticky surface of lollipops, impossible to resist for fluff and flies.

Zed sighs happily. He prods his cheekbone and lets the twinge take him back to that moment. Kisses and fists, fists and kisses, oh my!

Just then, the door flings open and Nancy bursts in, a whirl of spangled catsuit and ripe sweat.

'Zed. Zediah, Zediphous. You look like a total fucking celebrity.'

'Don't I?' He gives himself one last joyful look and then scrambles over to the bed. There's work to be done, of course, but a girl deserves a break now and again. Perhaps a little drink? Something candied to turn the afternoon all sugar town . . .

Nancy flings herself down next to him. 'Gloria's in the dirt.'

The air whicks out of Zed's throat. He wraps a careful arm around Nancy. 'Buried?'

She nods into his armpit. 'She's going to rise in half an hour. We're supposed to get to the tent.'

This is serious. Gloria doesn't go in the dirt often. She has other ways of seeing the future. Ones that don't risk suffocation or paralysis, ones that don't involve a single poison. The dirt is reserved for the game changers. The times when it's absolutely vital that the future comes back crystal clear. She hasn't been in the dirt since that time in Cornwall, by the stones – they got away with that one, just about.

'What is it?'

'I'm not sure, but I think –' Nancy huffs out a sigh – 'I think that man didn't like my special surgery.'

Despite everything, Zed can't stop the grin tearing up his face. 'Post-trepanation regrets? Missing those solid-skull days, when his brain was all strapped in tight?'

'No! He loved it. At least, the person he was afterwards did.' She shrugs.

'And the other—' says Zed, but that's as far as he gets. There's a stuttering knock, a pause, and then a flurry. It makes Zed think of fireworks at the Freakslaw parties, how you're always convinced it's the end and then there's another, and another, a sky-full explosion of psychedelic stars.

Nancy raises an eyebrow. 'You expecting someone?'

Another spatter of knocks and Zed bursts into giggles. He

can't help himself. But he mushes a hand to his mouth and swallows them as best he can. 'Come in!'

The door creaks open. And who's behind it but sweet Derek Geddes, the boy with the liquid stomach and the solid fists, shifting nervously as if he's about to piss his pants. Derek, with a matching black eye of all things! Beaten and bruised and delivered to Zed's door.

Derek looks at Zed – clocks his purple swollen cheekbone, the sexy blue stain in his socket – and he actually says it: 'Oh no.'

What a ridiculous cutie. Zed's heart might burst. This is a gift from the universe, that's what it is, a reward for the pure of heart.

'Really, come in.' Zed pats the bed, a soft comforting nest. But Derek just stands in the doorway. He's literally wringing his hands. Zed didn't know actual humans did that outside lines in books. He watches, fascinated, to see if they start dripping, but not a drop of blood or water falls. Derek's hands are dry.

'It's okay, you know,' says Zed. Derek looks like he's going to start bawling any second.

'It's not,' he says. 'It's my dad.'

Nancy makes a face. 'What does he want?'

'He's coming. But not just him.' Derek takes a deep breath. He steps over the threshold, back into Zed's caravan, back into this world of wickedness, the sweetest perversity, that irresistible candy. 'They're coming to get you,' he says.

When he's done telling them everything he's heard, the three of them sit in silence for a moment. It takes Nancy to break it. 'Gloria,' she says. 'She'll be coming up any minute.' She pushes past Derek – whose hands are, by now, a fetching puce. 'Zed?'

Zed and Derek look at each other. They don't say a word. The air between them turns shiny and drips with condensation.

'Fuck's sake,' says Nancy. Behind her, the door slams.

Zed gets up from the bed, moving like a lynx. The caravan is a tiny space and he crosses it before the blood has even had a chance to gather in Derek's cheeks. A hand snakes into Derek's hair. Fat lips soft lips ohmygod boy lips pushing against his. Two black eyes come together and the bloody bruises mix, oil stains on water, slick and rainbow iridescent. The kiss is a deep well.

Derek loves it. Many things fall in and disappear into blackness: his dad, school, Jack Haskett, fistfights, his missing mum, black toast crumbs, and every song he hasn't yet written.

When they hit the water, Derek can barely hear the splash.

THE WHOLE MAN

THE NEWS OF Gloria spreads like the flames that are waiting to burn, and everyone gathers in the tent where the rectangle of ground is sawdust bare. A low, frantic panic flickers. The Pin Gal shivers and her metal clacks together like teeth. The Twins needle each other furiously, stealing coins from each other's pockets, poking each other in the ribs. All the Strongmen are holding hands, crushing each other's fists with muscly fingers. Miss Maria dabs her forehead repeatedly with her purple handkerchief and Werewolf Louie yanks out the hairs around his centre parting and Derek stumbles inside, way-dazed and goofy dumbstruck – but even he, with his palm firmly in Zed's (this hand this hand!), can't give himself fully to delight. Fury is coming.

They flock from every corner to gather around the grave. No one says a word. June – pink-cheeked and breathless, Shona's arm snaked through hers – lets out a shriek when she sees her Derek, but even that's not enough to break the spell. Derek gives her a sheepish wave.

By the head of the grave, Mr Partlett leans against a gold-tipped cane, thinking: *It begins.* Nancy waits by its feet. She blows a pink bubble the size of a grapefruit then pops it with one lazy finger. When Zed catches her eye, she winks, but she's nervous, Zed can tell. The music starts up in the background, that jangly wind-up box song, and all the air in the tent is inhaled in a collective breath. Hold it there now. And wait.

Deep beneath the earth, something is happening. The worms are finishing their stories, the ancestors are howling. The dirt is starting to move. Hallucinogenic visions give way to exclamation-marked certainty. A liver metastasizes the final drops of the world's most toxic delicacy. A scrap of silk sucks against a mouth as the first breath in five hours is taken. Eyelashes flutter through grains of soil.

And then Gloria's hands are claws digging towards the surface. Up up up like a salmon coming home at last. The others can see the grave roiling, but no one makes a move to help. No. Gloria must do this herself. One of her nails prises back on a rock, detaching from the wet meat, and her teeth are gnashing. She bites at the dirt, devouring it, closing the gap between the darkness beneath and the light above. Her lungs burn. She can taste the muck, thick and wet in her throat.

Everyone holds their breath in solidarity. The music gets faster. One hand bursts through fresh earth. A second. The dirt behaves like the ground in an earthquake, a liquid, living thing. It parts for her.

Gloria sits up. Her eyes are blazing. Muck streaks her cheeks, her neck – there is soil clagging her lashes. Worms in her hair like Medusa. She looks around her family: so tense, so terrified, waiting. She takes a huge breath, one that rattles all the way down her lungs.

'Fuck!' It's a guttural ache of a word and it sends a gasp around the gathering. At their horror, Gloria pastes a smile across her mouth. A gold tooth, blinking. She inhales: a second rattle, a snake's tail. 'I'm back.'

This is met with murmurs of delight and a smattering of

applause. But Gloria looks down at the mess she emerged from.

'No,' she wheezes. 'It's bad.'

Derek squirms beneath the firm pressure of Zed's hand. He knows exactly what the bad is. He prised the door open and let the bad in.

'They're on their way,' says Gloria. 'No time for the plan. It's too late.'

Gloria's eyes meet Nancy's, but she doesn't elaborate. She doesn't say, *This is all your fault* or *Look what you've done.* Nancy hears it anyway. She looks at her filthy mother, caked in dirt and delirious. Reeking of the specific bitter sweat that comes from being buried alive. They hold each other's gaze for a long time, long enough for Nancy to hear twenty ways she's fucked it up and believe none of them.

Gloria looks away first.

'But wait.' Gloria runs her fingers through the topsoil. Blood seeps from her broken-off fingernail. She looks around, eyes glittering maniacally. 'There's another option.' A smile claws across her cheeks. 'A sacrifice!' Her voice leaps into demented sing-song. 'Why not throw the whole man away?'

'*Oooooh!*' say the crowd, who think such a thing sounds delicious.

'Why not? If our ancestors want revenge, let's give them a real one. Blood in the soil!' The gold tooth glints again. 'A most deserved offering!'

Mr Partlett thinks there's something she's not saying, something he'll prise out of her later. Nancy thinks this is what she wanted in the first place, but did they listen? Gloria forces out a laugh and it lands in the crowd, catching like a blown ember. Miss Maria is the first to let out a deep guffaw.

In a moment, Gretchen Etcetera is cackling with her. Surely, from deep beneath the earth, the ancestors are laughing too. Old bones are crowing. Derek sneaks a glimpse at Zed, whose face is all dimples and ecstasy.

But across the grave, peering from behind the Twins, June chews her lip. 'What sacrifice?' Suddenly there's a dark shape moving inside her stomach. She watches Mr Partlett start to laugh too, his scars slick and crinkled. Place one hand on Gloria, one on Nancy. The alligator in his smile.

June turns to Shona. 'What sacrifice?' she says again.

Shona grins. 'I dinnae ken.' She's like a little kid, firing up for a cannonball leap into the pool.

But June knows. She knows in her bones – not the psychic energy of Gloria, but something else. The kind of mindreading that comes from giving years of your life to a volatile husband, always listening, always predicting. Knowing when he needs quiet and when he wants the radio on, when he's hungry for dinner and when he'd rather be left alone. Knowing when he's been pushed too far. Knowing when he'll snap.

She stumbles past the Twins, into the circle where Gloria is kneeled in the dirt.

'What sacrifice?!' she shouts. Everyone's eyes are on her. She can see Derek, cringing, snuggled up close with a boy. *His fault!* she thinks. But she also knows that's a lie.

'June.' Gloria climbs unsteadily to her feet. 'Let me explain.' She dusts her hands on her thighs, smearing dirt into red velvet. 'They're coming. Angry men, men from your town. Men convinced they are owed.'

'No,' says June. 'They'll not do that.' As the words leave her mouth, she can barely stand how little they are true.

Gloria smiles sympathetically, but her face is pinched and drawn. She takes June's hands. 'They will.'

June shakes her head again half-heartedly. She looks to Mr Partlett, begging in her eyes. He's a man. He must know the way men get sometimes?

'The earth needs an offering.' Gloria's hands are quivering. 'They burned witches here, you know. Our people, our ancestors. Whole lines of our history, licked up in flames. Do you know how that feels?'

June is quiet.

'Brilliant women. The midwives and the alchemists. The freaks and the queers. The ones who knew how to bring hope. All gone, like that.' She clicks her webbed fingers. 'We lost so much. The ancestors want something back.'

'What will you do?' June looks from Gloria to Mr Partlett and back again. She sees the same gleam reflected in both their eyes. All around the circle, every face shining like funhouse mirrors. She can barely look at Derek but she forces herself to and yes, there it is. Her son is gleaming.

'An offering,' says Gloria again. Her gaze is firm. 'They'll come to punish us. They know, left to our own devices, we'll take their children. Their women. We have so many temptations, and they see it. Their families are already becoming ours. How could they stand that?'

June blushes. To hear it acknowledged, their capitulation spelled out? She doesn't know how to feel. She keeps coming back to that moment in the mirror: it felt *right*. Is it?

'They'll come in a furious mob. But they'll come willingly.' Gloria nods. 'That's part of it, of course. And when they get here, a sacrifice must happen. Just one, for all ours snatched away. Really, it's more than fair.'

There's that word again. Just like the man, that same dedication to weights and measures: eyes for eyes; teeth for teeth; checks, balances and a neat column for each one.

'But who?' It's all June cares about now.

And that's the question, isn't it? Gloria would like the answer too. Because it could go either way, that's the thing. Something beneath the earth has turned. As Lùnastal gallops in, the walls between the worlds are getting thinner. The dead are getting louder. They're down there, tossing and turning, screeching and howling, reaching out with their rotted fists. Grabbing on to whatever they can get.

If revenge takes the form of a man from the town, fantastic! If not, well . . . the ancestors will take whoever's in reach. When they get loud like this, they're not *fussy*. And Gloria can feel their fingers already inside her like a glove puppet, tightening around her organs. Squeezing on a liver. Yes, if they can't get the ancestors their pound of flesh, she has an inkling of who they might take.

She's about to speak when the tent flaps open and the girl tumbles through. Her cheeks paper-lantern red, her breath fast and ragged in her throat.

'Everything's fucked,' says Ruth. 'It's fucked, and you need to make it right.'

A TOTEM FOR
THE FUTURE

NANCY SQUATS IN the roiled dirt, scraping mud from her feet, delighted by everything. Things are really happening now. Finally! She watches Ruth stumble around the circle, one accusatory finger held out. She looks like a medieval painting, like Cassandra: a blighted woman driven mad by nobody listening. What a curse, to know the future yet to never be believed!

Ruth's eyes flick from Strongman to Strongman. It's no use. Nancy knows it's not. The Strongmen are cast from identical moulds, skin the same dense alabaster, eyes the identical shade of robin's-egg blue.

'Yours,' says Ruth. 'It was you.'

They blush in unison and shrug. The air is heavy with castor oil and grapefruit and a shared secret.

A miracle, really, that Ruth ever got one on his own. It wouldn't have happened if not for the moon, the feast. The spell of the night. If not for Nancy's meddling: a devilry of dolls, that childhood necromancy. But now look. Tatters! From her cloth bag woven with three-legged crows, she plucks out Ruth-Barbie and stands her up, chewed foot in the dirt.

'You bastards,' Ruth's saying. 'Tell me.' But the Strongmen just keep on shrugging. The who-knows moves around the circle like a swelling wave. Nancy thinks of a game, a person in the centre of a circle, blindfolded, flung between arms. She imagines Ruth bouncing from Strongman to Strongman, a pinball out of control. She smothers a laugh.

As the giggle escapes, Ruth's eyes meet hers and a wildness creeps into them. For a moment she is beseeching – clutching her arms to her chest as if trying stop herself spiralling. Then her eyes flick to the doll. The name scribbled in hectic black pen. *Ruth Ruth Ruth*, writ small nine times, a numerological spellwork.

'What the hell is that?'

Ruth pushes past the Strongmen, flicking them out of the way as easily as a line of paper men. Strides to Nancy and rips the doll from her hands. Confusion tissues her face as she takes in Barbie's stitched smock, her choking ribbons. Her name! Then Ruth turns her finger on to Nancy – a curse, a plague on all your houses. Nancy watches the ages pass through Ruth, sees her skip from maiden past mother and all the way to crone.

'You,' she says.

Nancy smiles. She takes handfuls of soil and sprinkles them through her fingers, sifting the dirt. 'Me?' What a coincidence. It's her favourite word in all the languages.

'What *is* this? What did you do?' Ruth's looming over Nancy. She holds the doll away from herself as if it might be radioactive, she shakes it, and all the while Nancy smiles.

Well, she planted a charm, of course. Burying things in the dirt was all very well, but this is better. The foetus, really, is no different from the baby tooth or the menstrual blood or the hair drilled to trees. A little witch bottle in the shape of a bean. A sweet hex for tricksy witches with big egos. The chance to toy with a whole damn town.

Barbie stares blankly at the roof of the tent. The funfair is silent: watching, waiting. Gretchen's filing a nail, leaning in for certain hot gossip. Gloria presses a scrap of fabric against her bleeding nail bed. Werewolf Louie slips his paw into Shona's hand.

'Ever since I met you, there's been trouble.' Ruth's expression is demented, eyes glittering. *'You're trouble.'*

'Well, someone needs to be,' says Nancy. It's only practical. If no one's shaking things up, the good bits sink to the bottom. The pot needs stirring so the bits don't burn. Simple! And Ruth needs to learn, that's the thing. She's like all teenage girls: a totem for the future. If they grow up to behave – never screaming baseball bats into the plate-glass window, never setting fire to office buildings, never yanking the loose thread of society and watching the whole thing unravel – then the world won't get anywhere other than where it's already going. A future that's already set. Wayward daughters are the grease slick in the egg white. It just takes a smidge for a good ruin of everything.

Nancy winks. 'It's for your own good, you know.'

Ruth stares at her for a long minute. Then she throws the doll down and leaps on Nancy, hellcat feral and out for blood. She digs into Nancy's shoulders and launches them both to the ground. Claws at her eyes, rains down with flat palms. Ruth fights dirty, a girl who has nothing left to lose. Their hair tangles with dirt and sawdust. All the air gusts out of Nancy's lungs.

She shrieks with delight. Here's that feeling in her stomach: the crest of the roller coaster, *clack clack clack* before the descent into freefall. Ruth's knees find Nancy's shoulders and pin her down. There's June's high, frightened voice – *Oh, oh, shouldn't we stop them?* – and the gleeful cackle of the others. Ruth's hand flails towards Nancy's throat and Nancy matches her family's laughter with her own.

'It's not *funny!*'

But it is, that's the thing. It is hilarious it is sublime the mechanics of a brain gone all awry a finger poking a cat paw pleasure pigeons erupting into the air . . .

'Shut *up!*'

Then Ruth is slapping her, wide palms across the face. Nancy keeps giggling, she can't help it. She's tipsy with her own brilliance. Her plan, come to fruition. Ruth with Nancy's charms buried deep inside her. A hook to hang her power on. Magnifying her magic, a whole new layer of control.

'Fuck you! What did you *do?*'

She did what she wanted. And if she could go back to the very beginning of summer . . . why, she'd do it all again! Ruth's hits hurt, but it's a good hurt. A reminder she's alive. Then –

'CHILDREN!' screams Gloria, and Ruth stops. Both look up; in fact, everyone turns. Gloria stands in the centre of the tent, a mad blaze in her eyes. 'We're out of time,' she says, gulping something down. 'They're coming. Can't you hear?'

The crowd is silent, craning their ears for the sound of footsteps on the breeze. In the distance, a crow hacks up laughter. *Caw! Caw! Caw!* The trees shuffle awkwardly, nervous about what's to come. And then a noise that makes them all freeze, a noise that has the power to change everything, send it spiralling off in the wrong direction.

The soft whump of sawdust, as Gloria's body falls to the floor.

BROKEN BIRD

NANCY EXTRACTS HERSELF from Ruth in the twitch of a limb, as if the only thing stopping her was the fun of the game, and scoots to her mother's side.

'Gloria!' She shakes her shoulder, hard enough to make Gloria's head loll wildly against the earth. 'What the fuck?'

Her mother doesn't say a word, can't say a word. Her lips are sealed or she has an ancestor's whole fist in her mouth or she's down in the between worlds with them now, collateral to ensure some kind of death comes out of this sunny evening. Or a little bit of all of that, all at once. Her eyes are moving beneath the lids, as if she's tracking planes across the sky. Her head splayed back, leaving the long quiver of her throat exposed.

Everyone crowds round: the Pin Gal cupping Gloria's scalp, Mr Partlett lifting a pale, limp hand that sits in his own like a broken bird. 'The fuck?' says Nancy again and she scrabbles her small hands against Gloria's chest, clawing away the last of the soil. Beneath her velvet suit, a heart still beats erratically. A wild tom drum, the panic of horse's hooves. The feel of it calms Nancy a smidge, but still, none of this is right. The game wasn't supposed to play out this way. Forsaking Gloria, of all people, for this shitty town! The most absurd kind of sacrifice, a queen for a whole swathe of pawns. If this is what the ancestors want, really, they can stick it.

Miss Maria scoops Gloria up in her arms and carries her to a bale, across the tent from the churned hole in the soil. Too much like a gaping grave, a thing that could suck her back down at any moment. Mr Partlett, worrying one papery hand inside the other, follows and frets. 'She took too much.' Nancy's never heard him sound so old before. 'Such a delicate balance, a drop too many.'

Zed's arms find Nancy from behind. He squeezes her tight, his breath warm against her ear.

'The hospital's thirty miles away,' says Mr Partlett. 'It's not too late, if—'

'I'll take her,' says Gretchen, the fastest, wildest driver of them all.

But Nancy shakes her head, wriggles off Zed's comforting embrace and steps forward. She can't believe she's the only one to see it, can't believe she has to be the one to give those ancestor cunts their due. All her delicious wayward intentions for the future, and in the end here it is coming back to the past.

'Leave her,' she says, and her own heart quickens to horses because if she's wrong and Gloria really needs medicine, well, then it'll be too late. But what else is there to do – as a witch, as a daughter – but follow your intuition and trust it will turn out right? 'Didn't you listen to a word?'

The others freeze in tableaux, turn to Nancy, who's standing there with all her mother's electricity careening through her veins.

'We need to complete the sacrifice. And then they'll let her go.'

KISMET

IN THE CONFUSION, no one notices Ruth turn on her heel,
no one asks where she's going as she slips out into the Freakslaw. Not a soul to follow her, to tell her she shouldn't as she
throws open the flap to Gloria's tent. To where this began.
Queen of Kismet. Find your Fortune, Discover thy Destiny! It's
just how it was the last time: that buttery candle glow, shelves
stacked high with odd things in jars. The liquids gleam. And
Ruth knows now, certain as anything, that it's all real. Whatever severed limbs and mutants are on display, they're real.
They were once as alive as her.

But who even cares? What's alive can be made dead at any
moment. What's here can be gone. What's planned can be
wiped out, no matter how firm and certain those plans were.

She can hear herself, when she waltzed in here two months
ago, at the very beginning of summer. *The future's not going to
fuck with me!* Those words will come back to her time and
again for her entire life. When her dad goes into hospital for
the third round of chemo. When she's standing at the Thai–
Laotian border with an eighth of grass in her rucksack. When
the man she doesn't really love gets down on one knee. Once
you know that the future's always fucking with you, that it
looks at your destiny like a mouse between its paws, it's hard
to go back to how things were before.

But for now, Ruth searches through the shelves, jars for

this spell and that, magic suspended in clear liquid. She saw it here, she's sure. Axolotl. Ayahuasca. Too far. Arnica. Amniotic fluid. Abortion. Yes.

Inside the jar, a smattering of seeds and torn red-orange petals. Ruth has no idea what the plant is. She's never read a botany guide to the peacock flower, never spoken to the Surinamese medicine women who use it as a cure for fevers, sores and coughs. She doesn't know a word of its history, has no idea it was once the ultimate escape route for pregnant women held in slavery. As for the correct dosage or contraindication, forget it.

All she can see is that single word typed in neat dymo letters, a talisman Gloria inscribed years ago to keep the future sweet. An escape.

She unscrews the lid and stuffs a whole handful into her mouth. The petals burst – a sweet tinge of spring onion, thin and green. The juice trickles. The seeds grind between her molars, bitter little harpsichords. Her cheeks bulge as the wodge expands, she gags, her mouth dry and puckered. There's the moment of a heave, but that's not an option. She's going to eat the vomit if she sicks this up. So she closes her mouth and swallows as hard as she can.

Gulp.

And it's down. Ruth stands there in the world of futures and fortunes, a hand pressed to her lips. That's that, then. Her throat churns. It's the feeling of something inevitable already done. A line crossed, a step you can never take back.

She walks out into a burning sunset, the sky all pink and lilac and gold.

HOT LICKING
NOSTRIL FLAMES

MEANWHILE, ACROSS TOWN, the mob is coming together. Whipped into an apocalyptic frenzy by a series of phone calls that leaped like frog spit, lily pad to pad. Boyd to Greg to Callum to Jim, all the way to the town council, to Norma Murray: a game of exquisite corpse, the story mutating with each fresh dial tone.

They are delirious, righteous. Brim full of fury. Not at themselves for failing to name the change before now, or at the history that left them closed as a fist. Not the church for teaching emotional restraint. Not their fathers for all those lessons about the deep-down spot where a real man keeps his heart.

No. They blame the funfair. The corrupting funfair, tricksy place of fancies and rampant grabberies, fat fucks and gobby bints. That gaping maw that fell open in the heart of the town. Enough's fallen in already. Time to stop it up.

Greg Haskett holds his big stick aloft. The end's swaddled in an old T-shirt and reeks of petrol, of chemical getaways. It reminds him of the glue, round the back of Tesco with a brown paper bag as a teenager, the bag a wild warmth, the inhale a hot licking nostril flame. 'Are we ready, then?'

'Fucking right we are!' yells Boyd. He hasn't felt like this for years, not since that time the lads went on holiday to Blackpool and drank Upgrades all night – half a pint of lager, half a pint of Red Bull, sticky-sweet and full of caffeine. His whole heart trying to leap out of his chest, and no matter how many he drank, the soft escape of unconsciousness never caught up with him. That's the same energy barking through him now.

'Undoubtedly,' says Norma Murray, who's got no concern whatsoever for Boyd Geddes or Greg Haskett or any men at all for that matter. She's still thinking about the fat woman, her audacity, the gall to laugh in her face!

'Aye?' Callum stares at the club in his hands. It's a bit heavy, like. A bit unnecessary. What they could do instead is take a seat outside the pub in the bonny evening light. Callum could really go a pint right now. A portion of crispy chips, fluffy and steaming in the centre, crackling on the outside. Globbed with mayonnaise. Since the whole business with the drill, he can't quite remember the old anger that used to thrum inside him. He's not sure what he's doing here, truth be told. But—

'Fuck them up!' says Mr Scott, the history teacher, who's always wondered how it might feel to be swept along by a righteous crowd (what, pray tell, would it take for an ordinary citizen to be seduced by rhetoric?).

'Pervert scum!' yells Phillip Burnstone, who's been waiting for this moment ever since he saw these freaks pigging out in the cafe all those weeks ago.

'Alright, let's go!' says Boyd Geddes, so their feet start to tramp across the dirt.

Twenty of them in all, a cluster rather than a crowd, but thirty litres of petrol with it. Lighters clutched in white-knuckled hands. Home-made torches silhouetted against the sunset sky.

The cans slosh with every step. Below their feet, centuries of tightly packed dirt, thick with memories. The plants, the roots, the soil, the rocks, the bones, the ash, the buried. The whispers of the ancestors start, but the mob is shouting too loudly to hear them.

They're on their way.

SUMMONING THE THRUM

ON THE HAY bale, Gloria's body lies motionless. Her pale skin mottled with patches of red, little fairy rings across her arms and neck.

Mr Partlett looks from her to Nancy and back again. 'It's not the poison,' he says. 'It's the ancestors?'

'Well, duh.' Nancy juts out her chin. She rolls her eyes, like the question's inane. And still, Gloria lies there, silently daring Nancy to prove him wrong.

'Are you sure?'

No, she isn't sure. Of course she's fucking not. Nancy's never been one to listen to the old guard and their endless rattling at the best of times. She's got her own brand of chaos magic. Every time Gloria hunkered down to press an ear to the soil, Nancy fucked off looking for a better spell. She didn't have time to learn any of the lessons her mother wanted to teach her. So it's just peachy-fucking-creamy that she has to start now, when the stakes are so high.

'Course I am.'

All the certainty she doesn't feel, she puts into her voice. What other choice is there? Because Gloria was sure, that much was obvious. She was the one down there in the dirt, who came up baying for blood. And that's something Nancy can get behind. Something she's been cawing for the whole summer long. Something she can make happen, too.

Nancy's got a hold on Pitlaw. She's sewn her charms here: in the soil, in the trees. That little bean deep in Ruth's womb. They're all winking out energy at her now, sending vibrations, crackling power into her veins. If anyone can control this place, it's her. It has to be her.

Nancy opens and closes her fists, summoning that thrum.

'They're on their way.' She stands to her full height, all five foot nothing of her. 'You heard what she said. The men are coming.' Her laugh is almost cherubic, a million miles from her usual cackle. Miss Maria enfolds Gretchen in a hug. The Twins intertwine their fingers and squeeze comfort into each other's palms. Werewolf Louie snuggles on Shona's lap and the Pin Gal glimmers with anticipation and June frets, wrings her hands, *The men, coming, oh god, please no.*

In the midst of it all, Zed catches Nancy's gaze and crooks an eyebrow and in that twitch she sees all the years of their friendship: the miles covered and the drinks drunk and the dawns welcomed, finishing each other's sentences and delirious with night sweat. A perfect grin for perfect trust. A grin that believes she's the greatest thing there's ever been. She's right, and she can do it. Doesn't everyone need a friend who'll look at them like that?

Nancy fingers her necklace: a dog tooth on a string of black leatherette. She brushes the tooth against her bottom lip; the brush of enamel and canine giving her strength. 'Let's be there to meet them.'

And sure, this isn't how it was supposed to end. There was supposed to be high glamour and temptation, a flute and a wink. Music like piped frosting, oozing soft from the bag. But who cares about what's supposed to happen? There can still be music, after all. It will still be a celebration. Offering, like torn entrails and destiny, the sweetness of family and blood.

Mr Partlett stares heavy at her with his ancient eyes that ask a dozen questions but still she doesn't look away, doesn't waver.

'Fine,' he says at last. 'If you're sure.'

The high whine of drill bits sounds up in her ears again, the red mist, the glory of the splatter.

'Bring them to me,' Nancy says. 'I'll take them out.'

And beneath their lids, Gloria's eyes twitch. Skipping from ancestor to ancestor, the endless squabble. Following the path of the moon.

TURNING AN ORANGE
INSIDE OUT

RUTH STUMBLES THROUGH the funfair, concentrating on one foot ahead of the other, heading for the gate. There's something wrong with this place, gone off-kilter. The waltzers are still whirling demonically, chairs empty, like a possessed children's toy creaking to life the moment you turn off the light. Not a soul to be seen, but alive all the same.

Her head is swimmy. The sawdust pathways of the Freakslaw disorientate, beckoning her down. She's all spun around. Ruth turns round the side of the Orbiter, a path she was sure would take her to the exit, but instead she emerges in the hollow by the Haunted House of Horrors. To her right, the Funhouse looms, hysterical mouths cackling at this hilarious plot twist.

Ruth tries to focus, but her eyes are loose in their sockets. The twilight is getting brighter, saturation turned to max. Her guts roil and the world undulates. Sweat is oozing from her pores, thick like plant sap. A hallucinatory wave swoons through her and she grabs a railing before her legs give out entirely.

She has no idea what's happening and then the bitter rush comes back in her gums and she does. *Oh god. Oh no.* It wasn't supposed to come on this quick. A dull, deep cramp lodged in the small of her back, a pain like a runner's stitch buried deeper within herself than she knew existed.

Ruth looks around wildly. This can't happen here, exposed to the world. She needs to get somewhere private: a bathroom, anywhere with a door that can lock. So she can get naked and howl. For a moment the pain slackens, and she thinks, *Yes, there's time, let's run* but that's before the steamroller hits her thighs, and

Oh holy fuck oh holy wow shit gasp shit gasp Jesus something grabs her deep in her womb. Gnarled and pointed fingers, and she pants and swallows and the cramp tightens, and she's going to die, and—

It's gone. The claw releases its grasp, all the agony washes out of her body. She slumps against the Funhouse wall, basking in sweet relief. But she knows it won't last. The pain is hiding, not dead. Waiting to be reanimated in zombie horror, preparing for the moment Ruth thinks it's over to drag a fingernail across a rusty scimitar.

I'm BA-ACK!

She clenches her vagina. Tightens it like a fist. Rams her fingers into the front of her womb, pounding the muscle. *Fuck you, then. Get out if you're going.* She slumps to the ground, trying not to think about all the feet that have stamped here, the spit and chewing gum, knee scabs, burned popcorn. Boak. Her jeans are tight against her crotch and she has time to wonder what would happen if you tried to give birth with trousers buttoned, whether the baby would tear through the denim or just stay stuck inside for ever, whether—

And then: thwack.

It's back, screaming down like snakes, and there's only this, oh holy fuck, there's only this.

She pushes, it's trying to turn an orange inside out with her fingertips, pith stuck in the skin.

Ow, ow, holy fuck, it's inside her, and then – it's gone again.

She loses track of how long it lasts. Each time, she's convinced this is it. She prepares herself to push everything out, but her body clutches on. Time swells and dilates. A whole day passes, a month, ten years and Ruth is in limbo, straddling the realms, incapable of stepping off the ledge. She stares at the darkening sky, black dots pulsing. Maybe she'll die. Maybe this is it. God's been watching all along, tapping his long fingers on his God chin and thinking, this won't stand. Her punishment is about to be meted. The panic comes on her, a whole flock of black birds, and—

Bam. Those gnarly fingers, back in her womb. Her body slackens. One moment she's clutching herself, and the next it all catapults from her, a feeling like she's shit herself and she's wet herself and she's let go of everything.

WHOOSH.

Like footage of fishing trawlers when the net's released and the fish spill out, so live and close and clumped they're a single wriggling beast – this is like that, it's totally like that, except it's not, because it has nowhere to go. Whatever was inside her splashes into her crotch. Her underwear is sodden, a wet slosh as she shifts her weight.

Ruth looks down at the blood leaking through the denim. Somehow, in the darkness, it's sparkling. A bioluminescence, an oil slick of red glitter.

Inconceivable that it was ever part of her, that it could have ever been inside.

She sits for what feels like a very long time. Her head light and swoony, her heart impossible. Ruth unbuttons her jeans and dabs at herself with tissues and throws the slimy things as far away as she can. Bloody icebergs scatter the ground. She edges back, as if any moment they might reanimate, come crawling towards her, calling her name.

They say nothing. She tells them everything.

You didn't get me. I'm still here. My heart is beating. I'm fine.

AN APOCALYPTIC SNOW

THE WHITE WOODEN teeth creak in the breeze as Boyd Geddes leads the mob beneath. No one is on the ramparts to defend the castle. No buckets of boiling oil, no arrows slung in quivers, not even a sentient pigeon waiting to seize the news and relay it to the defending army.

Good.

Let's see how they like it, someone sneaking in their business when they're not paying attention. He angles his big stick before him like the prow of a ship. The balmy night air breaks upon it and they sail inside.

'Alright.' His voice is a gravelled whisper. It's church all over again. This is biblical shit right here, the proper Old Testament stuff, your Sodom and Gomorrah, that daft cunt's salty wife. If God is watching (and he probably is, because God likes to peer over his reading glasses and see what the weans are up to today) then what's coming Boyd's way, when this is all over, is a hearty clap on the back. God's hand is gonna feel so big and so heavy. The big dad's gonna know Boyd came good at last.

'This it?' asks Mr Scott. They shuffle to a stop next to the Tilt-A-Whirl, by a day-glo-yellow ticket booth with nobody inside. No one's strapped in the dangling carriages either, though they're still tilting and whirling through the air.

'Aye,' says Boyd. This is it. He's really doing it. And he's not afraid. He's excited, is what he is. The weight in his palm feels devout. 'Come on, then.' He turns to face the others. They cluster round and he holds the lighter out, he flicks his thumb. The first flame's a tiny orange flicker but the moment he touches it to his torch, that hungry petrol mouth gobbles it right up. Gulp!

And – 'Ohhh!'

Just like kids watching the fireworks. They lean in, hypnotized, stunned drunk by the hot hallowed fire. The flame gathers strength. Their cheeks scald red, their eyebrows singe. The men shuffle back, never breaking eye contact with that burning torch, but Norma Murray leans even closer, orange-faced and ravenous. The stick grows heavy in Boyd's hands. It's like holding a bone for a pack of dogs, watching their tongues unravel as he decides which direction to fling it.

Last chance, Boyd. It's not too late to put the burning torch down, to take this home and talk it out. But he thinks of that moment at the kitchen table again, how his stomach dropped out to see her gone. The fear that licked at him. Like: maybe he *is* weak, maybe he doesn't have it in him to hold his family together. So what choice does he have? She's his wife. And if she's not coming home to him, she's not coming home at all.

Greg gives him a nod, a nod that says he's letting Boyd take this one – Boyd, who has been so grievously fucked over, who deserves the chance to set things right. But Greg's right there by his mate's side, a sadistic grin smeared across his chops, and he's going to relish every moment of what happens next.

'What are you cunts waiting for?' Boyd hisses.

That does the trick. Suddenly, the mob leaps to life. They

take their own torches, hastily bound and drenched in petrol, and hold them up to Boyd's. For a moment, he thinks they should have done this bit back in town, tramped over here already blazing, charring the sky orange. They should have had a chant. But it's too late now, and when the other torches take light, he realizes it doesn't matter.

Whump! Whump! Whump!

An electric delight seizes Boyd. 'Get in!' Greg yells – and he pours his can of petrol all over that dumbfuck yellow ticket booth. Boyd touches his flame to rickety wood and it's as simple as switching on a light. The booth is swallowed whole. Hungry blue tongues lick across the trodden grass, follow the drizzled path of petrol the men are spreading. It makes him think of the Road Runner sprinting along, kicking up a cloud of dust at his heels.

Boyd feels like a boy again. He wants to shriek, to giggle, to click his heels in the air. Is it acceptable for a man in his position to shout the word 'wahey'?

Well, why not? This is the fair, after all. A place for kids and eejits, and isn't that fun?

Norma Murray is cackling now, rushing ahead to find new stalls to burn. Lewis scurries after, gushing petrol across the building bases. And Greg is having the fucking time of his fucking life: that smirk on his face like someone's going to hurt tonight, someone's going to get theirs. Only Callum is frozen at the back, holding his can all awkward-like, wide-eyed at the turn things have taken, but what did he expect?

The mob is generous with this liquid gift, offering it all to thirsty walls. The shacks gobble it up and transform into ripe wicks.

The fire chases in hot pursuit.

It's catching faster than Boyd could have imagined. At first it just slicks over the surface of the Tilt-A-Whirl, turning the frames a quick blue, but soon this gives way to a deep, soulful orange. The sides of the Haunted House catch, the roof takes; suddenly, the Mummy ignites. Tattered bandages flicker in the updraft. They burn off and gust into the air, falling in flames like apocalyptic snow.

For a moment, Boyd is too star-struck to move. He didn't know how much he needed this until it was happening. He didn't know it would be so fucking pretty. A poofter thing to admit and he never would, but Christ, what a treat. His face is hot. The buildings are tearing up. The only thing that could possibly feel any better would be to see some of those freaks burn up with it.

With that thought, his feet remember how to move. 'Come on, then!' he shouts, as he pushes past the others, taking his rightful position by Greg at the head of the mob. This is just the beginning. There's so much more to come.

MEETING THE MINOTAUR

ABOVE THE FREAKSLAW, a pink moon peers down. The moon wants to take in as much as possible before those gathering storm clouds block her view. For the first time in almost nine weeks, the constellations are smothered. But for now, she can still see what's below.

At the west boundary, a series of fires have taken hold. From up here, they're infinitesimal: tiny flares of struck matches. But the moon knows something important is beginning. Fireworks, from the moon's perspective, are the smallest sparkles, after all. We can't judge human affairs by how large they appear from the sky.

Electricity thrums the night. Two cumulonimbus the size of icebergs careen into each other's arms. Their kiss is a jaguar clearing her throat. As the panorama is swallowed, the moon huffs and turns her attention to other things. In the distance, the drums begin.

Ba-dong-ba-dong-ba-dong-ba-dong, the sound threads through the dark. Boyd Geddes pauses, jerry can held high. The drum keeps time with his heart. 'Fucking-A!' cries Greg as a board of pink teddy bears catches fire, plastic faces curdling, lattices of cracks shattering across their wide, horrified eyes. The mob hoots, takes another step towards the Freakslaw's beating heart, where the future is waiting.

*

There, the funfair folk are already in formation. They stand two by two in whatever ruffled finery they could grab before the mob's arrival. Muses queueing for Mardi Gras. 'Ready?' says Mr Partlett, and the freaks holler back: 'READY!'

'Then let it be done!'

Upon the crash of the Pin Gal's cymbals, the freaks disperse. Only Nancy is not among them – and Gloria, of course, sprawled on her hay bale, halfway between there and the underworld.

Nancy is walking alone, bare feet padding sawdust streets. She's not afraid. Not very. Or, truthfully, she's a little afraid. Her fear tastes of burned cloves and lemon pips. It's a good reminder. It'll keep her quick when fast feet are necessary.

Overhead, the thick smoke joins the gathering storm. From town, there's a high howl: a dachshund, perhaps, who can smell the future. Who'd like to warn everyone what it smells like: Bad Meat! rotten no-good Bad Meat! soaked in the Bad Smell! that makes dog bellies eat themselves and cry.

And oh, it's fitting for this to end in a parade. To go out dancing, a last hurrah! That jangling music catches the breeze. Feet stamp dirt, knees rise up. Carnival beads are flung into an imaginary crowd. Winking purple sequins sprinkle the dirt. The family scatters, towards the Orbiter and the Kraken. To the candied nut stand, to the gate where the teeth blow in the breeze.

By now, the mob has reached the Freakslaw's innards. Behind them, the flames dance their favourite waltz. Ahead, shadowy tents, lanterns swaying in the soupy air. The sign winks – *DISCOVER THY DESTINY!* – and Jim leans down to set one corner ablaze. Greg's all lit up, red-faced and glittering, more alive than Boyd's seen him in years. Norma's hair is haloed, her expression twisted in a snarl. She looks like that picture from the school textbook he never could get out of his head: an engraving of conquistadors, burning the heretics. The sign catches and a caterwaul cuts through the Freakslaw, setting their hair on end. Wind or a howl, it's impossible to tell. It sounds fucking mental.

The mob freeze. A tableau of shocked fury, torches aloft.

And then it happens: the sky explodes in a huge CRASH-BANG! A jag of lightning cleaves the night and Norma Murray screams. Perhaps it's the scream that starts them all going or perhaps it's the sudden sound of chanting, that demented cacophony. Voices layered on top of one another in an incantation that calls to mind ancient ritual and sacrifice. It bounces off the funfair shacks, echoing and repeating, until it's impossible to tell where the noise begins and ends. Still, it sounds as if it's getting nearer.

The locals look around at the destruction they've set in motion, goose pimples prickling at the threat of retribution, and begin to run. Greg is last to move, searching for what final mayhem he can cause, but as the flames lick ever closer, even he takes his cue to leave. They thud past the tents, deeper into the fair, then swerve north. There, the funfair edge and the road back to town. They're making for it, *let's get out of here*, but at the end of this hollowy avenue, Miss Maria steps out, skin glowing, her illustrious bulk quivering. A wall of sensuality any fool could fall inside. 'That's right. Come here,' she says, and spreads her arms wide. This hungry woman, asking for everything, unencumbered by shame. It's that invitation, that swell of want, which stops the mob in their tracks. They cut right instead, down a path overgrown with charred streamers.

Once again, the boundary looms. A hundred short metres and they'll be out. Greg's at the front now, covering ground, when his feet are brought to a screeching stop. What the ever-loving fuck? The ground is *writhing*. Something's oozing, pink and wriggling, a rank gack chugging up from the dirt. Clammy sweat breaks out on Greg's neck as Lewis bashes into him. 'It's a'right,' he says, 'it's just worms.' But worms aren't a'right, worms haven't been a'right since Greg was wee, since his big brother squished a handful between two slices of gummy white loaf and made him choke that sandwich down.

'No. No fuckin' way,' and Greg shoves Lewis back. In the confusion, they stumble deeper into the Freakslaw, towards the distant chanting. As they turn, the Pin Gal steps into the fray, a million piercings winking. She holds one hand flat before her, purses her lips and blows – the Sandman sending dreamdust flying – but what emerges is a perfectly round ball of fire. 'Oh!' she says.

The meteor falls gently to the ground. The clouds rumble. The trumpets crescendo. But it's not too late. Callum's been here before, he remembers the route. 'This way!' and they bellow after him, past the Orbiter, round the back of the Houses of Horror and Fun. Where Nancy's waiting: a hot streak of red, a tight bundle of trickery. Ready for what's been sent her way.

Ready, and furious. These people have crossed her dribbled boundary. Stepped over the bloody threshold and into her home. They've hurt her family – easily, carelessly, as if such a thing meant nothing. For that, they'll pay. The flames are here now, catching at the back of the Funhouse. The beasts have been corralled. Now it's her turn. She steps out of the dark and Callum screeches.

'Fuck me! It's you.'

She nods. 'How's the scalp?'

Callum's hand flies to the bandage. Greg takes it in.

'You wee bitch!' Greg says, the riot momentarily forgotten. 'You cut up my mate's skull!'

Callum turns pink. Boyd gasps: a ridiculous, theatrical sound. The flames lick on in the background, the drum beats *ba-dong-ba-dong-ba-dong-ba-dong*, and a thought coalesces: How the fuck did that happen? The girl's nothing, she's just a girl.

'I did,' agrees Nancy. 'And he loved it.' Her sharp teeth twinkle in the night.

'That's a problem.' Greg's breath has turned harsh. 'You don't fuck with our mates.'

Callum twitches. 'Ach, Greg, leave her be. Let's get out of here.'

'She's just a girl,' says Boyd. That's what he can't get over: she's a kid. She's no older than Derek. What's she doing having sex with a man like Callum, and what's he doing having sex with a girl like her? This is what the funfair's done to them, this perverted place. Tempted them, goaded them, taken them away from themselves and what's decent. Boyd feels the sick rise up at the thought of his own family here, lured into depravity. He pushes past Callum to the front of the crowd. 'Did your da never teach you to behave?'

She laughs. 'Who?'

The way she says it, like the man's less than nothing, sends fury rattling through Boyd's skull. 'Your ma, then?'

And really, that's the stupidest question Nancy's ever heard. Gloria's taught her a hundred things: how to scry and how to mix a Tom Collins; which phase of the moon is best for apotropaic magic; who's more trustworthy, the crows or the foxes. But she's never, *ever* taught Nancy to behave.

'She knows better. Don't you? Or are you the kind of deluded that thinks your kid actually listens?'

Boyd moves fast. Fast for someone carrying the bulk of those shoulders, fast for a man who's been stuck so long in the same small ways. One minute he's stood by Callum, the next he's up for Nancy's throat, all sixteen stone and broken capillaries of him. His fist about to connect with her cheek . . . when she scoots out of the way, little contortionist witch! When she's somehow stood two feet to the left. An old acrobatic trick, a classic. Nancy slopes her weight into one red glittered hip and smirks.

'Was that punch meant for me? Oh dear.'

The disrespectful bint! Boyd launches again, quick with fury, but Nancy moves faster. Slipping down the side of the Funhouse: *slap slap slap* on the dirt, while the worms wriggle, hoping their girl's come good at last.

Boyd's right behind her. Callum's shouting: 'Stop, mate! Leave it be.'

Parade music is approaching, a hideously jaunty summer song, so jarring against the drums and the chanting. So inappropriate, surely, given the turn the night's taken?

Ruth's slumped outside the Funhouse, dazed and crampy, watching the chaos approaching, a wild and ravenous thing, and what on earth is going on?

What on earth, indeed. Nancy screeches to a halt, narrowly avoiding crashing into Ruth and sending them both sprawling. There's a second of double vision – two girls, two destinies, two forces of pure will galloping onwards – and that's when she sees it. The red sop of Ruth's crotch, the scattered tissues. Wet blood and what the fuck?! The seeds she planted, the power she sewed, all dug up by meddling forces. Strewn over the ground.

Nancy can hardly believe it. For a moment, she just stands, violated to her bones. It's like someone's gone rummaging through her bedroom drawers and nicked the best bits, but worse. It's her magic! Her fucking charms! How could she?

Boyd skirts the corner. Nancy gives one last death glare at Ruth then ducks into the Funhouse, swallowed into that terrible laugh riot. Already, the back is beginning to smoulder. Nancy can hear him right behind her, his Darth Vader pant. Each step makes the metal struts of the Funhouse ring out like a bell: *A plague, a plague, warn the villagers!* The shoogly stairs dance and the corridor whirls all magic eye, and Boyd's there, a bull primed for red cloth.

Nancy's run the Funhouse a million times. She's ahead of him. It's fine, it's fine. But as she crests the stairs, the image flashes back to her: her charms spilled, the circuit board broken. A distraction and a curse. It's with this picture swamping her mind that her foot hits the edge of the spinny platform and skites out beneath her. She tumbles to the patterned vinyl. Boyd lands with sure feet and then he's upon her. His hand finds her throat.

And Nancy screams and twists, but it's too late. She's pressed against the ground. Time slows to a standstill. She can hear every note of the parade plucked out of the air. She has time to think of Zed's grin, the broken tooth and the devil-may-care. Time to watch the blood glisten, hear Ruth's screech from below: 'What's happening? What are you doing?'

The metal is getting warm. The fire is catching, contagious as a yawn. She senses it in her bare soles, the warning signal: get out while you still can.

'How you gonna talk to me like that?' Boyd hisses, thinking of her smirk, her suggestion that as a dad – as a *man* – he doesn't matter. The little bitch wasn't a bit afraid, in her laughter was every cunt who's ever made Boyd feel less than. Well, he's not going to take that any more, he doesn't need to take it, so he lifts his other hand and smacks her one. Right in the face.

Nancy's world explodes into fractals, kaleidoscopic. Her plans shatter and scatter across the floor. A sharp one cuts through and what was she doing? Getting out, the heat, the scorch on her soles. But how? There was a way, remember . . .

'Oh it's not so funny now is it? It's no a fuckin' joke?'

Boyd's hands tighten on her throat. He jerks her body wildly and she lets herself rag-doll, an animal playing dead, but even as she does, she knows it's no use. They don't stop until they've got proof, it's always been the way. Survival's just one more piece of evidence in the great case against you.

If you dunk the witch and she doesn't drown, that's when you'll know she's really magic.

If you press a thumb at precisely the right spot on the carotid artery, that's when any girl will swoon. It's where the word comes from – and Zed told her this, Zed and his fucking etymology – carotid from the Greek *karōtides*: for drowsiness, for stupor, for the lights to turn off.

It's what she's thinking as they plink out of being. Oh such a lovely darkness! The thumb pushes her soft spot and the fire climbs the stairs, she can hear purring footsteps, and there was something she was supposed to do, after she led him here.

Escape.

But the room is very small and very warm. The way they came has already been eaten. Her lungs turn hot and frantic. Brain cells send Morse code emergency messages: *Help us stop send oxygen stop the troops are failing stop*

She can hold on a little longer. Can't she?

No. The dark closes in from all corners like an old TV set turning off in slow motion. It comes over her, velvet soft, cat tongues and quivering. A silent gulp, and there's nothing.

Nothing at all.

Darkness.

THE WELL

NANCY DROPS DOWN a deep hole. Nancy becomes a coin falling, a thing to place wishes upon. Nancy plummets and plummets, waiting for black water, letting damp stone whip past. She falls all the way to the centre of the earth, landing in a place that's wet and hollow.

She's alone. She sits in the dark.

If she can hear anything, it's the *hush hush hush* of brain cells quietly giving up the ghost. Boyd is far away, the funfair is far away, Gloria is furthest of all. Here in the deep well, it's quiet. In the silence, she whispers a goodbye and an apology. She fucked it up. She lost her charms and got distracted.

I'm sorry, Gloria.

I'll see you, Zed, on the other side.

But that's when she hears it. An old voice from deep in the dirt, a voice so long dead it takes unconsciousness for her mind to shut up enough to let it penetrate. There are other ways, of course, Ayahuasca and meditation and fasting and being buried alive, but the simplest trick is the same it's always been: the holy swoon of a hand on the throat.

YOU! croaks the ancestor and the voice batters her wildly, sending her heart tumbling down inside herself. In an instant, the voice becomes a chorus: COME DOWN, hiss the ancestors, COME DOWN AND LET US OUT. The voices are huge and unfathomable, louder than they have any right to be. She can hear the hunger inside them, feel grabby hands reaching out. Clawing at her, squealing with dirt-pig glee as they find a bone to cling to. For all her cool, all Nancy feels is terror. Uncontrollable fear, the fear of a hole when you don't know its depths. There could be anything down there, thrashing in the dark, ready to pull her into the fray. A black place clotted with writhing bodies, each trying to rise to the top and smother the others.

Here they are, the ravenous long-dead, who've already taken her mother and now want to snack upon her too. Who don't know when to shut up and let a thing go. The past who've had theirs and weren't satisfied, who want to drag the future down with them. Who can't tell the difference between a plump offering and the ones on their side.

As these thoughts whirl through Nancy, the fear changes texture, getting thicker and more electric. It catches in her throat, it claws her fists, it hocks up as a big Fuck You.

COME ON, goad the ancestors and a new power crackles into Nancy, the strongest of motivations, one that tramples the rest to dust.

Pure spite.

Because fuck if she's going to quiet down. Fuck if she's going to let them take her, or her mother either. As if she wasn't right all along, as if she didn't call it that things had to end like this. Blood and death and ritual. A handover. The end of the old and the beginning of the new.

With the last of the strength she can muster, Nancy flings open her eyes. Her body is a trick, and she folds herself into herself, a magical napkin, until she's out from under his hands. A tablecloth whipped aside. All the glasses quiver, but they do not fall.

By now, the smoke is very thick. Boyd's breath is coming in ragged wheezes. His meaty hands grasp but Nancy's moving now, on her toes, she darts towards the platform at the top where the slide begins. That snaky green and purple tunnel: an escape route for children and tiny contortionists, a helter skelter, a reckless plummet. On the ground, she can see the parade all gathered, her family's eyes wide. She can feel the animal thrum of terror but when she catches Zed's gaze, he's smiling. A perfect grin for perfect trust. She smiles back and takes a step towards the slide.

It cuts through the flames, a hole bored straight to hell. From the tiny circle, black smoke billows like a chimney. Every second she waits, the flames creep higher, the tunnel gets hotter. Death waits with her sickle, testing the breeze.

Nancy wraps her hands around the hot metal, and catapults into the heart of the flames.

EVERY CELL SCREAMING

THE FREAKSLAW IS a held breath as Nancy careens down the slide and lands knee-first in the dirt. She crumples into a blackened ball. Mr Partlett can't look. It was a risk; it's always a risk to dance to the precipice of the chasm in a gale-force wind. But what other choice is there? They were born to the precipice, it's the only place they'll ever call home.

Still, if they've misjudged, he will never forgive himself.

'Nancy!' Zed throws himself on her, wraps his arms around her back. For a moment, there's nothing. Zed can't tell if the thudding is his own heart or Nancy's pulse or the feet of the oncoming riot. This perfect human lies motionless. A tiny, precious thing – hard as a diamond, but still possible to break. He shakes her. He holds his breath. Then Nancy unfurls. There's blood on her chin, black smudges across her cheekbones. Her eyes glitter madly. Her dimples deepen.

'Did I do good?'

Glee floods Zed, liquid and bathwater warm.

'Holy shit. You did—'

The animal screaming swallows his reply. They look up, and he's there, that angry man, perched on the whirly plat-form of the Funhouse balcony.

'Help me, oh god, you fucking cunts, help me!'

Demonic orange ghosts dance beneath him. His voice cuts through and everyone stops what they're doing to stare.

Zed wraps an arm round Nancy's shoulder and Nancy snuggles into his armpit. They turn, clutched together, warming themselves in the crackling, cheeks turning a pleasant pink.

'It's burning oh fuck it's so hot, oh Christ, do something!'

The funfair gathers before the manic glow. Miss Maria starts to giggle, a sweet cake-crumb laugh that's terrifically infectious. Gretchen drags a file across one fingernail and blows the dust. And the mob from the town drop their petrol cans, fling stakes to the dirt. They push through the funfair folk, screaming and oh-so hysterical.

'Oh shit, Boyd, what the—?'

Boyd Geddes is standing above a wall of fire. He claws the air, reaching for a zip wire, a trapeze, a magic escape route. He grabs a strut then lets go, screaming. He brings his ruined palm to his mouth.

Greg grabs Gretchen by the shoulders. 'Do something!' His voice already halfway to a punch.

'You do something.' Gretchen shoves him and he stumbles back, eyes goggling. 'You made this bed.' A lickety grin takes her lips, and she sings: 'We didn't start the *fi-ire*.'

Greg looks at his fists as if he's no idea where they came from. There's still violence in him, in all of them, but at the sight of Boyd trapped, it lacks direction. Brutality leaps from man to man and fizzles out wetly. It's Norma Murray who steps forward and gestures frantically to Boyd, framed in his glowing wreath.

'Just hold on! Somebody will call the fire brigade!'

Gretchen rolls her eyes. Lewis starts sprinting back to town. Four others turn heel and follow. The remaining townsfolk yell conflicting instructions, like it's a game show and they're desperate for him to get his hands on the crystal.

'Stay where you are, Boyd, help's coming.'

'To your left, mate, the flames are only wee there.'

'Boyd, don't be a fucking pansy, just jump. Jump!'

Nancy feels a helpless laugh frothing out like freshly activated yeast. It's too late for that. The flames are caught on the updraught, a hammering wall of heat. Like leaning over a volcano, but still the men shout, 'Jump!' as if it's like leaping off the diving board, just frozen limbs keeping him back.

Anyone who hasn't been in a fire always thinks they know shit. They'd run straight towards the molten core if they needed to. They'd see through the black blindfold, scream for help while smoke battered the oxygen from their lungs.

Well, Nancy knows otherwise. How logic and direction shrivel before the Great God Fire, the primordial lizard grabbing hold of your reins, turning the human meatsack towards one thing and one thing only: air. Every cell screaming *Breathe*, screaming *Run*.

Boyd's shrieks are rising. The metal platform has taken on an orange glow. It's burning through his shoes, surely, turning his soles a bubbled black. Nancy sniffs, but she can't smell the char. Not yet.

Beneath the earth, the worms wriggle deep, to where the soil is cooler. Across the Freakslaw, a discarded Barbie starts to melt. The plastic turns slack, the hair incinerates in a chemical pop. Her mouth falls open. Her lips dissolve. In the crowd, Ruth gasps as a grip slackens in her chest, a breath she didn't realize she'd been holding until now.

And Boyd stands over the funfair like a prophet. The metal gets hotter. He lifts his feet: first one, then the other. He is jumping on the spot – now, when it's already too late. Trying to leap higher, to dance himself away from his destiny.

The funfair folk stare up, wide-mouthed, but Werewolf

Louie is the one who starts. A terrible giggle escapes him as he lifts his own feet: one, then the other. Foot to foot, in perfect time with Boyd's. Miss Maria sees what's happening. A beatific smile breaks open her face and, one ear cocked to that atavistic drumbeat, she too begins to dance. Her flesh moves like lava lamps and molten wax. She turns her face to the sky.

The others follow suit. All of them, gathered around the flaming Funhouse, stomp their feet and dance. The Twins clap their hands. Seven shaved Strongmen bob their heads in time to the music. Mr Partlett eases from foot to foot, and Gretchen vogues and the Pin Gal shimmies and the fire lights their sweated faces. Nancy sits alone, palms on the dirt, on a spot where not so long ago a single baby tooth was buried. She looks at the burning man, at her wild dancing family. She thinks of Gloria, alone in the tent. She sends a message down to those ancient fuckers: *Take him. Let her go.*

Boyd is still screaming.

June is watching him, hands clutched to her mouth. That's him up there, her husband. The man she's shared a bed with for twenty-five years, the one who took her on holiday to Blackpool on the off season, nicked a bottle of fizz from the hotel bar, and kissed her in the bathroom while they drank it from toothpaste mugs, laughing and feeling like they were getting away with the world.

He looks like a fish gasping on a rock, eyes bulging. June remembers going fishing with her dad as a lass, the way it felt to clutch that shimmering creature, how the bones moved beneath the scales. It would thrash and thrash, gills flapping, but all it took was a single dull thud, right on the back of the head. An end to the misery.

And then Jim's in front of her, stumbling out of the smoke. 'June, you cannae watch this. C'mere.' He's still clutching his stick, dragging it behind him, a toy dog on a wooden leash. He's crying. Or it's the smoke, sure it is, caught in his eyes.

June looks past him to the Funhouse. Her own eyes are dry. There will be tears later – the first as small and sharp as shards of metal, and then, once the seal is broken, a flood that comes like absolution, wiping the plains clean. But for now, her insides are empty polished glass.

Boyd is a black silhouette. He will die, that's the truth of it. He's probably almost dead already. He'll never again eat her tatties or roll over in the night to fling his heavy arm over her, sweated and secure.

Jim lets the staff fall from his hands, grabs June by the wrist. 'Come *on*.'

'No! Let go of me.' She yanks her arm back. June needs to stay, that's the thing, she needs to see this. She has to stop closing her eyes, even when she can hardly bear what she's looking at. Especially then.

She pushes past Jim towards the hungry flames. Tiny particles of ash fall in her hair like snow. Her skin prickles. Her heart is rabbiting in her chest but it's still beating, there's that. She's here and she's alive. One more thing, and plenty to be done.

'Oh, Boyd. What were you thinking?' she says.

Boyd doesn't answer. For the first time in her entire life, June Geddes gets the final word.

Derek finds he's forgotten how to swallow. Big huge feelings are globbing up in him, barfy and impossible. That's his da up there, he's on fucking fire!

He should do something. He should run in there and rescue him. That's what a man would do, any decent son. Fat orange flames spit at the sky. In their midst, a shadow puppet writhes. And fuck, it's going to be so hot, it's going to hurt so bad.

Derek takes a stumbling step towards the Funhouse. Before he can get anywhere, a callused palm slips into his own. Those long bony fingers close, the cold scuff of silver presses down. And he should shake him off, he should run in there screaming, but Zed yanks him back. Zed wraps his arms around Derek, holding him firm in the earth.

'Burn! Burn! Burn!'

The crowd chants, the voices swell. They're full-throated, lungs honed from years of shilling: *Roll up roll up you're all invited!* Except it's not the freaks that are the entertainment this time, it's not magic or illusions. It's real.

'Burn! Burn! Burn! Throw the man away!'

What a terrible thing to chant! Derek can hardly believe it. This crowd is totally on Team Fire. And they're right, that's the horrible thing – in this fight, the fire is winning. The people are ecstatic. And there, up in flames: his dad, his dad, his dad.

He should—

Zed cups a hand around his face and turns his eyes away. Derek's stomach heaves wildly. There's a part of him that made this happen, he knows: the dirty-boy part of him, the one that wanted to get away with everything, revenge for the fist and the black toast crumbs on the floor. And now he's actually got it.

'Burn! Burn! Burn!'

The chant is rolling now, a regular pound like the ocean.

338

Derek is swept into its waves. He lets the scream fill his ears. His whole world narrows to two things: *Zed!* and *Burn!*

Burn! takes over his brain, *Burn!* licks his skin. *Burn!* becomes a curse, a mantra, a law of nature. And Zed pulls him close, their bodies pressed against each other, so Derek can feel the taut certainty of his embrace, something firm and sure.

How could this possibly be wrong?

Derek closes his eyes and kisses Zed hard.

For her own part, even as she watches it happen, Ruth's sure there'll be some last-minute reprieve. A third-act deus ex machina, a helicopter descending from smoke-clagged skies. She's waiting for the unfurling rope ladder, Sean Connery's heroic palm.

There's nothing. Her eyes are streaming. Her insides all wrung out.

Still, she can't repress a flicker of joy to see the Freakslaw burn. What happened here will be swallowed, so everything can go back to normal.

Or it could do, if she wasn't actually watching a person die. In fact, nothing's going to be normal after this, absolutely nothing. Reality's gotten too big, the world's skipped out of kilter, and what the very fuck? The man is dying. The people are dancing.

They're delirious for it to happen.

It doesn't feel real. It's too big, that's the thing, too big and too close. How are you supposed to grasp the whole thing at once? She thinks of a comic: a submarine, a porthole filled with a single blinking eye. Anything with an eye that big must fill half the ocean, but that's as far as imagination can take you. The tentacled implications are endless. Things down here go on for ever.

'Burn! Burn! Burn!'

The Pin Gal is chanting. The Twins, pink-cheeked and gleeful, holler as one. And folk from town too: Shona in the centre of them, of course, but also Euan Cruikshank from school, fearless and furious now, part of something bigger than himself. He has his hands balled in fists, red-faced and screaming. There's Lesley MacDermid who works at the supermarket meat counter, clambered on a Strongman's shoulders to get a better view. It hasn't taken much. And Ruth would judge but she can't look away either.

She wants to see it happen. She needs to know: what's it like the moment life snuffs out of a body? Will they know the instant it happens, or will the world go on screaming, only to realize they've been yelling at a corpse? That would be terrible, but not as terrible as turning away.

This will still happen, that's the thing. If she closes her eyes, it'll go on. And she'll never know what it was like to see.

Her stomach loops dangerously. The fire gusts higher. Surely, it can't be much longer?

'You're not dancing.' Nancy's voice is soft. Ruth turns. Nancy's face is streaked with ash. The skin around her nostrils is cracked and black.

'Neither are you.'

Nancy shrugs, reaches a hand to massage her own shoulder. Her body seems small and stiff in the dark. 'It's beautiful,' she says.

'He's *dying*.'

The fire casts orange shadows across Nancy's glistening

cheeks, her sharp little teeth. 'We're all dying. Just some of us faster than others.'

'He's dying *now*.'

Ruth can't see the silhouette any more. He's fallen to a blackened crumple, or the fire is too high. One part of the Funhouse is starting to collapse, wooden boards falling like a domino rally. The crowd shrieks in delighted terror. Hands grab one another. That furred man takes Shona the hairdresser in a hungry embrace. And Lesley MacDermid rips her shirt open, baring her breasts. She screams.

Nancy's eyes are long black tunnels, two tiny flames dancing at the end. 'Someone had to.'

Ruth can't listen. She wants to press her hands to her ears, to grab Nancy and shake her hard. They're better than this, surely. Glee feels like sinking to their level, the same as the mob, letting something inside that will divide and multiply, a Xeroxing of cells until everything's swallowed by hate. But what about the flicker of excitement in her own stomach? It licks at her and the tongue is soft, the tongue could be delicious.

'This feels bad.'

Nancy leans in, breath hot against Ruth's ear. 'It *is* bad. Do you think we started this? Do you know how fucking exhausting it is to be always fighting back against people who want to destroy you?'

Ruth shakes her head. There's a popping as a new part of the building bursts into flames. From the crowd, a shirt is flung into the air. A screech of laughter rings out, high-pitched and wild.

'Everything we could get done, if we weren't always on the

defensive. You wouldn't even recognize the world. But him?' She shrugs again, smiles a dreadful smile. 'Who gives a shit?'

As she says this, there's a great roaring, a hewing, and the centre of the Funhouse collapses. The building falls into itself in slow motion. Metal warps and buckles, wood crumbles to dust, swathes of floor fall into the pyre. Everything is swallowed in a single hot gulp. And, if the body of Boyd Geddes had still been alive, it's not any more. He is gone.

A gust of heat ripples through the crowd, the shockwave of an explosion. Eyebrows are singed. The chanting stops. Dizzy townspeople lift their hands to their faces, smear ash into their own sweat. A series of grins light up the funfair folk, gleaming teeth over scorched dirt.

And in this moment – the presence of death so close – a cardinal electricity crackles, infecting everyone who breathes it in. The throng becomes a feral animal, driven half mad by ancient impulse. Moved to clutch each other close, drunk on the impossible preciousness of life.

'Got to go,' says Nancy, and she turns from that thrashing carnival of bodies, off in the opposite direction.

Ruth stands at the outskirts, hugging her arms to herself. She has no idea what she's going to do. Nothing in her life has prepared her for this moment. For every constellation she's ever picked from the sky, none of them looked a thing like this.

Before her, the crowd has given itself over to primal glee. Bodies dance and writhe, squeezing one another so tight they may snap under the pressure. There's a whoop, a keening that sounds like something being born. And laughter so long and loud it rends her heart.

Ruth sits on the grass and hugs her knees to her chest. The

animal reek of her body rises off her. Her bloody crotch, the tang of sweat. She's going to go home, in a minute. She's going to let what happens happen.

For now, it's enough to just sit in the aftermath, and watch all the people pass by.

LÙNASTAL

THE FIRE BURNS hot and heavy. The bodies find absolution in each other's arms. The fat of Boyd's corpse hisses and spits. As the great wheel of the year ticks into Lùnastal, the ancestors catch a whiff of barbecue and drop the toy they've been playing with to snack upon some sweeter bones.

On the hay bale in the Freakslaw tent, Gloria falls back into herself. A holy whoosh as consciousness returns. She flutters her eyes open the same moment Nancy yanks back the flap. Her daughter skids to the sawdust by her side, flinging her arms around Gloria's neck.

She beholds her glorious wayward child, her jagged hair and beating pulse, the reek of smoke on her skin. Gloria doesn't need to ask what happened. She can feel it. The end of a cycle, marked by ritual, commemorated by blood.

Deep beneath the earth, the ancestors smack their lips and make their beds. Gloria lets them leave her, holds her daughter close.

Her chest is loose. Her heart is light.

And silence, at last, in her skull.

ALL THAT'S LEFT

One Week Later

THE TRUCKS PULL into the rest stop like a troop of exhausted dancers with swollen feet. Gloria yanks her handbrake and flings open the door, leaping out into the scrub. Nancy follows, ducking immediately behind a cypress tree to piss. It comes out in a jet and is swallowed into dry earth.

Hot engines tick and sigh. The air here is parched and smells of rosemary.

'Fifteen minutes,' yells Gloria, and Mr Partlett's headlights flash to show he's heard. They could afford to take longer, really – they've been making fine time on the road, but Gloria has a yearning to keep pace. She can feel the tug of the south, another ocean. This migration is patterned in her bones. Besides, it couldn't hurt to place a distance between them and Pitlaw.

By the time the fire engines had arrived, there hadn't been much left of the man to salvage. Still, the bones told their own story, along with the charred remains of the rides. The men with the petrol cans, drifting back to reality. Dazed with regret at an impulse got out of hand. Call it death by misadventure – not that they waited for the verdict. The Freakslaw left in the thin dawn drizzle, and Jimmy's field turned back to mud.

Still, there are certain plants that need a bushfire to reseed.

Sometimes it takes being razed to the ground for crops to grow back stronger.

Gloria sits on one of the concrete bollards and presses her hands to her thighs. Her mind is quiet today, a glorious tundra with no landmarks left to define her. It won't last for ever – but for the moment, it's sublime. She closes her eyes and lets the sun beat down on her. That night will be something to come back to, when the world gets too overwhelming. A tonic to fortify her soul.

The others stretch and pace, loosening their muscles after the long drive. The Strongmen are massaging each other again. The Pin Gal glints in the sunshine, radiant; her tattoos luminescent in this light. Cass, who's barely paused her chatter while the miles whipped out from under them, is lulled into a moment's contentment by the warmth on her arms.

Derek and Zed wander back from the cantina, a paper bag of pastéis de nata clutched between them. Zed tears off a crust and feeds it to Derek, who blushes, but lets it happen. Yellow goo smears his lips. His teeth ring out from the sweetness.

June, watching, can't help herself fussing. 'Derek, you'll ruin your dinner,' but Shona shushes her. She hands June a tart from her own bag. 'Go on, try it,' and June does. The custard tastes like sunshine.

'Oh well, I suppose it's alright.'

June tests the smile out on her own lips and finds she can stand it. This, whatever else, is a fresh start. A break with the past. The sky looks very big here, the horizon low to the ground. You could drive all day and still not get close.

Nancy is still squatted in the dust. She plucks something from her bag – Gloria's scrying mirror, bejewelled with mother of pearl. She angles it from the sun, convinced she'll get the knack of this trick soon, and all the secrets of the past, the future, and the distant will be revealed to her.

But nothing happens. It's a shame, really. If she could catch a glimpse of what was happening in Pitlaw, it would bring a smirk to her lips. A smug satisfaction to watch the town attempt to piece itself back together from all the detritus that's left behind.

Take Norma Murray, who's tried three times to chair a town council meeting, only to lose herself to unfinished sentences. The woman's mulish certainty is all gone. Now, she can barely formulate a thought without spiralling through every potential consequence. The Freakslaw may have moved on, but its repercussions remain, and what momentum can gather when you start just a single rock rolling . . .

Sooner or later, this saga will play out all the way to its logical conclusions. The town council disbanded. Regulations lost to unthumbed paperwork. Eventually, Curl Up and Dye given over to a new leaseholder, the boarded shopfront prised down. The locals will huff and gossip about the woman who runs the place – the sparkly rubbish she sells, that patchwork hippy skirt – but eventually they'll find themselves drifting inside. The crystals in the window are so shiny, after all. They might not have a use, but Lord if they don't catch the light nicely!

As for Greg Haskett, he'll be sat down the pub, sinking pints, trying to drink fast enough that the past can't catch him. Blocking out a certain night, that distant pop as something wet in the Funhouse exploded. One day soon, he'll drive all the way to the animal shelter in the next town over and sit in the car park for an hour, thinking. He could go in there, get a cat to take home. A soft kid, or a second chance.

A new beginning. Or just the same old thing for ever, again and again.

In the fields of Pitlaw, the rain will fall heavy on the soil. Brambles and greengages will fatten on their vines. Roots burrowing deep into the earth, listening to the worms giggle in the way only the worms can.

And somewhere out there Ruth is on a bus, her forehead pressed against the window, eyes reflected in the glass. Big white headphones over her ears, while the world whips by. And though the Freakslaw will never witness the unfurling of her destiny, never know if their actions left Pitlaw irretrievably broken or primed for regeneration, it doesn't matter. There's plenty of new magic to occupy them, new old grudges to stoke and vengeances to reap. Plus the plans for next summer, and the one after that.

Nancy takes one last look at the mirror, then throws it into the dirt. Stomps on it with one heel. A crack appears, shattering the sky in two. She tramps back to the cab where Gloria is waiting, one elbow leaned out the window, dust in her hair.

'All done?' her mother asks.

The engine's already running. Nancy nods briskly and yanks herself into the seat. She flips the visor down. The road reflects endlessly behind them, spilling backwards, unravelling.

'Ready,' she says, and the wheels begin to turn.

ACKNOWLEDGEMENTS

Writing a publishable book, it turns out, takes an obscenely long time, and there is not enough room on these pages to thank everyone who held my wayward heart upright on the twisting path that led to this point. I feel incredibly lucky to have had the support of so many excellent humans over these years. Love goes to all of you, and special gratitude to the following people.

Marina de Pass – your utter joy for *Freakslaw* from the start and uncanny ability to make me feel calm throughout the publishing process have been a gift. Thank you for being my fiercest champion and making it happen.

Charlotte Trumble – in my wildest dreams, I never conjured an editor who understood my book the way you do (or who'd duet the Singing Kettle with me in a Soho restaurant). Thank you for always pushing me to make this story the best version of itself.

Bobby Mostyn-Owen, for adopting *Freakslaw* with such enthusiasm and bringing your brilliant mind and ruthless dedication to this project. Working with you has been a complete delight.

Beci Kelly, for somehow crawling inside my brain and designing a cover from its feral depths. I could not love it more.

Everyone at Transworld who helped this book on its way,

especially Georgie Bewes, Fraser Crichton, Sara Roberts, Chloë Rose and Barbara Thompson.

Victoria Gosling: my most incisive editor, my Queen of Swords, my dear friend. I wouldn't be the writer or person that I am without the care you put into the world, and I'm grateful for it all the time.

Sarah Van Bonn, Sharon Mertins and Jessica Miller – gleeful coven of novel club – who read this story as it was written, pushing me to go weirder at every turn. You are such glorious creatures.

Ambika Thompson, bizarre genius of my heart, for always making me do the thing I'm scared of. My life would be so much more boring without you.

Dan Ayres, my beloved travel gremlin, for the constant reminder that *everything is really beautiful* when I was in that dark query hole.

Alex Highet, you are the best person and I love you so much.

Sophie Raphaeline, queen of Another Country and all-round good witch. Thank you for carving out a space in the city where the deviants could gather. I miss you.

Ryan Van Winkle, who has been waiting for this dedication for sixteen years. Thank you for taking me in the van when I was a baby poet and making me believe I was a real writer.

Samar Hammam, who found my words before they were ready and told me one day, I would have a book.

Mark Flett: my brilliant brother, the hottest doctor, and one of the kindest people I know. I'm so proud of you.

Mum and Dad, who brought me up to believe I could do absolutely anything I set my mind to. Thank you for a thousand trips to the library and for letting me forge my own strange path.

The Scottish Book Trust, whose early support made me think this peculiar career was an excellent idea.

The Berlin Senate for Culture and Europe, for the rare gift of a year in which to write.

All the residencies who offered me brain space away from Berlin's delectable chaos: Zvona i Nari, Can Serrat, Moniak Mhor, Villa Sarkia, the New Orleans Writing residency (Tim Raveling, you perfect angel), and my happiest of happy places, Foundation OBRAS. Ludger and Carolien – I started and ended this book with you, and I'm endlessly appreciative. May we all have a one-eyed cat to watch over us and a clear blue pool to dive into while we draft our books.

And to all my friends, lovers and exes who shaped the person I am and the book this became – if you think you belong on this list, you are correct, of course. Let's go sit under the fairground lights and stake our hearts on the moon.

ABOUT THE AUTHOR

Jane Flett is a Scottish writer who lives in Berlin. Her fiction has been commissioned for BBC Radio 4, featured in Electric Literature's Recommended Reading, Highly Commended in the Bridport Prize and performed at the Edinburgh International Book Festival. She's a recipient of the Scottish Book Trust New Writer Award, the New Orleans Writing Residency and the Berlin Senate Stipend for non-German literature. *Freakslaw* is her first novel.